In Appreciation

Now that this story is written and printed, thanks are in order for the many persons who have assisted me along the way.

I'm not going to attempt listing the names of anyone except my wife, Gerry. I offer my gratitude to my children, relatives, friends and a few strangers who have helped and offered encouragement as I struggled toward its completion. My reason...chances are that I would overlook someone which would offend them and me.

Whether or not this novel is accepted by readers is unknown. I have devoted three years in completing it as well as simultaneously learning the intricacies of operating a computer. So, to those of you similar to me who have reached or passed three quarters of a century's existence on this planet, don't give up. There is still time to make an accomplishment of some nature before you meet your Maker. In my case, I always wanted to write a book.

D1207730

death under tall pines

Copyright 1998 by Horace P. Landry
All rights reserved.

Especially to Fuentes a first Leader. Congratulations

Horace P. Landry
_10/7/00_

Cover Art by T.W. Jaaskelainen

Printed by The Foot-Print
20523 S. Tamiami Trail
Estero, Florida 33928

Fourth Printing

i

Foreword

The portrayal of Jacques and his pet bear in this novel is based on a true story while the other characters are fictitious. And except Middleton and Bear Lake, the names of all places are authentic.

This story relates to life in the Northeast during the 1940's when World War II began to change the way of family living. Its setting is in Maine that offers unlimited beauty and quiet life style which remains today. Known as the Pine Tree State for its vast forest acreage, it has miles of rocky coastline, hundreds of lakes, beaches and mountains. Thousands of tourists invade the region each year helping Maine to maintain its image as a vacationland.

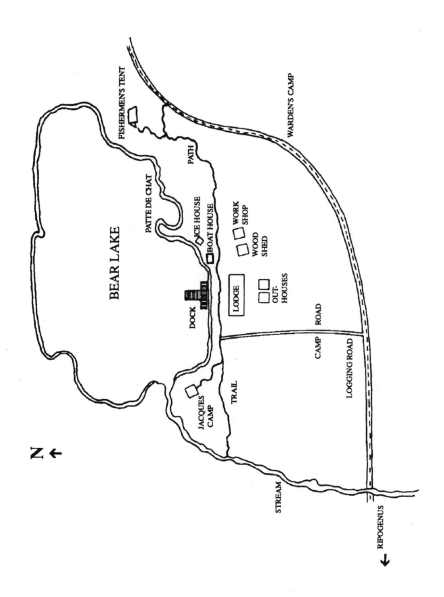

Chapter 1

Racing toward the lodge to escape the storm's wrath, he was suddenly aware of a figure shadowed by heavy rain with a weapon pointed at him. He waved his arms frantically and shouted but his cry was drowned by a bolt of lightning hitting a tall pine creating sounds of snapping timber and gunfire. Screams pierced the early morning tranquillity as a beam of light revealed a grotesque face with eyes wide open staring hopelessly toward the heavens.

Trapped under the brush of fallen pine trees, a frightening distorted figure horrifies searchers groping in the darkness for a missing companion. The shrilling cries climaxed a night of thunder with torrential rains and menacing bolts of lightning miles far away from a thriving community where the unexpected disaster originated.

Middleton lies peacefully in an armful of lovely lakes and farmlands. Railroad tracks and a highway pass through its center while a meandering river flows along the outskirts.

Not noticeably different from any small city, however, it has two things to boast of... Chamberlain College, once Hawthorne but named for a Civil War hero, and The Daily Guardian, an award-winning newspaper.

The 25,000 or more residents comprising the city are comparable to populations of other municipalities. They are descendants of families from many countries who migrated to live and raise children in Maine. Workers in the textile and wood industries crossed the border of their northern Canadian neighbor to become American citizens.

A legendary proverb about the history of Middleton discloses there are the good, the bad, and the indifferent. The do-gooders included educators, enforcers, and soul-savers. The not-so-gooders were often found out to be adulterers, blackmailers and an occasional murderer.

In 1949, four years after the end of the World War II Middleton rapidly became the magnet for thousands of midstate citizens seeking professional and business services. The cosmopolitan city owes its growth to resources from the lifeline of the Kennebec River. The rushing waters generated electrical power for its industries while strength from its currents drove logs felled in forests hundreds of miles to the north. In

1

the community's infancy, the river also provided transportation and abundant salmon for its settlers.

Today's modern structures are vast contrasts from the log cabins that encompassed a primitive Indian village centuries ago. Hospitals, churches, schools, and business blocks rise along the streets that originally were paths for natives and animals.

Outside of the business district, crystal clear lakes offer recreational facilities for natives and tourists. The farms, many that have been homesteaded for generations, uphold a tradition of providing crops and livestock. It is a city of beauty, wealth, and joy along with pains and disappointments. Journals record the growth as progress.

It was an exceptionally warm day in Maine. A summer unprecedented in recorded history with an early morning low of seventy degrees and an afternoon high reaching the nineties, temperatures seldom prevailing here. A local wag pronounced you could fry an egg on Main Street.

The season began slightly more than a week ago as the solstice in June officially heralded summer. Exceptionally warm weather didn't usually make its debut until later in July, but for some inexplicable reason, this year decided to be different.

A twenty-nine year-old journalist, Ted Graves, sat at his desk in *The Daily Guardian's* editorial room writing articles on the morning's activities at city hall. With his six-foot frame and long legs, he had difficulty manipulating his knees under the desk. He was uncomfortable today, affected by the humidity as perspiration covered his face while his arms stuck to papers on his desk. It reminded him somewhat of the hot temperatures in the African desert, but at least in that region humidity was not a dilemma.

The young writer had returned to his hometown a few years before working for a New York City newspaper. A Middleton native and Chamberlain College graduate, Ted had often thought of coming back to his native state and jumped at the chance to serve on the staff of a daily in his hometown when a new position was created on the Guardian. It didn't take long for this amicable newcomer to adjust here.

Across town in one of Middleton's oldest buildings, the district courthouse was turned into a sweatbox by the intolerable heat. Presiding Judge Bernard Collins had already removed his robe and rolled up his sleeves but that wasn't adequate for the venerable jurist. Exasperated, he declared, "This oven isn't a place to administer justice. I'm adjourning this session and postponing the docket cases until the rooms become habitable again."

When Ted entered the *Guardian* shortly before noon, the place was relatively quiet with only a few of the staff at their desks and an elderly proofreader seated behind a stack of newspapers. Ted stopped at the society editor's desk and spoke to Bertha Cronin.

"Having a quiet day?" He asked. "Most women in the city must be spending their time at the beaches."

"No way," she replied. "A few women's clubs are having dinners or meetings today. Obviously, they weren't aware that summer temperatures would come so soon when they scheduled their meetings. It's a hot day but we'll get through it. What brings you here this morning? Where's Scoop, the reporter who's usually here in the mornings?"

"He called in sick. "It wouldn't surprise me if he's snoozing under a shade tree near a lake. I'm going to find a cool spot when I get out of here," Ted concluded as he continued to his desk.

The stillness during the morning hours was only interrupted by the clacking of teletype machines, ringing of phones, and the whirring of a dozen or so fans trying to keep the place livable. In the afternoon, this scene would be bustling with activity as the news center became alive with the arrival of others reporting for the night shift who would also share the misery of this heat.

Although the *Guardian* was considered a small city newspaper, it had a spacious facility located near the downtown district of the city. An unusual large editorial or newsroom comprised the entire second story of the building. Sixteen desks, eight in two rows, took up most of the space while five teletype machines bringing up to the minute news and photos from around the world were lined along the wall behind the copy desk. The city and state editors" desks were set at the head of each row and the managing editor occupied a sizable office on the other end of the rows that had a long glass window where he commanded a view of the entire room This setup portrayed a run-of-the-mill newsroom as a day progressed at the *Guardian* with odors of ink, paper, tobacco smoke, and the sounds of noisy chatter and teletypes.

As he continued his article of this morning's activities at city hall, Ted thought of his friend, Father Timothy O'Toole. Last night he suggested that a fishing trip to Bear Lake might be one way of beating the heat. The writer and this Irish priest who had studied law as well as theology, had become fast friends since both realized Middleton was

3

their place to live. Also, supplementing the relationship was their mutual interest in police investigations and a curiosity of the increasing usage of forensic medicine in criminal investigations.

Father O'Toole left a small parish in an Irish section of New York City. He had a colorful speech pattern with a picturesque Irish dialect intermingled with a thick brogue that kept listeners attentive while relating unending metaphors. With a twinkle in his eyes he shrewdly affirmed the presence of leprechauns in the old country. A popular figure in his new environment, he explained to friends that his interest in criminology developed as a result of his parish location in New York. Father O'Toole related that much of his leisure time was spent with detectives at the precinct a few blocks from the church rectory. Modest, he never mentioned his association in any police activity, but a former precinct commander, Dan Mahoney, who stopped in Middleton while en route on a fishing trip to visit the retired priest revealed a couple of his secrets.

Father O'Toole brought him to the local police station to meet Chief John Davidson and much to his chagrin, the New Yorker discussed incidents in which the priest had participated. He told the chief about an event that took place in 1920 during the Empire City's heyday when a horsedrawn wagon came up Wall Street and stopped in front of J. P. Morgan & Co. The driver left the wagon and walked away. At noon, the wagon exploded killing thirty eight people and wounding more than one hundred. According to Mahoney, Father O'Toole was among the first on the scene, administering to the dying and wounded, and later he became involved in the investigation. This crime was never solved. Officials theorized it was the work of anarchists displeased by Wall Street's influence on the city's financial success.

Another time, Mahoney related, the retired priest participated in the investigation of a murder. This crime resulted in the most famous picture in tabloid journalism about the time when these half size newspapers were becoming standard.

The officer said he was only a patrolman at the time, but he remembered Father O'Toole's name mentioned often in the department as officials conducted the investigation.

"A murderess with the help of her lover conceived a plot to eliminate her husband," he said. "Not only was she a conspirator in the killing, she was the active planner and a participant. After the couple tried several times to murder him in numerous ways including poison and carbon

4

monoxide, she chloroformed him and ultimately strangled the victim with picture wire. To cast suspicion elsewhere," the former cop added, "the lover tied up the wife so when police arrived she told them she had been attacked by burglars.

"Because of Father O'Toole's close relationship with detectives, he was allowed to join with investigators at the scene of the crime," Mahoney said. "And he, along with the police, became suspicious because her bindings had been tied rather loosely as though to save her from any discomfort," he added. "Other evidence found in her possessions indicated she knew her conspirator well. They were convicted and sentenced to death in the electric chair, a fate they met a year later at Sing Sing prison," Mahoney continued.

"As the executioner pulled the switch on the murderess, a photographer sitting in the front row with a camera strapped just above his ankle crossed his legs and snapped a picture. The next morning, the New York Daily News devoted the entire front page to the horrifying shot of the current coursing through her body," he concluded.

Besides Dan, the retired priest had made countless friends in New York including J.T., a Wall Street investor who owned a lodge in a remote region of Maine. The successful financier made the lodge available to Father O'Toole, who shared its facilities twice a year with local friends.

Since he was retired, Father O'Toole established a policy with friends insisting they eliminate the title of Father that had preceded his name for half a century. It was difficult for Ted to accept this change, but soon it became routine as their friendship warmed.

Ted knew Timothy was a special friend of Chief Davidson's and probably shared information no one else in the city knew. He also believed Timothy had more knowledge relating to state criminal activities than anyone was aware.

Last night Ted spent a couple of hours chatting with him at Harry's, a local pub where customers included college students and writers from the *Guardian*. Pub was misleading as a description for this place as it included a separate coffee shop, an attraction for many of the city's downtown employees.

Reflecting on the fishing trip, Ted thought of the group of Timothy's friends which included Brett Hartman, a photographer with a studio close to Harry's, who Timothy had known while in New York. Brett opened his business here about ten years ago. He was always well dressed and articulate and became a familiar figure in the business district of

5

Middleton. Tall with a slim nose and sporting a well-trimmed mustache, Brett was still trim at fifty.

Another was Linda Breton, one of Ted's attractive dates, who was on the reporter's mind more frequently during the past weeks. Not a part of the newspaper staff, she worked for the college that had a close relationship with the *Guardian.*

Also, three others who were original members of the group on these trips included Randolph and Ruth Perry, a college professor and his wife and Alec, who was Ted's boss and managing editor of the *Guardian.* And, the newest addition to the local newspaper staff, Janice Robinson, who didn't hesitate to say what was on her mind when an occasion arose. But she didn't know if she should make a play for Ted in spite of a close friendship with her roommate Linda Breton.

Ted temporarily forgot about last night as he finished a couple of pages on a city awards article which he thought was sufficient. And, it was enough to satisfy the mayor's ego and Alec, who should be making a boisterous entrance soon.

Nothing of special interest appeared on the police blotter with the exception of a call shortly after midnight from a mother who reported her fifteen-year-old daughter missing. After an hour of searching, the girl was discovered walking from the downtown section of the city toward her home. The teenager had neglected to tell her mother she was spending the evening with a friend.

This item on the police log wouldn't make good copy, Ted decided. He dismissed it as a naughty girl's brief adventure.

His timing was right about the boss as Alec Johnson entered the room. A big man with a ruddy complexion, he stood over six feet while his broad shoulders filled the door frame. Although he never mentioned his weight, there was little doubt it well exceeded two hundred pounds, a little more weight than he carried when he played fullback for Chamberlain College. His size and knowledge of the newspaper business left no doubt who was in charge of the newsroom.

The editor's voice carried above the clamor of teletype machines and telephones. He didn't require an intercom to attract the attention of workers in any part of the editorial room. Alec had no sooner reached his office when Ted heard the anticipated roar.

"Get in here, Ted!"

Ted examined his copy as he walked to the city editor's desk to put it in the news basket before entering Alec's office.

Expecting to learn about this morning's assignment, Ted was amazed when Alec brought up the subject of Timothy's conversation last night about the trip.

Noting Ted's surprise, Alec explained he had just left Timothy at Harry's.

"I understand Timothy is planning a trip at the northern retreat," he added. "This year, he sounds excited about this jaunt." "I wonder what's so different about going there in July," Ted said.

"He's usually more interested during the hunting season," Alec replied. "He probably brought back an exotic fish recipe from his visit to New Orleans last week that he wants to try out. We had better be prepared for a hot and spicy menu."

Although Timothy acquired a gourmet appetite, his culinary skills were limited to fish and wildlife, his cooking specialties at the lodge.

Alec was settled in his cushioned swivel chair with an unlit cigar in his mouth, a cue for Ted to reach for a match. The boss was another smoker who seldom carried a light.

With a red ash and puffs of smoke rising toward the ceiling, he looked up at Ted. "Are you ready for that trip, Graves?"

"Anytime to get away from this heat," was the reporter's quick response. "July probably isn't the best month of the year for angling although Bear Lake offers more features than only casting lures in the water."

"Don't try to kid me, Graves. You'll be casting lures but not necessarily in the waters," Alec remarked. "You're planning on taking your new friend along, aren't you? What's her name?"

During the conversation last night with Timothy and now with Alec, Linda's name had surfaced. He hoped she would be interested in this venture. He met Linda more than a year ago when she joined the administrative staff of Chamberlain College and their dates had developed into a more serious romance although he never closed the field to the many other women who sought his attention.

"Why not? Dr. Perry's wife would have a female companion for a change," Ted challenged. "Linda Breton is her name as if you didn't already know. She would be more acceptable to an invitation at a not so male-dominated party."

Alec chuckled.

"I was only trying you out, Ted. I've met Linda at a couple of college functions. She's an impressive girl. Linda and Ruth Perry have

7

apparently become good friends and I understand she's invited to most of the Perry parties," Alec related. "And, they appear to be numerous for an educator with a heavy academic schedule. Enough for now. We'll discuss the trip later," Alec concluded.

With that remark, Ted was dismissed.

Most everyone on the campus knew that Dr. Randolph Perry, a popular professor of mathematics at the college, was nearing the half-century mark and Ruth was about twenty years younger. Regardless of their age difference, they appeared compatible and carefree.

Randy, as he was called by friends, was also a large man weighing nearly two hundred pounds but not as tall as the others in the group except of course, Timothy. He was a dedicated educator who spent many hours with students who experienced difficulty with their assignments.

Ruth, a Middleton High School math teacher, appeared less serious than her husband and she loved to be the center of attention at a gathering. She was a well-built attractive woman slightly taller than Linda and Janice with hazel eyes and an ever-flashing smile. Usually Ruth was the life of a party.

Returning to his desk, Ted made a few phone calls and finished a couple of articles for the city edition.

This completed his day's duties, an unusual occurrence for this reporter who preferred to work the night shift.

Ted reached on his desk for his pack of cigarettes and a pen and stuck both in his shirt pocket. He was headed for the door when Janice, the newcomer, entered the room and approached him.

Smiling, she greeted him. "Hi, good looking," as she sat on a nearby desk. "How's your day been?"

Janice Robinson had many qualities, not the least, her shapely legs. Sometimes it was difficult to look directly at her face. Although she smiled frequently and displayed her beautiful white teeth, this expression would change quickly when her unpredictable temper was aroused. Jan, as she became known at the *Guardian*, not only had a keen sense for news, she normally possessed a blooming personality. At twenty six, she was a graduate from a prestigious school of journalism and already had several years of experience on several dailies in the East.

Ted was amazed how Jan managed to smile in this sweltering room. Of course, her only exposure to the elements were bare legs, a skirt slightly below her knees, and a sheer blouse.

She was aware of what Ted was seeing.

"You should have been at the beach today. The sun blistered everything except my arches.

You haven't seen me in my new bathing suit yet."

"No, I haven't been near the lake for a week," Ted responded. "I'll find time soon if this weather doesn't change. You mentioned a beach. What beach?"

"I spent most of the day at Randy and Ruth's cottage at Cedar Lake. We had a good time in spite of the miserable heat. I was kidding you a few minutes ago. I kept out of the sun or I would look like a boiled lobster. Perhaps, I do anyway," she added.

"I'd like to visit with Randy and Ruth," Ted remarked. "It's been some time since I've seen them. Did you spend much time in the water or just stay in the shade?"

"Only the three of us and Brett were there today," Jan related. "I swam a little but we sat on the porch most of the time. Brett did most of the talking. I found him interesting. Randy was not his usual self today. He was restless and it appeared he had something on his mind that was bothering him," Jan continued. "I think that he and Ruth would like to get away from the city for a spell. It was not like Randy. He hardly took part in the conversation today."

"Well, Jan, nothing seems to have troubled you. The lake must be just what the doctor ordered for you. You look fit and, unlike the rest of us, comfortable. Of course, being young and beautiful, it's much easier for you," Ted added.

Ted was aware Jan had something on her mind.

Could it be the trip?

There was no way she could have known about it so soon. He and Timothy had only discussed it last night, and with the exception of Alec, no one knew the plans.

"What's on your pretty mind Jan," Ted asked, "now that we have covered the day's activities?'

"I can't keep a secret from you," Jan answered. "I overheard a conversation between Father O'Toole and the boss while I was having coffee at Harry's. Could it be that a trip is being planned that might include women other than Ruth Perry this year?"

"Our plans weren't intended as a secret, Jan, but I did have a reason for not revealing them so early," Ted continued. "We wanted you along knowing you'd be a lot of fun."

9

"Are you trying to tell me your intentions are less than honorable, Ted? You certainly aren't trying to put the make on me. I would like to think so but I'm sure that's not the reason. You wanted me along so it would be easier for you to ask Linda. Aren't you the crafty one. All the time, I thought you were making a pass at me. It's all right with me. I would like to be a part of the group if that's possible. I would also like Linda's company. I don't suppose there's another reason why Alec mentioned my name. I will have to wait and see, won't I?"

"Do me a favor, Jan. Please keep this quiet until I have a chance to talk with Linda. I want to surprise her."

Now that he and Jan had a good rapport, he thought this might be the time to bring up another subject, but maybe not.

He was about to forget it when, ironically, Jan opened the conversation by relating Brett had invited her to his studio tonight to look at some photos. "Etchings, he called them, " she added.

"Jan," Ted retorted. "Brett has photos in his studio that could make Satan blush. I don't want to throw cold water on your invitation, but there's something I'd like to tell you."

Suddenly he realized that he was out of line. This was none of his business.

Not knowing exactly what to do, he got up and pushed his chair back.

He couldn't find the words at the moment, but on the way out he leaned over her desk and quietly said, "Jan, try to find an excuse to avoid Brett's invitation tonight and plan to have dinner with me tomorrow. I have something that I'd like to tell you. We'll meet at the Rendezvous Restaurant at noon. Please let me know if you can make it?" He asked.

Ted was oblivious of anything excepting the miserable heat as he walked out of the room and down a flight of stairs to the outside.

He went quickly to his car at the end of the parking lot and drove out of the city.

Something about the proposed trip troubled him. Yet, he couldn't figure out why, it would only be the same friends who had spent a week together on previous occasions. Why should this outing be different?

Chapter 2

Instead of going directly to Harry's, Ted drove to an area along the Kennebec River. One of the state's great branches of water, it flowed through three large counties from Moosehead Lake on its journey to the Atlantic Ocean.

His favorite spot was only a few miles from Middleton overlooking the river, a good place to stop. He turned off the highway on to a winding dirt road that led to a pine grove. He got out of his car, took off his shirt and tossed it in the back seat. Afterward, he took a narrow trail several hundred feet to a place above the Kennebec where the view was spectacular.

Ted walked slowly along the high ground watching the river running below. It was a breathtaking sight as he looked across the rapid waters to the other bank.

A couple of white-tailed deer, a doe and her fawn, were lying on the grassy shore taking advantage of shade from huge oak trees. A squirrel unaffected by the warm weather scampered through patches of yellow and white daisies.

As he continued, his mind drifted back to a conversation with Chief Davidson. During his last phone call before leaving the office today, he talked with the chief who said that the missing girl last night was walking near a photo shop on her way home. Beyond that, the chief told Ted there was nothing unusual about the incident. This only increased Ted's suspicion of Brett's extracurricular activities.

He continued his casual walk and felt the hot sun burning his shoulders. There was hardly a breath of air so he moved farther upstream along the river bank until he found shade under a tall pine. He stretched out on the grass where at last he found some comfort.

How long could this intense heat continue, he wondered as he scanned the sky for possible signs of a break in the weather.

Soon he was aware of a darkening sky in the south. Ted removed his sun glasses and stared at the distant horizon where a glimmer of hope appeared. No question about it. A storm was brewing and a change in the weather pattern was imminent.

It didn't seem possible this place could be so peaceful and tranquil when only a few miles away life was bustling in Middleton. The only interruption of silence this afternoon were sounds of the river ever-flowing southerly with its water dashing wildly over the rocks.

How beautiful it must have been a few centuries ago, he thought. But it wasn't always peaceful, Ted remembered from his history class. During the second Indian War, trade centers along the river, occupied by traders before the seventeenth century, were laid waste by the natives. The area remained in Indian hands until the early 1700's when a stone fort was erected, the strongest fortification on the river at that time. It was destroyed by Indians later and settlers left the region until another was built a quarter century later. It was about this time when a detachment of troops explored the region north of this site, and another fort was built large enough to accommodate a four hundred-soldier garrison.

Civilization came back to the Kennebec Valley as protection was afforded settlers. Gradually life changed as the white men began to occupy the shores of the river forcing the natives to retreat from their heritage.

Ted read a lot about the Kennebec Valley when the rich lands were purchased from the Indians for mere trifles, and the natives were driven from their hunting grounds. Before the century had elapsed, the remaining three families of a once-powerful Indian tribe were forced from the valley. The weakened remnant moved to the northern portion of the valley where they asked English permission to dwell but were refused, and the tribe was driven from the valley. Although some of the early settlers suffered from the hostilities of the natives, most generally the white men started the trouble.

While Ted was enjoying the serenity of the surroundings, he still faced a minor detail of explaining to Jan about the missing girl who was found near Brett's studio. Perhaps he should forget about it. On second thought, he would discuss it with Linda.

It seemed his eyes had barely closed when he heard the sound of a twig snapping, indicating someone was approaching. The footsteps were quiet and were moving slowly toward him.

Suddenly, a light breeze carried a whiff of perfume that only one person would be wearing. It meant Linda was nearby.

When he opened his eyes, Linda was standing motionless looking down at him.

A tall, slender brunette with long, black eyelashes, she smiled as their eyes met. A gentle wind moved the dark hair touching her shoulders.

She spoke softly.

"Where have you been? It seems ages since I've seen you?"

"I've been here, honey, waiting for you," he answered as he reached for her with outstretched hands.

Her delicate frame fell on him and he wasted no time in finding her lips. Neither backed away from the embrace until she murmured breathlessly.

"Let's come up for air. Don't be so eager." "This was worth the wait," Ted replied as they embraced again.

This time, their grasps were tighter while they gradually moved on their sides. Slowing he reached under her blouse for a soft breast while shifting his body on her. They continued their embrace as Linda began to breath heavier and she pulled his head to her face. Their lips pressed tightly together and she felt her body relaxing under him.

Instantly, Linda began to realize what was happening and pushed him away. She really didn't want to move from his grasp so quickly but she was aware where they were heading. And this wasn't the place to continue.

"Come on, Ted. Not here."

Slowly withdrawing, they sat up.

"You must have left your office early, Linda. What happened?"

"Today's heat made it so uncomfortable that Mrs. Thompson decided to close the office. I think she plans on returning tonight when it might be cooler. I drove to the apartment to change and here I am."

"Linda, this is a great place to share with you," Ted said. "I didn't think anyone would bother us here."

"I'm sure other ideas entered your mind when I arrived but you can forget them. I imagine that you're here for other reasons," she remarked.

"I came to do a little thinking and to get away from the unbearable temperatures downtown but I didn't expect to see you," he said. "However, your timing is perfect because I have something to ask you."

"What's on our mind, darling, because I have something to say and a question for you." She replied. "I love you. You know that, don't you?" She whispered staring at him with her warm brown eyes."

"I sure do, honey," he replied as he pulled her toward him again and pressed his lips against hers.

This time, a louder sound of thunder cut short their embrace.

"We had better get back before a storm arrives," Ted remarked.

I'll answer your question first," Linda said. "Why I'm here? Well, it's been more than a week since we were together, and I was afraid that something was wrong. Either you didn't want to see me or you had a problem. What was it?"

"Neither, Linda. I have been busy but the question I have in mind refutes any idea of not wanting to be with you. Would you like to spend a week with me at a lodge on a Maine lake? Not alone but with a group on a fishing outing."

"I'd love to, Ted. With or without others. When do we leave?"

Timothy and I haven't decided on the time for the trip but it would be in July," he answered.

"As long as it doesn't conflict with my work, I'm raring to go anytime. Do I know the others?"

"I think you do. Does it matter?"

"Not a bit as long as you're there," she replied smiling. "Just let me know the dates so I can make arrangements at the office. Now. You had something else on your mind?"

"I'm going to have dinner with Jan tomorrow at the Rendezvous to talk about something that's been bothering me."

She reached for his hands and softly asked, "What can be so important as to require my attention about a dinner with Jan? You don't need me to suggest a menu."

"A couple of things have happened since last night that trouble me. Although they don't directly affect Jan, something she told me today may if she keeps an invitation to visit Brett at his studio tonight," Ted replied. "More of a hunch than a fact. It seems the studio is becoming a focal point for attractive girls," he added. "Last night, police were looking for a teenager who was supposedly visiting a girl friend. This afternoon when I was talking with Chief Davidson, he mentioned the girl was seen near the studio. He couldn't say she had been in the building. The chief told me something else. Several of his officers noticed two vehicles in the studio parking lot. They were Brett's Ford V-8 and Dave Paxton's Lincoln convertible. Adding to events relating to the studio,"

Ted continued. "It was something I found among notes on my desk this afternoon. There was a newspaper clipping about Brett concerning an appearance in a court where he was exonerated on a child pornography charge. I have no idea how the news item got in my notes. Obviously, someone at the *Guardian* had to leave it there. There was no dateline, and names of the city and people involved were removed."

"What does all of this have to do with Jan? Certainly she didn't bring that girl to the studio. I don't think she ever had anything to do with Brett."

"Perhaps you're right, Linda. However, this afternoon, Jan told me she was invited by Brett to his studio tonight to look at his pictures. That's why I asked her to dinner tomorrow and I plan to explain the other incidents."

Linda was obviously upset.

Annoyed, she retorted. "Jan is not only my roommate but also my friend. Are you implying that she is associated with Brett at the studio?"

"I'm trying to avoid that, Linda. She is an attractive woman, and I don't want her portrayed in a different light by his studio cameras. You know what I mean. If you could ever see some of the photos Brett keeps in his files, you'd flip your lid," Ted remarked.

"Ted, Jan's a wonderful person. She's mature and intelligent. I'm sure she knows the facts of life and what it would mean if she did anything stupid. Now, don't you agree?"

"All right, Linda! You're right. I'll call her tonight and cancel my invitation. Hell, what's the matter with me? Why don't I take you to dinner instead? "

Smiling, Linda replied. "It's a date. Now, let's join Timothy at Harry's."

With his arm around her waist, they walked slowly back to their cars.

"Really, Linda, How did you know that I was here?

"A little bird told me," she whispered as she gave him a quick kiss and got into her Ford convertible.

He leaned toward her, asking, "Why did you come here?"

"I thought I told you. I missed you." Ted reached in the back seat for his shirt and put it over his shoulders.

Before they got underway, another rumbling of thunder was heard as a storm front approached the city.

Following behind her, he thought of the two friends who shared an apartment downtown. When they walked together on the sidewalk, many pairs of eyes focused in their direction. Both were attractive. Linda was a slender brunette, while Jan was not as tall and had short auburn hair and weighed a little more. Something else. They were intellectual. Jan, a thriving news reporter, and Linda, a competent secretary to a college president. It appeared they had promising futures.

Neither Ted or Linda was hurrying to Harry's. With their car windows down, the outside air was becoming more tolerable as the storm clouds began to obscure the sun. Winds were shifting slightly westward signifying a sou'wester was en route.

And this one could be furious, Ted thought. Linda's ride in an open convertible was not a good idea with threatening weather .He sounded his horn until he got her attention, then pulled to the roadside. As he got his head inside her car and moved upward to place the car roof to an upright position, his face rubbed against her breasts and again he pulled her toward him. Their eyes met momentarily but this time she quickly pushed him away.

It seemed likely Harry's should be quiet today because of the storm and today was Wednesday, the afternoon of the week, most city professional offices were closed. This was the day doctors, lawyers, and other chiefs went to lakes and golf courses.

The streets were nearly empty of traffic and pedestrians as Ted and Linda entered the city. The condition would soon change. Hundreds who flocked to surrounding lakes earlier in the day to escape the weather would soon be returning to avoid the storm.

As anticipated, Middleton resembled a ghost town when the couple drove the remaining blocks to Harry's.

They had no problem finding parking spaces. With the exception of three vehicles in front of the building, the area was vacant. Behind the restaurant several cars were visible, most likely those belonged to Harry and his employees. A familiar aged Ford sedan was among three automobiles parked close to the building. Timothy was one of the few customers who had chosen to remain downtown in spite of the weather.

Ted and Linda had just turned into the parking lot when a roar of thunder preceded the opening of rain-laden clouds. Rushing out of the coffee shop, a waitress was running to Timothy's car to roll up the windows. She was drenched before returning to the restaurant.

Flashes of lightning streaked across the darkened sky as the storm moved closer to Middleton. Rain was now pouring across the parking area while both Linda and Ted stayed in their vehicles. Not much sense to make a run for the coffee shop during this heavy rain. Nothing to do except wait. Unfortunately, they weren't in the same car.

After sitting a half hour, there was a slight break in the rain. Ted sounded the car's horn and waved to Linda.

Inside the restaurant, Timothy was watching through the window as the couple made a dash for the door. He had been waiting patiently for an hour for Ted to show and he was pleased when Linda appeared with him.

"Linda," the retired clergyman exclaimed as he rose from his seat to greet her. "Well now, a pleasant surprise it is. Seeing you is always a pleasure."

"Father O'Toole, it's nice to be in your company again," Linda replied as she greeted him with a hug.

"You know, a dear you are, "Timothy said. "You're prettier each time I see you. It's no wonder Ted keeps you to himself."

"Father, you haven't lost your line of blarney since we last met," she added. "I'll bet Harry pays you to patronize this place just to attract customers."

"All right, all right," Timothy added. "It's you who always has plenty of nice things to say, young lady. What part of Ireland is it you're from? Oh, yes, something else. All my friends call me Timothy."

"I'll try to remember," Linda responded.

Harry interrupted the conversation. "Would you like a larger table or will this one do, Timothy? " "Fine, it is. I don't believe anyone else will be coming. Your company, we'd enjoy if you have time, Harry"

"Thanks, Timothy, but it's almost supper time and there's work to be done in the kitchen," he answered.

Harry started this business many years ago. No one remembers how many and no effort was made to find out. Most of his customers and friends didn't know his last name or his age. His three customers today knew that Greenwood was his name, but his age was a little more difficult to determine.

As the story goes, Harry boasted many years ago when he reached sixty, he was going to quit the business and spend the rest of his days in the sunny south. According to Timothy who arrived in Middleton nearly six years ago, Harry had passed three score then. This was a mystery someone might eventually solve.

Ted pulled up a chair for Linda, and the three of them sat for a quiet discussion which would certainly involve next month's trip.

Harry interrupted again before the conversation began.

"I almost forgot, Ted. Jan called earlier and asked me to relay these messages to you. First, she will be unable to make it at noon tomorrow, and secondly, if you saw Linda, tell her to call Mrs. Thompson at the office. Now, what will you have?"

"Before I do anything, I'll call the office," Linda said as she headed for a phone.

"Use mine in the kitchen, Linda," Harry offered. "It will save you a nickel."

"Harry, please bring me a glass of iced tea, and I'm sure Linda will have the same," Ted said.

"May I buy you another coffee, Timothy? "

"I'm all set for now," he responded. "Shall we talk a little about the trip while Linda is on the phone? By the way, did you invite her?"

"I sure have and she would like to join us if her work doesn't interfere."

"That's wonderful. Now, shall we go over the names on the list. The lodge can accommodate a dozen persons or more. But, I don't think we want to go beyond that number. "What do you think?"

"It's your party, Timothy. However, if you want my opinion, and apparently you do, I think eight and not more than ten would be about right," Ted replied. "It's still a sizable group. Also, keep in mind you always like to do the cooking and you don't need a lot of mouths to feed."

He knew Timothy never thought of cooking at the lodge as work, but this was still a lot of work for anyone, especially a seventy-year-old retiree. He often wondered how Timothy could accumulate so much energy.

If Timothy gave any thought to the almost totally different group from prior years, he never let on. This is the first time that there would be almost as many women as men.

Linda returned from her phone call and joined them at the table as a waitress brought their drinks.

"This is refreshing," she remarked, taking her first sip. "Evelyn, Mrs. Thompson, who's the administrator of the college president's office, asked if I could return to the office tonight. It seems Mr. Damon has a series of supper meetings scheduled and invitations must be mailed. Timothy, I've seen you only twice since I came to Middleton. And that was more than a year ago. It seems Ted joins you often here but he seldom brings me along. He didn't forget me entirely because he invited me on the fishing trip that you are planning. It sounds exciting. I'd love to go if I can make it."

"We'll try to arrange the outing so it doesn't interfere, "Timothy replied. "We'll set our sights on the latter weeks of July. That should give everyone a chance to prepare. What do you think, Ted?"

That's all right with me. Does that give you enough time, Linda?"

"I'll know after I talk with Evelyn tonight. I don't believe there'll be any problems," she replied. "I've got to leave now to do a few errands that I had intended to do later. Hope to see you again real soon, Timothy."

Linda hurriedly finished her tea and whispered in Ted's ear before making her way to the door. It was still raining as she rushed to her convertible and drove to the campus. "I didn't get much of an opportunity to talk with Linda, Ted. I'd like to learn more about her work at the college. And being inquisitive, I intended to pry more into her life. Just an old priest's nosy habit. Hang onto her, son. She's a winner," Tim said.

Ted was pleased with Timothy's interest in Linda.

"Frankly, Timothy, I can only tell you a few things about her past. She came to Middleton from Watertown, Massachusetts, early last year after learning of a vacancy on the president's staff at Chamberlain College. She applied for the position of secretary to Mr. Damon. Both the president and Mrs. Thompson were so impressed with her resume and qualifications they hired her on the spot. Since we've been dating, she told me her education included a degree from a secretarial college in Boston and that she was a secretary to an insurance executive in that city for two years. On a personal side, her father's graduation gift included an extensive tour of Europe and the Middle East. Besides these travels, she has visited all our states and most of the Canadian Provinces. Does that give you some idea of her background?" Ted asked.

"Just what I surmised, Ted. I hope I'm around for the ceremony."

"You will. You'll be performing it," Ted responded.

"That will be a pleasure, Ted. Now, I'll be going home. It's getting closer to supper for the Haneys. Helen will be looking out the window for her lost lamb. A cold meal, she doesn't want me to eat. Now, as far as the trip is concerned, I believe the only thing left to do is to extend invitations," Timothy remarked.

"That shouldn't be difficult," Ted said." As it stands now, you are the host with three persons from the *Guardian*, Alec, Jan, and me. Three of the others are from the college campus, Randy, Ruth, and Linda while Brett completes the list of eight."

"We'll let Alec invite Jan? He really wants her on this trip," Timothy proposed.

"Good idea," was the reporter's reply. "We'll get together on the logistics of this safari later."

Timothy rose from his chair and walked slowly to the door and out in the rain. The storm appeared to have gained momentum as the rainfall was heavier and the wind had gathered strength.

Ted wasn't particularly worried about Timothy driving to the Haneys. He was a good driver and it was only a dozen blocks away on the outskirts of Middleton.

The retired priest had found a new home at the hands of the Haneys who catered to him like a child. He was provided with a large bedroom with ample room for a desk besides having run of the house. Needless to mention, both Helen and Mike made certain their guest was comfortable.

While the storm outside intensified, Ted was trying to make up his mind how to spend the evening. Only a few customers remained in the coffee shop so he decided to have a drink in the pub.

Harry's place was actually two buildings. The coffee shop with an L-shaped counter and a dozen tables was built adjacent to another structure housing the pub. Under that arrangement, customers who wanted an ale or those desiring food had to enter separate buildings. A canopy over the sidewalk along the front of the buildings provided protection from the elements.

"See you later," he said to Harry as he walked out the door. "I'm going to the pub."

Torrential rain was falling as he stepped outside. The parking lot was vacant except for his vehicle. Shoppers, vacationers, and others were seeking shelter in other places, Ted reasoned.

The odor of stale brew prevailed when he opened the pub door. After adjusting his eyes to the dim room, Ted saw that the only person present was Don, a bartender who had become a fixture in this place. Ted remembered that someone once said Harry had brought him along when he opened the business, but that was questionable.

"Wild time out there," Don uttered while Ted walked toward the bar. "We need the water but not so much at one time."

Ted agreed as he sat on a stool. "Kinda quiet, isn't it?"

"It's been this way most of the day," Don replied. "First, the heat kept most everyone away from downtown and now the storm is keeping them at home. The usual ale, Ted ?"

"Sure. And then, I'm going to the movies. Nothing else to do."

As they chatted, mostly about the weather, another customer entered and sat at the other end of the bar.

Wiping his face with a handkerchief, the new arrival ordered a martini.

"Wow! Is it ever rough outside!," he exclaimed.

Ted easily recognized the newcomer as Dave Paxton, better known in Middleton as the newlywed husband of a much older woman with more cash than she could ever spend. Unquestionably, he was a handsome man which would make him easy prey for wealthy women. Gossip had it that she came by her millions as heiress to an industrialist. Besides a Florida home in Palm Beach where the couple wintered, she owned a sizable estate at the head of Cedar Lake in this city.

Ted and Dave exchanged greetings, only mentioning the weather. Alec was better acquainted with Dave, who was not a popular person. What surprised Ted was his appearance here tonight, especially in a place he rarely frequented. And when he did come here for a drink, Alec was usually with him.

Ted knew little about Dave, only what Alec had told him. His wife, Phyllis, had spent most of her life in Florida. During the winter, she devotes most of her time hosting charity functions and keeping close watch on Dave. Alec said she was extremely jealous and Dave was aware of it. One slip and he would become a member of the working class again, Alec had remarked. Ted didn't now how well Dave knew Brett but he went to his studio occasionally, probably only for business.

Ted finished his drink and left for the movies. It was still raining as he ran to his Chevy and drove to the theater.

He sat three hours through a double feature, and he was relieved when the last reel came to an end. However, he did like the antics of Marjorie Main and Percy Kilbride in *Ma & Pa Kettle* and *A Letter To Three Wives*. Linda Darnell was in this movie and Ted thought she was sultry. Anyhow, it was as good a way as any to spend an evening.

Rain was still falling as he headed back but instead of going directly home, he drove downtown which was a common habit for him. As he neared Brett's studio, he slowed his car to see if any vehicles were parked behind the building. Peering through the rain, he saw two vehicles but they were not distinguishable. So, he entered the driveway to the lot and passed by them. One was Brett's and the other belonged to Ruth Perry.

How could that be he thought, looking at the dashboard clock? It's nearly ten o'clock. What would she be doing here at this time of night? Not only was it a late hour for the studio to be open on a normal schedule day, but this was Wednesday when almost every business establishment in the city had been closed since noon.

He left the lot and continued down King Street. A vehicle was approaching and, being a curious reporter, he slowed down to see the driver. It was Jan and she would be passing the studio. He stopped and looked back as she made a turn into the studio lot. Well, he thought that was her prerogative. She had refused his invitation for dinner and accepted Brett's suggestion to view his work at the studio indicating she preferred to be with him..

But more puzzling, he wondered, how does Ruth fit into this triangle?

Chapter 3

A bright red sky on the eastern horizon was an omen of yet another hot day in Middleton. Looking out the bedroom window at his home with the Haneys, Timothy knew the red sky was a harbinger of a storm later in the day, similar to yesterday. He recalled the adage, "Red sky in the morning, sailors take warning. Red sky at night, sailors delight."

He arose slowly from the bed and walked to the door where he knew Helen had put the morning newspaper on the hall carpet.

Timothy returned to his favorite chair, a rocker he brought with him from the parish rectory in New York, and began the day reading about yesterday's world events.

Timothy was a small person, slightly taller than five feet and weighing about one hundred pounds. His silver-framed eye glasses rested on the edge of his nose while an unlit pipe extended from his mouth. His pale face was the result of his profession that kept him indoors most of his life.

He turned the pages of the *Guardian* scrutinizing them carefully. Nothing of any consequence attracted his attention in this morning's edition as most of the stories related to the weather. If the present temperature continued, he assumed tomorrow's newspaper would be a replica of today's. He finished reading the paper, and he had nearly completed the day's crossword puzzle when there was a light knock on the door with a familiar question.

"Are you all right, Father? "

"Yes, Helen, " Timothy answered. "I'll be down shortly."

"There's no hurry, Father. Breakfast will be ready when you are."

The Haneys were friends of Timothy's who refused to eliminate his title when addressing him.

"Anyway," both Mike and Helen said emphatically, "Father is who you are and Father is what we will call you."

About a half hour later, Timothy was sitting at the table enjoying his usual breakfast...a bowl of cereal, toast, and two cups of coffee.

Helen usually joined him for his second coffee while she most always insisted he should eat more.

His response would be. "I've had enough to eat and I'll be having a snack at Harry's."

After he finished his coffee, he got up from the table and walked toward the front door.

"Another hot day, it is, Father," Helen warned. "Don't stay in the sun," he heard while leaving the house for his morning visits downtown.

Timothy's first call would be with Chief Davidson just in case he missed something in the *Guardian*. He often told him that he was "only a nosy old priest."

Helen was correct. The day was becoming warmer without a breeze or a cloud in the sky. He parked in front of the police station and climbed the cement stairs to the chief's office. The open door was Timothy's invitation to enter although he gave a slight knock on its frame.

"Come in, Timothy," the chief shouted. "Don't stand on ceremony."

"Morning to you, Chief. Only passing by and wanted to say hello," Timothy grinned.

"Your hello means you want to know what's taking place in Middleton that the Guardian didn't know or print," the veteran officer responded. "Frankly, it's been awful quiet the past few days. Last call of any interest, and that wasn't much, was the report of a missing girl who turned up within an hour. Ted must have told you about that."

"No, that he didn't. I was with him briefly yesterday but no mention was made of a girl. That's understandable because he was with Linda Breton and we were discussing other matters. Anything unusual about this incident, you say?"

"Nothing excepting she was only fifteen years old and walking alone after midnight," the chief related. "We have learned it wasn't the first time the girl was late getting home, but it was the only time to her mother's knowledge she was in the downtown area at night."

"Something you're leaving out, John," the retired priest commented. "You and Ted had something on your mind."

"Timothy, nothing of importance occurred, only the girl's tale didn't make sense. Although her mother was often working late at night, a friend said Dawn didn't stay home alone. She and a companion were away from the house on many occasions. On this particular night, she told her mother she was going to visit a friend, but her mother doesn't recall the conversation. Two officers in a cruiser who located her reported she was near Brett's studio but she was heading toward home.

"An officer who was on foot patrol thought he saw someone coming out the rear door of the building a few minutes earlier. Another patrolman on this beat mentioned activity in this area at night but it usually involved older women.

"There isn't much we can do about operating a photo studio at night or any other time. We know that some women like being photographed nude. It takes place all over the country. I'm sure there are other similar incidents in this city from business offices to private homes.

"However, this type of photography involving juveniles is a horse of a different color. We aren't going to allow it in this city.

"Returning to this incident, there were a couple of other related matters, none of which are incriminating. Two vehicles were in the studio's parking lot, and there were no visible lights in the studio. One of the cars was Brett's and the other belonged to Dave Paxton," the chief said.

"A coincidence, it could be," Timothy added. "She could have been passing by the studio while the two cars were there. That child could have been anywhere during those hours. A boy friend, she could have?"

"She had many according to her friends, "the chief replied. "She apparently wasn't selective about male companions. Let's get down to facts, Timothy. The child as you called her is fifteen but the age is deceiving as she is only a month away from her sixteenth birthday. Describing her is something else as the age doesn't match her body. She is larger than most fifteen-year-olds, about five feet six, weighs about one hundred and ten pounds and well developed. Doesn't that present a different perspective?"

"It's a young woman you're describing, chief. It's difficult to suspect Brett would get involved with a girl although he and Dave are rumored to have roving eyes."

"That ends that story, Timothy," the chief added as he rose from his chair and walked over to close the office door.

"You didn't close the door because it was too cold in here, did you, Chief? Something else, you have to say?" Timothy inquired.

"This has to do with Brett. Timothy, we have been friends since you arrived in this city and our police conversations are confidential. I understand Brett is over his head in gambling debts and I believe he's a friend of yours. Last week, a local bank executive told me he is having financial difficulties and it's becoming worse. He's heavily mortgaged," the chief continued.

"To hear that, I'm sorry," Timothy said. "He's had problems before coming to this city but not that serious. I truly hope he can live with it."

"And, that may not be long," the chief added.

"What's going on? What's that, you mean?"

"The worse is yet to come, Timothy. A couple of days ago, one of my detectives was in the studio area when a car with Rhode Island number plates stopped in front of the building. One of its occupants went inside and returned with Brett at his side. Brett entered the vehicle and talked to someone in the back seat. He then returned to his studio. He reported that the photographer was visibly shaken. When Sgt. Davis returned to the station, he called the state police and learned the vehicle was registered to a business firm in Providence. The only address was the city name and post office box."

The cop and the priest looked at each other for a minute before Timothy broke the silence.

"He'll not come to a good end. Our knowledge of this type of operation places Brett in a dangerous situation. What do you think will happen now, Chief? "

"Only speculation, Timothy, but he's got to find a way to raise quick cash or the lid may fall. Those boys play rough and have exceptionally long arms. Nude photos of attractive girls command top prices," the chief continued. And, inasmuch as photos of girls are more lucrative than school and family portraits, I think Brett is after the big money to get himself out of the hole with the syndicate. In the department, we aren't going to take this incident of the missing girl lightly. This is one case, as insignificant as it may appear, we plan to solve. There'll be no publicity about it, but believe me, Timothy, I want to know where the teenager was on that night before our officers discovered her walking on the street," Chief Davidson emphasized. "I won't tolerate business of this nature in my city."

"There was another subject pertaining to this affair. And, of course, it's classified," the chief said. " I have a suspicion that state police are preparing a raid on Charlie's Cigar Store on Water Street. The owner has been taking book for years, and he's associated with out-of-state gamblers. I don't know, but he could be Brett's outlet."

Rising from his chair, the chief extended a hand to Timothy saying, "I've got paper work to finish. Drop in again soon."

"And I'll be saying good bye to you, Chief," Timothy replied as he thanked him and left the office.

As Timothy strolled down the hall, he stopped for a chat with the desk sergeant in case the chief had omitted an item of news from their conversation.

"How's the day going, Sergeant?" Timothy asked.

"Unusually quiet," the officer answered. "Combination of the extra warm weather and the vacations seem to have kept both the pedestrian and auto traffic down. According to our log, it was quiet last night. I can't recall such behavior in all of my days at this desk."

"Let's hope it's not the calm before an impending rash of stormy events to disturb your vacation from crime," Timothy said. "However, I have an idea things will soon return to normal."

With these parting words, Timothy walked from the building.

The heat was becoming worse as he crossed the street to the book store for a copy of the *New York Times*. Ordinarily, he would sit on a bench in the city square to read this newspaper, but today's temperature was too much for him. He got into his car and headed for Harry's where Ted might be having a coffee.

Ted hadn't witnessed the early morning sunrise because he didn't awake until after ten. However, he was aware that last night's rain hadn't helped weather conditions. It only intensified the heat and humidity. It wasn't the weather that bothered him this morning; it was remembering what took place last night.

Could it be possible Ruth Perry was involved with Brett, not that he wasn't surprised about the photographer's morals? But Ruth? He couldn't believe she would step out on her husband. There had to be another explanation.

Perhaps her car had engine problem and she left it in the studio lot. Or possibly, she loaned it to someone. He thought maybe Ruth would tell Linda what happened.

Now, how about the other end of the triangle? What was Jan doing there? He saw her car entering the parking lot.

Suddenly, he realized he had a dinner date with Linda and he had planned to meet with Timothy for coffee.

He reached for the phone and called Linda's office.

"Hi, beautiful," he said when she answered, "our date still on?"

"Yes, dear. I'll be at the Rendezvous about 12:30. What have you been doing?"

"I just woke up. Haven't got out of the sack yet. I was thinking of something that happened last night when I remembered we had a date

27

today."

"What happened last night, Ted?" She asked.

"It's too long a story to talk about now if you want to keep that date with me. I'll tell you later at the restaurant."

"Now, you've made me curious. Can't you give me some hints, " she appealed.

"No, darling. You'll have to wait. Sorry."

"All right, Ted, if you want to be that way."

Then, she added, "Forgive me, honey. I want to know but I can wait to satisfy my curiosity. See you soon," Linda concluded as she put the phone down.

Ted got out of bed and walked to the bathroom. He stretched out in the tub as cool water slowly covered him. This was refreshing but he couldn't stay here long. He wanted to see Timothy before he met with Linda at the Rendezvous.

It was getting late when he finished dressing so he only glanced at the newspaper that was left at the front door and left for downtown to do a few household errands. If he didn't meet too many acquaintances it shouldn't take long to make these stops. He was lucky today. The weather had kept most everyone away from the shopping area so he wasn't interrupted on his rounds except at the drugstore where a second bit of luck surfaced.

He heard a group of girls talking and laughing about someone being lost. Curious, he walked closer, trying not to be noticed when he heard one say, "Being lost wasn't too bad. I had fun."

One of the girls started to tell the others more but she spotted Ted as he moved closer to them. She whispered something and they made a hasty retreat from the store.

Then, it dawned on him. This could be the missing girl. Ted was surprised at her size since police reported she was only fifteen. This girl was really stacked.

Completing his purchases, Ted hurried back home to straighten his room. He still lived with his mother and father in the family house in this city where he grew up. The three of them liked this arrangement of being together where Ted still had his freedom and they had their son. Although they had only been away on vacation for a few days, he missed them.

The house was warm and quiet when he entered. He put the items he had just bought in the cupboard and went upstairs to make his bed.

Afterward, he gathered his soiled clothes that were scattered about the room and the wet towels in the bathroom and brought them downstairs to the washroom. After he finished these chores, he went outside to his Chevy and headed downtown again.

Ted and Timothy arrived at Harry's a few minutes apart. When Ted entered the restaurant, his friend was seated at a table near the window reading the *Times* and where he could also see what was taking place outside. On this day, there wasn't much activity as the climbing temperature kept customers away.

"The weather apparently is the top news again today," Timothy said as his companion neared the table.

"And if the proverb of 'Red sky in the morning and so forth' materializes, there's going to be a lot of it to talk about. Did you see the sunrise this morning? "

"No," Ted replied. "I slept later than usual so our coffee break will have to be brief. I almost forgot my date with Linda this noon. I had some errands to do downtown and things to do around the house. After we end our talk about the trip, I've got something interesting to tell you that took place in the drugstore.

"Now, Timothy, lets get back to the drawing board. I believe we've decided on the size of the group although Jan hasn't been invited yet. Do you want me to ask Alec to do it as you suggested or will you call him?"

"I'll probably see him here this afternoon when he drops in for coffee and, if not, I'll call him before Jan reports for work," Timothy replied.

"Good, Timothy. Now all we have to do is set a date and, of course, another important detail, logistics. Let's do the easy part now. Setting the date. How about July 13, unless you're superstitious?" Ted suggested.

"That's fine with me," Timothy replied. "I have an idea, Ted. I'll include Randy while making the other calls this afternoon, and I'll try to get him involved in the preparations. I'm sure he'd like to take part in the planning stage."

Randy and Ruth had never missed a trip to Bear Lake with Timothy. They loved the outdoors but preferred the hunting season more than the summer outing. The couple's cottage at Cedar Lake was a popular place where they entertained friends during the summer. In the academic part of the year, they hosted numerous parties at their residence near the campus.

They were good hunters and excellent marksmen. During the past two hunting season since their arrival in Maine, both had tagged a deer.

Timothy liked these outings too. That's when he had a chance to display his culinary art of preparing dishes with fresh venison as the entree.

"There's no question about it," Timothy said. "Randy and Ruth must be at the next meeting."

"All right, Timothy. I plan to meet Linda at the Rendezvous in an hour and I've got to make a quick stop at the *Guardian* before then."

"I'll finish my coffee and go home where it'll be cooler under the maples," Timothy replied. "I did my errands earlier and visited with the chief for a few minutes. He said the city has been quiet lately with hardly any activity which surprises him since hot weather usually breeds trouble."

Ted was about to leave when he realized he hadn't discussed the missing girl with Timothy, and he had promised to tell him about the incident at the drugstore this morning.

"Timothy, there's an item missing from the *Guardian* that was listed on the police blotter yesterday. It didn't appear to have any significant news value since no crime was committed. As only a teenager was involved, I disregarded it .However, there's something about the incident annoying me."

"You're talking about the missing girl, aren't you," Timothy answered. "The chief told me about it. Although there's nothing criminal about the incident, as you mentioned, it seems to have created an interest for him also."

Timothy was reminded he must keep only to the facts of this incident as his conversation with the chief was confessional privilege as he liked to put it, or confidential, relating to Brett's other activity.

"I don't know how much the chief told you, Timothy, but something I witnessed this morning adds more interest to it."

Ted related details of his experience at the drugstore earlier.

"Something odd is taking place and I can't put my finger on it. Do you have an opinion? "

"I will have to wait and see. Everything thus far is circumstantial. As I told the chief, it is difficult for me to believe Brett would get involved with such a young girl although he does have a way with women. As far as Dave Paxton is concerned, I don't know enough about him or his habits," Timothy concluded. As he was finishing his coffee, Ted left for the Rendezvous and his date with Linda.

Chapter 4

An early bird, Linda watched the colorful spectacle of the sun's ascent in a cloudless sky. In her travels she had learned the maxim of a pink horizon leading to a storm later in the day. She remained in bed looking out the window while thinking of the brief encounter with Ted yesterday at the river. She had only been in his arms yesterday for a few minutes but she couldn't get him off her mind.

She was now aware how much she loved him, more than she could ever have imagined. She wondered if his love for her was as sincere. Linda was also aware that taking Ted for granted would be a mistake. A handsome man with sandy wavy hair and steel gray eyes, he was one of the top-sought after mates in the city. She also remembered the words that she had whispered in his ears yesterday. "I'll make it up to you later, dear," she told him. When would she keep that promise?

Linda realized that dreaming wasn't getting her anywhere. She would be seeing him at dinner. Her main concern at the moment as she opened the closet door was selecting something light to wear. Naturally, it had to be appealing for her date at noon. She moved quietly about the apartment trying not to disturb Jan. While getting dressed, she remembered last night's conversations.

They had arrived at their apartment about the same time and stayed up talking about their day's activities. Jan said she didn't meet Brett last night, mainly because of the storm.

Jan told her that a special women's meeting she was assigned to cover was canceled so Alec let her go home before ten. Ordinarily, it would have been near midnight. That's the hour she told Brett she might stop at the studio.

However, she told Linda her decision had been made earlier about seeing him. She said it would be late and she had doubts about such a visit after talking with Ted.

It did appear strange to Linda that Ted's suggestion not to meet with Brett last night was so effective. His brief chat in the afternoon seemed to have left an impression because Jan had been eager to see Brett.

As Linda recalled last night's conversations, she thought of Jan's remark about how light traffic had been downtown. And, Jan's response when Linda asked her what she was doing in that area instead of coming directly to the apartment.

"It was raining hard when I approached the intersection and I missed the turn on High Street, "Jan related. Realizing she could have taken other turns before heading downtown, she quickly added, "I guess my thoughts were somewhere else. I wasn't paying too much attention to my driving."

Without trying to appear too inquisitive, Linda asked, "Did you have a sudden change of mind about meeting Brett?"

"Maybe," she said.

Linda decided it was time to change this subject and brought up the fishing trip.

"You must have heard about the outing planned next month by Father Timothy. I've been invited and I'm sure you'll get an invitation soon."

"It sounds like a lot of fun," Jan replied. "Until now, I believe Ruth Perry has been the only woman on these trips. Apparently she has privileges. As you mentioned, I'll get an invitation, one that I'll readily accept although I don't know who's extending it."

"Don't be coy with me, Jan. You know who's beginning to keep an eye in your direction. Hasn't Alec made any kind of advances yet?"

"No, he seems to be more interested in his farm than anything," Jan replied. "I doubt if he knows that I exist except when it's time for news assignments."

"You may be surprised, Jan. This might be Alec's first move in your direction. Wait and see."

Although Linda didn't grasp the significance of Jan's earlier remark referring to Ruth's privileges, she continued talking about the trip.

"I'm sure you will receive your invitation before the day is over," Linda said. "And I'll learn the date of the event from Ted when we meet at dinner. I'm positive Father O'Toole and he have made a decision.

"You'll know when you get to the *Guardian*," Linda continued. "I don't know how well acquainted you are with Father O'Toole, but he insisted last night we drop his title in future conversations and just call him Timothy. Seems awkward but if that is what he wants, I'll do it."

"I'll follow suit," Jan added. "What do we take on this safari, Linda, besides insect repellent. I understand this could be the time of year when flies are bad. We never had that problem when Dad and I hunted elk back in Wyoming."

"I never knew you were an outdoor person, Jan. Did you shoot any?"

"Sure. Dad took me on hunting trips while I was in high school. I killed five elk during those years. I don't want to brag, but I'm pretty good with a rifle. I kind of wish this were the hunting season instead of fishing."

"You never cease to amaze me, Jan, with your past experiences. For some reason, I thought you were brought up in the northeast. Perhaps it's because you worked on newspapers in New England. Anyhow, you should feel right at home in the Maine woods where there are plenty of animals," Linda added. "Obviously, we should see wildlife on this outing."

"Besides mosquito dope," Jan said, "there is clothing to think about, particularly footwear. The lodge is a long distance from a main highway. We will ride most of the way but if a storm arises, we'll probably have to do some walking. That's the impression I got while listening to Ted and Alec talk about previous trips," Jan related somewhat surprising Linda as she brought up the subject first.

"Jan, you are more familiar with details of the trip than I, "Linda said.

"In a way, I should be. These trips, both hunting and fishing, are talked about frequently at the office when Timothy drops in. And Randy and Ruth are always wondering when the next one is scheduled. But we still have to make our own plans."

"From a female point of view, we can talk with Ruth and ask her advice, "Linda added. "She must have a lot to offer."

"I'm sure she does," Jan quipped. "Now, I'm going to turn in."

She went to her bedroom while Linda was still trying to understand what was meant by her last remark. It was the second time tonight Jan had uttered something odd when Ruth's name was mentioned.

Linda tried to forget the previous night's talks as she finished dressing. She didn't want to wake Jan, so instead of eating breakfast in the apartment, she drove to a diner near the college.

It was a clear morning but the heat was overwhelming. With the mercury rising every hour, Linda wondered how high the thermometer would get by late day. The weather was certainly playing a role in the activities of Middleton residents with little traffic on the street and few customers in the diner.

She sat alone at the counter where she ordered a light breakfast. There was no one she knew among the patrons which was uncommon. Apparently most of the working people were on vacation. Another factor was the ending of the college semester two weeks ago. With that, hundreds of students and school personnel vacated the campus which was located less than a mile away.

Without anyone to talk with, Linda finished her coffee and left for her office although it wouldn't officially open until another hour. She drove to the campus where she parked her convertible in front of the administration building.

With plenty of time on her hands, she strolled under the shade of trees to a small pond. It was peaceful here. Linda sat on a bench watching a duck and its flock of ducklings glide gracefully in the water creating ripples on its surface. The ripples, as they reached shore, and the occasional chirping of birds were the only sounds to interrupt the morning silence.

She was hopeful a similar environment prevailed at Bear Lake in a few weeks when she could share this kind of beauty with Ted. She was happy when he was around as they enjoyed many of the same things.

Thinking back since her arrival here eighteen months ago, she thought of their dates at college concerts and hockey games. Whatever he was doing, it seemed that she wanted to be a part of it.

Their backgrounds were similar in numerous ways, she thought. They each came from a one-child household and lived in cities of comparable size. Both were educated in small colleges and they had traveled extensively. At twenty-six, she was only a few years younger than he. More important to her now was the possibility they were in love. She was sure of her feelings but not certain of his intentions. His popularity kept her guessing.

For the second time this morning she found herself dreaming about Ted. If ever there was an ideal place to dream, this was it. She decided to leave the bench and walk along the shore. There was still plenty of time remaining before the office opened. If only it weren't so warm, she would enjoy walking around the campus. The heat was getting the better of her as she returned to the original seat waiting for time to pass. If only she had bought a newspaper at the diner, at least she could be reading.

Now, her thoughts shifted to Jan. Yesterday, Ted was the person who was concerned about her roommate and a probable association with

Brett. Today, Linda was wondering why Jan had made a couple of remarks when Ruth's name was mentioned. What could have happened since yesterday morning when Ted said Jan had visited Randy and Ruth at the lake? Everything seemed all right then. Something had to take place last night. But how and where? Maybe Ted would have an answer.

A sound of a car broke the silence as it entered the office area and parked next to Linda's convertible.

She and campus custodian Ron Goodwin reached the administration building about the same time. They ascended the stairs together, and Ron unlocked and held the door open as she entered.

Although the original college was founded around the turn of the nineteenth century, today's campus consisted of mostly new buildings. All the structures were impressive including the administrative headquarters. A spacious foyer provided entrance to the first floor where paintings, artifacts, and memorabilia were displayed.

Usually Linda hurried through the area to her office, but today she had plenty of time and Ron for a guide. It would be awhile before the rest of the president's staff arrived so she walked slowly in the hall examining some of the exhibits.

Ron was knowledgeable about Civil War history and, particularly, Col. Joshua Lawrence Chamberlain of the 20th Maine infantry, who later was promoted to brigadier general on the field.

In the center of the foyer was a bronze bust of the college's namesake, not only a Civil War hero, but a four-term governor of Maine.

Ron enjoyed guiding visitors through the foyer and expounding the feats of this Maine hero. Linda was impressed with the custodian who related the general's movements with the Army of the Potomac from Antietam to Appomattox.

He pointed out the inscription mounted below the bust recording his exploits at Gettysburg. The highlight of the battle occurred when he led his men, who had exhausted their ammunition, on a furious bayonet charge. This action broke a Confederate onslaught and held Little Round Top for the Union.

The message concluded, "Although wounded, Chamberlain continued to lead the charge until the Confederates retreated from the hill. Thirty years later, the nation recognized him for his valor by awarding him the Medal of Honor." It was no wonder, Linda thought, that the college was named in his honor.

She also learned from Ron, prior to the war, Chamberlain was a

34-year-old professor at Bowdoin College who secured a sabbatical supposedly to study in Europe, but instead of traveling became an officer in the Maine 20th.

"Where did you learn so much about the exploits of this soldier?" Linda asked her escort.

"I was interested in American history while attending Middleton High School, especially of the war between the North and South. So when I became a custodian here, it seemed like a good idea to learn more about General Chamberlain for whom the college was named. Now, I enjoy recalling the life of this hero to both college students and visitors."

Linda thanked him and walked to the college president's office where other members of the staff were arriving.

"Good morning, Linda," Mrs. Thompson said as she greeted her near the door. "What a pretty dress you're wearing. Is it new?"

" The answer is yes and no. I bought it a few weeks ago when I went home to Massachusetts over a weekend. However, it's the first time I have worn it."

"Anyhow, my dear, you look lovely. It would seem that you are going on a date instead of work."

"I do have a confession to make," Linda replied blushing. "I plan to meet Ted for dinner at the Rendezvous this noon."

Mrs. Thompson smiled, adding, "We will have to be careful not to work you too hard this morning."

They entered the office together and Linda went to her desk.

The sun was at its height when she and Ted approached the Rendezvous from opposite directions. It was blazing hot, not a leaf in the trees was stirring, and streets were void of traffic. Although the early morning sky indicated a storm was forthcoming, there wasn't a cloud anywhere.

It was difficult to get excited about a break in the weather following a storm as yesterday's rain hadn't alleviated temperatures a bit. Actually, it had only increased the humidity.

Literally and figuratively, it was a warm greeting as the couple embraced after leaving their cars. An onlooker might have guessed that they had been separated for months, not less than twenty-four hours. A minute later, they loosened their hug and walked into the restaurant.

A hostess greeted them as they approached the dining room and she offered them any table. Smiling she added. "Take your pick. This weather is not conducive to the eating business. If it doesn't pick up soon, all of us can go on vacation."

Not only was the outside heat keeping patrons away, it was not comfortable inside either. Several large fans helped circulate the air but much of the warmth still prevailed. Linda thought that the only place to keep cool was in a lake, a place where neither of them would be today.

Anyhow, Linda was pleased because Ted was with her.

"My day's work is half over, Ted, and yours hasn't started. I feel sorry for you. But, what the heck, you're a big boy."

"That's all right, honey. Having dinner together will help make this day pass more quickly," he said.

"In a few weeks, we'll be vacationing far away from this place. I'll bet the hours will pass faster then. By the way, Timothy and I set July 13 as the day for the trip. I hope it meets your schedule. If not," he laughed, "we'll choose another date."

"I'll check with Mrs. Thompson, but I'm sure it's all right. We talked about the trip last night, and it appears next month should be quiet here. So, dear, we can be together for a whole week. Isn't that wonderful?" she gleamed. "Have you got ideas of how we can be alone most of the time?"

"I'll work on it," he replied. "Now, what are we going to eat?"

That wasn't a difficult decision. The Rendezvous was noted for its excellent lobster salad so they agreed on this entree along with iced tea.

Then, they resumed their conversation.

"Did you miss me?" she teased, reaching across the table for his hands. "I thought of you often last night."

"Of course, I missed you," Ted smiled. "Looking forward to the trip makes it easier. As you said, we'll have a week to share together."

"I'm sure it will be fun," she added. "Is there any other news of interest? "

"I don't think so. Jan visited Brett's studio last night as she planned," Ted added. "It's her life so she can do what she likes. I only hope she doesn't get hurt on the way. Oh, I'm sorry Linda. I agreed not to say anymore about her affairs."

"Ted, you're wrong. Jan told me she changed her mind about seeing Brett last night, and she came home directly after she left the office last night. We arrived at the apartment about the same time, shortly after ten o'clock. Alec let her off early because an assignment was canceled. Jan said the heavy rain obstructed her vision when she approached High Street and she missed the turn. So, she drove through the streets downtown and returned to the apartment. Jan said she had decided not to go to the studio after you spoke to her at the office. Anyway, she said it was too late for a visit."

"That's odd, Linda. When I passed the studio last night after the movies, Jan was driving on King Street and when she drove past me, I stopped and looked back. I saw her enter the driveway leading to the studio parking lot at the rear of the building."

"Well, she must have had a change of mind at the last minute," Linda surmised.

"Or, something she witnessed could have initiated a sudden switch in plans," Ted responded.

They were silent when the waitress brought beverages to the table.

"I don't understand your logic. Who could she have seen at that hour? It was past ten o'clock and the studio office was closed long before that. In fact, the studio is closed on Wednesday afternoons."

"Perhaps it was not who she saw but what she saw," Ted replied.

"Now you're talking in riddles. What do you mean?"

As he was about to continue, Dave and Phyllis Paxton became the restaurant's third and fourth customers. They were seated close to a window at the other end of the room.

Mrs. Paxton's hair was almost snow white, and the heavy makeup didn't cover her wrinkled face even from this distance. On the other hand, her husband was comparatively young and still tanned from a winter in the sun.

"Ted, I don't intend to be catty, but she looks much older than I imagined. Gad, she's old enough to be his mother."

Amused by Linda's remark, Ted commented, "Obviously, age doesn't affect Dave's relationship with her."

"I didn't know Mrs. Paxton had returned from her business trip to New York," Linda said.

"How did you know she was away?" Ted inquired.

"The other day at the office, Mr. Damon was trying to contact her for a fund raising meeting. We were told by her personal secretary she would be away for a couple of days. We were also advised she would be on an extended business trip in July."

When they were about to resume their conversation, the waitress again interrupted them as she brought the salads. During the break, Ted thought of Dave's presence on a couple of occasions this week. It now occurred to him how the playboy could spend two consecutive nights away from his wife, a privilege that according to Alec, would be rare. He also wondered if he would be given carte blanche while she was away for a longer period of time.

"Let's return to the mystery of what happened last night at the studio parking lot," Ted said. "Jan told you she did not see Brett last night but I saw her turning into the studio driveway. That means she was there but not necessarily in the studio. The time element verifies this. She left the newsroom about ten. You said both of you arrived at the apartment sometime after that hour. That allows only fifteen or twenty minutes to make the trip. She had time to talk with someone but not for long. Nor would she have had time to visit anyone in the building," Ted continued. "Linda, I'm only theorizing, not presenting conclusive evidence. What made Jan have a change of mind about meeting Brett was visible to me when I drove through the parking lot only a few minutes earlier."

"What in the world did you see, Ted? " she asked curiously.

"Now, don't get upset, Linda. I saw Ruth Perry's car."

"No! I can't believe Ruth would have anything to do with anyone except her husband," Linda answered vehemently. "She isn't that type of person."

"Hold on, Linda," Ted responded quickly. "Just because her vehicle was parked there doesn't mean she was in the studio. When I saw it, I felt the same as you. I was shocked! However, Ruth could have loaned her car to someone. I'd like to believe that happened," Ted remarked.

"I hope so, Ted," Linda replied. "It would really hurt if I thought for a moment she was stepping out on Randy. Ted, now I have to be honest with you about Jan's attitude last night. Naturally, what I have to say doesn't mean Ruth was with Brett, but on two occasions last night, Jan made derogatory remarks when I mentioned her name."

"That makes sense, dear," Ted said. "Jan saw Ruth's car and she reached a conclusion they were together in the building."

"I wish we knew the truth, "Linda added. "This bothers me. I don't intend to mention it but hopefully she may volunteer the information when we get together again."

"That could be tomorrow or Sunday," Ted said. "Timothy wants to have a meeting with the group to arrange details on the outing. That may be your opportunity, Linda. There's something else you may as well know although it doesn't involve Ruth or Jan."

"Let's hear it, Ted. This seems to be a day of surprises."

"I've already told you about the missing girl the other night who was located near the studio. What I didn't tell you, there were two vehicles parked in the studio lot belonging to Brett and Dave," Ted related as he glanced at the Paxton table across the room. It appears Brett is entertaining more company at night lately. When you said Mrs. Paxton was away, it explained how Dave was alone for a couple of evenings."

"However, both of these incidents could be merely coincidental. Brett's car was in the lot most of the time, although we don't know if Dave visited him often, particularly at night. As for Ruth, we don't know," Ted concluded.

A similar thought occurred to both of them, but Linda spoke first.

"Let's hope none of these events lead anywhere. It could ruin our outing next month and I don't want that to happen."

They were quiet while eating dinner. Although neither admitted it, both were concerned.

Ted broke the silence.

"I don't plan on seeing Timothy this afternoon before going to the Guardian. I intend to stay at home.

"I've got to return to the office," Linda said. "There's plenty of work to do although the college isn't open. Why don't you give me a buzz later at the apartment? Let's do something exciting over the weekend. But, come to think of it, I'll probably see you at the meeting if it's on," she added.

They finished their dinner and left the restaurant.

"See you later, honey," Linda said.

She kissed his cheek before getting into her convertible.

Ted stopped at the dry cleaners to pick up a pair of slacks en route home to Manley Street where he had spent most of his twenty-nine years. This was a friendly small family neighborhood with well-kept homes. Elm trees lined both sides of the street providing ample shade which was a blessing today.

It was becoming warmer as Ted stepped from his car. As soon as he got into the house, he changed from slacks into shorts. Then he reached in the refrigerator for a Coke and took a big swallow before he walked to the back lawn.

With a few hours remaining until it was time to leave for work, Ted lay on the grass gazing at the cloudless blue sky.

As he relaxed, his mind wandered back to his early life and the birthday parties he shared with friends on this lawn.

Those anniversary events continued until that infamous December day in 1941, eight years ago, when the way of living began to change for most everyone. In the military, men and women who had never been more than fifty miles from home would find themselves thousands of miles away in places they never knew existed with names they couldn't spell or pronounce. Islands like Eniwetok and Kwajalien in the Pacific Ocean to the Moroccan town of Port Lyautey and the Kasserine Pass in the Tebessa Mountains of Tunisia became familiar words to GIs.

On the home front, common commodities such as coffee, butter, gasoline, and tires soon became limited and scarce.

Everywhere, probably the most significant change was the disruption of family life. As the necessity for defense weapons increased, more workers were attracted to factories, a tradition that would linger long after the war ended. Now fewer family members were seated around the table for supper, and quiet evening gatherings in the living rooms gradually disappeared. Few were aware this variation in family life eventually would lead to a lessening of moral values. This appeared to be one of the greatest changes this generation would face.

As the country entered war, Ted had only two semesters remaining before receiving his degree from Chamberlain College. Upon graduation, he enlisted in the Army Air Corps and he was sent to an officers training school. After receiving his commission, he was assigned to a navigation school at a California base to prepare him for combat duty. When Uncle Sam decided he was qualified the Army gave him a two-week leave to spend in Maine. It seemed that he never became as close to his parents as he did during this brief period when they realized that he would soon be leaving for combat.

His parents alternated their work schedules and remained home to spend time with him during the day. In the evening they would invite neighbors to a specially prepared supper at home or dine out, taking in a show or a sporting event.

As he looked back, they were some of the best days of his life. His Mother, staying home from her duties as a nurse at St. Agnes Hospital, would sit with him on this lawn remembering his childhood days or entertaining some of their friends.

And, on other days, his Dad, taking time off as superintendent of the city's water utility works, would take him for rides in the country, stopping occasionally to visit friends and recall past experiences.

It was on this lawn where many of his companions and college mates gathered with his mom and dad for a bon voyage party on the last night of his leave. It was also here that he said farewell to his Mom on the final day of his leave. After a tearful parting, his Father drove him to the railroad station and he left him with these words.

"Son, do what you have to do."

The following days and weeks passed rapidly as he joined with nine other airmen to form a B-17 bomber crew. They trained together regularly during the coming days. He was relieved when the time finally arrived when airmen of this bomber group were told to pack their gear for duty that would take them to unknown lands.

It was a long but uneventful flight from takeoff on the West Coast to a familiar stop at Presque Isle in his home state. He took his last look at Maine and the United States in late August as the planes flew across miles of woodland beyond the Canadian border in the Province of Quebec. Many miles were still ahead over the rough seas of the North Atlantic until they reached Greenland for a stop prior to a landing at their destination in the United Kingdom.

He was impressed by the beauty of the English countryside as his plane flew low over the neatly trimmed hedges and white roof tops that were intermingled with countless trees. It wouldn't be long before he would also be overwhelmed by the friendliness of its people.

No sooner had the crew stepped from their planes onto English soil than a cup of tea was handed to them.

"We're stopping the war for a spot of tea with you chaps," a laughing Royal Air Force officer proclaimed. "Cheers," he shouted lifting his cup high. "We'll have a little stiffer taste later."

There were many similar greetings in the days ahead as allies began to know one another. But, there were also serious matters facing the nations. Although Ted was only a second lieutenant he, along with others on the air base, surmised something big was in the making.

Military duty was strenuous during the daylight hours with increased emphasis placed on training missions, while the evening hours were usually free.

Limited trips to London were available, but Ted usually went to the officer's club for a couple of hours, particularly after a long day in the sky and another early morning call facing him. In early evening he enjoyed riding a bike to the village pub not far from the field for a pint of bitters. Here he would chat or play darts with the civilians. That is, until one of his friends, Grant Holiday, his crew's bombardier from San Francisco, California who persuaded him into taking a two-day leave on a sight-seeing trip to the country's largest city where he met someone who he would always remember.

Chapter 5

It was a clear September day when they boarded a train a few miles from their base that took them to King's Cross Station in the heart of London. Ted was accustomed to seeing servicemen and women in this country but he was amazed at countless military personnel wearing uniforms of allied countries as they disembarked in this capital. It was almost elbow to elbow traffic on sidewalks as they made their way downtown. His companion cautioned him to stay close as they could be easily parted in this throng as they entered Picadilly Circus, the Times Square of London.

"If we become separated in this jungle, I'll see you at the American Eagle Club tonight," Grant grinned. "If you don't know where this Mecca for servicemen is located, ask any GI." Although this was only meant as an idle thought, it became a reality. A short time later as the airmen made their way among hundreds of sightseers and stopping frequently to look in shop windows, Grant's prediction came true. They became separated.

Ted had several places in mind before he left the base that he was anxious to visit beginning with Hyde Park which he learned was a meeting place for soapbox orators. Others sites on his mind were Westminster Abbey, Buckingham Palace, and Big Ben. He assumed he was now headed toward Hyde Park.

A book caught his attention as he passed a small shop so he stopped abruptly for a closer view. As he turned, he collided with someone who was walking close behind him. Glancing back, he saw a woman on the sidewalk and bundles scattered about. Embarrassed, Ted was apologetic as he bent over and then kneeled on the pavement to comfort her.

As Ted continued to stare at her, his heart skipped a beat. Instantly he realized that she was the most gorgeous woman he had ever laid eyes upon.

"Are you hurt?" He asked as he reached for her hands. "Is there anything I can do?"

As a crowd gathered, she said quietly, "I'm all right. I can get up by myself. You can get my packages if you will."

Although she said that she didn't need any help, Ted gently placed his hands on her shoulders and helped her to her feet. Onlookers had already picked up the packages.

"Please forgive me," Ted explained. "I'm sorry to have caused you this trouble. I should have been more careful. Guess I'm just a clumsy Yank. Would you like a refreshment of some kind? There's a cafe across the street."

"That would be nice. I would like a cup of tea," she replied.

They walked slowly across the street and entered a small but quaint cafe where an elderly woman led them to a corner table. The waitress said that she had been outside and saw her fall. "I hope you're all right. I'll bring tea if you like."

"Please," Sheila responded while Ted said he would also like the same. When the waitress left, Ted finally had the first chance to examine this stranger.

Wow!, he thought. Was he ever glad that he lost his friend in the traffic. He stared at the lovely girl seated across the table and it seemed for the first time in his life, he was lost for words.

Unquestionably, she was a beauty. The golden blonde hair that touched her shoulders was a faultless blend for her peach complexion. Her gentle blue eyes resembled sapphires when she smiled.

"You appear timid for an American," she said. "My name is Sheila Wakefield. What's yours?

"I'm Theodore Graves. But I'm not shy, just embarrassed," he remarked. "To be honest, as long as you aren't hurt, I'm glad we met."

"Now, you're sounding more like a Yank. You say what you really think and I like that. I've met a lot of you lads during the past six months, particularly airmen. You're in the Army Air Corps, aren't you? The insignia on the wings attached to your tunic tell me that you're a navigator so I'm certain that you're attached to a bomber squadron."

"Right. I 'm assigned to a group stationed about fifty miles north of here. I haven't accomplished much since I arrived in your country, not even flown on a combat mission. And, this is my first visit to London."

The smile on her face vanished when Ted mentioned he hadn't seen any combat. She turned somber and avoided looking directly at him as she took a sip of tea.

Ted noticed the sudden change in her demeanor and unhesitatingly inquired, "Did I say anything to annoy you?"

"Heavens no, Theodore," Sheila replied. "I was just thinking there'll be plenty of flights ahead so don't be too eager. This war has a long way to go.

"A lot has changed in London during the past year," she continued. "A year ago German aircraft were bombing us nightly and our underground shelters were filled. Now we have occasional air raids with little damage and most families have found safety and comfort in other areas. We've acquired a more optimistic view of the future. No doubt many more will lose their lives before the war is over, but we'll be the winner if there is such a thing," Sheila said.

Ted was impressed with her soft voice as she talked about life during the war without fear or anger. He hadn't guessed her age yet but she couldn't be more than twenty. She was about five and a half feet tall with a shapely figure that revealed itself in a dress. She was one of the few young women who was not wearing a uniform in England which aroused his curiosity. Somehow, Sheila surmised what Ted was thinking as he stared at her necklace and earrings.

"I have a suspicion that you're wondering why I'm wearing a dress instead of a uniform as most women? During the blitz, I wore a Red Cross outfit while driving an ambulance but since the bombing subsided, I've been a recorder in a barrister's office.

"Theodore, I've been doing most of the talking. Tell me something about your life and the girls you left behind. Surely a handsome young airman in that striking uniform has caught the attention of American girls. And don't tell me that I'm the first woman you've met since you arrived in this country. It didn't take long for us to learn of GI's and their flirting habits after they landed here."

"Of course, I dated at home," Ted replied. "When I was in high school and college, classmates kidded me as a Romeo. But I didn't leave a girl behind holding a noose. This may be hard to believe but since being in the service, the army has kept us on a busy training schedule.

I found time for dates near our bases but not in this country. You're the first English girl with whom I've talked this long."

"Come now, Theodore. We're accustomed to hearing that line. You're pleasant company but I don't know about meeting again. I can only stay a few more minutes now before I go to my flat and pick up things for mother. She lives alone in a village north of here. I don't have time to explain but she was injured during the blitz."

Can't we arrange to meet when I get another leave, Sheila? Although they seem to be pushing our training, I'm sure I can get away again. Honestly, I just can't let you disappear from my life and these aren't meaningless words. Already, you're special to me."

"Let's not get too involved, Theodore. There are reasons why I can't. You' appear to be a good chap. I'll try to see you another time if possible. It'll be a fortnight before I return from the country so probably we can meet in this same place next month.

"Really, I've got to rush but my telephone number is on this card. Call me. I'm not making promises but maybe we might meet again. Cheers." With those parting words, she headed for the door. Ted had hardly time to say good-bye before she disappeared among the throng in the sidewalks of Piccadilly Circus.

He spent the remainder of the day touring the city and went to Hyde Park where he heard soap box orators berating members of the British Parliament or condemning sinners for lack of faith. Before he found his way to the Eagle Club to join his lost friend, Grant, he toured Westminster Abbey and later got a look at Big Ben. The only thing on his mind now was Sheila and he knew she wasn't in the city. He was concerned that he would never see her again.

Ted lost interest in the city as he and Grant made a round of several pubs in total darkness later that night. Dense fog and blackout restrictions attributed to the limited visibility. They called it a day a couple of hours and several pints of English bitters later.

Sheila was still on his mind when he awoke in the morning and he decided to return to the base after having breakfast with Grant.

"You don't mind if I go back to camp," Ted asked. "I'm sure you'll find plenty of excitement without me."

"Go ahead, Ted. You really caught the bug yesterday when you met that girl. She must be terrific. There are others from our group here and we'll find plenty to do until I return tomorrow. See you then," Grant remarked.

Although training intensified, the days seem to drag as he couldn't forget Sheila and wondered if she would meet him in London again. He was also concerned if his group would still be in this country as rumors were quickly spreading about something big taking place soon. No one knew when or where. His squadron had yet to take part in any raid across the English Channel. He thought that perhaps they were being saved for a bigger operation,

As the weeks passed in October, Ted couldn't delay any longer in making a call to Sheila. His heart was pounding and he was apprehensive when she answered the phone. "Sheila, this is Theodore. Remember me?

"Why, of course. I've been expecting your call and wondering if you would be coming to London. I'd like to see you. What are your plans?"

"Sheila, I'll be there tomorrow afternoon. I'll meet you at the same cafe. I can only have a couple of days leave at this time but I believe I can make another visit in a few weeks. Is that okay?

"Theodore, that's fine. I'll see you about four o'clock. I have a full evening planned. Cheers"

Ted was prepared for his visit with Sheila. He had written to his mother after his return from London last month asking her to send something that an English girl would like. It wasn't long before he received a package from home with nylons and perfume.

It was still dark when Ted arose on the morning of his date with Sheila. Not a soul was stirring. He took a shower and went outside before the dining room opened. To kill time, he walked to the flight line where the bombers were parked and chatted with a GI on guard duty.

"You're up early this morning, aren't you, Lieutenant?" the guard asked. "I wasn't aware of any early morning missions today."

"There's no flying for me today," Ted responded. "Just couldn't sleep any longer. I might as well be guarding these planes. It must get lonely out here in this darkness."

"We get accustomed to it. The first three hours aren't too bad but it gets a little edgy toward the end of the tour."

Ted thought that it was going to be a long day as he headed back to his quarters. To his surprise, the day passed rapidly as he took in many of the various sights in this metropolis from the time he stepped from the train until he arrived at the cafe. He didn't have to wait long before Sheila entered and came directly to the table. She was more lovely than he had imagined as he stood and reached for her hand.

"Sheila, it's great seeing you again. I was afraid you might change your mind."

"I wouldn't do that to a handsome American flier," she replied. "I'm sorry that I had to leave you so soon the last time but I've been looking forward to seeing you again I rushed from the office to get here. Have you been waiting long?"

"This is my first cup of tea and I've only had time to take a couple of sips. Oh, I brought something that my mother sent from the States. I asked her what she thought a beautiful girl from England might like.

You can decide if she made a good choice."

"That was thoughtful, Theodore. May I open the package now?"

"Of course," he answered. "I hope you like them."

Sheila's eyes sparkled when she saw the gifts. "I love them. Your mother must be a dear. She certainly knows what are missing on our store shelves and what lies in a girl's heart. I could kiss you for this, Theodore. Maybe later?"

"I'll have a tea and then I know of a nice restaurant where we can also dance. I hope you like to dance. These are the plans for this evening and tomorrow night we can do the same things or go to a cinema. However, I won't be able to see you during the day."

"That sounds great," Ted replied. "We'd better make the best of what time we have. I'm not sure if there will be other leaves available. There's something big going on as you're probably aware but I have no idea. The staff officers don't invite me to their conferences."

"I haven't told you much about my family," Sheila said. "But my father is a naval officer aboard a British cruiser in the South Atlantic. No different from your officers, he doesn't confide in me either but I have a feeling from reading between the lines in his letters that unpredictable times are ahead for all of us. Let's not talk anymore about that now. I'm hungry."

Any further mention of the war didn't surface until their night's enjoyment of fun was nearing its close. It had been a wonderful evening and Ted could sense a growing affection for this woman and he felt that it was becoming a mutual relationship. It was then that Sheila became serious as she took Ted's hand and looked directly in his eyes.

"Theodore, when we met a month ago, I said that I had a reason why we probably wouldn't meet again. I've got to be honest as I'm becoming fond of you. When you gave me the gifts earlier I said I should kiss you. After spending the evening together I could kiss you for more reasons than the gifts but that wouldn't be fair. Theodore, I thought that I was in love with one of our pilots whose aircraft was shot down during a raid over Germany two months ago. A crew member in another plane reported he saw the plane go down in flames but he thought he saw several parachutes open. There's a chance Charles, that is his name, could be a prisoner of war and that he also could have been wounded. I must know the truth.

"I had promised Charles that I would be waiting for him. I can't go back on my word. If he's alive and wounded, he'll need me more than ever. I'm not going to fall in love with another airman. It could be a situation with a similar scenario.

"If we are going to meet tomorrow night and possibly once more before you leave England or worse still, are lost in enemy territory, we must keep our relationship as friends. Do you think that's possible?

"Sheila, for the first time in my life, I have met someone who has captured my heart. Please don't walk away from me. I must see you as often as we can get together. I want to hold you again as we did tonight while we danced. I want to love you as I think you are beginning to love me. Whatever lies in our future, can't we make the most of it?

"I really don't know," she replied. "I'll see you tomorrow night and we'll talk more about it. Can you meet me at the restaurant about six o'clock? I've got an errand to do after work. Do you mind if we say good-bye here? It's only a short walk for both of us to our quarters."

Disappointed, Ted agreed. "I'll see you then. Goodnight, Sheila."

She walked out the door when Ted stopped to pay the cashier. As he stepped on the sidewalk in the darkness of a blacked-out London, a soft kiss met his lips briefly and he was alone again.

It was nearly noon when Ted decided to get up but there was a good reason not to hurry outside. Overcast skies and drizzle blanketed the city when he looked out a window, hardly a good day for sight-seeing.

After dressing, he donned a raincoat and left the building. He had only walked a few blocks when heavy rain began to fall and he hurriedly entered a nearby restaurant. There wasn't any particular reason to rush his dinner so he bought a newspaper and ate slowly as he scanned the Daily Mirror. It was apparent that rain would continue so he asked the waitress if there were any cinemas nearby.

"Right down the street," she answered, "and the film playing is *Gone With The Wind.*" He had seen it but it was a good way to spend a rainy afternoon until he met Sheila.

She was waiting at a table when Ted arrived shortly after six o'clock. Even on a dreary day she was beautiful, he thought. Their eyes locked and she gazed at him steadily as he approached. "The rain hasn't changed your loveliness, Sheila. I've been waiting all day to see you."

"I hope it was worth your while, Theodore. I'll try to be cheerful tonight. Let's order a drink now and I'll tell you what I learned today." After the waitress brought two glasses of stout beer to the table she asked Ted to bear with her until she knew more about Charles.

50

"It shouldn't be much longer before we know where his aircraft was shot down and what happened to him," she continued. The errand I mentioned that I had to make earlier was a visit to the War Office where I have a friend who is in charge of locating missing fliers whose planes were shot down over the continent. They aren't certain yet but from the information they had gathered, it is likely that Charles is in a German hospital in occupied France. They don't know how seriously he was wounded but knowing the enemy practice, it must be bad or they would have taken him to a hospital in Germany. My friend said they should get more information soon from the Red Cross.

"So, Theodore, let's enjoy this evening together. Please be patient. I know that you are going back to your base in the morning but I'll call you often and maybe we can get together again before you're shipped out."

No more was said during the remainder of the evening about the war. This would be a night of dining and dancing, one they would always remember. Ted and Sheila made an impressive couple as they jitterbugged to the popular fast tunes of Glenn Miller's arrangements of *In The Mood* and *The American Patrol* until closing time. As the evening waned, they held each other tightly when they danced the last waltz, hoping that this wouldn't be the last time they would be in each other's arms.

Scuttlebutt was widespread at Ted's bomber headquarters about the group's first raid across the channel prior to a larger unknown strike. Word also had it that all leaves would soon be canceled and personnel restricted to base.

He was afraid that his chances of seeing Sheila again were becoming unlikely since he hadn't heard from her since his visit to London two weeks ago. Ted didn't believe that she would walk away from him but she did ask him to be patient. He thought that it would be unwise to ask the pilot of his crew about a leave before he received word from her. As he pondered this dilemma, the situation was abruptly resolved when announcement over the loud speaker system requested all flying crews to report to operations. His heart pounced. At last, he thought, the time had arrived for action, and he suddenly forgot about London.

A lot of eager faces filled the crowded room as the group commander walked to the podium to make this announcement:

"Gentlemen, this is the news you have been waiting for. Within two weeks this group will begin bombing missions somewhere over Europe. Obviously, I can't tell you where but you will learn of the target on the morning of the briefing. All of you will be granted an overnight leave to London before our missions begin but make certain that you return within the allowed twenty-four hours. I suggest that you keep this information to yourself. You can make your requests anytime now. That's all."

Ted was elated with the news, though apprehensive. Now he knew that he could see Sheila but he was fearful of what decision she might have regarding him. He was sure that she didn't want to abandon their relationship. However, it was understandable that Sheila would not break a promise that she had made to Charles.

Mindful that he didn't want to live with this anxiety any longer, he decided to see her regardless of what she had learned from the War Office. All phones in the officer's quarters were being used as other airmen were making plans for their leaves. It wasn't a long wait before Ted was talking with her.

Enthusiastically, he said, "Sheila, we have all been granted a leave to London anytime during the next two weeks. May I see you again? I have something to tell you."

"Of course, Theodore. That's wonderful. I was going to call you later as I have news for you also. When can you make it?"

"I'll have to call you when they decide what day I can have," Ted said. "Does it matter?"

"No, anytime," she answered, "Only let me know. I'll be waiting."

Without wasting any time, Ted went directly to the officer's quarters and made arrangements for his leave on the following Tuesday. He called Sheila again to tell her the news and said that he would meet her at the same restaurant where they had dined on his last leave.

"I'm so happy that we can be together again," she said. "And, Theodore, don't make any reservations to stay overnight. I have a place for you."

Ted got off the train at the same station late that Tuesday afternoon. It had been a beautiful day in late October with clear skies and a prediction for a full moon that night. The station was always crowded but on this particular afternoon there appeared to be a larger throng of servicemen and girls holding hands as they walked toward the heart of the city. If everyone felt as Ted did, London would be a happy place to be tonight.

Sheila had arrived ahead of him again and she was seated at the same table they had occupied the other night. "You're a sight to see, Sheila. More lovely each time we meet."

"Go on with you. You Yanks say that to all the girls you meet." she laughed. "But I love to hear it."

"The eagle flew yesterday which means payday to American servicemen. I got my first pay since coming to this country so why don't we spend it on something a bit more tasty." Ted remarked. "We'll begin our evening with a bottle of champagne."

"That would be nice, Theodore. I haven't had a taste of vintage wine since Charles left." She suddenly realized what she had said and quickly apologized. "I'm very sorry. I didn't intend to say that."

"Don't let it bother you. That's why I like you so much. You're beautiful and honest." Then he asked the waiter to bring a bottle of their best wine. "This is a special occasion," he added.

As they sipped their drink, Sheila said, "Theodore, I have something to tell you and I believe you also have something to say. Don't you think we ought to get these things off our mind?"

"You're right, dear. What I have to say won't take long. This is not exactly confidential information as American bombers are flying over the continent daily. We've been alerted that soon our group will be included so I will be seeing action soon. It could also mean that these raids are a prelude to action that may take us out of the country."

"I knew it wouldn't be long before your group would be included in the bombing raids and that something else is in the wind," she remarked. "I had readied myself for that. But, I wasn't prepared for a report from the War Office." Sheila looked down at her glass and when she glanced up again, her eyes were filled with tears. Sobbing, it was hard for Ted to understand all that she was saying but he knew that it involved Charles.

"He was badly wounded and I have no idea when or if I'll ever see him again," she spoke softly. "I can only wait and hope."

"I've lost someone I loved and you are leaving with our chances of never meeting again. Guess I'm not a lucky person. Let's make the most of tonight and let tomorrow take care of itself," she added as she wiped the tears from her face.

As the evening came to a close, they left the restaurant and strolled slowly arm in arm under a moonlit sky to her flat several blocks away. When they arrived at the small apartment, she reached into her handbag for a key and gave it to him. After he unlocked the door, she walked ahead but before turning on a light, she went to each window and closed the blackout shades. It was quiet as he locked the door behind him and took her in his arms. He held her for several minutes and not a word was spoken.

Finally, she said, "Darling, I'll be back in a few minutes."

When she returned wearing only a negligee, Sheila turned off the light. She reached for his hand and led the way to her room where she opened a large blackout curtain. As she stood in front of the window, her shapely body was revealed by a bright moon that illuminated the room.

"Now, it's time for bed," she whispered.

The moments were for love while they lay in passionate embrace. Their breathing was the only sound except the clanging of Big Ben as each hour passed. The couple were aware that dawn would have another meaning. Ted felt that he would never see Sheila again and that their brief encounters would be a love affair to remember.

Morning came, they left the flat and walked slowly to the railway station gate where a tearful Sheila kissed her new love a final farewell. After Ted stepped aboard the train, he glanced back as she waved and quickly vanished in a mass of uniforms.

Chapter 6

More fighters and bombers were arriving daily in the British Isles, landing in airfields scattered across the country. Word was circulating that a convoy assembled in Scotland was sailing in the Irish Sea. Farther south in the Atlantic, occasional sightings were made by German U-boats of warship groups. However, information was vague and scattered to prevent Germans and Italians from knowing that Allied armies were preparing for an invasion of North Africa.

Ted flew his first bombing mission over Rouen in Northern France in November without incident, as American heavy bombers began strikes against submarine pens. He would fly only eight missions over these targets. Ted had often wanted to visit France, but he wasn't going to see many of the country's historical sights from this altitude.

Later that month, the group left for North Africa after Allied troops had secured its airfields. His flight landed on a base in the Sahara Desert near Biskra in Algeria.

He witnessed the results of a dangerous mission late in the afternoon of his first day on this continent while standing in line for chow. A lone four-engine bomber approached the landing strip after a long mission over enemy-held territory. It was flying low over the desert sands while a crew member dropped red flares signaling there were wounded aboard. The Flying Fortress had been badly damaged over a coastal target. The aircraft's tail section was split in half by an enemy fighter plane that had gone out of control after being hit by machine gun fire. As airmen on the ground watched, the crippled plane barely made the edge of the strip before grinding to a halt near the end of the runway.

A few hours later Ted got his first taste of hostile gunfire when German bombers made their appearance, strafing and bombing the American base.

Long before the sun rose over the desert on the following morning, his flight became airborne from this strip, and took a northeast course to a German-held port city on the Mediterranean coast.

His first two missions were milk runs, so-called by airmen when sorties were completed without encountering enemy fighters or antiaircraft fire. Ted's luck ran out on his third flight from the North African base. Over another enemy-held city on the coast, his squadron encountered both enemy fighters and heavy flack from antiaircraft guns.

Ted remembered seeing bombs as they fell on a ship below, but suddenly a flash of light filled the plane, followed immediately by flying metal as shells from enemy antiaircraft guns hit the plane. His memory faltered from here to the end of the flight back to Africa recalling only excruciating pain in his arm and shoulders on the return trip to the base. He vaguely remembered being taken from the plane after it landed in Biskra. His next recollection was looking up at a face hidden by a white mask in a hospital room.

"You're going to be all right," a muffled voice behind the mask said. Your next flight will take you home."

And so it was.

He had almost forgotten the flights back to Maine, the longest across the ocean to Walter Reed Hospital in Washington, D.C., where he spent months recuperating from his wounds. He would always remember the flight to Bangor where his parents were waiting to greet him. This ended the war for him.

As Ted continued laying on the ground, his thoughts now switched to conversations with Timothy and Linda today. The events involving Brett and Dave were vague without revealing anything of importance.

Of course, Jan's conversation with Linda saying she didn't see Brett last night was mystifying.

Sitting up, he finished his Coke and went into the house to get the morning newspaper that he had only glanced at earlier. There was nothing of particular news except the weather and that didn't interest him. He was enduring the heat like everyone in the city.

The next daily routine before going to work was checking the oil in the Chevy and giving the tires a couple of kicks, a habit he acquired from a neighbor, Sam, who jokingly remarked that it would make the car run better.

With everything in order, he went to his room and changed his clothes before leaving for work.

He could smell the heat rising from city pavements as the Chevy entered the *Guardian's* parking lot. It was almost vacant but he knew that would soon change.

Stepping out of the car, he heard the rumble of thunder. There wasn't a cloud in the sky as he looked toward the heavens, so he walked from the lot to the other side of the building. He stared at the western horizon where yesterday's storm originated trying to detect signs of a storm. Ted realized something was brewing as the distant blue sky began changing its shade to a darker hue. The weather was developing into a repetition of Wednesday's performance. Just as if a bugle had sounded for reveille, people gradually began to stir on the sidewalks and traffic increased on Middleton streets.

Ted was not the only person to notice the sky changing its color or hear the sound of a thunderstorm as it approached the city's outskirts. Similar to animals in the wilderness when a fire threatened, residents were preparing to seek shelter from a storm about to erupt. He was not in a hurry to get to the newsroom where the air would be stifling. He took his time, walking slowly toward the doorway.

Other news workers were also milling about the area anticipating a whiff of fresh air in advance of the storm. However, the front was at least an hour away and typewriters and telephones would be busy before there was a dramatic change in weather. He took a last look at the darkening horizon before entering the building, an agony that couldn't be postponed any longer.

He climbed the stairs leading to the newsroom where whirling fans had created a mixture of air he once experienced while serving in the Mediterranean area. That air mass was known as the sirocco, a hot, dust-laden wind from the Libyan deserts blowing on the North African coast. The prevailing air in this room was obviously not as severe, but it was still uncomfortable.

He was surprised to find Jan standing near her desk, apparently waiting for others who would soon be entering the newsroom.

What a difference in appearance she was, he thought, as compared to yesterday when she was sitting on the same desk. Then, she looked as though she had just stepped out of a shower. Today, she looked like she had been through a wringer. He was aware today's temperatures could affect anyone.

"Apparently you haven't been to the lake today," Ted commented, trying to avoid being derisive. "The weather appears to have taken its toll on all of us."

She avoided looking at him as she reached in her desk drawer for facial tissues.

"I decided to remain at the apartment this morning instead of driving anywhere," she answered. "However, I would like to be near a lake at this moment."

"I don't think so, Jan. In the next hour there's going to be a drastic change in the weather and waters on any lake will be treacherous. It will be a welcome relief when it cools this oven into a more comfortable habitat."

Instead of going to his desk, Ted walked over to a window still searching for more signs of the storm.

Thunderheads began to appear among the cloud formations and occasionally a streak of lightning flashed in the sky. It was difficult to hear any sounds of thunder in this room because of the noise of teletype machines.

He hadn't noticed Jan standing near him. She must have followed him quietly as he went to the window.

As they both looked out the window, Jan opened a conversation.

"I didn't meet Brett last night. I thought you would like to know."

This remark came unexpectedly and he wasn't prepared for an immediate response.

"Jan, I probably was stepping out of line meddling in your affairs. Frankly, I'm glad you didn't go to his studio."

Nothing else was said about last night's events. They remained near the window without talking for few minutes until Ted remarked he had some calls to make.

"What's on your schedule tonight, Jan? I hope you don't have an assignment that will take you out in the weather. It's going to be a bad storm as you probably have surmised."

"I don't have any specific event to cover unless a women's meeting canceled last night is rescheduled for this evening. I can do my stories by phone. If the weather is going to be bad, it's questionable if that meeting will be held tonight."

"What have you got going?" she asked Ted.

"Unless something spectacular happens I can work from my desk. I have a feature to write which should take part of the night.

They returned to their desks to begin articles for tomorrow's edition as phones started ringing.

While Ted was making a call, Kevin Leonard, a *Guardian* reporter who regularly covered city activities during the day, came to his desk.

"What took place in Middleton today," Ted asked the young reporter after he had completed his call.

"It was pretty much routine," Kevin replied.

"Most everyone was on sick leave or on vacations in the city departments. Because of the high temperature in the courtroom, Judge Collins again postponed all cases on the docket until tomorrow. It was even quiet at the police department," Kevin reported. "Except, Ted, I think there's something going on about that missing girl the other night but no one is saying anything. That is, not to me. Perhaps you can make something of it."

"Thanks, Kevin. I'll look into it. You had better head for home before the weather worsens. See you later."

Alec resembled a storm as he came thundering in the room complaining about the "damn heat."

"There's got to be an end to this sometime," he roared, his voice carrying above the noise.

Almost in the same breath but in a lower tone, he said. "Jan, come in my office."

Well, Ted thought, Timothy has contacted him about Jan's invitation.

Ted admired Alec. His bark was louder than his bite. Ted knew little about his past except he had been an outstanding fullback for Chamberlain College. A bachelor, he lived on a small farm on the city outskirts where he raised a dozen or so head of Hereford cattle. During the war, according to the few who were more acquainted with him, he was awarded a silver star while a captain in the Marines.

Ironically, he knew Dave Paxton when serving in the Corps. They were about the same age which probably accounts for their being in the service together. Alec was Dave's commanding officer in the Pacific. But, he never discussed it with anyone. They must have had some contacts following the war because Alec was aware of Dave's marital status. During one of Ted and Alec's few extended conversations, Alec said that Dave went to Florida after leaving the Corps where he became acquainted with a wealthy widow. Later, he heard they were married and Dave was living like a king. Beyond this, Alec never mentioned Dave although he came to the editor's office occasionally. Ted theorized their reunion in Middleton was coincidental.

Alec kept to himself although he attended special gatherings at the college and often he was a guest at Randy and Ruth Perry's home for parties. No one knew about his personal life but he appeared to display an interest in the *Guardian's* newest staff member. And she was in his office now listening to an offer she couldn't refuse.

Ted knew it was coming.

"Ted, come in here," Alec shouted.

Smiles were on Alec's and Jan's faces when he entered the office so he was certain Jan had accepted Alec's invitation, and they were waiting for the date of the venture.

Before Alec could utter a word, Ted said, "We plan to leave on July 13. Hope that's a lucky date for both of you."

"You're pretty sure of yourself, Ted," Alec quipped. "How did you know Jan was coming with us? "

"Even from my desk across the room I was certain she was going to be a part of the group," Ted laughed. "You resembled a pair of Cheshire cats. What other conclusion could I have drawn? "

"I guess I asked for that, Ted. Anyhow, what plans have already been made and what can I do to assist?

"I'm expecting a call from Timothy," Ted replied. "He planned to make contacts with others in the group to arrange a meeting sometime over the weekend. We hope then to finalize arrangements. In the meantime, Alec, you can teach Jan how to tie flies to catch those clever fish in Bear Lake."

"Although I like to fish, I would like to spend more time swimming and canoeing," Jan interrupted.

"It certainly would have been a perfect time for swimming in Middleton today," Ted related. "However, Bear Lake is larger than any of the area lakes. Even in the middle of the summer, water temperatures often fall below sixty degrees. You may have to wear your overcoat for a dip in that lake."

"Well," Alec interjected," I'll instruct her how to handle a canoe. And before this outing is over we'll challenge any couple to a canoe tilting bout."

"One fact is certain," he continued. "After listening to her elk hunting expeditions, she won't need any lessons in outdoor survival."

"I never knew you were a hunter," Ted remarked as he tried to avoid staring at her legs. "I thought you were a product of the Bay State. And I know there haven't been elk sighted in Massachusetts during this century."

"Apparently you never saw my resume, Ted, so I'm not surprised you weren't familiar with my high school years in Wyoming," she replied. "You didn't know I lived near Boston only part of my life. However, it never occurred to me Alec wasn't aware of my past when he hired me. He seemed amazed when I told him of my hunting experiences in the mountains with my Dad. I have a feeling both of you concentrate more on my legs than my mind," she continued. "That's not unusual. I've experienced that scene countless times," she added smiling. "Let's return to the outing. Is there anything Linda and I should bring besides bathing suits?" she asked. "That is, if the water is warm enough for swimming?"

"Don't place too much emphasis on sun exposure, "Alec replied. "The nights can be cool in that part of the country. You had better take warm clothing along."

"Now, let's get back to your resume for a moment, Jan. I knew you lived in the Rockies. But nowhere in your qualifications did it refer to your experience with a rifle," Alec remarked.

"I didn't see a spot for this question and answer," she chuckled.

Abruptly changing to another subject, Alec explained the Guardian work schedule for the week when they would be away.

"Newspapers have to be on the street every morning while we're gone. Your replacement, Jan, will be our college intern, Betty Osgood, who will help with society and local news. Ted, sports will cover for you."

"Obviously, you had this situation well in hand before tonight, including Jan's substitute," Ted added.

However, he was careful not to mention who would replace the managing editor during the interim. He probably could get away with that question over a drink at the lodge.

Alec's offer to hold a meeting at his farm was disrupted by an intense clap of thunder. Immediately rain began pelting against the office windows and a few seconds later, lightning streaks crossed the sky. The storm had arrived.

This interruption also concluded the briefing session and they returned to their desks. Ted started to uncover his typewriter when another blast of thunder shook the room.

Everyone rushed to close windows as strong gusts of wind blew papers off the desk tops. Heavy rain turned to hail that sounded like firecrackers when it hit the glass. Flashes of lightning brought temporary daylight to the darkened sky. Suddenly, teletype machines and fans were silenced and the room was without lights except for the emergency units.

A bolt of lightning had struck nearby trees that fell across power and telephone lines leading to the *Guardian*, disrupting all communications from the outside world. It was still daytime, but visibility was limited in the newsroom with only emergency lights providing minimum illumination.

Ted approached Jan at her desk.

Jokingly, he inquired. "What happens when the lights go out? Do we play post office? "

"If you wish," she laughed. "Do you want to kiss me first?"

"That's a wonderful suggestion," Ted replied. "But I don't think it would be advisable."

"You're right. Especially since we're going on a trip with Linda in the party. She would find a way to get even in the wilderness."

"Linda wouldn't do anything to harm you, Jan. Besides, she'll be lost most of the time in the woods. The closest she has been to a forest is a city park."

"I know, Ted. She's a wonderful person. I'd try to steal you from her but I don't think that's possible. I've got a confession to make," she continued. "Last night, we both passed Brett's studio about the same time. I know you were watching me enter the studio parking lot because I saw your brake light in my rear view mirror before I made the turn. I didn't lie to you earlier, Ted. I only said a half truth. However, I didn't tell Linda the truth last night at the apartment. I told her the reason I didn't meet Brett was because I had earlier changed my mind. That wasn't exactly correct."

Ted interrupted.

"You don't have to explain to me. I know what you witnessed as I saw the same car when I drove through the parking lot a few minutes before you did. Let's hope that both of us have arrived at a wrong conclusion."

"What on earth do you mean, Ted. Neither of us is blind. It was Ruth Perry's car."

"That's right. However, she could have loaned her car to someone. Or it could have had mechanical problems when she was downtown shopping so she left it there overnight. Let's hope one of these explanations is correct. There could be other possibilities."

"Oh, Ted, that never occurred to me. I do hope you are right."

"By the way, Jan, Linda is aware of this. She replaced you at dinner today and we discussed the incident. Linda had difficulty understanding your attitude toward Ruth last night. You hadn't mentioned anything about the car but Linda was suspicious. She had to hear it some time and I thought that was the best opportunity. I hope you'll overlook it."

"I forgive you and I hope Linda forgives me, too. That was very unfair of me."

After sirens began wailing, they walked to a window where they could see flashes of red lights on outlying areas as emergency vehicles rushed to troubled areas.

Close by, flickering of amber lights indicated Central Maine Power along with New England Telephone and Telegraph crews were repairing downed lines connecting the *Guardian* to the outside world.

Lacking phone service and without lights, the newsroom staff was helpless. It was obvious that other business operations in the city were also hit but not as severe as the Guardian.

As Ted was trying to decide what to do, Alec, who was sitting in for Howard tonight as city editor, had already made a decision. He approached Ted and told him to find a staff photographer.

When Ted returned with Hank Davis, Alec's instructions were clear.

"Go to fire headquarters and remain there until our electrical service is restored. This is going to be a bad storm. There certainly won't be any power here for at least an hour. Phone service won't be out long but there's little we can do in the editorial rooms without energy for lights and the teletypes," Alec said. "You'll know what's happening in other sections of the city through the department's radio system. You can make your moves accordingly. We'll call you when our power is restored."

"Okay boss," Ted replied.

Turning to Hank, Ted added. "We'll take our own vehicles. I'll meet you at the station."

Ted took foul weather gear from a rack in the hallway and hurried out the door with Hank close on his heels. Pouring rain left puddles of water throughout the parking area. Long before reaching the car, his feet were soaked and water was running down his face. The storm was moving toward the east but strong winds and heavy precipitation continued in the city. With windshield wipers turned on high, it was still difficult to see through the heavy rain. Gusts of wind occasionally made the Chevy sway as Ted headed for Central Headquarters where most of the city's fire-fighting equipment and men were stationed.

Autos belonging to permanent and volunteer firemen filled the yard when the Guardian staffers arrived. Quickly they jumped from their cars and raced for shelter. Only four persons and a lone piece of fire apparatus were left in the station. Jim Grady, a regular, along with three call men were the only men left behind.

Ted's watery footwear left smeared tracks on the cement floor as he sauntered inside and sat on the back of the fire engine to remove his saturated socks and shoes.

"What's happening?" Ted asked as his feet touched the cool cement floor.

"Three lightning strikes during the past hour are keeping the department busy," Jim replied. "Four pieces of equipment with the chief and crews responded to the first alarm at a dairy farm on the Old Bennett Road," he said. "This call was followed quickly by an alarm sounded by the pastor of the First Baptist Church on Summer Street. A fireman was injured while fighting the blaze that damaged the steeple. He was taken by ambulance to City Hospital with a fractured collarbone where he's reported in good condition," Jim continued. "A slate shingle fell from the steeple to cause the injury.

"The third call dispatched fighters to WMID Radio Station's broadcasting tower on the Old English Road. Station Manager Hewitt Jones told the men when they arrived at the scene that lightning didn't cause a fire but it did damage the tower. He reported that the station would not be back in operation for at least a day," Jim added.

Jim related that the most serious damage to structures took place at the Ganeau farm on the Old Bennett Road which was aflame when firemen arrived at the scene.

Jim said Fire Chief Joe Blanchard reported by radio that the barn was a total loss. Fortunately, the chief said that the fifty or more head of cattle were being herded back from the pasture when lightning struck the building.

"Fifteen minutes later, they would have been in the barn. Ironically, it was past the usual milking time but Mr. Ganeau and his family went for a swim at a pond near the farm and they were late getting back. Another stroke of luck," Jim continued. "Many Maine farms are built with barns connected by sheds to the house. This barn was more than one hundred feet away from the family living quarters."

"That explains why one of the ambulances and most of the other apparatus are not here," Ted said. "Where is the other ambulance?"

"That unit responded to an auto collision and an engine was dispatched to a smoke-filled room at an apartment house on Bell Street," Jim reported. "As far as we know, there was only one injury but there was a lot of damage. As expected, there are power outages in scattered sections of the city where utility crews are making repairs."

After listening to Jim, Hank had left to take photos of the damage, and he told Ted he would be looking for other storm-related pictures before returning to the office. There was not much Ted could do except to wait for the fire chief for information about the calls and for power to be restored in the newsroom. He walked to a window and watched water flowing down Main Street as heavy rains continued.

Jim came out of the office and spoke to Ted. "The chief radioed that the fire was under control and he was returning with a few men and equipment. He said although water was pumped from the pond on the Ganeau farm at the beginning to fight the blaze, heavy rain was responsible for quelling the fire. A pumper will remain at the site until morning but it didn't appear embers would rekindle in this weather. Just a matter of precaution," he said.

Jim finished his conversation with Ted as an ambulance and rescue vehicle returned. While they entered the station, two other trucks were approaching. Unless something drastic took place, the worst was over for this day, Ted believed.

As he sat on the back of the engine waiting impatiently, two of the units dispatched to the farm fire returned and backed into the station. All of the equipment had returned from the three calls.

Fire Chief Joe Blanchard approached Ted and he repeated his report that was sent earlier by radio.

"Mr. Ganeau was a lucky man," the chief said. "If his herd had been in the barn at the usual milking time the loss would have been greater. Come in my office, Ted, and I'll give you details of the farm fire with exception of the damage estimate. You will have to get that information from Ganeau. He knows the value of his building and equipment. You can talk with Captain Fred Mathews about the church fire. He'll be here shortly. And I suggest you ask the radio station manager about damages at the tower. Now I'm going to the hospital to see how Bob McMahon is making out. I hope he wasn't hurt too badly," the chief concluded.

Finishing his interview with the chief, Ted returned to the truck when Jim shouted from the office door that power had been restored at the Guardian and the newspaper was back in business.

Anxious to get back to the newsroom, Ted would have walked out of the station barefooted if he hadn't tripped over a helmet on the floor

65

en route to an exit. He returned and sat on the rear of the truck again, forcibly putting his wet shoes on his sockless feet.

Three elements were noticeably different when he stepped outside. The rain and wind had subsided and the temperature had dropped 20 degrees. At last he enjoyed fresh air again as he rushed to his car.

It only took a few minutes to reach the *Guardian*; he ran up the stairs to the newsroom where everyone was busy at their desks following the two-hour delay. When he neared Jan's desk she told him Timothy had called.

Ted didn't hesitate in returning the call when he reached his desk.

"What's on your mind," Ted asked when his friend answered.

"Ted, I have tried to reach Randy or Ruth at their cottage but apparently the lines are down. As you know, I would like to arrange a meeting over the weekend at their place if possible. If they can't make it we'll have to wait until another time. I think that it's important at least one of them attend. Could you possibly see them tonight?"

"I'll do my best, Timothy. Unless Alec has something planned for me, I'll go to the cottage. You'll be hearing from me later."

He went directly to Alec's office to inform him of the past hour's activities.

"It's been a rough night, Alec. A fireman is hospitalized, the Baptist Church steeple and WMID Radio's tower have been damaged, and a farmer has lost his barn. All of this, plus a multitude of downed trees and power outages along with a minor fire and auto accident sums up the results of tonight's storm."

He explained that Hank covered the fires and that he would be looking for pictures of other storm-related damages before he returned.

"You seem to have the situation in hand," Alec said. "Do you need help with these stories?"

"I can do it," Ted answered. "I have most of the information already."

"Good, Ted. There's a hearing in progress at city hall about construction of a building close to city park. Could you drop in for a few minutes and try to get a handle on it? You don't have to remain for the entire session. You can make arrangements with the committee chairman to call you later after it's over."

"All right, Alec. However, first, I'm going home to change my footwear and then I'll go to city hall," Ted said. Timothy wants me to contact the Perrys to arrange a meeting on the outing so I'll make a quick run to their cottage before returning," he added. "He can't reach them by phone because of the storm. I won't be long, Alec."

After leaving Alec's office, he spoke to Jan while passing her desk. "I'll see you later. I plan to see Ruth and Randy at the lake."

He was almost out of the room when he heard a familiar phrase. "Ted, come here!"

Now what, Ted thought as he walked back to Alec's office.

"I'm going to save you a trip to city hall," Alec said. "I just got off the line with the mayor. The committee meeting was canceled so you can continue with your other errands."

It was still raining when Ted left the *Guardian* and drove home. En route many trees were damaged by the storm with limbs lying across the sidewalks. Utility crews were clearing power and telephone lines along his way. He realized that tomorrow city maintenance workers would have their work cut out for them.

It didn't take long for Ted to change shoes after reaching his home and in a few minutes he was on his way downtown again.

Chapter 7

The Perry cottage was about two miles from the business district in a sparsely populated area of the lake. There were several other camps on this road, but he didn't encounter any traffic and no lights were visible during the last quarter mile leading to the lake.

It was a dirt road, rough at times pitted with many pot holes as a result of the rain.

Ted could see a faint light in a window of the Perry summer home as he neared the lake. Apparently, the lights were lamps or candles, most probably lamps, he thought. Lighted candles would flicker in a draft and with the high winds outside, an unexpected opening of a door could be dangerous.

Ruth's coupe was parked in front of the cottage although Randy's Kaiser sedan was not there. Ted drove his auto next to hers leaving the engine running with the headlights on high so he could find his way on the porch. He knocked on the front door several times but there were no sounds. He walked around the far side of the porch to a rear door that opened to the kitchen. His car's headlights didn't hit this part of the building and it was pitch dark.

The window shades hindered any view inside but he could see shadows moving in the living room beyond the kitchen. Simultaneously, he heard muffled voices and it was apparent more than one person was in the cottage.

Now, he tried turning the door knob. The door was locked.

Finally, he heard a sound and he saw a shadow in the cottage. This time, he pounded on the door with his fists while shouting. "Randy or Ruth! Is anything wrong? This is Ted. I would like to talk with you."

Slowly, the door opened a few inches and a soft voice asked.

"Is it urgent, Ted?" Ruth asked.

"No, I only wanted to arrange a meeting over the weekend to discuss our outing next month."

"Randy's not here and I don't feel well. May I call you tomorrow?"

"That's all right," Ted replied. On second thought, Ted asked, "Is there anything I can do or get you?"

"No thanks. I'll take a couple of aspirin and go to bed," she responded. She was still careful not to open the door any wider.

The door closed behind him as he made his way to the front of the porch.

As he turned his car around toward the rear of the cottage, the headlights picked up another vehicle. He stopped and looked at it. There was no doubt who owned this new sedan. It belonged to Brett.

Ruth was shaking when she closed the door.

How stupid, she suddenly realized. This was the second time in her four years of marriage she was with another man while Randy was away. It was hardly a good record. She thought of a similar incident in Illinois resulting to their relocation to Middleton.

Brett walked out of the bedroom while she was still standing at the door trying to analyze her situation. She pushed him away as he placed his hands on her shoulders.

"Go. Get out of here," she cried. 'Our tete'-a- tete' and maybe our lives are over."

Abruptly, he grabbed her arms.

"What do you mean by that remark?" he asked nervously. "Do you think Ted knew I was here,"

Looking up at him, for the first time she saw a different Brett Hartman. He had lost his composure. Facing her now was a frightened man who was beginning to realize this was a serious predicament.

In the dim light, his face became ashen when she told him of Randy's threat if he ever found her with another partner.

His voice trembled when he spoke, "I wasn't aware you were seeing others."

"I don't make a practice of it, "she remarked. "You are the second and last man to interfere with my marriage. I swear to that." Then, she added, "That doesn't matter now. If Randy even suspects, we're in serious trouble. Now, about Ted. He's no fool. He knew someone else was in the house. That's why he turned his car around so the lights would screen the back of the house. He wanted to see the other vehicle because he knew that it wasn't Randy's."

Whatever she had seen in Brett suddenly became a mystery. As he stood, his hands were shaking and his voice cracked when he tried to speak. More annoyed than ever, she didn't give him a chance to open his mouth.

"If I were you, I'd be giving serious thought about the future. Maybe a hitch in the Foreign Legion. Go look at yourself in a mirror," she cried.

"You're disgusting! Better still," raising her voice, "just go!"

Brett started for the outside but stopped short of the door. Attempting to regain his composure, he walked back to Ruth. "We must be calm. This isn't the way to end our affair. Hadn't we better face reality with a plan? "

"The only alternative we have is to suffer the consequences," Ruth concluded as she grasped his arm and hurried him to the door.

After he left, she walked to the living room and sat on the edge of a sofa. Near her on a coffee table, there was a photo of Randy taken when he was awarded his doctorate at the University of Illinois. What a handsome and kind person, she thought. How had she become so inconsiderate?

Her thoughts drifted back to her days as a student at the university when she made it customary to occupy a front seat during his lectures. She wondered how she had ever completed her collegiate education because she spent more time watching him than studying. That's what it seemed, but somehow she must have acquired some knowledge to receive a degree in mathematics. She learned enough to marry him a year after her graduation and they had many happy days in Champaign.

During the following year, she found excuses to visit him at his impressive office in Altgeld Hall on Green Street more often than she should during the day. Usually close to noon when she knew he would take her to a nearby restaurant. When the day was over, she would be waiting at their home on Florida Avenue, often preparing a candlelight supper. Or, they would dine at Katsinan's, a popular restaurant, and occasionally drive a few miles east of the campus to Wheat's Steakhouse to enjoy both dining and dancing. There were many pleasant memories just doing things together around the house.

In the fall of the year, along with neighbors, they would rake bushels of leaves on their lawns that fell from big elms lining the avenue. Afterwards, the odor and smoke of the fires from the burning piles would fill the evening air as they gathered on the sidewalks and chatted.

This was the nostalgia she felt tonight. The sprawling campus of the university extending through the cities of Urbana and Champaign included students from many countries in its 15,000 enrollment. She was happy to have been among this group along with Randy, who loved his work here and the people in the Midwest, especially Chicago, where both of them were born.

She dwelt on her responsibility for their move from this environment as she continued to reminisce. She couldn't forget their favorite sport, hockey, and the train trips to Chicago to watch the Black Hawks at the stadium. Joined with other faculty couples, they often boarded the Illinois Central for an afternoon trip to the Windy City for a night game when the Hawks were entertaining one of the league's six teams. It was a long but enjoyable day, not returning from the three-hour ride until nearly two o'clock in the morning.

Their enjoyment for hockey continued in Middleton where they attended all college games, home and away, and managed to catch the Hawks games in Boston Garden when they played the Bruins.

Tears filled her eyes as she remembered many wonderful moments together until she committed the biggest mistake of her life. A pitfall so easy to stumble into when you have too much leisure time.

That affair began innocently enough. A former classmate happened to bump into her in a nearby store. Same old preliminaries, she remembered. "Ruth, let's have a coffee," he asked, is how it began but it didn't end that way. The next meeting included a drink and eventually the one-drink meetings occurred more frequently. One afternoon when Randy was in Chicago for the day, the one drink led to several. Soon they left the lounge and went to a nearby motel.

She sobbed as she recalled her unfaithfulness. Ruth knew she couldn't face Randy when he returned home later that night so she went to bed pretending to be asleep when he entered her room. The following days only deepened her guilt until she thought she couldn't stand it any longer.

Also, coinciding with her remorse, was fear. She was well aware of Randy's temper. She had witnessed an incident at the university when he had caught a student stealing exam papers from his briefcase. Randy, who was nearly the size of Alec, grabbed the young man and threw him over a desk.

Unfortunately, it wasn't a long wait before her transgression became known. A friend of Randy's informed him about seeing Ruth at a motel. When he came home that night he approached her with glaring eyes. Shivering and frightened, she moved back toward the wall not knowing what to expect.

"Ruth, if you don't know me by now, you will! I cannot tolerate cheating," he shouted as he a threw a book that he was holding across the room. "You deceived me."

She fell to the floor covering her head with both hands awaiting a

71

blow that never arrived.

Instead, the room became quiet as he hurriedly left and went upstairs to the bedroom slamming a door behind him.

Slowly, she got up and made her way to a couch where she lay sobbing.

She wasn't aware how long she had been alone when sounds of footsteps coming down the staircase broke the room's silence. Somehow, she wasn't afraid any longer as he approached the couch and a hand touched her on the shoulder.

She turned with tears in her eyes and looked up at him as he spoke.

"I'm going to forgive you, Ruth, because I love you. We all make mistakes. "However," he continued with a threatening voice. "Let this be the last time."

What a relief, she thought to herself. Randy was well known for his kindness in spite of his temper. She was getting off easy, it appeared, until he finished his absolution with this ultimatum.

"My resignation will be on this university president's desk tomorrow morning, effective at the end of this semester," he declared. "In the meantime, we will prepare resumes for positions at a college or university in the northeast. With both employed, you will have less leisure time.

"Now, Ruth," he added with a smile. "Why don't you go upstairs and open the package on your bed. You can wear it tonight when we dine at the Urbana-Lincoln Hotel."

All of this was clear to her tonight as she sat alone. She hadn't forgotten the pleasant hours with Randy. What troubled her was the way she had blown her second chance.

At the moment, the selfish idea of 'saving yourself' developed in her thoughts as a paramount goal. She vowed nothing like this would ever happen again but first she needed another opportunity to prove herself.

As much as she disliked Brett at this moment, she agreed a plan or at least an excuse was necessary if a defensive occasion arose. It was unlikely Ted would mention tonight's events to anyone but unexpected encounters may take place similar to her experience in Illinois. She would have to swallow her pride and contact Brett in the morning. After all, she was as much to blame.

Sitting in the dimly lit room, many thoughts entered her mind how she could escape this embarrassing if not fatal situation. Instead of a solution, another terrifying oversight unfolded. Suppose someone had seen her last night at Brett's studio? Nothing had happened there but it would be difficult to explain to Randy, especially at that hour.

It was another experience with an innocent beginning at this cottage yesterday morning.

She and Randy were sitting on the dock when Jan came for a swim and later Brett joined the group.

Only idle conversation took place with the exception of Brett who invited Jan to visit his studio that night after she finished her shift in the newsroom. Jan said she usually left the office about midnight and jokingly said if the studio was open, she would probably drop in.

Before Jan and Brett left, Randy mentioned he was leaving for Boston that afternoon on a business trip and would be away for a couple of days.

Later in the afternoon, Brett called her and said Jan would be at the studio at ten o'clock. He asked her to join them instead of remaining at the cottage alone.

When she arrived shortly before ten, Jan was not there. She had been in the studio only a few minutes when a power outage left the place in darkness. Over his objections, she walked to the studio exit and glanced out the window before opening the door.

She stopped instantly when she observed two vehicles approaching on the street in opposite directions. To avoid being seen, she waited until they passed.

Instead of continuing down the street, the first car turned into the studio driveway. Within a minute, the other car also entered the driveway. Both vehicles drove through the parking lot in the rear of the building and continued on their original courses.

The frightening aspect of last night's turn of events finally dawned on Ruth. Ted's Chevy was the first car to enter the studio lot while the other belonged to Jan. And both passed by her Plymouth coupe and Brett's Ford. Undoubtedly they knew she was in the studio.

She survived last night without any noticeable scars but tomorrow could be a different story. Tonight's happening wasn't a lover's tryst. It was an unplanned meeting between a bachelor and a woman who had too much leisure time. A once forgiven person who promised she would never betray her husband again.

Brett came to the cottage at the height of the storm indicating he was looking for Randy which she knew was a lie. He was aware Randy

73

was away and this bachelor was after loving which he easily found from a lonely woman on a stormy night.

Ashamed and frightened, she extinguished the lamps and went to her room where she fell on her bed in a mist of tears. The tears soon turned to sobs as she thought of her affair tonight.

How could she have crawled in bed with a man known city-wide as a philanderer? A person, no less, supposedly a friend of everyone who was included in a week's outing together.

Worse how could she have been deceitful to Randy again? What had been sobs, now became cries as she remembered her promise that nothing like this would ever happen again. As she continued to dwell on tonight's actions, she became more emotional with tears covering her face. Soon she became hysterical, pleading aloud. "My God, help me. I'll never be unfaithful again."

Unexpectedly, a flash of light filled the room and she slowly rose from her bed. Peering through tear-filled eyes, nothing seemed unusual. It must have been lightning from another developing storm.

But the approaching storm would not be as dangerous.

Suddenly, she realized the room was illuminated from headlights of a vehicle stopping in front of the cottage as she heard a door open. Frantically, she found her way through the lightless living room bumping against furniture until she reached a window.

Looking out in the darkness, she knew the vehicle and she recognized Randy with the inside dome light on. He had returned earlier than anticipated. Frightened, she watched as he stepped out of the car into the rain and reached in the rear seat for his suitcase.

She suddenly realized her predicament but she was thankful for the power outage. In the dim light, he wouldn't be able to see her tear-swollen red eyes and anxious face. An idea quickly entered her mind. She moved fast but carefully to a liquor cabinet in the living room and took a bottle of wine along with a glass from a shelf adjacent to it. Hurriedly, she moved to a lake front window and sat on a chair.

Listening to Randy's footsteps as he approached on the porch, she opened the bottle and took a couple of drinks from it. Then, she filled the glass and waited.

This way, she thought, it would be easier to explain why she was sitting alone in a dark room. She would explain she was just sitting and having a drink while watching the storm pass by.

But another terrifying thought occurred to her. What if Randy had seen Brett's car as he drove from the cottage road to the highway?

She felt the warmth of the wine as she remained quietly waiting for Randy to unlock and enter the kitchen door. Not accustomed to consuming alcohol rapidly, she felt a tingling in her head that induced a bit of courage which she so badly needed.

Her immediate response to the impending problem had so far been effective. She was now prepared to answer coherently when he called.

"Are you awake, dear?"

"Yes, Randy, I'm in the living room. Just a few seconds, and I'll light a lamp so you can find your way. The electrical power is out so I've just been sitting here in the dark."

He left his suitcase and the rest of his belongings in the kitchen and came into the living room where he gave Ruth a brief hug and kiss.

"Was the seminar successful? Did you meet anyone I know?" she asked.

"Answer to both questions is yes. The meeting was worthwhile and I saw Gordon Chase from Illinois and, of course, John Kenney from Boston University. They both inquired about you and send their best."

Changing the subject, Randy questioned why she wasn't reading instead of sitting in the dark.

"Oh, I just wanted to be sentimental, I guess. Just enjoying a glass of wine and listening to sounds of blowing wind and rain. Would you like a glass of wine or may I mix you a drink?"

"Thanks. I'd like a scotch with water."

Now came the question Ruth feared would arise. "As I was approaching the road to our cottage, I saw a car coming from this direction and turning on the main road toward the city. Did you have any visitors?," he asked.

"Ted dropped by for a couple of minutes inquiring if we could arrange a meeting soon to complete plans for the outing in July. I said you would give him a call when the phone lines were back in order. Timothy couldn't reach us because of the storm so he asked Ted to drive down."

"Was that the only car?" Randy inquired suspiciously. "It didn't look like Ted's Chevy."

Prepared for this question, Ruth was cautious with her response. "Earlier, a utility vehicle turned in our driveway," Ruth answered. "And,

75

I believe there were lights from cars in the other camps, too."

"It could possibly have been one of them, "he said. "It was difficult to see clearly in the rain."

Now, Ruth could only hope he was satisfied with her answers to his question. However, she was more convinced a meeting with Brett was essential to overcome any personality clashes. Where and when would be the problem unless he attended the weekend meeting.

How could that be arranged? Instead of Randy calling Timothy, she would find an excuse to talk with him and suggest that Brett attend.

As they sat with their drinks, Ruth said she had to get a few groceries in the morning and would stop at Harry's for a coffee.

"Chances are I'll see Timothy," she added. "Do you want me to offer an invitation to meet here either Saturday or Sunday afternoon for a meeting or would you rather talk to him? "

"No, you do it. Let's try to make it Sunday."

The couple finished their drinks. Randy took care of his luggage while Ruth took the empty glasses to the kitchen.

Returning, she went directly to her room and slipped into bed. After an exhausting night and a few drinks, she soon fell asleep while Randy remained in the living room reading.

Returning to the *Guardian* was a nightmarish ride for Ted after he left the Perry's cottage. During his association over the years with many acquaintances, he had never witnessed a betrayal involving a close companion.

Unbelievable, insouciant Ruth had become too free with her attentions, catering to whims of a Middleton Casanova. The consequences could be disastrous for Randy as he was highly respected on and off the Chamberlain campus.

Ted always considered Brett untrustworthy but Ruth's actions seemed inexplicable.

Only yesterday Alec remarked how close friends Linda, Jan, and Ruth had become, and how much the trio would enhance the fun of next month's outing.

Abruptly, a monkey wrench had been thrown into the machinery. This affair couldn't linger a secret long, Ted surmised. It was the second questionable encounter of Ruth and Brett within a few days.

For the first time tonight, Ted had his windshield wipers turned low as only a light rain was falling, a reminder the heavy storm was now moving east through the Canadian province of New Brunswick.

He drove slowly on his return to the Guardian where he knew Alec and Jan would be curious about the date of a meeting. A time yet to be scheduled, if ever.

Alec was sitting at the city desk editing copy when Ted made his way through the newsroom toward his desk. He grinned when he glanced down at Ted's feet curious as to whether his writer had changed his soaked shoes. Quickly he looked up and inquired if there was going to be a meeting of the minds over the weekend. "

I don't know yet," Ted answered. "Randy wasn't at the cottage tonight but Ruth said when he returned from Boston she would ask him to call Timothy."

"You're saying Ruth was alone at the cottage during this storm? It must have been wild at the lake," Alec remarked.

"She handles it well," Ted quipped as he continued to his desk.

He was interrupted another time by Jan as he passed her desk wanting to know when Ruth expected Randy home.

"She didn't say," he replied, cutting the conversation short.

Before he could sit, Alec called him back to his desk. "I hope you're prepared for a wrap-up story on the storm. It's going to be a page one feature tonight. Hank has some excellent damage photos besides the fire pics. Nothing else has happened in the area or in the state for that matter to justify a better news story."

"I've got to make a few more calls to emergency units and police in the city which will give me enough material for the story," Ted commented. "I'll have more copy within the hour."

On the third attempt to reach his desk, he was uninterrupted and he finally began making phone calls.

A call to Timothy had slipped his mind until now. He hoped the phone wouldn't disturb the Haneys at this hour but he felt sure Timothy wanted to know what Randy had to say.

Timothy answered the phone immediately indicating he had been waiting for Ted's call.

"What did you find out, Ted. Can Randy and Ruth make a meeting over the weekend? "

"I only talked with Ruth," Ted answered. "She said Randy was in Boston and that she would have him call you tomorrow."

"Good, Ted. Now, I've got something amusing to tell you. I think most everyone will get a chuckle from this bit of news."

" I sure hope so. I could stand some humor after this day. However,

Timothy, I've got a deadline to meet so your news will have to wait."

"What's happened, Ted. I hope it's nothing serious."

"It's nothing we can talk about tonight but I'll see you at Harry's in the morning. Briefly, what do you have to tell us?"

"It's a long story, Ted. It involves an individual that J.T. in New York has hired to take care of the lodge. When I called earlier tonight about our plans, he told me about Jacques, a real northern woodsman, who would meet us at Bear Lake. His given name, Jacques, is not unusual in Maine," Timothy emphasized. "But his surname will allow you something to think about. It's Silver Seven."

Realizing Ted was limited on time to spend on this conversation, Timothy only said that J.T. had not elaborated why he acquired a new handyman.

Jokingly, Timothy added, he was explicit concerning Jacques's abilities to handle the job. Qualifications, he has, including guiding, bear taming, fishing, logging, and about anything essential for a person to survive in the forests," Timothy continued. "He even mentioned something about hockey but I don't understand why he included that game in his conversation. In the morning, it's more I'll tell you," Timothy said as he hung up the phone.

Silver Seven. Where had he heard the name before, Ted pondered momentarily. He didn't have time to dwell on that now. The newspaper was waiting for a story on the storm.

A few hours later, Ted's activities for the day terminated. It had been a long day, Ted thought as he went to Alec's desk and handed him the final page of the article for the *Guardian's* Friday edition.

Completing his assignment he turned, faced the remaining writers who were sitting at their desks, smiled, bowed, and said goodnight. Then he walked silently out of the newsroom and into the darkness of Middleton.

Chapter 8

A comfortable cool morning greeted citizens of Middleton with a clear blue cloudless sky and temperatures in the sixties.

For many, it was another working day. For others, a continuation of vacations, and to some, a migraine.

Brett Hartman looked at his desk calendar for the day's appointments, noting it was Friday but not the thirteenth. In his mind, however, it had earmarks of a doomsday. He was thankful for only one reason today except being alive.

His calendar indicated all appointments were scheduled in the afternoon which allowed him the morning to clean his desk, certainly not his soul, of unfinished business. He'd felt Ruth's anguish last night but it was insignificant compared to the other problems facing him. Unlike her, he felt no remorse.

However, they both faced uncertainties if Randy learned what happened last night. He dismissed this possible reaction temporarily as this wasn't his first extramarital relationship. Taking advantage of his affability and physical attractiveness, he had entered the hearts and beds of many women. Somehow he had managed to avoid confrontations with upset husbands but Ruth's fears of Randy's reaction were frightening. Randy would be an unpredictable adversary. Results of last night's incident was one of two and possibly three serious problems he faced immediately. Similar to others who had dug themselves into a hole, his thoughts drifted to whence he came, Rochester, New York.

Too late to think about it now, but if he had remained with Eastman Kodak where photographic miracles originated, would he now be reaching for schemes to save what was left of his life?

During nearly twenty years working at the Eastman facilities, he became adept in photography and won many awards for his stills. Unfortunately, he learned techniques with cameras rarely used by reputable professionals.

He barely escaped a prison stretch during this period when he teamed up with a photographer in New York City. They had a lucrative photo business involving young boys and girls. These kids would do anything to earn a few bucks, and they had a growing market for pictures portraying sexual activity.

Business was brisk and money was rolling in until they became careless about the subjects they used. His partner knew a man employed at a nearby girl's summer camp who sometimes had to take girls to a dentist or other necessary errands in the city. It wasn't long before the two men schemed, and without Brett's knowledge, began using several of these girls as participants in obscene sequences.

Word began spreading and it soon reached a camp counselor. One of the girls was persuaded to reveal the name of the studio and, without warning, police moved in as the photographer and his cohort were filming boys and girls in lewd scenes.

The partner and his friend along with Brett stood trial, but Brett managed to avoid punishment with the aid of political acquaintances and most of his savings on the premise that he wasn't in the studio at the time of the police dragnet.

Since he arrived in Middleton his business grew rapidly. It was again his extracurricular activities for monetary greed which were leading to a downfall. Highest on the list was gambling, mostly horse racing at Narragansett and Lincoln Downs in Rhode Island.

A vile concept of photography to pay his debts had lingered in his thoughts but until now he had dismissed it.

Never in the half century of surviving on the planet had the future become so bleak, he realized. A smooth talker who survived many pitfalls in New York, he had managed to manipulate friends to help him through sinister ploys and criminal prosecutions.

Last night's affair was problem number one. Could it be possible to talk himself out of this if consequences warranted?

Problem number two was an imminent threat. He owed the mob. There was only one solution. Pay or else!

His losses from track wagers had emptied his coffers leaving mortgages on everything he owned. Gambling had caught up with him and the syndicate now demanded $20,000 for unpaid bets.

Today, he planned to see Charlie Matix at his store where he most always placed his bets by phone. Last week's visit from the Rhode Island bill collectors was not a social call. Charlie laid Brett's bets with them and now they wanted cash or collateral. Maybe the local bookie could get the mob off his back until he had discovered other ways to pay them.

Brett knew he had to make a personal visit, not a phone call. Hopefully, he could escape the wrath of Randy's fury if the professor did learn of his cottage visit. If he could stall his creditors, he might pull through this scrape.

He had finally realized that raising cash to pay off the debts couldn't come from putting more bets on the ponies. That would be ultimate suicide.

The knowledge of acquiring funds from sources other than banking institutions was what he learned from photography. Pornography and modeling. These were the quick ways but he knew the possible consequences of the former method. His previous attempts in smut hadn't been successful in Middleton due primarily to the age of available attractive subjects. He was apprehensive about using younger girls. And the market demanded both of these qualities. Thus far he had located subjects less photogenic who would do about anything in front of a camera. He had found a few attractive young women who didn't object to modeling but they didn't want anything to do with pornography.

As he pondered over this predicament, he suddenly remembered a girl that he photographed last year for a beauty contest. She met the criterion but would she do it? Oh, what the hell, he thought. Nothing gained, nothing lost. First he had to locate her but that shouldn't be too difficult in this small city.

His options of amassing twenty big ones were limited with a camera or anything else with the possible exception of a gun. He was too smart to go that route. Regardless, it was imperative to hold an ace-in-the-hole. He had reflected on this perilous course months ago when it became apparent his ship was taking on more water than she could hold. There didn't seem to be a plausible solution to his dilemma.

The idea occurred one day when he heard Dave Paxton boasting about his life-style and Phyllis' millions. That was the moment he decided to risk blackmail. It wouldn't be easy extorting money from an ex-marine who had been around the Horn a couple of times. There seemed no other plausible answer to his dilemma. Then a stroke of luck came his way to make this possible, when the former beauty pageant contestant appeared unexpectedly on the scene. He was holding a good hand as he drove to Charlie's Cigar store. It seemed unbelievable how easy it had been to set up Dave.

The die had been cast and the act occurred by coincidence only a couple of nights ago in this studio. Now, he could use Dave Paxton for collateral if all else failed.

The setting for this performance had its beginning early that afternoon when Brett was standing on the sidewalk near the studio talking with a mail carrier. The girl he remembered and photographed last year was approaching.

Unbelievable, he thought. She smiled while walking by but instead of continuing, hesitated and stopped a short distance away pretending to window shop.

Brett knew she was delaying until he ended his conversation with the postman. He assumed correctly as the girl retraced her steps after the carrier left.

"Remember me?" she asked sweetly. "You took my picture for a contest last year."

There was no way he could forget this attractive teenager. She wasn't shy when she posed last year making sure her legs were well exposed.

"Sure, I remember you but I forgot your name," Brett answered. "What is it, and this time I'll remember it."

"You're kidding me. You'll forget it again. When I had my picture taken, I had to tell you a half dozen times. It's Dawn. Dawn Gronorski. Do you want me to spell it?"

"Dawn, I won't forget it. Come inside and I'll write it on my appointment book. A pretty thing like you should have a picture taken often. How about a sitting? "

"I sure would love to have pictures taken but I don't have any money," she replied.

"Don't worry about that. Come in," Brett said.

As he was opening the door, the idea to arrange a frame-up tonight involving Dave entered his mind.

He recalled Dave saying the other day that Phyllis was going to be away Tuesday and Wednesday nights this week. Tonight would be perfect, he thought.

"Dawn, something occurred to me. Why don't we take your photo tonight instead of making an appointment? Can you make it ?" "I won't have any trouble getting out. I'll tell mom that I'm going to visit a friend." "Dawn, I would prefer that this sitting is known only to us," he added.

"I won't tell anyone," she replied. "Perhaps you can take a lot of different pictures. That would be fun," she said.

"Dawn, perhaps I had better explain this type of photography. You will be paid for posing but that means you must remove some of your clothing. You won't have to take off your skirt but everything above your waist will have to be bare. Do you understand?"

"Sure I do. That's fine with me."

"Then, I'll see you tonight," Brett told her. "Come in the studio by the parking lot door."

"O.K., honey I'll be here," she laughed, leaving the studio and hurrying down the sidewalk.

Brett locked the front door and went back to his office to call Dave. As he reached for the phone, fate handed him another trump to play this hand. The phone rang and the caller was Dave. Two breaks in one day didn't seem possible but the cards were being dealt in his favor. "Are you busy, Brett? If you aren't, I thought I might drop in after I take Phyllis to the airport."

"I'm going to be tied up the rest of the day but I've got a photo appointment tonight that might interest you," Brett suggested. "I have a subject who is a nice looker and she's eager to try more revealing photography. I might need some help with her attire," he kidded.

"That sounds good to me," Dave responded. "What time? " "Make it after dark, about nine o'clock. Use my parking lot entrance."

"All right, I'll see you then."

The remainder of the day passed rapidly with a photo sitting and a realtor's order for photos of several dwellings in the city.

As twilight approached, Brett sat at his desk reviewing the procedure he had taken to install a hidden camera in the studio lounge when he remodeled the building last year.

He would capture Dave and Dawn's movements tonight with a plan to leave the couple alone.

A camera had been rigged on a shelf between the wall of the lounge and darkroom. From the darkroom, Brett could observe any activity through the view finder and release the shutter that was adjacent to it.

The ceiling light was kept low but adequate to provide essential lighting. A switch for this light was also in the film processing room to avoid a chance it would be turned off.

An expert photographer, he had synchronized the aperture and speed settings. The camera was focused on the couch and the precise distance was also adjusted. Loaded with film, the camera was always ready for action.

Now all that remained was waiting for someone to spring the trap.

Within a few hours an unsuspecting victim would be seduced by alluring bait into a cleverly programmed lair with incriminating results.

Unfortunately, it never occurred to him this girl was a minor which would become a disturbing factor for both him and Dave later.

It didn't matter who arrived first as the plan was foolproof. If Dawn was first on the scene, he would delay filming by showing her photo albums of models in a variety of settings. Chances are Dave's arrival would be early as he had plenty of time with Phyllis out of sight and the thought of a new playmate. Brett knew he would be anxious to make time with Dawn when they met.

The sound of a vehicle entering the parking lot meant Dave had arrived so he left his office and went to the rear door to let him in.

It was a solemn playboy who entered the studio.

Immediately aware something was wrong, Brett asked. "What's wrong, Dave? It looks as if you just lost your best friend."

Shaking his head disgustingly, Dave responded, "Same lecture every time Phyllis leaves on a trip. Don't do this or don't do that. And make damn sure you don't find a playmate while I'm away or you'll be playing with yourself. The worst part is that she's serious. She makes my life both enjoyable and miserable. But I like this life-style anyhow," Dave added. "Well, I asked for it. It's a great way of living if you can handle the restrictions. It reminds me somewhat of my time in the Corps, but she barks more orders than a drill sergeant. Now, I'm more interested in this photo session. Brett, I always thought of you as a portrait photographer," he added. "What turned your talents in this perverse direction?"

"Dave, I've got to get some money quickly. My creditors are becoming anxious."

"You mean bookies," Dave interrupted.

"You're right," Brett remarked. "How did you know? "

"I'm not a recruit anymore. Your gambling habits are well known by most bankers. Here's a bit of advice if you aren't already aware. Don't let your situation get too far out of hand, especially if your slips are held by Rhode Island bookies. You could find yourself trying to swim in Narragansett Bay wearing concrete shoes.

"Let's get on with tonight's session," Dave continued. "Are you trying to provide entertainment for me while the cat is out of town? What's the price of this shenanigan? "

"Nothing. I thought you would like to meet someone new. Forget it, if you're not interested."

"You know damn well I'm a sucker for dames, particularly if they're good lookers," Dave responded. "What makes this one so special? "

"I photographed her last year for a beauty show. She's a cute chick with a lot of imagination and body. By chance, she walked by the studio today and indicated a desire for more photos. That's all, excepting it may provide an opportunity to attract more young models. Does that satisfy your curiosity?"

"O.K. Another question. How old is this girl? "

"I don't really know. I never asked. She must be a senior in high school, probably about eighteen. That would be my guess."

"So, Brett, you expect a pretty girl to arrive soon to be photographed. What do you want me to do besides look at her?"

"Do what you usually do when you meet someone on the make but move a trifle slower. Suggest different poses for the settings and assist in sitting positions. I'll tell her you photographed models in California."

"After I finish," Brett continued," I'll go to the darkroom to process the film and you can remain in the lounge together until I return with the proofs."

For a person who has been around as much as Dave, it obviously didn't occur something was amiss with this arrangement. During his thirty-nine years he had conned and been conned often enough to realize he was being taken. Now he was about to swallow the bait, hook, line, and sinker like a country kid on his first city visit.

There was a light rap on the door as they ended their conversation. Brett opened the door for the teenager.

"Hi," she said with a smiling face revealing her eagerness for adventure.

"Come in," Brett welcomed her. "The camera is ready and waiting for a pretty face."

When Brett closed the door, she noticed Dave sitting on a chair at the far side of the room. Even in the dim lights of the lounge, she recognized him instantly.

"Hello, there," she exclaimed. "I know you but perhaps you don't have any idea who I am." "Of course, I remember you," he lied. "You were a participant in a talent contest last summer, weren't you? "

Surprised he knew her, she excitedly replied, "I never thought anyone would remember me. I only ended up as a second runner-up. I might've done better if I had some talent. Guess the judges had to decide on other things besides looks. Everyone said I was pretty."

"You're attractive. Another time you should enter a contest where only beauty is necessary. There are contests in other towns where special talents are not necessary," Dave explained. "I thought last year's contestants had to be under sixteen years old," he added but he was interrupted by Brett before she had a chance to answer.

"We had better get started if you want pictures taken tonight," Brett remarked.

"I'm ready anytime, "she said.

Then she said to Dave. I'd like to know your name. I've often seen you driving that big convertible around. I would like to have a ride sometime. Usually you have your mother with you."

Both Dave and Brett ignored that last remark although Brett turned his head to pretend he didn't hear it.

"I'll give you a ride next time I see you on the street. By the way, my name is Dave. What's yours? "

"I'm Dawn Gronorski. You must be a friend of Mr. Hartman. Are you a photographer, too?" she asked.

"Dave photographed models in California several years ago," Brett intervened. "He might be helpful to you in selecting the best poses. Is that all right with you, Dawn?"

"I would love it. You mean you really photographed models? "

"I took pictures of many girls. Some of them became stars in Hollywood," Dave replied.

"Let's get on with this," Brett concluded.

"Dawn, are you sure you want to do this? You'll have to undress," Brett told her.

"I understand," she said. "Will I get paid much for posing and who will see the pictures? "

"I'll pay you well when I receive my money next week from a buyer in New York. No one around here will see the photos. You understand, you are not to tell anyone about this. If the buyer wants more photos, you'll get more money."

"Now, if you're ready, go into my office and remove your clothes. There's a robe on my desk you can wear between scenes."

The next hour was spent taking photos of Dawn in various positions.

When Brett finished, he said it would take about an hour to process the film and he started for the darkroom.

Addressing both of them, he suggested they could leave now or wait in the lounge until the proofs were ready.

"Dawn, you can dress now," he added.

"O.K. I'll only be a minute dressing but I want to stay and wait until the proofs are ready. I want to see them tonight", Dawn replied excitedly.

"Do you want to stay with me until they are ready," she asked Dave.

"I'll wait with you," he answered.

Brett left for the darkroom but Dawn didn't go to his office to change. Instead, she sat on the lounge next to Dave.

After he closed and locked the darkroom door, Brett went immediately to the camera and looked into the view finder. He watched as Dave tried to locate a wall switch to turn off the ceiling light.

He gave up the search and he walked to the couch and sat next to Dawn.

Brett couldn't hear their conversation but soon Dave placed an arm around her shoulder while pulling her toward him.

It took only a few minutes before Brett was recording his fiendish evidence.

Brett thought of a French phrase suited to the occasion.

"Voila. Fait accompli."

Brett felt more comfortable as he made the turn on High Street only a few blocks from Charles's. However, this was only a brief respite that would soon end with bad news.

Suddenly, three cars in succession whisked pass him. He glanced in his rear view mirror and saw another car rapidly approaching with flashing blue lights.

He stopped and pulled to the side of the road to let the vehicle pass when he noticed other cars reaching the intersection ahead near Charlie's Cigar Store.

He couldn't imagine what was happening. There were no sirens or emergency vehicles so it couldn't possibly be a fire or accident. And there were no local police cruisers, only unmarked cars. As he reached the intersection, he saw Charlies' building surrounded by vehicles.

It didn't require a Philadelphia lawyer to solve this mystery, he concluded. Any hopes of negotiating with Charlie today vanished.

This was a police raid of the bookie's establishment, and everyone inside would be questioned and arrested if they possessed any betting slips. He had no further thoughts of talking to Charlie now.

When he reached the crossroads, he made a turn and headed back to the studio where he spent the remainder of the morning licking his wounds and trying to analyze the next move.

He was left with only two choices now that Charlie was out of the picture. Concentrating on young models or blackmail, both dangerous ventures leading to either the possibility of incarceration or a grave.

Chapter 9

Timothy awoke at his usual early hour on this Friday morning but unlike yesterday, he breathed cool refreshing air. And this sunrise was different without a bright red sky, but with a blue background indicating a storm-free day ahead. Looking out his bedroom window, the landscape reminded him of earlier days of his life in Ireland.

He watched cattle grazing in the pasture of a nearby farm which was a familiar sight in far away Cork County where pastures and cropland comprised most of the country's total acreage. However, unlike this state, half of the livestock were sheep. Although the view from this house away from the metropolitan area appeared similar to his hometown, it differed greatly overall to Maine. Woodlands here occupied ninety percent of the state's acreage while only five percent of forests covered the Irish countryside. Regardless, it did bring back memories of his homeland.

The last time he saw Irish soil was nearly forty years ago aboard a steamship with a contingent of other priests sailing out of Queenstown, a principal point of embarkation for emigrants to America. The tall spires of St. Colman's Cathedral were the final landmarks on the horizon he saw as he left for the new world. On this side of the ocean, St. Patrick's Cathedral towering above fashionable Fifth Avenue greeted him in New York City.

He often considered returning to Ireland for a visit but somehow he found other excuses not to make the voyage. Between religious duties and his increasing interest in police investigations, he couldn't find the time. Now, that he had the time, perhaps after next month's outing he might convince Ted to travel abroad with him.

After dressing, Timothy picked up the *Guardian* from the hall floor where Helen had left it and returned to his rocker to learn what happened yesterday in Middleton and elsewhere. He read Ted's account of the storm noting there had been only one injury. With the exceptions of power outages, no serious damage occurred except the fire at Ganeau's farm. On the world front, NATO, the North Atlantic Treaty Organization formed a couple of months ago, still dominated the international news.

In this country, columnist Ed Sullivan was planning a television show in the fall featuring special guest stars. Although few in the city had television sets, he thought it wouldn't be long before that would change.

Another article attracted his attention. After taking a cue from self-service retail stores in San Bernardino, California, Richard and Maurice McDonald opened a drive-in restaurant last December featuring hamburgers with standard condiments. They reported the idea has yet to attract the public. He turned to his daily routine of solving today's crossword puzzle before going downstairs for breakfast.

Helen was seated at the table when Timothy entered the kitchen.

"A good morning to you, Father," she greeted him. "It's a more comfortable day, you'll be enjoying. And, I hope, a bigger breakfast. I made corned beef hash for Mike and there's plenty for you. A bit you'll have, won't you? "

"Thank you, Helen. I'll have a small serving. You know, it's a little I eat in the morning."

"Helen," he added. "I was thinking a few minutes ago about visiting Ireland. I had thought Ted might be interested but I thought you and Mike would enjoy the voyage more. Besides, your folks came directly from the old country, didn't they? "

"Yes. My mother arrived in this country a year after her closest friend in Ireland survived that awful Titanic sinking."

"They had planned to sail together on this new liner but mother wasn't able to save enough money for the voyage," Helen said. "So she had to wait until the following year to leave. She said her friend told her how survivors shivered and sat numb in a lifeboat several hours on that cold spring night and cried as the ship disappeared into the ocean.

"My father came to this country several years before she arrived and they met at a church gathering in Malden, Massachusetts," Helen continued. "A wedding it was, two years later.

" Let's talk with Mike when he comes home, Father. I would like to go and I'm sure he would enjoy it. Lord knows he needs time off. He never took a vacation in his life."

"Very good," Timothy replied. "We'll discuss it with him tonight. It's probably too late to make arrangements this year, but plan, we can, for next summer."

Timothy finished his breakfast and left for downtown to get his copy of the Times and to make a visit to Harry's where he would meet his newspaper friend.

Ted awoke in an empty house. He missed talking with his mother or father although they had only been away on vacation less than a week. He wanted to talk with someone today but he couldn't have discussed last night's incident with either of them. There was only one person who would be interested and who might offer some explanation. That was Timothy who he would see at Harry's.

As he closed the door to leave for the coffee shop, it was difficult to understand what had taken place at the Perry cottage. If he hadn't been there, it would be hard to believe.

While walking down the front steps he heard a phone ringing in the house so he rushed back on the porch. He returned and hurried to the kitchen phone. It was Alec calling from his home.

"Ted," he exclaimed, "I'm glad I reached you. Our reporter called from city hall and said something is going on at Charlie's Cigar Store. I would like to have you at the scene. Could you get down there now?

"Sure, Alec. I'm on my way!"

When he was nearing the store, traffic was stalled along the highway. He couldn't see the building from his car so he parked off the road and started walking toward the intersection where most of the activity appeared to be taking place. The parking area in front of Charlie's was filled with vehicles and a crowd was milling in the parking lot at the rear of the store.

Ted saw an off-duty Middleton police officer he knew among the curious and he approached him.

"What's happening, Jack?" he asked.

"I don't really know, Ted," he answered. "I was going downtown and came upon the scene by chance. But, I think both of us have a good idea what's taking place. This is a state police show and to my knowledge, no one in our department was aware of it. Which means," he continued, "Charlie won't be making book for awhile."

"Have you seen him since you arrived? "Ted asked.

"No, I haven't. You'll get more information if you talk with the sergeant. You know Barry Davis, don't you? "

"Certainly. But, I don't see him anywhere. If this is a state police action, he wouldn't be in the store, would he?"

"Ted, I don't know. Why don't you look for him? He would be your best local source of information, and he could tell you about someone to contact."

"Thanks, Jack. I'll track him down."

Ted knew a fire or a parade attracted spectators and he learned today a police raid was just as effective. How so many people learned about this raid so quickly was difficult to understand. Especially since nobody on the Middleton police force knew about it.

Ted moved through the crowd, occasionally stopping to talk to persons he knew as he made his way to the store's door. Standing in front of it was a uniformed state trooper who he didn't recognize. He continued to the side of the building where he saw Sgt.. Davis talking with a trooper in plain clothes. They both recognized Ted as he approached and apparently they were prepared for his questions.

"You got here quickly, Ted. How did you learn of this raid so soon?" Sgt. Davis asked.

"You're got to be kidding, Barry. Half of the city beat me here," Ted responded.

"It's amazing," the trooper interjected. "With no sirens and advance warning how so many people can congregate in a relatively quiet part of the city. A lot of residents must be on vacation. You're not here on a sight-seeing tour, Ted," Davis said. "This is Sgt. Melvin Cook from Augusta. You probably have met before because he knows you. Regardless, he's the person who can tell you about this morning's state police involvement in this case."

"I'm glad to meet you, Sergeant, "Ted said as he extended his hand. "I have seen you on a couple of occasions but never had the opportunity to talk with you."

"I have seen you too, Ted," he remarked. "And, I've read some of your news stories. Good reporting."

"About what's taking place now. It's all a state police action as you are aware. We rarely do this on our own but sometimes we think it best to act alone to avoid any possibility of word slipping out beforehand," he continued. "There's a lot of preliminary investigation involving many days of work and we don't want that time and work wasted. I'm sure you understand."

"I'm aware of the situation, "Ted responded. "I've heard about similar events."

"All right, Ted. This action or raid if you prefer, involved eight plainclothes officers with seven unmarked vehicles.

"We wanted to secure the building area to avoid anyone getting away when we neared the store so our cruisers approached from four directions while one was already close to the area. Two vehicles drove directly to the front of the store and officers rushed to the door. The officer in the car already near the building covered the back door," Sgt. Cook explained.

"At this moment, "he continued, "only the owner of the store, Charles Matix, is in custody, charged with conducting illegal gambling. More charges may develop and possibly other persons could be held as we continue our investigation."

"What kind of gambling activities was Charlie carrying on? "Ted asked. "And, how did you suspect him? "

"Preliminary investigations from sources in Middleton lead us to believe Mr. Matix was taking bets or booking as it is commonly known," the sergeant said. "Acting on this information, we obtained a search warrant and conducted the raid this morning."

"Where is Charlie now? "Ted asked.

"Mr. Matix is still being questioned in the store and will be taken downtown to be booked. Chances are he will be released after bail is set and posted."

"Thanks for the information, Sergeant. There's nothing I can do here, "Ted concluded as he started to leave for his car.

"If you wait a couple of minutes, Ted, I'll walk with you, "Sgt. Davis said.

"O.K. Barry, I'll wait down the road for you."

As Ted walked slowly toward his vehicle, cars were passing him and he turned to look at Charlie's store. Most of the crowd had disbanded and only a few vehicles with the exception of several unmarked cruisers were in the parking area.

Charlie's would be closed for the remainder of the day or until he was released from custody.

Apparently, Barry wanted to discuss something with him about this incident, but he wondered what local police knew that the state police didn't tell him.

Of course, most everyone in Middleton who was knowledgeable about city activities was aware Charlie was a gambler, and he had booked since starting business here. The mom & pop store with a cigar name was only a front for the main purpose of this establishment. State police must have known also but in a few minutes he would get some additional local information.

When Barry caught up with him, the sergeant explained that whatever he said was only for Ted"s information and not for publication.

"Chief Davidson and your friend, Timothy, visit frequently to discuss local affairs, but I don't know how much Timothy tells you because a lot of their conversations are kept between the two of them. However, here's something I don't think is hush that might be of interest to you in the future. That is, if Charlie stays out of the bookie business for a long period of time. But, let's keep it to ourselves," he suggested.

"All right with me, Barry. What's on your mind? "

"Earlier this week I happened to be talking with someone near Brett's studio when a limousine stopped in front of the building while one of its occupants went inside and returned with the photographer. About five minutes later, Brett got out of the car and went back to his studio. The vehicle was registered in Rhode Island. It was obvious the passengers were not tourists or customers making an appointment to have their pictures taken."

"What has this incident got to do with the raid at Charlie's today? " Ted questioned.

"Oh, I thought you were aware of Brett's financial problems, Ted. He owes a lot of money locally and apparently out of state, too. Are you trying to tell me you didn't know Brett was a heavy gambler and that he did a lot of betting with Charlie? "

"Guess I'm a lousy newsman," Ted admitted. "I thought women was his only problem. Do you think Timothy was aware of his gambling problem, Barry? "

"I don't really know. You'll have to ask him. I can't give you any more information about the raid than you already got from the state police. Hope what I told you about Brett might be of value," Sgt. Davis concluded as he walked back to Charlie's store.

Ted had plenty to think about as he got into his car and drove to Harry's for his morning coffee and visit with Timothy. There was certainly much to discuss particularly about Brett who was joining them on the outing. He now felt certain Timothy knew of Brett's meeting with the gamblers but he didn't know about the affair with Ruth. He realized this morning's coffee break could develop into an interesting game of chess. Which of the two of them was going to reveal secrets first.

The traffic was heavy as he made his way downtown indicating vacationers were taking advantage from a day at the lakes to do some shopping. He had planned to go directly to Harry's but he thought he should stop at the *Guardian* to pick up any messages.

Ted received a surprise beyond his expectations in the next few minutes. It was quiet when he entered the room with the usual exception of clamoring from teletype machines. He hadn't made any noise when he went to his desk looking for messages. There were no signs of anyone in this desk-filled area and no notes on his desk, so he pulled out the top drawers in case a personal message had been left. As he continued his search, he heard the sound of a voice coming from Alec's office. It couldn't be Alec at this time of the day, he realized. But who would be occupying his office when he wasn't around?

Ted walked quietly near the editor's office and carefully peeked through the long glass window. Sitting in Alec's swivel chair was Sarah, one of the *Guardian's* proofreaders, talking on a phone. It was difficult to hear the conversation, but what he heard was clear when she angrily exclaimed, "Keep away from the studio. That man is up to no good."

In a calm voice, Sarah continued. "I know something he did and left a news story about him on a reporter's desk. Wait and see if I'm not right."

The conversation ended abruptly as Sarah dropped the phone and rushed out the office when she heard sounds of footsteps mounting the stairs.

Ted quickly returned to his desk keeping out of sight of Sarah who had disappeared behind a stack of newspapers at a proofreader's desk. He pretended to be rummaging through his desk drawer when the Guardian's paymaster entered the room and walked desk to desk leaving envelopes containing employees paychecks. He looked up at the courier as he left his envelope on the desk but didn't speak. After closing the drawers, he took his check and left the newsroom.

Now, he knew how the news clipping appeared on his desk but didn't know why. That was a mystery to be solved and soon, if he wanted to know more about Brett. As if the past twenty-four hours hadn't revealed enough.

Leaving the building, he drove directly to Harry's for his first morning coffee. The parking lot around the restaurant was filled for the first time this week. Luckily, a car backed out, opening a parking space, and Ted drove in. The coffee shop was filled as Ted made his way to a table at the back of the room where Timothy usually sat. He wasn't there this morning but Ted finally saw him sitting at the counter talking with Harry. As Ted approached, Harry moved from his seat explaining he had to get back to work.

"Ted. Harry offered to bake a batch of apple pies to take on our safari. Thoughtful of him, wasn't it?" Timothy asked.

"Sure is," Ted replied. "Everyone loves them. They won't last with this crowd."

"Talking about food," Ted said, "I'm starving. I haven't eaten anything this morning and it's near lunch time."

Reaching for a menu, Ted asked Timothy if he would like something.

"Thanks to you, Ted. It's more breakfast than usual that I've had and at least three cups of coffee. And Helen will beg me to have a bite with her."

"What's it going to be, Ted?" the counter waitress asked.

Ignoring the menu, Ted said, "Give me the big breakfast. Ham, eggs, and the works."

Looking at Timothy, Ted related, "We've had an interesting morning. I assume you heard about the raid at Charlie's."

"I overheard someone talking about it," Timothy replied with tongue in check. If anything was far from the truth, this remark was it. Hardly anything happened in this city that Timothy wasn't among the first to know.

"I haven't learned any details, and, what if anything, happened to Charlie," he added.

"The bottom line is Charlie has been taken into custody," Ted continued. "But I guess he's the only one. I still don't know how many charges are being brought against him or how long he will be held."

"I doubt if it will be long, "Timothy added. "If he's in the booking business, someone will be coming to his assistance soon."

"Timothy, I would like to discuss something with you. Let's see if we can find a table away from the others."

"Joan," he said to the waitress, "Will you please have my breakfast brought to me at the table across the room?"

"That's no problem," she answered.

"You must have important things on your mind," Timothy said. "Do they involve Charlie?"

"No," Ted answered as they walked to the table. "I'll tell you over coffee."

Before their discussion began, Timothy remarked that Ruth Perry had dropped in for a cup of coffee while doing her errands this morning and had invited the group to their cottage Sunday afternoon to make plans for the outing. He said that she hoped everyone would attend and asked if I would call all of them including Brett and Alec as their phone lines were still out of order.

"Did she specifically ask you to invite Brett?" Ted asked.

"Yes, she did. She said that he had been on most of the other trips and he could be helpful in preparing this larger gathering. Why do you ask, Ted? "

"Well, Timothy, you and I have some serious talks ahead and they don't involve Charlie as much as Brett. He's been associated in several awkward situations during the past week. So, we had better lay our cards on the table."

Timothy seemed surprised as Ted began with his knowledge of Brett's indebtedness and his visit with men from out of state.

"You have sources of information also," Timothy remarked. "A sign of a good reporter, that is."

"We cross paths often," Ted said jokingly. "It would be interesting if ever an occasion arose when we could solve a mystery together. But this city doesn't present any opportunity."

Returning to their original subject, Ted said, "Both of us know something about Brett's serious financial status and the money he owes bookies."

"You are correct, Ted. I am aware of Brett's problems and of the consequences if he doesn't meet his obligations to his creditors soon. What I cannot understand is how he ever got himself in such a mess. He has been around long enough to avoid these pitfalls. Now, Ted, you obviously know something that so far has escaped me. Do you want to tell me about it?"

"Timothy, what I am going to tell you is delicate and no one else knows about it except Brett and the other person involved. I don't like to disclose this type of information as it hurts to think about it, and I'm certain you'll feel the same."

"What in God's name are you trying to tell me, Ted? It can't be that bad."

"I'm afraid so, Timothy, and I wouldn't reveal it now if it weren't for the outing next month. I feel that you should know so you can make the decision if everyone in the invited group should be included."

Ted hesitated as a waitress brought his breakfast to the table.

"Is there anything else I can get you, Ted? " she asked. "No, thanks. I'm all set now," he answered.

"Well, Timothy," he continued when the waitress left. "It's Ruth Perry. Thursday night, her car was parked at Brett's studio about ten o'clock. Both Jan and I saw it behind the building as we drove through the parking lot. I'll explain Jan's presence there later. Last night, you asked me if I could contact the Perrys at the cottage as their phone lines were down so, I did."

"When I went on the porch to talk with Ruth," he added, "she didn't answer the door. After knocking and finally banging on it I heard someone inside. I identified myself and she reluctantly partially opened the door, saying she didn't feel well. After explaining that we would like to arrange a meeting, she said that Randy would be in touch.

"Timothy, I knew someone else was in the cottage but didn't know who until my headlights flashed on Brett's car when I backed away from the cottage. I made a special effort to identify it so there would be no question about the owner," Ted declared. "It's bad news, Timothy, but they were together." Accustomed to bad news, Timothy, however, appeared dumbfounded by this revelation.

He had many associations with Ruth and Randy since their arrival in Middleton, including outings twice a year at the wilderness lodge. A wonderful couple, he believed, and Ruth was a lovely individual. It was difficult to imagine she would become intimate with anyone but Randy.

Timothy sat silently, attempting to absorb what he had heard. Minutes passed before his friend spoke.

"First, Ted, I believe what you said but I would rather not. My only response is there must be an explanation for her actions. There are a couple of other considerations to be taken into account if news of this affair leaks out. I think our first obligation remains with the Perrys.

"We must keep the secret among the four of us, meaning Ruth and Brett. I wouldn't guess what would happen to Ruth or Brett if Randy learned of this affair. I know Randy quite well and although a gentlemen, a violent temper he has.

"During one of the numerous functions I attended at the Perrys, Ruth confided in me about an incident when Randy caught one of his students searching in his files for answers to an examination. She said the student required medical treatment afterwards. Ruth mentioned there were other occasions when his temper erupted but she didn't elaborate. It is my opinion that Brett's odds of survival would probably be better with his gambling creditors than with Randy.

"The other consideration is simple. Any change from our plans might trigger suspicions and obviously, we could not refuse to allow Ruth on this outing. Let's hold that meeting Sunday and continue with our original plans. My opinion, that is, Ted."

"As usual, Timothy, your opinions are wise. I plan to talk with Jan, and with your permission I would like to tell her about last night's affair. She is already suspicious of Ruth. However, no one besides the four of us and Jan would know. Is that all right with you?"

"That makes good sense, Ted."

" I wonder why Ruth wants Brett to attend Sunday's meeting," Ted continued. "Certainly, they aren't going be chummy with everyone around. The other possibility is since the Perry's phone line is not working, Ruth has something to discuss with Brett and there's no way to contact him. Sunday's meeting would allow the opportunity.

"As I mentioned earlier, Jan and I saw Ruth's coupe at the studio Wednesday night as we happened to be driving on King Street. It was only curiosity that made me drive through the studio lot. Jan had been invited by Brett to drop in after work but she changed her mind after seeing Ruth's car."

Brett's activities involving women always annoyed Ted and the affair with Ruth compounded the situation. It appeared Timothy was also losing his patience with him and he had known Brett many years. The incidents were getting closer to home and becoming more personal.

Ted hadn't forgotten his talk with the police chief concerning the missing teenager. If Brett was associated with this girl, he was really driving a nail in his coffin. As Ted finished his breakfast, it was noon and downtown employees were entering the restaurant for dinner.

"I've been here long enough, "Timothy remarked. " About time that I leave and make room for customers. I'll probably see you tomorrow but if not, I'll see you Sunday afternoon at the lake. There's nothing we can do about the situation and our best course is to continue as planned."

"I'll see you later, "Ted said. "You don't have to contact the others as I'll see them this afternoon."

Chapter 10

Jan didn't awake until late Friday morning, long after Linda had left the apartment for the college. Probably like most in the city, she discovered that cool refreshing air was conducive to sound sleep. Besides, she didn't have to report to work until late afternoon. She stayed in bed, being reminded of the mountain air in Wyoming where her early life was spent.

She reached over and turned on the radio, listening to the recorded music of the Glen Miller Band playing "Moonlight Serenade". Listening to music by the Big Bands always brought her back to days at Boston University where she spent four years studying for a degree in journalism.

Her family had moved from their hometown of Rock Springs when her father was appointed vice president of a bank in Boston and had settled in the neighboring city of Newton. Ironically, Linda was born and grew up in Newton, but Jan and Linda didn't become acquainted until they met in Middleton.

It wasn't long after graduation when her father told her a friend in the bank revealed that there was an opening on the Boston Globe staff. She wasted no time in getting to the personnel office and within a week she was on her first assignment in Beantown.

It was interesting and exciting working for a large daily newspaper in New England's largest city but having been brought up in a less populated community, she would rather be in a more rural area. She searched the classified ad sections of Boston newspapers every day for openings on smaller dailies in the northern part of New England without success.

She vacationed in Maine on the following year and fell in love with the place. It was now only a question of time before she could find a job on a city newspaper in the state.

Jan had returned from an assignment at the courthouse when the city editor called her to his desk.

"I have news that you have been waiting to hear, Jan. A friend of mine from Maine was at the New England Associated Press meeting last night and he remarked there was an opening on his staff for a good reporter.

"You have been looking for a chance to relocate in that state and you are a good writer so I took the privilege of telling him. His name is Alec Johnson and he's managing editor of *The Daily Guardian* in Middleton, an outstanding daily in a fast-growing city. You will like all three. Alec, the newspaper and the city."

He gave Alec's business card to her and added, "Give him a call now." Jan thanked him and returned to her desk to make the call and soon she became a member of the *Guardian* staff.

She was still reminiscing when the phone rang. Quickly jumping out of bed, she rushed to the phone in the kitchen of the small apartment. A familiar voice said, "Hello" and her heart skipped a beat when Alec asked, "What are your plans for this noon, Jan? "

Certain he was inviting her to dinner, she happily responded, "I'm free as a bird."

"That's good," he replied.

"Then, you won't mind covering the Women's Literary Club meeting at the Central Hotel. Our women's page editor forgot about it and she was scheduled at another event taking place at the same hour. I'll give you the night off as a reward."

Disappointed, however, she answered. "Sure, Alec. Anytime I can be of help."

"Thanks a lot, Jan. I'll make it up to you sometime. Lunch is scheduled for twelve-thirty with a meeting and speaker to follow. It probably will last about two hours."

"All right, I'll cover it and have a story ready by the time you get to the office."

Why doesn't he pay more attention to my features instead of my mind, she wondered dropping the phone in the cradle? Most men whistle but he gives me orders, she observed. I'll wait until I get him in the wilderness. Hopefully, I might change his way of thinking.

Suddenly, all the extra time she originally had was shortened. She had to hurry to get ready as her day for the *Guardian* would begin soon. But she would have the night off.

As she soaked in the bathtub, it dawned on her that perhaps Alec was becoming interested in not only her work but also in her as a person. Or why was he so anxious to have her along?

Smiling, she realized how naive she had been and how cleverly he was making up to her.

After all, he was the boss and it might create a negative image among the staff of the newsroom if the relationship became too obvious.

The office personnel were leaving their desks for the day while the news staff began to enter the editorial room as the *Guardian* neared its end of another week.

Jan completed her afternoon assignment and she was waiting at her desk to talk with Ted before going home.

"If you're expecting good news, Jan, I'm not the person to deliver it. Bad reports are becoming more common lately even for Charlie who had a poor start this morning at his cigar store. He probably would have had more success if he placed his emphasis on promoting tobacco products instead of horse racing."

"I don't know what you're talking about, Ted. You mean something happened to Charlie?"

"Haven't you heard about the police raid?" Ted asked. "He's been arrested for booking."

"No," Jan replied. "I attended a women's club meeting this afternoon and I returned to write the story and to finish another article I started yesterday. Nothing exciting took place here today. The only good thing that happened is I'm all through work for the week due to good behavior. Alec gave me the night off for covering the meeting."

"I don't like what I'm going to tell you, Jan, but since we both had suspicions the other night, it wouldn't be fair to leave you in the dark. I told Timothy this morning but I won't tell Linda or anyone else. It involves Ruth. On such a beautiful day, I dislike talking about unpleasant subjects," Ted continued.

"You knew I went to the Perry cottage last night for Timothy because the phone lines were out. Ruth answered the door and said Randy was away but he would contact Timothy when he returned. She didn't offer to let me in the house. In fact, she was cautious not to let me see inside by partially opening the door. "Jan," he continued, "I felt someone else was in the cottage and when I left the driveway my car's headlights flashed on a vehicle parked near the rear of the building. It was Brett's."

Jan was stunned. It took a little time before she spoke.

"This is awful hard for me to believe," she finally said. "I would like to talk to her about it, but it's hardly my place. Anyhow," she continued, "What about our outing? Will this affect it, Ted? "

"I don't think so. I discussed it with Timothy and he suggested that we keep this information to ourselves."

"All right, Ted," she replied. "It's shocking, you know. The other day I thought Brett was an interesting person but you were right. He's not to be trusted, not that I can blame everything on him. It takes two to tango.

"I'm going home, Ted. I probably won't see you again until we meet at the Perry's cottage. I hope I don't give myself away when I see Ruth. It's going to be difficult concealing my feelings when I see her."

"I'll see you, Jan," Ted responded.

She had almost reached the exit door when Ted remembered something.

"Hold on a minute, Jan," he shouted. "I'd like to ask you something about our proofreader."

Jan returned and they both sat on her desk.

"Which proofreader?" she inquired.

"Yesterday, I dropped in here to check on messages that might have been left on my desk. I thought I was alone in the newsroom until I heard someone talking in Alec's office. It was one of the proofreaders, Sarah, who was talking on the phone. I wondered what she was doing in Alec's office when there are so many phones in the newsroom. The only part of the conversation I was able to decipher was in reference to a studio or words to this effect, 'Don't go near there. I left something on a reporter's desk about that guy.' Well, Jan," Ted continued, "last week I found a news clipping on my desk relating to Brett's court appearance somewhere in which he was exonerated on a pornography charge. What I would like to know is with whom she was talking. Do you know anything about her, Jan? "

"Not very much. On a couple of afternoons, a high school girl with some friends came in the newsroom and she talked with Sarah. I'm not sure but I think she called one of them Dot or Dawn. Some name like that. It could have been a relative or friend. If you're really interested, I'll talk with her the next time she's on duty. That's no problem."

"Thanks. Will you try to find out something about the girl? Now, go home and make the best of your weekend!"

After she left, Ted walked to the coffee pot and brought a cup to his desk where he began making calls.

Although most of the Guardian staff frequented Harry's during the week, it was seldom if ever any of them were there on Sunday mornings.

On this day, the restaurant attracted a different clientele other than the usual customers of downtown office and store workers. They were mostly church members who stopped in for coffee and doughnuts on their way home.

After early morning Mass, Timothy picked up the *Times* and *Portland Sunday Telegram* at the news stand and returned to his room. He usually remained in this room most of the morning with the exception of an hour when he went downstairs for a breakfast of bacon, eggs, and homemade blueberry muffins with Mike and Helen. On this morning Timothy went downstairs early. During breakfast, he brought up the subject of a possible visit to Ireland which he had forgotten to mention the other night.

"Mike," he said. "Helen and I talked about taking a voyage to the old country next summer, realizing none of us has returned to those shores since we left many years ago. Does that interest you?"

"By gorry, that's an excellent idea, Father. We could take a whole month off and travel the entire island. A vacation, I've never taken since I've been at the mill for thirty years that I've worked there. No trouble, I'll be asking for one. My boss, Jack Mahoney, has always been giving me the devil for not taking vacations. Now, a surprise it will be to him. A wonderful thought, it's an enjoyment for us. Don't you think so, Helen?"

"Of course, I do," she replied. "Father Timothy and I thought you would never consider going on a trip. You certainly surprised me. I always thought to the grave you'll be taking your life savings."

"Now, don't you try to be funny. Not as bad as all that, am I. We take trips often, don't we? "

Helen laughed as she responded to this remark.

"Trips, you say. We visit your cousin in Massachusetts once a year and we get up before the light of day to get there. And, then we leave before dark to return home. You call that a trip? "

"Helen, darling. Making it all up to you, I will. We'll sit down with the Father Timothy and look at a map of the country. We'll visit places we have never seen. And we can go to other countries, too. We'll make a big one out of this trip. And, Father, this voyage on us, it will be. I want to pay all of it and no more do I want to hear about it. All you have to do," looking at Timothy, "is make the plans."

Timothy smiled. He knew it was useless to argue with Mike about paying his way.

"All right, Mike, we'll start preparing for it during the winter months when there's not much to do." "I'll be returning to my room to catch up on the news before going to a meeting at the lake," Timothy said as he left the table.

When Timothy arranged this meeting today he forgot that three members had to report for work at the *Guardian* later in the afternoon. None of them had mentioned it during the discussions so apparently it didn't matter. He assumed that since they were accustomed to limited times on Sunday afternoons, they never planned a long event.

It would take nearly an hour for Timothy to reach the lake at the speed he drove which allowed him plenty of time to think about the meeting. Reflecting on Ruth and Brett, he was certain nothing would be mentioned about Friday night. It was going to be interesting to watch Brett's facial expression as discussion included the raid at Charlie's and the missing teenager. He intended to nonchalantly mention that the girl was only fifteen years old. Beyond this, conversations would be limited to details of the outing and he wanted to tell the group about the new lodge handyman. Timothy was anxious to hear more about this interesting character.

His thoughts about newsmen having limited time on Sunday afternoons was correct as vehicles from the Guardian staff were parked near the cottage when he arrived. It also made him aware that this session should be brief to allow them time to return to their homes early.

Only one person hadn't arrived and that was Brett. Timothy knew he was usually a latecomer.

Randy was steering his boat toward the boat landing when Timothy got out of his car, while Ted and Linda were waiting to help him with lines to secure the craft. On the porch, Jan and Alec were talking with Ruth but Alec left when he saw Timothy and approached him.

" I see you often for a few minutes over a coffee, "Alec remarked. "However, it appears we are going to have more time to talk in a couple of weeks. You're welcome at the farm anytime Timothy. I wish you would visit me some time. I would like to show you my place."

"The offer, I'll accept some day , Alec. I have stayed away thinking busy you'd be. A lot of courage you have. Taking care of your herd and maintaining a farm plus running a newspaper."

"I only have ten head of cattle but it's enough. Like you said, it keeps me busy but I enjoy it, perhaps with the exception of housework. Farming is a great contrast from the newspaper world but much more unwinding. What have you been doing with yourself?"

"I manage to find things to do, Alec. Obviously, I'm not as young as the rest of you so I don't keep as active physically. However, I spend a lot of my time visiting friends. Something just occurred to me, Alec, what you need is someone to take care of your house. Have you given any thought to that?"

"Timothy, please don't try to be a matchmaker. I've thought of it before but I haven't discovered the right one yet. Maybe time will prove differently."

Changing the subject, he said, "It seems everyone is looking forward to this outing. Perhaps we all need a break from our long winter. Have you been to the lodge since the hunting trip last fall?"

"No, Alec. Sometimes I take an early fishing trip in the spring, but this year I went to Louisiana instead. I thought that I told you about it. I realize I would have enjoyed the Maine woods more than the heat we suffered down south. Anyhow, I had a good time. Have you been anywhere?"

"No, this will be my first break. I have only been out of the state once this year and that was to Boston for a Bruins game."

"Is there anything going on in the newspaper business I should know about?" Timothy asked.

"You're kidding, Timothy, "Alec replied. "I'm sure Ted keeps you informed on everything taking place in the city. Besides, you have your other sources. Sometimes, I think you know more about what's going on than anyone including the police."

The final member of the group was arriving as Brett's car neared the cottage. Ruth walked from the porch to meet him while Jan joined Timothy and Alec on the lawn.

"Lovely as usual, you are," Timothy told Jan. "Life and color you'll be adding to the outing, won't she, Alec? "

"No question about it. Besides being attractive, she's quite an outdoor person, Timothy, if you're not aware of it. I don't know about her fishing qualifications but I've heard she is a good hunter. Jan, you should tell him about your elk hunting expeditions in Wyoming. I'm sure he would be interested."

"Of course, interested I am, Jan," Timothy remarked. "I wasn't aware that such a young woman was an experienced elk hunter. How did you manage to hunt in the Rockies?"

"I was born in Wyoming," Jan responded, I grew up and went to school in Rock Springs not far from the mountains where Dad and I hunted. I have a trophy at our home in Massachusetts. You'll have to visit me there if you want to see it."

"I doubt if I'll have the opportunity of visiting your home, but I'm surprised you did so much hunting. If we have a fall trip to the lodge, which we usually do, you should consider joining us. Incidentally, a cook you are, or do you live out of a can?"

"I love to cook, Timothy. From my childhood days, Mom, Dad, and I spent much of our spare time in the kitchen preparing different dishes. I think Dad is the best chef."

"That's interesting," Timothy replied. "Cooking is my second hobby. You can give me an opinion of the entrees that I'll be preparing with fish if we have any luck with a rod at Bear Lake. I'm anxious to try a Cajun trout pecan fish recipe I brought back from New Orleans. We'll fix it together at the lodge."

"That ought to be fun, "Jan replied. "I'd like to help."

"Timothy," she asked. "you said that cooking was your second hobby. What's your first? "

"You don't know Timothy very well, Jan," Alec interrupted. "By the time we return from this trip, you'll know that Timothy is a clever investigator. Don't ever try to hide anything from him. "

She didn't have time to speak as Randy shouted from the dock.

"Everyone is here now. Let's take chairs from the porch and we'll hold our meeting on the lawn."

As they gathered, several conversations were occurring simultaneously so Timothy decided that if something was to come of this meeting, it needed more coordination. He took over and raised his voice.

"All right, friends, let's simmer down and get this discussion started."

"Most of you know the date, July 13, and with the exception of only two, everyone has been at the lodge on previous outings. For the benefit of Linda and Jan, the lodge facilities contrast drastically with what you'll be leaving behind.

"Drinking water is hand-pumped from a well while other water is taken by buckets from the lake. Lighting is provided by candles and oil lamps and before I forget to mention it, everyone should bring a flashlight and extra batteries.

"You won't have to be concerned who will pay toll calls as the nearest phone is more than thirty miles away at a tiny settlement called Ripogenus.

"A hired hand at the lodge will cut and store wood for the kitchen

107

stove and logs for the fireplace, "Timothy continued. "I'll tell you more about the handyman later. There are two half-moon buildings labeled in the rear of the structure for your toilet conveniences.

"Bathing is available in any section of the lake you prefer.

"Now, let's get our transportation schedule settled. For more convenience, we probably should use three vehicles including Alec's. Does that sound reasonable?" he asked.

"My station wagon has more space to carry supplies and another passenger or two if necessary," Alec volunteered.

"Good. I know Randy and Ruth would like to travel alone as they plan to stop for visits in Millinocket and Bangor on the return trip, so that leaves only six of us to occupy two vehicles.

"I'd like to ride with Ted and Linda while Brett can go with Alec and Jan. As we all know the way, it's not necessary that we leave or return at the same time," Timothy suggested.

"There are several ways to reach Bear Lake including two famous trails, Moosehead and Arnold. The Moosehead Trail heads east toward Bangor and turns northwest passing through towns with beautiful lakes including Sebasticook in Newport and Wassookeag at Dexter.

"It continues toward Dover-Foxcroft along the Piscataquis River where you can see one of the few remaining covered bridges in Maine on the way to Guilford and Greenville.

"The Benedict Arnold Trail is longer but probably more historical extending on Route 201 through Skowhegan, Bingham, The Forks, and Jackman.

"From this town, a single lane dirt road is passable but more difficult as it extends east about thirty-seven miles to Rockwood.

"From there, Route 15 goes through Greenville and then to Lily Bay and Ripogenus as does the other route I mentioned."

"The Arnold Trail sounds more interesting, "Ted exclaimed. "This will allow the newcomers a chance to see more of the Maine beauty and learn more of the state's past."

"And as it will be a long ride, I will hear more about Alec's farm life as well as the state's history," Jan remarked.

"If you don't object, Timothy, I'd like to deviate from details of the trip for a couple of minutes," she said. "I'm interested why Alec chose farming as an extracurricular activity and why he selected this particular breed of cattle instead of the common stock most farmers raise in this area."

"I can tell you now if the rest don't mind, "Alec replied. "It's not a long story."

"Go ahead," Randy interjected. "I'm sure we're all interested. Timothy can get back to the trip afterwards."

"First, and perhaps most important, my father left me the property when I was a graduate student at Columbia University and not ready to settle in Maine. So I put farming on the back burner while pursuing my career. In the meantime I became acquainted with a couple in New York who wanted to live in a rural area so I made a deal.

"For a minimal rental fee and an agreement to maintain the property until I returned, they could reside at the farm. They farmed until I came back after the war leaving the place in top condition," Alec related.

"You aren't a Maine native, Alec? Was your home out of state?" Linda asked.

"You're right. I was born in Philadelphia and lived with my parents until they separated. My father came to Maine when he retired and lived on the farm while my mother and I remained in Pennsylvania. When I attended Chamberlain College, I lived on campus and visited him at the farm often. That's when I acquired my fondness for country living. I hope that satisfies your curiosity, Jan and Linda?

"Now, the other reasons for living at the farm are obvious. I enjoy it and it's a great way to relax after a day in the office. There's some financial benefit from operating a farm, but I'm not utilizing all of its capacity yet and probably I never will. I plan to double my herd within the next year if I can find some spare-time help.

"Jan, you asked why I don't raise the same breed of cattle as most farmers. I have a good reason for keeping Hereford beef stock.

"They don't require the constant care of dairy cows. In other words, I don't have to baby sit them. There are no milking chores twice a day. And I enjoy steaks and this English bred cattle offer the best. And the most important reason of all. I don't have the time."

"I understand now how you came to live on a farm," Jan said, "But I would still like to know more about farm life. We can talk more about it on the way to Bear Lake."

"Now that we have placed some of Alec's past behind us, we had better get on with our plans," Timothy said.

"There isn't much work involved for everyone," Brett said. "I can buy most of the necessities when a list is compiled. Most of them can be bought at stores near the studio."

"You're right, "Timothy stated. "The main purpose of this gathering was to become acquainted again and to hear suggestions for meals and so forth. To avoid confusion, why don't all of you write your choice of food on this sheet of paper I'll pass around. Then, we'll let Brett take over and we'll reimburse him for the costs the next time we get together.

"Now that the food requests are resolved, let's be reminded we are responsible for individual sheets. Blankets are available in the lodge.

"And don't forget to bring along warm and foul weather clothing. Although the weather is nice now, things can change rapidly at Bear Lake," he concluded.

"I have a suggestion," Ruth added. "Why don't we meet at Harry's on the morning of departure for breakfast and we can leave from there. If Brett is going to have the supplies, we can swing by his studio and get them."

"That's a good idea," Alec said. "But we must keep in mind it's going to be a long ride. We should leave Middleton near dawn which should be about quarter past four if we want to take advantage of sights along the way."

"Besides the food Brett will get, I want to stop at a store or roadstand to pick up some fresh vegetables and milk before we hit the wilderness," Timothy said. "However," he added, "let's keep in mind Brett is not going to get all the personal necessities such as fly dope, sun tan lotion, and other minor but important items. These are our responsibilities.

"Jacques Silver Seven will supply oil for the lamps, candles, matches, and so forth. Of course, some of the best food we hope will be caught in the lake by our skilled anglers and we'll bring fresh meat from here."

"How do you keep meat and other perishable food from spoiling if there is no electricity at the lodge? Obviously, there isn't a refrigerator, "Linda questioned.

"Well," Randy said smiling. "Here's a person who certainly hasn't done any camping in the wilds."

"Linda, there's an icebox in the lodge that will be filled with blocks of ice. For your information, ice covering the lake during the winter was cut in blocks and kept in a separate building by packing and covering it with sawdust."

Embarrassed, Linda replied. "Sorry, I should have known."

"Anything more to discuss, Timothy?" Jan asked.

"Perhaps one of the most important items of all. We haven't decided how long this trip will last and Brett can't buy supplies until he knows this. How many days do we intend to stay?"

"I had assumed a week," Alec replied. "We'll leave on a Saturday morning and return the following Saturday. That's all the time any of us working at the *Guardian* can spare. The rest of you can remain as long as you want. Those staying longer will have to make arrangements for a ride home."

"Randy and I plan to leave the lodge on Friday so that we can spend a few days with friends in Millinocket," Ruth said.

"Apparently, we had all better plan on that schedule, "Timothy said.

"All right, Brett. Why don't you buy enough provisions for a week's stay?"

"Now, is there anything else to discuss before we enjoy Ruth and Randy's hospitality which they have so kindly offered? Oh, yes. One more item. Harry is baking a batch of apple pies for us."

"That's thoughtful," Ruth said. "We should repay him somehow. I'll try to think of something."

"Excellent suggestion, Ruth. Now, I have another question," Linda added. " I hope this one is not as silly as the other. There's going to be a lot of meals to prepare. Who does all the cooking and how is that arranged?"

"Linda, you don't know Timothy well either," Alec said. "He's our master cook and gourmet chef par excellence. But, there's going to be need for dish washers."

"If the question and answer period is over," Timothy said," let me tell you what I know about the handyman at the lodge.

"My friend called this morning from New York saying the former lodgekeeper, Joe Lebec, moved from the area. Before leaving, he recommended a man to take his place and he told me a little about his past. He said when we meet him he'll tell us a lot more because he has a habit of talking a lot.

"This is interesting, and particularly so, if you are interested in hockey. As I told you, Jacques Silver Seven is his name and he was born near Notre Dame de la Paix in Quebec about the turn of the century. He was the son of an Iroquois Indian mother and a French Canadian father named Narcisse Paquin, who was so fond of ice skating, hockey became a passion.

"So, after the Ottawa's Silver Seven team beat the Yukon's Dawson club in the Stanley Cup challenge, he decided to visit the capital and try out for next season's team.

"Narcisse went to Ottawa in 1924 when he was nineteen traveling mostly on snowshoes where by luck he found Silver Seven Coach A. T. Smith talking with his star player, Frank McGee, near the Parliament. He interrupted their conversation and asked Smith for a chance to play for the team.

"Smith gave him a negative reply but McGee, still excited over having scored fourteen goals in the final game against Dawson, urged the coach to give him a chance.

"As Jacques' story goes, the trio went to the Rideau Canal where an area was cleared of snow and Narcisse tried his best to display his skating abilities but the coach felt he couldn't skate backwards well enough. So that ended his attempt to become a hockey player.

"Disappointed but appreciative, he gave his thanks and returned to Quebec. He was still infatuated with the Silver Seven and their three Stanley Cup wins, so when his son was born the following year he named him Jacques Silver Seven which he reasoned was a perfect blend of French and Indian cultures.

"There's a lot more to his exploits and talents and we'll hear about them, I'm sure. Before we end our meeting, is there any news of consequence taking place in Middleton that we should know about?" directing his question to Alec.

"You should be asking Ted. He's the person who covers the exciting beats. How about it, Ted? Are we leaving anything out of the Guardian?"

"The latest news was the police raid at Charlie's but he posted bail and reopened his store," Ted replied." I doubt if he's still making book. I guess he's facing a big fine, or a prison sentence, if not both.

"There's another story circulating about a girl reported missing the other night. It hasn't been in the newspaper because no crime has been committed and also because of her age. She is only fifteen."

Brett's face turned white as Ted finished but he didn't utter a word. Timothy and Ted's suspicions were confirmed as they saw his expression. They were now both certain the missing girl had been in Brett's studio Tuesday night.

"It's strange, a young girl walking alone in the city streets late at night," Linda remarked. "What do the police think, Ted?"

"No one is saying anything. I only said there is a rumor circulating in the department and no one's talking. Obviously they have a theory that it's more than a teenage date. Officials haven't closed the incident."

"O.K., that's enough news for one day. Let's take advantage of Randy and Ruth's hospitality," Timothy said.

The disclosure by Ted earlier of the missing teenager's age shook Brett as he had no idea the girl was a juvenile. This meant Dave could face a statutory rape offense if charged. He didn't know what faced him for his involvement. Suddenly worried, he became deep in thought temporarily ignoring the others.

He was concerned not only about that evening with Ruth, but also more importantly with his obligations to the gamblers as he knew time was running out to pay the debt. Charlie certainly was not in a position now to alleviate pressure for him from his gambling creditors. Uncertain when and how to put the bite on Dave, it would require a lot of finesse. Twenty thousand dollars was a lot of cash.

A plan entered his mind that Dave could invest in the studio and became a partner. Under this plan, Dave would probably encounter less resistance from his benefactor, Phyllis. She would certainly be reluctant to hand over twenty grand without collateral. The more he thought, this appeared to be the most logical maneuver. He had to complete the deal before the outing as he was afraid collectors from Rhode Island would be making another visit, especially since Charlie was out of business.

And, now, the worst if Dave wouldn't loan him money. His only alternative would be blackmail exhibiting photos of Dave and Dawn having sex. The scenario with Dave, beginning with a suggestion of investing in the business or an outright demand for cash would have to be played soon.

Reflecting on the possible problem with Randy, he didn't have an opportunity to talk with Ruth before the meeting to discuss an alibi and it looked hopeless now. Each time he approached her someone intervened. As he strolled toward the wharf, Randy walked toward him.

"Haven't seen much of you," Randy remarked. "The photography business must be good."

"No complaints," Brett responded. "This is a busy month for weddings. I'm booked solid. Had a great spring season with graduations from the college and area high schools."

"That's good," Randy replied.

Changing the subject, Randy said, "Thought I saw your car Friday night when returning from Boston. You were driving out and turned at the state road toward the city."

"That's right, Randy. I came to visit but changed my mind when I was half way down your road. I remembered the other day that you mentioned being away for two days. So I turned in a driveway and returned to the city. It was about ten o'clock."

"The time seems correct," Randy remarked as he dropped the subject and walked to the cottage. Turning around, he said. "There's plenty of ale in the refrigerator Brett, if you would like one." "Not right now," Brett answered. "Perhaps later."

Randy continued to the cottage but his mind centered back on the other night after he saw Brett's car and later Ruth sitting in the dark at the cottage. He was sure something had taken place. The thought remained as he continued to the wharf where Ted was steadying a canoe while Linda was gingerly trying to board it. In a few minutes, Ted pushed and maneuvered the craft out into the calm water and headed across the lake. Randy watched as the couple skillfully paddled the canoe leaving only a little wave behind.

Now that two guests had found a way to entertain themselves, he looked around and saw Jan and Alec sitting on a rock on the other side of the lawn. Not wanting to disturb them, Randy glanced toward the cottage as Timothy was coming down the stairs in his direction. Standing on the porch in the background, Ruth and Brett were engaged in a conversation.

"Timothy, I was looking for you, "Randy exclaimed. "Thought we might have a drink together and talk about the new man at the lodge. Without knowing much, he sounds fascinating. From your description he's got to be an interesting character. He must be a guide? "

"Can't tell more than you already know. As J.D. said, he likes to talk. He mentioned this woodsman has many yarns and undoubtedly knows a lot about Maine wilderness," Timothy continued. "There's something else I forgot to mention. At some time in his life Jacques tamed a bear. We'll find out more in a couple of weeks."

"Well, Timothy, everything is shaping up to be a pleasant vacation. Hope fine weather prevails. Did your friend mention anything about fishing? We know July is not the best month for good catches but we've always gotten our limits in past years at this lake, which reminds me that we should bring back a couple of togue for Harry. That's one way of thanking him for the pies he's contributing."

"J.T. didn't say anything about the fishing but I agree with you. We shouldn't have any problem catching enough for our meals and a few for Harry."

"By the way," Randy remarked, "Ted said Charlie was arrested for booking. Won't that hinder Brett from placing bets? Understand he's quite a gambler."

"If he is," Timothy responded, always careful not to commit himself, "he'll have to find a new bookie."

The conversation ended as they walked slowly back to the cottage to join Ruth and Brett on the porch.

While Timothy and Randy were talking on the lawn, Brett finally found a chance to meet with Ruth to collaborate on stories to tell about the affair Friday night if it became necessary. Brett explained what he had told Randy indicating the issue seemed resolved. That is, if Randy believed both explanations, Ruth's on Friday night and Brett's, a few minutes ago.

During their brief visit, Brett acted apologetic although Ruth was aware he was deceitful.

"I'll never know how I ever got involved, but I regret meeting you, Brett. For our salvation and the love my husband has for me, I must continue a friendly relationship. But, there's no misunderstanding on my part. Deep down, you're a first-class heel."

"Don't give me that "holier-than-thou" routine. You enjoyed every minute of it. Whether or not you regret your actions is your decision. I'll never bother you again," Brett declared.

With this assertion, their dialogue ceased as Timothy and Randy neared the cottage. The conversation terminated but not Ruth's anger. She was infuriated but she couldn't respond at this moment. Her feelings suddenly turned to thoughts of revenge.

Then she realized there's no better place than the wilderness to accomplish it. Too bad it wasn't hunting season. Yet, it's always open season in the woods.

"Friends, you have a choice of any refreshment. Name it," Randy offered.

"I'll have a Coke," Jan replied while Ruth said she would like the same. Timothy and Brett settled for a brew.

Randy was serving the refreshments when a CMP utility vehicle drove into the yard. He excused himself and went outside to talk with the driver.

"I don't usually work on Sunday afternoons, Dr. Perry," the company worker said. "I was checking lines and it appears there was no damage from Friday's storm. Your service was restored early yesterday morning without problems. I came here during the storm and turned in your driveway before returning to the city. I saw your vehicles but there was no need to talk with anyone."

Apparently the lineman knew Randy as he addressed him although the professor didn't recall ever meeting him. But Randy picked up quickly when he mentioned the vehicles.

"Was there more than one car here at the time?" Randy inquired.

"There were two vehicles but in spite of pouring rain, they looked like them over there. The Plymouth coupe and the Ford. Is there a problem?"

"No," Randy answered. "You must have been here before I came home."

"I'll see you again," he remarked. "If you have any power problems, call anytime."

The remarks about the vehicles opened the festering wound. Now Randy was quite certain Brett was here with Ruth but he still didn't know what took place.

He wondered about Brett. It required gall to fool around with a married woman in her own home with the possibility of being seen. Of course, there's a chance nothing did take place but why did both of them lie?

How to heal the wound was developing into an obsession. Several years ago he moved from a city to get away from a similar incident but he wasn't going to leave here. It was far better that the problem be resolved or eliminated, he believed.

He thought that another talk with Ruth might discourage her from future associations with Brett. But the cause of the irritation would still exist and make its presence known.

There was only one way to eliminate an obstacle and that was to destroy it. A thought entered his mind but that was ridiculous. Better to let such an idea wane than to give it any consideration.

While returning to the cottage to join the others, he dwelled on this ludicrous idea. What if something happened to Brett?

Many fishermen have been lost when a boat capsized.

Chapter 11

There's a saying in New England that was believed to have originated but never confirmed, with the landing of the Pilgrims at Plymouth, Massachusetts, when John Alden's niece remarked after she was drenched during an unexpected rain shower, "If you don't like the weather, wait a few minutes and it will change."

Storms passing through the area last week changed the favorable weather pattern Middleton had experienced during the past two months. On this first morning of the work week, the blue skies with floating, fluffy, white, cumulus clouds that had prevailed almost daily disappeared and were replaced with a dreary gray cloud overcast. Rain was forecast for the next few days and it was anyone's guess when the sun would appear again.

Brett was expecting two callers at his studio sometime this week. He was sure someone from the syndicate would be making a call to remind him of his gambling debt, and Dawn would be dropping in to get paid for posing the other night.

Brett hadn't decided how much he should give her. He was reluctant to hand over too much cash to a teenager who might boast of her earnings to friends. Anyhow Dave should be paying for her performance, but Brett was hoping to borrow some money from him.

Another thought entered Brett's mind. He should have taken other photos besides the modeling scenes. After all, Dawn must have an excuse to visit the studio again. When she arrived, he would make arrangements for another sitting, this time during the day. He decided to give her ten dollars and promise her more later. Thus far, he hadn't sent those photos to anyone. The only negatives printed the other night were the scenes of Dave and Dawn together.

As he sat at his desk waiting for the first appointment which was scheduled in two hours, he thought of Ruth's parting remarks at the lake yesterday and also Randy's curiosity about seeing his car Friday night on the camp road.

Brett wondered if Randy believed his explanation but he was certain the Perrys had acquired a repulsive conception of him. It wasn't the best way to begin an outing particularly in the wilds of Maine. He wasn't certain if this togetherness at the lodge presented a physical threat although Ruth indicated her husband had warned if ever he was aware of an affair with another man both would suffer severe consequences. The animosity he created with Ruth and Randy was probably insignificant compared to the problem Dave would face if the truth was revealed about his relationship with the teenager.

"Well," he thought, reaching for the phone, "this is as good a time as any to talk with Dave about his proposal and to inform him of the girl's age."

Phyllis answered the call and she was surprisingly amicable to Brett, a mood he had never experienced on previous occasions. He remembered her as curt but today she was exceptionally friendly while discussing his photography, the weather, and particularly, her business trip next month.

"I'm going to be away for a couple of weeks and I believe Dave would like to discuss your plans during that time," she said. "He'll talk with you about it when he sees you later this morning. I hope you can plan something to do together."

"I'm sure we can find things of interest," Brett replied. "A group of us have a fishing outing arranged for one week in July. I have no idea when your trip is scheduled but maybe Dave and I can work something out around those dates. We'll talk about it when he gets here."

"That sounds fine, Brett. Thank you. Please don't be a stranger and come to the lake to see us when you have an opportunity," she added.

Well, that was a switch, Brett thought as the conversation ended. He couldn't imagine why her attitude changed so much. She was probably laying the ground work for her two week absence from Dave trying to keep him busy and away from women. She had to be blind not to know he wasn't the ideal person for this task.

As for inviting him to her lakeside home, that was a laugh. Only the wealthy and prominent were welcome at the Paxton inner sanctum and he didn't fit into either category. Maybe Dave would have an explanation for her change of behavior.

At least it hadn't been necessary to ask Dave to come here. Phyllis had already convinced him to make the visit. That decision already alleviates the pressure Brett thought he had to use for Dave to listen to his proposition. If he could believe Phyllis might have softened and would listen to his business venture, his future might not appear so bleak.

However, he possessed no such illusions. A rough road still lay ahead.

He looked at his watch noting there was plenty of time before his first client was scheduled to arrive. There was some paper work to be completed but he didn't feel like doing it now so he left the office and went outside. Traffic was light this morning while a light rain began falling.

He walked across the street to a newsstand and bought a copy of the *Daily Guardian* and returned to the studio.

Back at his desk, he read the newspaper thoroughly, looking for any article referring to a reported missing juvenile last week. Ted told the group yesterday police were placing more emphasis on the investigation because other girls had been reported in the downtown area late at night. However, no mention was made of the incident in this morning's edition so he put the paper aside and decided to finish the postponed bookkeeping.

A sound of a door opening caught his attention. He glanced at his watch and knew it was too early for a family photograph slated at ten o'clock. The door closed softly but there was no further noise from the reception room. Standing, he placed the daily records inside the ledger, closed the book and walked from the office to the larger room where Dawn was sitting on a reclining chair.

Surprised at seeing her so early in the week, he abruptly asked, "What are you doing here this morning?"

"A few of my friends and I are going shopping in Lewiston today, and I thought you would have money to give me for the photographs you took the other night. Aren't you happy to see me?"

"Of course I'm glad to see you but I didn't expect you would show up so soon. I haven't heard from the outlet in New York yet but I can give you something until they let me know how much they're worth."

He took his billfold from his pocket and reached for a couple five-dollar bills and passed them to her. She looked disappointed when she took them only saying, "I thought I was worth more than ten dollars."

Suddenly, realizing his offer was too little, Brett smiled and said, "I told you I haven't heard from my buyer and I know you will receive more cash. I was just giving you some spending money for now." Wanting to be certain he didn't make a second mistake, Brett said, "Here's another ten dollars, which should please you, Dawn."

"Oh, Mr. Hartman, that's much better. I'll let you take pictures of me anytime you want. Now, I can go shopping and have dinner in that nice restaurant in Auburn."

"Now, remember, Dawn. Don't you tell anyone where you got your money."

"I won't, Mr. Hartman," she answered as she walked from the reception room.

Brett interrupted her departure remembering she should have a better reason for visiting the studio in the future.

"Dawn, why don't we make an appointment to have a set of pictures taken for your friends. It won't cost you anything and we'll do them during regular studio hours."

To make certain of her exact age, he added, "You'll need pictures for your graduation next June, won't you, Dawn?"

"Not next year, Mr. Hartman," she quickly responded. "I'll be a junior next fall and I have two years before graduating. You see, I'm only fifteen. My next birthday is on the first day of August."

"All right, Dawn. Let's make an appointment for next week. How about Tuesday afternoon at two o'clock? Will you be able to make it?"

"Sounds great to me. I'll see you then," she said hurrying out of the studio and into the rain.

After the family portraits were completed, Brett took passport photos of four couples who were going on a voyage to the British Isles, and as he was returning to his office, Dave entered the rear door. For some reason, he preferred that entrance rather than the front door.

"Guess we both wanted to discuss something," Brett said. "Phyllis said you were coming down to find out how busy I was going to be next month. What's on your mind?"

"You already know Phyllis is going away for a couple of weeks in July on a business trip so I thought we might do something together. You don't have any more eager young women looking for action, do you? "

"Dave, both of us have got to locate other bed partners as it's obvious we're both in hot water. Boiling water, and that's no joke."

"You'll have to run that by me again, Brett. I have no idea what you're talking about. I didn't do anything the other night I haven't done before, and as long as Phyllis is not aware of it, how serious can it be? "

"More than you are aware, Dave, if word leaks, regardless if Phyllis learns of it or not. Kind of bad for both of us. Dawn is only fifteen years old which means she is a juvenile and what you committed was statutory rape, with or without her consent."

"You are kidding me, Brett. Fifteen years old. She is at least eighteen or I'll eat my shirt."

"What kind of sauce do you want on it?" Brett retorted.

"She left here an hour ago after I paid her for posing the other night. I tried to make arrangements for a normal sitting explaining she should be thinking about class pictures for her graduation. She said she was fifteen."

My God," Dave murmured. "What in hell have I done. I'm forty years old and never fooled around with San Quentin Quail. Can't believe it."

Continuing, Dave asked Brett how much he paid her and if she mentioned him.

"She wanted more than the ten dollars I originally offered. But, when I gave her another ten she was pleased. She said she was going shopping with friends in Lewiston.

"No, she didn't ask about you. Apparently, she only expected money for modeling," Brett added.

"Brett, you said I could be charged with statutory rape for my affair with her. What does that mean in terms of penalties if I were convicted?"

"I'm not familiar with the laws but I'm sure it would mean a prison term or fine or possibly both. I guess it depends on the judge and most courts in the state are harsh on punishments for juvenile crimes," Brett said.

"You said she didn't say anything about me, Brett, so chances are nothing will happen."

"Just because Dawn didn't include you in our conversation today doesn't mean she has forgotten you. The only thing on her mind this morning was money and she went away satisfied.

"However," Brett said, "Ted told us yesterday at the lake that police are investigating her disappearance last week. I don't know how far they plan to continue with the investigation but they are suspicious of her story. They feel she's not telling the truth. What really baffles me is why they are so concerned about a girl missing for only a few hours. That's a common occurrence."

"Well, there's nothing we can do about it now," Dave said. "Let's get back to the reason I'm here. Do you have any plans for the second and third weeks of July? That's when Phyllis will be away."

"Our group who regularly make trips to Bear Lake twice a year is leaving the second week of the month. Besides the usual crowd, Timothy, Ted, Ruth, Randy, and Alec, there will be two newcomers, Janice Robinson and Linda Breton. Have you met them?"

"I've heard of them but we haven't met," Dave answered. "I've seen the others on occasions. I know Alec. We served in the Marines together."

It didn't take long before a thought entered Dave's mind.

"Do you suppose I could go along with you? That would make a good week," Dave asked. "Could you convince someone to invite me?"

"That's not easy, Dave. Timothy is head of the group because he is the only person who has access to the facilities. He is careful not to disrupt the usual harmony and he's kept the group small until now when he invited two others. That perhaps is the result of his friendship with Ted and Alec.

"I guess he thought it might be better to have more than one female along. I think your best bet would be to ask Alec to intercede for you. He has more influence than I."

"What's the matter with you, Brett? You have been on past trips and had no problems, haven't you? "

"Well, Dave, earlier I mentioned we both had better change our line of bed partners. I did something the other night that might disqualify me from making any suggestions and it might affect my going along on this or other trips.

"Friday night I was with Ruth at the Perry cottage. She is boiling mad and I am afraid Randy is suspicious of me. Maybe not, but I'm not in a position to suggest you or anyone who would rock the boat at this time. As I said, Alec is in solid with Timothy and he would be the best contact."

"All right, Brett, I'll get in touch with him. Now, what did you want to see me about?"

"My problems are compounded by finances as you are probably aware, Dave. I suspect it's becoming known in the business world, too. However, no one except me and the bookies know I owe $20,000 in racing bets. Now my creditors are becoming anxious to collect my debts and want the payoff or a schedule of payments."

"Twenty thousand big ones. That's a lot of dough, Brett. How in hell did you ever let yourself get into this mess? I thought you had some business sense."

"Apparently, you never did any gambling, Dave. Once involved it's easy to catch the bug when you make some good hits. Then you begin losing but the bookies don't care how much you bet and lose. Occasionally, you make some good bets, big ones, but the money rides only to pay off what you owe. Someone gives you a tip and you double your bet to make up, but instead you lose and you're deeper in debt. The process continues until your credit is shut off. Suddenly, it's payoff time.

"That's where I am today. The syndicate would rather have my ass but they'll take both if necessary."

"What do you expect me to do, Brett? I haven't that kind of money to hand out. Even if I did, it would have to be on a business basis. No different from a bank. I would expect collateral. And, I'm sure you don't have any or you would go to a bank. What in hell do you have to offer? "

Brett was taken aback by Dave's attitude. He hadn't expected to hear those harsh words. For a moment he thought of laying his ace on the table by showing the print of Dawn and him on the couch in the studio reception room.

However, he kept his cool and instead of displaying his reaction to Dave's remarks, he suggested the partnership he had originally planned.

"Why would I want to become involved in the photography business or any venture for that matter?" Dave asked after listening to Brett's proposal. "I have all the money I need and almost everything I want."

"You like female companionship and an expansion of my proposed photo business would involve many attractive women. The demand is growing for this type of photography. The prettier the girls, the bigger the profits," Brett said. "

It sounds interesting but there's no way I could sell that proposal to Phyllis. She's the person who makes the decisions and handles all the cash," Dave remarked.

Brett could see he wasn't making any headway with his proposal of modeling photography alone so there was no need to continue with this idea. However, the expansion of photography in school systems throughout the state might be the logical course to pursue. This was the line intermingled with modeling he needed to attract Dave's attention.

"Dave perhaps business doesn't interest you but it might appeal to Phyllis if we expanded to more schools outside of Middleton. That would develop into additional graduate portraits and extracurricular activities.

"The potential for discovering young models could develop into a sideline enterprise. Both businesses would return a profit, especially the models. But I've got the idea you aren't interested."

"That does present a different perspective, Brett. All right, I'll talk with Phyllis about your proposal. That may have possibilities but I'm not promising anything. We can continue to pursue this venture during the fishing trip, if I'm invited."

"I've got to know before then," Brett said. I must raise cash soon or present a reasonable proposition. I'm in deep shit."

"No doubt about it, Brett. You're in serious trouble. As you said, both women and money have created your problems. No promises, but we'll discuss it on the trip. That's the best I can offer."

That was not the response Brett wanted but without a final threat there was nothing more he could do. It was obvious Dave had to be invited to the lodge but he felt Alec would do that. When his creditors appeared, he would have to stall them until after the trip. He thought another week wouldn't make any difference but he must have a sound plan when he returned.

"That sounds fair enough," Brett responded. "Now, why don't you pay Alec a visit this afternoon. If the decision is between Alec and Timothy, I'd say you're in."

"Good. I've got to leave now. I'm meeting Phyllis in the bank at noon," Dave said as he walked from the studio.

Jan left early for the Guardian this afternoon in hopes she would see the proofreader Ted mentioned. Whatever Sarah had to say wouldn't matter to either Ted or her. Only the police might be interested.

Rain was becoming heavier as she neared the downtown area, and she hoped the skies would be clear when they were at Bear Lake. She and Linda discussed the trip this morning and were anxious for the departure day. They were getting tired of unpleasant news lately, and they thought a change of environment might alleviate the tension everyone had been feeling lately. They agreed Brett wouldn't be any problem.

Jan had been on numerous hunting trips and she always welcomed the opportunity to get away from city life. The reason she came to Maine was to enjoy the outdoors. She never had any experience fishing but she knew it wouldn't be difficult to learn, especially with Alec nearby.

Somehow she was beginning to think of him more seriously lately. He was a great guy, ten years or so older, but nevertheless a person she believed could fit into her life although she realized that was not her reason for coming here. After her conversation with Sarah, and with Ted afterwards, she had decided to dismiss Brett from her mind. In fact, she thought while smiling, "I'm going to dwell on Alec."

Jan raced across the *Guardian* parking lot in a heavy rain and into the building where several people were standing near the front door trying to decide whether or not to rush out or remain until the downpour subsided. With water covering her face and dripping from her coat, she laughed as she told the group, "It's a great day for ducks."

It was quiet when she entered the newsroom with only the sounds of teletype machines. After hanging her wet coat on a rack, she walked to her desk and noticed Alec sitting in his office with someone. It was surprising to see him at the *Guardian* this early which aroused her curiosity as to the identity of the visitor.

As she reached her desk, Sarah was walking from the far end of the newsroom where the proofreaders office was situated. What a break, she thought. Instead of trying to locate her, she had to pass her desk to leave the room. Jan greeted her with a friendly, "Hello, Sarah. You're leaving at a poor time. It's raining cats and dogs out there."

"I know," she responded. "I've been looking out the window the past hour hoping it would let up but I can't wait any longer. I've got several errands to do before going home so I might as well get wet now as later. You're in early today, aren't you?"

"Yes," Jan replied telling a small falsehood, "I had a story to finish and a couple of calls to make. Besides there was nothing to do at the apartment on this dreary afternoon."

"Oh, by the way, Sarah. I wanted to ask about the pretty girl who visits you occasionally. Is she a relative?" Jan knew it wasn't her granddaughter as Sarah was never married as far as anyone knew.

The proofreader came to Middleton three decades ago and was employed at the city library until she joined the *Guardian* staff last year. A quiet person who kept pretty much to herself, she lived alone in a small house outside the city.

"No, she's not related to me, only a neighbor who visits frequently. I enjoy listening to her telling what she does in school and about her friends. She is a vibrant girl filled with life and emotions. Unfortunately, she doesn't have much of a home life. Her mother who is divorced works afternoons and evenings as a waitress at the Pink Cafe on Winter Street."

Continuing, Sarah explained the girl would borrow a few dollars once in awhile when her mother forgot to give her spending money before leaving for work.

"She came in around noon today and paid me back five dollars she borrowed last week. She's honest. I believe I'm the only adult companion she has in the city. She never mentions anyone else."

"She's a pretty girl," Jan said. "What's her name?"

"Dawn Gronorski and she is an attractive youngster. Maybe too pretty. The other day she told me the man who owned the studio downtown offered to take her picture free. I told her to keep away from that place although it's none of my business."

"You don't like Brett Hartman. I thought he was a popular man in Middleton," Jan remarked.

"Maybe so. Well, I've got to go," Sarah responded as she started for the door.

Jan realized she had received all the information about Brett she would ever get from Sarah so she turned her attention to Alec's office, still wondering who was with him.

She made a phone call to a city hall office confirming information she received for an article and turned her attention to Alec's office again after she had finished. It was a man but his back was toward her so she still didn't know who he was. It wasn't too serious a conversation she thought, as Alec laughed occasionally as he talked with his visitor.

While she waited to talk with Ted, Jan decided to call Linda to find out what they could do tonight now that she didn't have to work. As she reached for the phone, she saw Alec's guest rising from his chair and walking to the office door. All her curiosity had been in vain. It was no surprise to see Dave Paxton with Alec although she now became interested why Alec would arrive early to meet him.

When Dave left Alec picked up his phone.

Jan was reaching for her phone again to talk with Linda as Ted entered the newsroom door wearing the same foul weather gear he took from the clothes rack the other night during the storm. He removed the wet garments, hanging them back on the rack and wiped the water from his face with a handkerchief. He walked in the room glancing at Alec's office and stopped at Jan's desk.

"It's kind of damp out there," he remarked. "I hope this weather ends before our vacation begins. By the way, what's everyone doing here so early?" when he noted Alec at his desk.

"I don't know about the rest of you," Jan answered. "But I came early to see Sarah which I did. Apparently Alec arrived before his usual time because he had an appointment with Dave Paxton. How about you, Ted? What brings you here at this time of day?"

"I got bored sitting around the house. Earlier I called Timothy to see if we were going to have coffee at Harry's, but he wasn't planning to leave the house today in this weather. He said all of the details of the trip were complete and he was going to give Brett the list of items to buy which should wrap up everything."

"Thank heavens for that," Jan remarked. "All we have to do now is to wait and pray for good weather.

"Sarah told me the girl who visits her occasionally is a neighbor whom she has befriended and her name is Dawn Gronorski. Her mother is a waitress at the Pink Cafe and appears she doesn't spend much time with her. She didn't elaborate on Brett only to mention he didn't impress her and that he had offered the girl a chance to have her picture taken. Sarah didn't say anything about the news clipping, so as far as I'm concerned let's ignore him and let the police continue their investigation if that's what they want."

"Jan, I agree. Let's get ready for the outing and forget his activities. I'm getting a little tired of it also. We'll see enough of him at the lodge."

With that remark, Ted went to his desk.

It seemed everything had been done to prepare for the big day when eight hardy souls would leave for vacation in one of Maine's most beautiful regions. On the surface, anyhow, it all appeared serene. Unknown to the others, Alec was now making a phone call, not to alter scheduled plans, but to request that an additional individual join the group.

Dave had called Alec this morning asking his former wartime commander for a favor. He said that he would like to discuss it with him so Alec told him to be at his office after three o'clock.

"What do you want that we couldn't discuss over the phone," Alec asked when Dave entered his office.

"Nothing that serious, Alec. I just wanted to ask you something in person."

"Then let's hear it," Alec said.

"I heard that you and some friends are leaving on a fishing trip in a couple of weeks and I would like to go. Phyllis will be away on a business trip and I'll be alone in the city. Obviously, I'm willing to pay my share of the expenses and take my car if necessary. I know some of the people involved, not too well, but I believe we can become acquainted."

Alec didn't respond immediately. Dave's request astonished him.

"What's the matter, Alec. Did I say something wrong?"

"No, you took me by surprise. For a moment I thought you were applying for a job," he replied laughing. Dave, I can't invite you as Timothy is in command of this operation. As we did in the service, I can only submit your request. I have no objections, but I would remind you of your escapades in the Corps. I assume you have outgrown these antics but if I ask Timothy, I want to make certain you won't be making passes at any of the women. He runs a tight ship."

"What can I say? Of course, I'll mind my manners. Alec, I only want to go fishing while Phyllis is away. There's nothing else on my mind, I promise you."

"All right, Dave. I'll give Timothy a call and if he says you're welcome, I'm certain the rest of the crowd will agree. They don't know you as well as I do so there's no reason why anyone would object. I'll call you as soon as I have Timothy's decision."

"Thanks a lot, Alec. You won't regret it. I'll behave like an altar boy."

After Dave left the office, Alec reached for the phone and called Timothy.

Timothy was his normal self as he answered Alec's call, friendly and talkative.

"What is it I can do for you," he asked. "It's certainly not time to leave for the lake, thank heavens. It's not many who hope this kind of weather prevails the rest of the summer."

"No, that's not the reason I'm calling, Timothy. And I agree we don't need this kind of weather in July. I have a favor to ask. Dave Paxton just left my office after asking me if it were possible for him to go with us. His wife plans to be away that week, and he would like to do some fishing. What do you think? "

"I have no objections, Alec, if you would like to have him along. You know him better than the rest of us. I heard he has an eye for the opposite sex," Timothy chuckled, "but I doubt if he can make any headway among the three women on this junket. They all appear to be well chaperoned, including Jan. However, everyone should be told that he'll be coming along."

"All right, Timothy, that's fair enough," Alec said. I'll call Dave tonight."

"While I've got you on the phone," Timothy interjected, "I think we're all set for the outing. I'll meet you at Harry's for breakfast on that Saturday morning.

"Alec, why don't you tell Ted and Jan about Dave and I'll inform the rest."

"They are both here. I'll call them in my office right now," Alec replied.

"Thanks and a good day to you," Timothy said, ending the conversation.

"Ted and Jan, come in here," Alec barked from his office.

Shortly, both of them were standing in front of Alec's desk awaiting his command.

"Sit down," Alec said. "I want to tell you about the new addition to our expedition. I hope you approve.

"Dave Paxton was in earlier and asked if I could arrange to have him invited on the fishing trip. I explained that it was not in my jurisdiction but I would call Timothy for his decision. I talked with Timothy a few minutes ago and he said it was agreeable with him. He didn't think anyone else would object but that they should be notified."

Ted and Jan looked at each other but neither spoke.

"Do you two mind if Dave goes along?" Alec asked.

"I don't care," Jan answered while Ted nodded his approval.

"Well," Alec continued, "it appears our group has grown to nine. I'll take him in my car along with Jan and Brett. After we leave Harry's, I'll meet Brett at his studio when we'll load the wagon. Ted, I assume you'll pick up Jan and Linda along with Timothy for breakfast. The Perrys will be coming in their car. That just about winds up the show until all of us meet together at Harry's on July 13.

"Now Ted and I can get back to work while Jan takes the night off."

As the couple left the office, Ted glanced at Jan and remarked. "Another Casanova in this group won't make any difference. A fox is already in the chicken coop."

Chapter 12

Hot and dry weather prevailed in Maine as the calendar turned its pages to July and to the departure date of Timothy's safari on the thirteenth.

Timothy awakened shortly after three o'clock, long before the sun rose. He turned on a light and moved quietly as he got out of bed. He didn't want to disturb the Haneys as he went downstairs to the porch. His quiet maneuvers were in vain as the couple followed him as he walked to a couch to wait for Ted.

"It's a bite and coffee you'll be needing while you wait, Father Timothy," Helen suggested.

"My thanks to you, Helen, but it's a breakfast all of us will be having when we get to Harry's. Why don't the both of you go back to bed. I'll be all right. Ted will be along shortly. By the way, Mike, if the trout are biting, I'll be bringing some back."

"I'll be looking forward to it, Father. I enjoyed the other fish you caught last year. They were bigger than trout. What did you call them?"

"They're called togue and some weigh over twenty pounds. I never caught any that large but I've seen other fishermen with their catches. They're tasty, too.

"And," Timothy added, looking at Helen, "I have a special recipe when it's time to cook them."

"We'll be seeing about that, Father," she remarked.

It was still dark when they heard the sound of Ted's approaching car. Helen had helped Timothy pack a small suitcase last night and Mike carried it to the porch before they retired. As Ted entered the driveway, Mike picked up the case and brought it to the car. Ted stepped out of his vehicle as it stopped in front of the porch while Linda and Jan got out to greet Timothy and meet the Haneys.

"A good morning to you all," Timothy said as he extended a hand to Ted and reached out with both hands to the passengers.

"It's a pleasant day to begin our week away from the city. Now," he continued addressing Jan and Linda, "meet my good friends and keepers, Mr. and Mrs. Haney. You're not seeing much of them because they are always catering and taking care of me."

"Be gone with you, Father Timothy," Helen smilingly remarked while greeting the new couple. "He's a lot of the blarney."

Mike also reached for Linda's and Jan's hands, adding, "You'll have to take light of the stock what the good Father says.

"Like Helen said, he's a flatterer, he is."

"I'm aware of his smoothness," Linda smiled." And Jan is slowly catching on to his Irish lines."

Grinning, Mike passed the suitcase to Ted who put it in the trunk with other belongings while the other passengers got in the car. With only four occupants, there was plenty of room for luggage.

"We're ready to go," Ted said as he stepped into the Chevy. "We'll see you next Saturday.

The sky was beginning to lighten when the four neared Harry's and Ted drove in front of the restaurant. The only vehicles in the parking area belonged to Alec and Randy so apparently Brett hadn't made his appearance. Timothy was humming an old Irish tune as he emerged from the car while the rest joked as they strode toward the door. It was a wonderful way to begin an adventure.

Harry appeared to have everyone's attention as he stood before a table of customers laughing and gesturing with outstretched arms, apparently indicating the length of a fish. It had to be a big one as his arms were more than a yard apart. The laughter continued as the others approached.

"Well, anyway, he got away," Harry concluded.

"It must have been a whopper," Timothy injected as he walked to the table where Alec and Brett rose to greet him.

"Timothy," Alec said. "Brett, Dave, and I were here earlier and went to the studio to load supplies in my beach wagon. Brett left his car in his parking lot so we don't have to return. We can leave from here when everyone finishes breakfast."

"That's great, Alec, "Timothy replied. "Now I have an idea that would save more time and I'll make the suggestion when we're seated."

As the late arrivals found seats around the table, a waitress began taking orders and it became quiet again allowing Timothy a chance to speak.

"Friends," he said, "I received a call last night from my friend who said Jacques Silver Seven would meet us at the lodge later this afternoon upon our arrival. He said the weather has been warm in the woods as it was in the rest of the state. And mosquitoes are plentiful in dry weather.

I assume you're prepared with plenty of fly dope. Also, we're reminded the woods are exceptionally dry and we must be careful about fires. He also added that Jacques is anxious to meet this group and he's brushed up on his stories. This guy must really be a character," Timothy added.

"I had a thought during the night, mind you," Timothy continued. "When we met at Ruth and Randy's cottage a couple of weeks ago, we agreed it would be all right for drivers to take any route to reach the lake. They still can if they choose but after studying the map again, it appears easier if we all went the same way on Route 201 from Skowhegan to Bingham and travel northeast to the town of Abbott above Guilford. It's a more direct highway and we would be traveling together. If any of the vehicles experienced mechanical problems, we could help each other."

"That makes sense," Ted said. "If we follow the Kennebec to The Forks, we would travel north over the mountain to Jackman and then east along Moose River for another 37 miles to Rockwood. It's another 40 miles to Greenville. We would be missing the beauty of the river but it's a longer trip as Timothy said."

"I'll explain logging operations and history of the Arnold Trail to Linda while Alec can describe them to Jan who will be riding with him," Ted continued. "We can always take the other route on the return trip if we wish."

"It sounds great to me," Alec responded while the others didn't object. It was a happy and agreeable group who gathered at tables this morning enjoying ham and eggs while laughing and telling stories. If there was any dissension, it wasn't obvious.

Randy indicated it was going to be a long trip but they should be at the lake before dark.

"How long should it take? "Jan asked. "I really don't know," Randy replied. "It depends on road conditions. Most of the way to Ripogenus should be good traveling and the only rough road is from the dam to the lodge. But without any rain for the past two weeks, those roads should be good."

"Perhaps, we can plan to have dinner in Greenville," Brett suggested. "That's about half way."

"Good idea," Timothy remarked. "Of course, we can stop anytime you'd like to stretch our legs and take pictures. I hope all of you have brought cameras. I know Brett, as usual, is prepared to take photos besides putting together an album for each of us."

"Oh, that's a wonderful thing," Linda said. "Do you mean we can

132

buy an album from you when we return? "

"There's no buying," Brett responded. "All of you will get an album with my compliments."

"That generous of you," Jan added.

Contributing to gifts for the trip, Harry made his appearance with a stack of pies in his arms and placed them on the table next to Timothy. "I hope these pastries will add to your joy," he said smiling as he left for the kitchen. "Thanks, Harry," Timothy uttered but Harry was already out of sight.

As the waitress was adding the checks for the breakfast, Dave took them and remarked.

"This breakfast is on me. I've got to begin earning my keep."

"That's not necessary, Dave. But we all thank you," Alec said.

"A fine day in summer, it is. Another hot one it will be," Timothy exclaimed as he walked from the restaurant ahead of the rest to Ted's car. "We can be thankful that it's a lake we'll be near, instead of a city."

Alec spoke to Ted and Timothy before they reached the Chevy.

"I'll lead the way in my wagon, you can be next, and we'll let Randy and Ruth follow. We shouldn't have any problems and I'll drive slowly along the river so the women can see all of the sights."

So it was. The three-vehicle convoy finally left Middleton and headed north for what they believed would be a week of fun.

Timothy sat in the rear seat with his unlit pipe hanging from his mouth while Linda was next to Ted in the front seat. She wanted to hear him talk about the various places and history of the Kennebec Valley.

Traffic was light on this early Saturday morning as they turned on Route 201 behind Alec who had a full car with four passengers and most of the gear. Instead of traveling straight north on this road, Alec turned west before arriving at Skowhegan and drove six miles along the Kennebec to Norridgewock, an area well known in historic Indian lore. Ted didn't elaborate on "Old Point" which was the home of the ancient Norridgewogs, but he mentioned to Linda it would be interesting reading if she would like to learn more about early times of the Indian tribes along the Kennebec.

They traveled along the river through Madison, Anson, and the towns of Solon and Bingham where pulp was flowing in the Kennebec to paper mills downstream.

"Timothy," Linda inquired, "you told us the other day about the Benedict Arnold Trail. Are we near it?"

133

"Oh, I'm sorry. We are on the route that Arnold took on his way to Quebec which was then occupied by the British. According to historical accounts, his Command followed the Kennebec north beyond the town of Bingham and left the river miles above it and entered the forests west along Dead River. They were underfed and poorly clothed, but his troops trudged to Lac Megantic in Canada. However, they were unsuccessful in reaching their objective. They had to retreat to Lake Champlain, a body of water that extends from the Province into Vermont.

"The Kennebec River," Timothy continued, "begins at the East Outlet of Moosehead Lake in Rockwood and flows one hundred and fifty miles south. It empties into the Atlantic a few miles from Merry-Meeting Bay near the islands of Casco Bay. This stretch of water was often called "Cradle of Rivers" because of its resources and the men who worked them played an important role in the expansion and development of our country. Linda, there are many stories about the dangers and hardships these adventurers encountered as they pushed westward," Ted added. "When you find spare time, I'm sure you'll enjoy reading articles about them."

The caravan continued on this route to the small village of Moscow where they turned northeast over the mountains and through the forests to the Moosehead Trail.

"I have another question for you, Timothy," Linda asked. "I believe there is another famous trail that ends somewhere near where we are going. I can't remember its name but it originates in Georgia."

"You're referring to the Appalachian Trail, Linda. It's a footpath for outdoor enthusiasts extending more than two thousands miles from Georgia. The route is primarily along the crest of the Appalachian Mountains. It's the longest marked continuous footpath in the world and at points reaches more than a mile high," Ted related. "You're correct in believing it's located near our destination. It ends about fifty miles east of Bear Lake at Mt. Katahdin in Baxter State Park."

"Does that answer your question, Linda?"

"Certainly does," she replied. "This state really fascinates me. It is so large and filled with exciting history."

The road improved as Alec puffed on a long cigar in the lead car. He made a turn in Abbott to a more northerly direction en route to Moosehead and their first stop at a vegetable stand. The conversations in his vehicle were less frequent than in Ted's although Jan was more curious than the other three. Alec explained to her about the logging operations that had been taking place on the river during the past century and injected his personal observations.

As they rode along the waters, he expressed his belief that within a couple of decades, thousands of logs and pulp now flowing downstream would probably cease. He contended that this wood some day would have to be carried overland by trucks.

"It's difficult to imagine," he said as he continued telling about the past, "that lumber filling the holds of countless schooners and vessels sailing the oceans years ago came from logs that once floated down this river to Maine coastal ports."

While Alec and Jan did most of the talking, Dave and Brett remained unusually quiet as the ride continued to the lodge. Naturally, it was impossible for Brett to learn of Dave's decision about the loan while riding with the others so he would have to wait until they arrived at their destination. Something else was on Brett's mind. The parting words of the syndicate's man who visited him yesterday and reminded him of the money he owed them were still on his mind.

"Don't forget us," Brett was warned. "We know where you're going and when, and if you'll be coming back." There was nothing he could do until he talked to Dave and that would take place later in the day. In the meantime, he might as well forget it.

Less than an hour later, Alec steered his car to the side of the road and parked at the summit of Indian Hill overlooking Moosehead Lake.

Ted and Randy drove their cars behind him and everyone stepped from the vehicles and walked to the front of the station wagon. All of them had witnessed this sight before with the exception of Linda and Jan who viewed the horizon with awe. Almost simultaneously, they exclaimed how beautiful and expansive it was as it loomed before their eyes.

"This is only a small portion of the beauty you will see before you return to Middleton," Alec remarked. "Another sight rests to the east. Does that mountain range remind you of something?"

"They look like elephants," Jan answered. "Could that be possible? "

"That's right, Jan. They are called Little and Big Elephant Mountains. Aren't they impressive?"

"Now, let's go downtown to Greenville and get something to eat," Alec remarked. "I'm starved and I'm sure you all must be, too."

No one realized how warm it was until they got out of their cars in front of a restaurant in the valley below Indian Hill. Not a breath of air was stirring. The mercury on a thermometer attached to the outside of a restaurant indicated ninety degrees, a reading seldom seen in this neck of the woods. Not a seat was available in Anne's Diner so they strolled down the street leading to the shore of the lake to wait for the patrons to finish their meals.

They watched a float plane take off from the cove and gradually disappear like a lone bird in the distant forest beyond the water. Outside of the drone of this plane, the air was silent and humid. Although hundreds of visitors must be vacationing in one of the state's largest tourists area, today they remained at lake cottages. While they continued their walk, Linda remarked how large a lake it must be.

"It's about forty miles long and twenty miles at its farthest width," Ted related. "Although it has never been officially verified, natives boast Moosehead is the largest fresh water lake contained within the borders of any of the country's forty-eight states."

Dave immediately took exception to this remark reminding everyone that Lake Okeechobee in Florida was much larger, but the question arose whether or not that lake's water was all fresh or it contained brackish waters. This discussion wasn't resolved and the group walked back to the restaurant where seats were now available.

A waitress approached the table arranged to seat the entire group. Alec motioned to her. Please make only one check for these meals and give it to me."

He turned to the group and said. "I don't do this often but I want to be your host today. Dave did the honors for breakfast and I can't let him get ahead of me."

"Thanks," Randy said. "Ruth and I will try to compensate for your generosity. Tonight, when we dine at the lodge on trout we assume Jacques Silver Seven has caught, Ruth and I will serve some special white wine we found for the occasion."

"How do you know Jacques has caught any fish?" Jan asked while Timothy responded to the question.

"Randy knows my New York friend wouldn't overlook such an event. It's bets I'm taking, mind you, Jacques is canoeing at this moment trolling for fish for our supper tonight."

Jan and Linda now joined Ruth and her husband at the end of the table.

"This sounds like a fun night," Linda said. "I hope it's not too far to the lodge so we won't be exhausted by nightfall."

"Don't worry about it, "Ruth replied. "After a dip in the cold water at Bear Lake and a glass of wine, you'll feel like sixteen again."

"Are we going to be there in time for a swim?" Jan asked. "How cold is that water?"

"Of course," Ruth said, "we'll get there in plenty of time. It's light until after eight o'clock and we should be there about five. Oh, the water temperature does get a little chilly but refreshing. It doesn't get as warm as the lakes in Middleton but you'll like it."

It became quiet in the uncomfortably warm restaurant as hungry patrons ate hurriedly, anxious to get to their destination.

The Perrys were last to enter their car because at the last moment Timothy said he had forgotten to list items for Brett necessary for his special sautéed trout or togue recipe.

Ruth volunteered to shop at a local market for a jar of pecans, cayenne pepper, and dried parsley. It wasn't long before she rushed from the store to join the rest. Alec's wagon led the way on a ride that would take them to Bear Lake before the afternoon was over.

All of the windows were rolled down in Randy's Kaiser to take advantage of the outside air even though it allowed the hot sun to shine inside. The trip was becoming increasingly uncomfortable as time passed slowly. Ruth lay her head back on the front seat and tried to close her eyes but frequent bumps in the road kept her from dozing off. The road was now taking them east of Greenville to Lily Bay where, if she managed to keep alert, she might catch sight of a moose foraging in a marsh outside the small village. She and Randy hadn't talked much today since leaving Middleton. However, that wasn't unusual, she thought, because she was accustomed to reading a lot while he was driving. However, she realized on this trip they should be talking more about fishing.

Her mind drifted back to the tryst with Brett at the cottage and worried if Randy suspected something. If he did, he hadn't shown any signs of it. Yet he appeared more reserved and quiet but she knew he was always exhausted at the end of an onerous year at the college. She was apprehensive as there was something else that concerned her.

As she was loading the car with their supplies last night, she noticed he had packed his .22 Caliber pistol among his gear. She couldn't recall if he had ever taken a weapon with him on other fishing trips to the lodge. Ruth knew he carried the smaller weapon on hunting trips although it had no hunting value unless it was fired at close range. It would be useless against large game. She hoped nothing would happen to affect their lives but she intended to keep a close eye on her husband during this outing.

At one point a few weeks ago, her hate for Brett was so intense that she felt like murdering him. She realized she was as much to blame as he and that kind of stupidity would never solve any problem. It would only create a bad circumstance for everyone. She also realized that if anyone were to undertake any drastic action it would be better that she do it since it was really her fault that she was in this mess.

"Randy," she asked, "have you given any idea of hiking to Bite Pond Outlet and casting for brook trout? We had some exceptionally good luck there last summer although it was a little longer jaunt than we had imagined. This would give you a chance to try out your new rod and the flies you tied last winter."

"I haven't forgotten about our luck last year. Certainly we should make another trip to the outlet. I would like to take Timothy along. You know how much he loves to fly fish. Do you suppose he could handle the hike? It wasn't easy walking."

"I think it would be too much, Randy, but how about taking him in an outboard and fish near the island at the head of the lake. There's good fly fishing there. He'd probably enjoy it more."

"You're right, dear," Randy responded. "Let's plan an early morning trip when trout are biting."

"Well, Ruth, we're coming into Lily Bay. Slowly but surely, we're nearing our goal. I hope we see a moose. Do you have your camera handy? "

"I sure have, Randy. I've been wanting a picture of a moose for a long time. It seems every time we see one, we don't have a camera. But this time I'm ready. Just find a moose," she laughed.

Again, the animals eluded them as they drove through the hamlet and on past another small settlement at Kokadjo.

While the vacationers were only hours away, Jacques Silver Seven was doing exactly what Timothy had predicted. Wearing a battered straw hat to protect his wrinkled face hardened by years outdoors, the 52-year-old handyman was quietly paddling a canoe close to shore at Bear Lake waiting for another togue to grab his handmade silver lure. He had already caught a big one and it was being towed alongside the canoe to keep it cool.

About a quarter mile from the site of the lodge, a mass of rock known as Patte de Chat extended far into the lake. Early French trappers gave this site its name because it resembled paws of bobcats that roamed the woods. When the canoe reached the point, Jacques released the paddle and grasped the fishing rod. The craft continued gliding through the water while the veteran angler waited patiently for a bite on his favorite lure. Within seconds, the line dipped toward the bottom of the lake and Jacques gave the rod a quick tug and then unlocked the reel letting the fish take the line. Then, carefully, he reeled in the line and a few minutes later a fish was brought near the boat where he netted it.

"By gad," he exclaimed, "this one is more big than the first one. Monsieur J.T.'s ami will have beaucoup fish for supper."

He began thinking of other things he had to do before the crowd arrived including cleaning the fish and keeping them on ice. He pulled the other togue into the boat and sturdily paddled the canoe to the dock yards away from the lodge's front porch. He brought the togue to an area away from the landing where he took his hunting knife and cleaned it. Jacques had prepared a lot of fish and game during his lifetime and finished this simple task in a few minutes. These beauties were ready for the pan so he put them in the kitchen icebox.

Everything was ready in the lodge for the visitors who should be arriving soon. Kindling and other wood for the iron cook stove in the kitchen had been stored in a wood box while containers of drinking water from the well were kept in the icebox. Logs for the living room fireplace were neatly stacked adjacent to its hearth although it didn't seem likely a fire would be needed during this exceptionally warm weather. All lamps in the dining and living rooms and kitchen were filled with oil as well as the smaller lamps in the loft bed rooms. Jacques made sure the lodge was immaculate and he had washed windows until they sparkled.

There was nothing left for the new handyman to do except to wait. He opened the icebox and saw a bottle of Canadian Black Horse ale someone had left. This was his favorite brew when he could afford it. He didn't think anyone would care so he took it and went outside and sat on a tree stump. He removed the cap from the bottle and took a long drink of the cold ale while wiping sweat from his face.

Mon Dieu!, he thought. It's hot, and this is good.

He was quite certain people coming would bring a lot of ale so he was anxious for them to get here. It seemed he was going to have a good time but kept thinking of the priest who would be here, too. He never went to church much but knew he would have to be careful of his words and what stories he told.

Another bottle of ale would taste good now but there wasn't anymore in the lodge and it was too warm to walk to his cabin. Jacques sat there thinking and waiting but not for long. Soon he heard the sound of cars coming down the camp road.

The fun, it was going to begin, he thought.

It was a weary group of travelers who stopped at the side of the lodge. Jan was first to get out of the wagon, expressing a sigh of relief as she looked upwards at the tall pines.

"Seems like heaven," she shouted to Alec as he moved from the driver's seat. "I thought we would never get here, particularly over the past few miles of rough roads. Did someone actually build the road or was it a wild animal trail? One thing is certain, we won't be disturbed by traffic at night."

Alec laughed as he got out.

"Jan, you won't be troubled by anything in this wilderness. Even the bears go to bed early."

"It's not that bad, Alec," she said smiling. "But I'm sure glad to walk again."

"That's the reason we're here," Alec remarked. "To get away from the hustle of city life and enjoy this solitude. And, hopefully, to catch fish."

Within a few minutes, the group had converged near Alec's wagon and heard Timothy's simple welcome instructions. While he was talking, Linda roamed around the building to stretch her legs but soon returned.

"We're here and the time has arrived to have fun. A lovely place, it is, and soon you'll be falling in love with it," he added.

"We'll be taking things to our rooms, and afterwards, you can do what you please. There's time for a dip in the lake if you choose and there are plenty of cold drinks about. There's room for everyone. I believe I told you where everything is located so it's on our way, we can go."

"Hold on a moment," Timothy remarked. "If it's help you'll be needing, I see it coming," as he saw a stranger approaching.

"You must be Jacques Silver Seven," he said. "I'm Timothy and friend of J.T. The rest of these people you'll be meeting in good time."

"Mon Pere," Jacques exclaimed excitedly as he removed his hat and stepped forward with a big hand well outstretched. "Monsieur Barker from Millinocket, who is also a friend of Monsieur J.T. told me about you. You must know him for many years, n'est ce pas?

"Very true, it is. We were friends when I lived in New York City."

At last, everyone had an opportunity to see the woodsman Timothy had mentioned. Unquestionably, he had spent much of his life in the outdoors as his rugged and tanned face revealed. About five-foot-six with broad shoulders and a thick neck, his body was brawny. He had piercing dark eyes and a full head of black hair. The name that his father had chosen suited his French and Indian character well while his accent left no doubt of his ancestry. Soon, this newcomer would become the center of attraction as he walked through the group shaking hands while his eyes lit up when he met the three attractive women. There was no doubt in anyone's mind that Jacques would become a welcome participant in the group.

When Jacques approached Ted and Linda who were taking things from the Chevy, Ted inquired if the fish were biting. "Oui, oui, monseiur. Fishing has been good since the season opened. Today, before you get here, I caught two big ones for supper. May I help carry things inside?"

"Thanks," Timothy replied. "It would be better if you helped the others in the station wagon. They have more to bring in than we do. With arms loaded, Linda walked beside Ted to the lodge that would be home for the next week. They were followed by the rest who entered with suitcases and bundles.

The lodge was a long building with a screened porch extending along the length of the north or front side facing the lake. A double door in the center opened from this porch to the living, dining room, and kitchen that comprised most of the lodge. There were three bedrooms on the lower floor, two on the west side and another at the east end beyond the kitchen. Adjacent to that bedroom there was a small wash room separated from the kitchen with a porcelain sink, cabinet with shelves, mirror, and towel racks. At the rear or south side of the structure, a door opened into the kitchen which had an iron stove and another sink with a hand pump that brought clear water from a hand-drilled well Stairs were located along the wall on the west side of the living room leading to a loft where four beds were located.

"This is wonderful," Linda exclaimed, as she put the items she was holding on the floor. Her head moved slowly while her eyes caught the charm of the huge stone fireplace with its antique andirons and tongs.

Resting on the mantel were a pair of century-old lanterns and an old Winchester rifle was placed below the mounted fierce countenance of a black bear a taxidermist had created. Along the rest of the walls, trophies of deer, moose, elk, and other wild animal species were displayed in the spacious room.

"The lodge and this room is so rustic and charming and the fireplace is stunning," she continued excitedly. "The fireplace must be ten feet long."

"At least," Ted smiled. "I believe it's more. Have you noticed the size of that mounted togue on the wall in the kitchen? That's no fish story."

Jan came in the room as Linda and Ted were studying the numerous objects and furniture. "Isn't this amazing," she said. "It isn't the most modern place I've seen but it is certainly more interesting than most."

"Have you a room for us?" she asked Linda.

"I suggest you and Linda share a room at the other end," Ted interrupted. "Timothy always wants to be on this end, and I believe the Perrys occupy an individual room. The rest of us will sleep in the loft."

"It's all right with me," Linda replied. "Jan, why don't we take our belongings to the room and go for a swim."

The couple went into the bedroom and placed their packs and blankets on the cots. There was a panel with hooks nailed to a log on one side of the room to hang clothes while a bureau with a large mirror and two chairs completed the furnishings. Both windows had shades but no curtains.

As they put items in bureau drawers, Jan began to laugh when she came upon a flashlight among the clothing. She placed it with a couple of batteries on the cot commenting on Timothy's advice to everyone to make sure they brought plenty of batteries.

"I know why Timothy was insistent for us to bring an ample supply. Linda, have you noticed how far away the outhouses are from this room?"

"I certainly have," Linda said joining in the laughter. "It won't be so bad making trips outside while everyone is up, but it will be scary walking outdoors in the pitch darkness. If we have to make visits during the night, we'll go together," she added.

"And," Jan remarked while still laughing, "we had better flash our lights above the door before we enter a half moon."

"I don't understand," Linda said. "What do you mean? "

"Linda, both buildings have mounted deer heads attached above the doors. The one with antlers, of course, is a buck identifying it as the men's room while the other is a doe. Need I explain more?"

"No, I understand," Linda replied. "I hope there isn't another building with a bear's head. You can bet your life I won't be making many trips at night."

"Did you learn about farm life or was Alec's conversation today limited to past events along the Kennebec?" Linda inquired. "I doubt if your discussions involved anything personal with two other men in the car."

"Alec kept it pretty much on a professional level. He didn't deviate from past and future activities on the river while the other passengers remained silent. Something unusual for them," Jan remarked. "I'll get him alone before this trip is over and open a new discourse. Do you think he's interested in me?"

"He personally invited you along so that indicates an interest to me," Linda answered. "Give him time. He'll make an unexpected move although that's what you're waiting for, isn't it?"

"You read me like a book, Linda. You and Ted must be getting along well. But it's different with you. Your relationship has been going on for some time."

"I probably won't have a ring when we return, " Linda said. "But I'm working on it."

After they finished unpacking, they changed into bathing suits and grabbing towels, headed down the porch stairs to the lake. Before they reached the ground, Jan said. "Just a minute, Linda. I want to tell Timothy I'll be back in time to help with supper."

In a few minutes they were at the water's edge where Ted, Alec, and the Perrys joined them. It didn't take long to cool off when they stepped into the sixty-degree water.

Jacques was showing Timothy his catch in the kitchen so Brett thought this was as good a time as any to learn what Dave had decided on his financial proposition. Locating Dave, he suggested that they go outside where it was more comfortable.

Leaving the lodge, they walked toward the camp road and Brett wasted no time in reaching the point.

"Are you going to invest in my studio so I can get those guys off my back?" he asked Dave. "Their collector was in my office yesterday, and they warned me that they wanted quick action on my account. You're my last chance of survival."

Dave didn't respond immediately, but instead stopped and looked down at the ground while shuffling the dirt with his foot. After what seemed like eternity, Brett got his answer.

"I can't help you and Phyllis will have no part of it. I'm not going to invest in a questionable venture. If I had extra cash, I would find something more profitable."

Brett's face flushed and he put his face close to Dave and asked, "Are you refusing to help me now that I'm in deep trouble?"

"That's what it boils down to," Dave answered. "You got yourself into this mess, now get out of it. You have no one to blame but yourself. Take what those guys are handing out and stop complaining."

The photographer was infuriated as he listened to Dave's response.

Almost shouting and trying not to be heard by anyone at the lodge, his voice boomed as he demanded, "Is this your final answer?"

"There's nothing more to say," Dave replied, now becoming annoyed by Brett's voice.

Becoming noticeably angry, Dave stared into Brett's eyes and uttered, "Sink or swim, Brett!"

"You son of a bitch," Brett shouted. "You know what they'll do to me. You don't give a damn."

"Frankly, I don't," Dave answered as he started to walk away.

"Hold on a moment," Brett remarked.

"You had better hear well what I have to say before hanging me out to dry. If I'm going out the hard way, you're going to follow a trail leading to cell bars at Thomaston. Your nonchalant life will come to an end."

"What in hell do you mean?" Dave shouted and now their voices were loud enough to be heard at the lakeside,

"I mean you're in deep shit, too. Enough to put you away for a number of years."

"I didn't do anything," Dave responded.

Oh, yes, friend. Can't you remember that night a few weeks ago in my studio with the young girl?"

"Of course, I do, but you wouldn't bring that up. You were there too."

"I may be involved," Brett answered, "but it won't make any difference. I'm in too much trouble already. I need your help."

"I'm not getting you out of anything," Dave shouted.

"If that's what you want, that's what you'll get," Brett emphasized. "Screwing a fifteen-year-old girl in this state can be incriminating. Just to make certain you understand me, here's a picture I took that night.

Think it over!"

Dave's face turned white as he took the print and stared at the incriminating photograph of him and Dawn. "Are you going to blackmail me with this picture, you bastard?"

"It's a matter of survival. You may have that copy. I've got another plus the negative. Phyllis will love that pose of you and Dawn," Brett smirked. "You had better cool off and give my proposal more thought."

Bitterly angry, Dave replied, "I've given it all the thought I'm going to. You had better change your thinking or those guys from Rhode Island won't have a job to do."

"And," Brett retorted, "you should think it over, too. A prison is not the most pleasant place to spend winters after being accustomed to your luxurious life at Palm Beach."

With that remark, Brett walked to the lodge as Dave remained on the camp road staring at the picture of Dawn and him on the studio couch.

After Brett and Dave left earlier, Jacques remained with Timothy and brought the priest's belongings to the bedroom. Then he unpacked food supplies and stored the groceries in the cupboard. The perishable items along with bottles of ale were put in the icebox.

"Why don't you have a drink to quench your thirst, Jacques?" Timothy asked after the handyman finished. "You certainly deserve it after the work you've done. There are two kinds, Croft and Ballentine. Take the one you like best."

"Thanks, mon Pere, it doesn't make no matter which one I drink. They all taste good," he replied.

"By the way, Jacques, it's not necessary to call me Pere. I'm retired from the priesthood and I have told my friends to call me Timothy. Please do the same."

"Oui, oui," he replied. "I'll call you your name from now on."

"All right, Jacques. Now that the supplies are taken care of, our work is finished until it's time for supper. Let's join the rest at the dock."

While heading for the porch door, Timothy walked to the fireplace and looked carefully at the 38-55 Caliber rifle. It was a unique gun with a hexagon shaped barrel.

He moved nearer the mantel and noticed rust on the plate of the gun stock which was probably caused by water leaking from the roof.

"Jacques," he asked, "would you come here a minute and look at the butt of this gun? I think water caused the rust on this plate."

Jacques put his drink on the table and looked at he rifle.

"You're right, Timothy, he replied. "Some water got on the gun somehow and made rust. As soon as I have time, I'll go on the roof and see what makes it leak. After that, I'll take care of the gun."

"No, Jacques, you don't have to bother with the gun. You can fix the roof sometime if you think it's necessary. I'm sure the leak has been there for a long time so there's no hurry about that. In the meantime, would you see if there is an oil can and cloth in the work shack? I'd like to clean ii."

"I'll go to the shop after supper," he replied.

It was still warm outside but more comfortable than the kitchen as they walked to the dock. The bathers were in and out of the water trying to decide whether or not it was better to be hot or cold. Apparently, they seemed to enjoy the water more than the sun.

"This dock, it needs some work done on it," Jacques said as they sat on the edge. "These logs have been here a long time."

"I imagine you keep busy repairing this place during the summer," Timothy commented. "And you must have many guests also."

"Not as many people come here in the summer as they do when it's colder during the hunting season. Then the place is filled all the time Monsieur Barker tells me. I don't know how many come because I have only been here a few months. He says all the people who visit here are friends of Monsieur J.T.

The swimmers were content to sit on rocks at the edge of the clearing near the lake's entrance. It wasn't much of a beach with many stones and not very shallow. This was a fisherman's haven, not paradise for sun worshippers .

Ted was sitting close to the dock where he could talk with Jacques and asked where he lived.

"I have a small place, a cabin you would call it, near a stream about a quarter of a mile in the woods," he said pointing in a westerly direction "I work here until the hunting season is over in November."

"What are those buildings?" Linda asked.

"The one near the lake is the boathouse and the others are the icehouse, woodshed, and workshop. You know about the small shacks," Jacques replied.

"I don't see any trucks or other vehicles How do you get around?" Ted questioned. "It must be at least three miles to the tote road and it's a long way to the logging road that leads on the main road to the dam."

Jacques looked down at his feet. "Le Bon Dieu give me these feet to use so I walk many miles every day, even when the weather, it is bad. When I go to the village or sometime to Millinocket, I often get rides on pulp trucks." "Jacques," Linda asked as she moved nearer the dock with the rest of the swimmers, "how do you carry all the things you need if you are walking? "

"I'm a strong man," he laughed. And, I have a big knapsack that fits on my back so I carry things I need for myself. Things for the lodge are brought in by Monsieur Barker or some of his workers."

"It must be lonely here," Jan remarked. "Don't you miss people?" Jacques smiled. "Mademoiselle, I live in woods all my life. I was born in a log cabin outside of a small village where I grew up. I fished and hunted with my Papa. After he and Mama die, I come to this country and built a cabin in Maine woods near Jackman.

"There I spent the years until I come and built another cabin outside of Greenville where I stayed for five more years. Now, I'll live here during the good months. Next winter, I'll stay with a friend who has a house near Millinocket. This winter will be the first time I live with someone except a bear since I left Canada."

"A bear," Ruth exclaimed. "You are telling a tall story now. How can you live with a bear?"

Timothy interrupted. "Ruth, I think what you are going to hear now is what J.T. told me about Jacques and bears."

"Regardless," Ruth continued, "How did you learn to tame wild animals?

"Madame," Jacques replied, "it was not animals but one bear cub that I found one day in the woods. He was caught in a trap and was hurt badly so I carried him back to my cabin and took care of it until he was strong again. He become so strong that one night he almost killed me."

Finally, the woodsman was pleased. He had everyone's attention so he continued with his tale while Ruth asked this question.

"Jacques, you aren't going to tell us that you shot the bear and nursed it back to good health again."

"No, no, madame. I wrestled the bear. He was big now and I knocked him down with a stick."

"Come on now, Jacques, this story is really a good one," Ted interjected. "Why don't you tell us what happened to make you fight with a bear?"

"Mon ami. Let me start from the beginning.

147

"After I brought the bear to my cabin, I washed his leg where it was bad cut and put some stuff on it that would make it better. It took many weeks before he could stand and walk. But soon he would follow me around the camp. Later, I got a rope and tie it around his neck so when I went into the woods to hunt or to the lake for fish, I would take him with me.

"As he get bigger, I couldn't let him run loose because hunters might shoot him. So I get long chain and tie him to a tree near the cabin. At night, I bring him into camp with me and tie him with a rope to a hook I put on wall. Then, I go upstairs to my bed.

"We had much fun together. I teach him to sit up like dog and stand on this hind paws and after a long time, I teach him how to wrestle. Sometime he put me on my back and another time I put him on his back. Then, when it was over, he would give me big hug and kiss."

To make sure they all believed his story, he reached into the hind pocket of his pants for a billfold. He took a picture from inside which he handed to Timothy who passed it along to the others. If there was ever any doubt as to the authenticity of this episode, it now vanished.

The pocket-worn picture taken decades ago revealed a bear and Jacques standing face to face. The bruin stood a few inches over him but close enough to plant a smooch on the stocky woodsman's nose.

While everyone was listening to this fascinating story no one noticed Brett as he joined the group except Jacques who was pleased because he was carrying a camera. He continued, quite sure he would have his picture taken when he finished talking.

"One night," Jacques related, " I was sound asleep when I heard big noise so I go down ladder and found bear loose. It is dark, but I could see his shadow as he tore doors off from the cupboard looking for something to eat. He had broke rope and was running wild in the camp.

"Then he saw me and came to grab me so I wrestle him to floor like I do many times before when we play outside.

"Soon, he was getting mad so I get big stick from wood box and kept hitting him on head. One of the blows must have hurt him so he stopped and laid down. I tie him with the rope again and went back to sleep.

"The next morning when I looked at him, one of his eyes was gone. I must have hit him hard. That's why he stopped fighting."

"He must have been mad and ugly," Linda remarked. "I would have been afraid of him."

"No, mademoiselle. I untie and fed him and we went outdoors and were friends again. We never had another fight."

"What a fascinating story," Ruth exclaimed. "You don't have him now, do you? What happened to him?"

"Oh, madame, he was becoming bigger and older so I decided he should live with other bears in the woods. He might find someone he liked to kiss better than me.

"So, one day, I put rope around his neck and we walk many miles through woods to other side of mountain where I'd seen many signs of bears. I untie him and let him go. He went a short ways, turned and looked back at me. Then, he went in the woods. I never saw the bear again."

"That's an interesting story," Randy said. "Maybe we should take Jacques back with us to give a lecture on humanities at the college."

"Jacques, it's a feeling I have, you'll be telling more stories," Timothy interrupted. "Now I must get supper ready. There's a Cajun recipe I want to try with togue so I'll be seeing you later."

"Wait a minute, Timothy," Jan remarked. "I want to help with tonight's meal."

A Maine woodsman is portrayed as Jacques Silver Seven in this fictitious mystery novel of *death under tall pines*. The photo taken around the turn of the century shows the lumberjack with a 400 pound bear that he rescued from a trap and trained to wrestle.

Chapter 13

Dave entered from the kitchen as Timothy and Jan were coming from the porch in preparation for tonight's special supper menu.

"An interesting story hour at the dock, you missed, Dave. You might have found it interesting," Timothy said.

"I took a walk on a wood path for a close look at the wilderness and to stretch my legs after that ride today. It was interesting when I caught a glimpse of the white flag of a deer as it disappeared into the brush. Later, I saw a porcupine clinging to the limb of a tree. I would have been at the dock if I had known. Who was the story teller?"

"Our new acquaintance, Jacques Silver Seven, entertained us with yarns of the wilderness," Jan said. "Dave, I've hunted elk many times but I have yet to see a deer. They must be faster animals than elk as you said you only saw the white flag which I assume was its tail. Elk usually move slowly. And something else strange for a hunter which I considered myself when I lived out West. I've never seen a porcupine."

"You won't find these animals in the western states, Jan. They are the Canadian species and they usually roam forests in this part of the country. There is something else you probably don't know. These rodent-type creatures that are protected with sharp quills covering their bodies are to my knowledge the only wild animal that man can catch without a firearm. Extremely slow, they can be caught and killed with a stick. `Good ol' porky' won't even cause a dog trouble until its nose gets too close."

" Dave, you mean they aren't vicious?"

"That's right but their quills can quickly penetrate a hound's nostril or anyone who gets close. They can't eject quills but these pointed objects that nature designed to protect them can penetrate the skin upon contact. It requires pliers or other tools to extract them."

"You seem to know about wild animals," Jan remarked. "Have you done much hunting?"

"Guess I've done my share," Dave replied.

"Now, Jan, tell me about Jacques."

"He's really a character. I wouldn't have believed the bear story if he didn't have a picture of the bear kissing him. I'm certain he'll show you the photo and tell you about his experiences when you see him.

"How do you like this place?" Jan asked. " I guess this is the first trip here for both of us."

"I like the lodge and the lake," Dave answered. "Now, I hope the fishing will be good."

"Jacques said it was," Timothy added. "You must have done a lot of fishing in Florida. Have you done much in Maine besides Cedar Lake?"

"Yes, I do a lot of fishing during the winter and I often fish in the Rangeley and Sebego Lakes. However, I've never been in this region. When Alec told me about the fishing success you and your friends have had every year at Bear Lake, I was eager to come along. I certainly appreciated the invitation."

"You can thank Alec for that. He knows you better than the rest of us," Timothy remarked.

"You must keep busy in Middleton during the summer with your own activities," Jan said. "I read numerous accounts of Mrs. Paxton in the Guardian columns but your name is never mentioned. Apparently, you don't attend these events."

"My wife is involved in many charitable functions and, of course, that's her way of life. I like sports and I play golf at least a couple of times during the week, weather permitting."

"What do you do outside of your work, Jan?"

"I haven't had too much extra time," she answered. "I've only been here a few months and getting settled has taken most of the extra hours. However, getting acquainted with Linda and having her as my roommate has made the transition easier. Also, as a member of the Guardian staff, I have met many people in a short period of time."

"I guess both of us find enough to keep busy," Dave added. "Now I'm going to join the others at the dock and listen to Jacques's stories. I'll see you at supper."

When he left, Jan remarked, " By the way, Timothy, did you hear those loud voices when we were at the beach? It sounded like someone was quarreling. Do you suppose it was Dave and Brett? Neither was with us."

"It could have been, Jan. But, let's get on with tonight's menu. First, we must have an entree title befitting the occasion. How does this sound to you?" Timothy asked. "A New Orleans treat, quick-cooked fillet with a meuniere sauce, or A' la sautéed Togue with Toasted Pecan Butter featured by Chef Timothy O'Toole and his lovely assistant

Mademoiselle Janice Robinson."

"Timothy, you should have been in show biz."

"Now mademoiselle, I'll get the ingredients from the cupboard. While I take them to the working table, would you make certain our dining facilities are adequate for the occasion?"

"Oui, monsieur," Jan replied as she took a few steps to the west of the kitchen and into the dining room.

When she entered the lodge earlier, she hadn't noticed all the furnishings in this combination kitchen, dining and living area. In the kitchen, along with the cast iron cook stove, there was a working table, icebox and plenty of cupboards.

The dining area consisted of a long oak table with a dozen chairs while the living area was filled with two large sofas. There were three stuffed chairs and two rockers plus four end tables and a large coffee table. A gaming or card table with chairs completed the furniture. Lamps were in place on shelves and several coat racks were located near the doors and at one end of the fireplace. Whatever the lodge lacked in modern conveniences was offset by adequate facilities.

Before returning to help Timothy prepare tonight's entree, she went to the cupboards checking on the dishes and other items for the dining room table. Jacques was more than a handyman and guide, she thought. He was a perfectionist in the kitchen. Everything was ready.

"I want to help you with supper, and if you don't mind, I'd like to make the Cajun meuniere sauce," Jan said.

"That's all right with me, Jan. I'll get the recipe from my room and you can mix the sauce while I fillet the fish."

"Of course," Jan remarked, "you must have something else to serve with the entree. Tell me and I'll get it ready after I finish this sauce."

"When we stopped at a roadstand in Abbot, I bought a peck of new peas and potatoes along with vegetables for a salad. You can prepare the peas and potatoes dish."

"My mouth is watering already," Jan answered. "Everyone told me you were an excellent cook and there's no doubt in my mind. All of this topped by Harry's apple pies will make this a scrumptious feast, much better than any restaurant menu."

"By the way, Jan, plenty of help, we have. Why don't you ask Ruth and Linda to make the salad?"

"Oh, Jan, something just occurred to me that would add more woods atmosphere to this setting. I was thinking about homemade biscuits and I know someone who has this finesse. It's more than likely that cooking goes along with all of Jacques talents. Do you mind asking him?"

"Not at all, Timothy," she responded as he went to his room for the recipe.

She walked out to the lake where Jacques was still holding the speaker's platform.

"Sorry to interrupt, Jacques," she said. "Can you bake biscuits? Timothy thought it would add to the supper menu. He was sure that a man who spent years in the wilderness would have this talent."

"Of course I can," he answered. "It'll be my pleasure. I'll stop talking and go to the kitchen with you, Jan."

This was the first occasion since Jacques met the group that he used her name instead of mademoiselle. It appeared he was becoming more at ease with the guests.

"You're a jack of all trades, Jacques," Brett remarked.

Jan turned to Ruth and Linda and asked them if they would make the salad.

"Of course, Jan," both replied.

"Before you leave, Jacques, let me get a photo of you alone and another with a couple of lovely women. We want to remember you."

This made the woodsman happy and he beamed when he stood for the second picture with Jan and Linda.

After the pictures were taken, everyone left for the lodge.

"Jacques," Timothy said as he entered the kitchen, "welcome, you are, to join us for supper and other meals. Would you like that? Besides, my friend, you are too good a cook not to use your experience."

"Merci, merci," Jacques exclaimed. "I would like that very much."

The kitchen was becoming busy with more taking part in the action. The saying "there was room for only one cook in a kitchen and too many cooks would spoil the broth" wasn't the situation here. Everyone was having fun.

"How many biscuits should I make," Jacques asked as he reached for a bag of flour. I can made a big batch in one big pan. Maybe thirty biscuits."

"That's plenty and there'll be enough left for breakfast," Timothy said.

Timothy handed the recipe for the Toasted Pecan Butter sauce to Jan who made a pan-full within ten minutes. All that remained was heating the sauce and serving it after Timothy fried the togue.

As Timothy was filleting the fish and Jacques was mixing the dough for the biscuits, Dave and Ted went to the cupboard for the dishes and silverware. They were joined by Brett as the table was set for the first night's supper.

At last, everyone was involved in getting tonight's meal ready as Randy entered the room and helped Ruth and Linda in preparing individual salad dishes. Timothy and Jan began heating skillets separately and soon the aroma of Cajun cooking permeated the lodge. When the cooking was done, Brett and Dave placed servings of the entrees on individual plates and brought them to the table. Jan spooned a portion of toasted pecan butter sauce over each piece of fish.

As everyone was seated, Randy opened a bottle of wine which he had put in the icebox earlier and walked around the table filling the glasses. When he reached Jacques's seat, he asked if he would rather have ale than wine.

"I don't drink wine much but I like ale," Jacques replied.

Randy walked to the icebox and returned with a bottle and filled Jacques's glass.

When all the glasses were filled and Randy was seated, Timothy rose from his chair and offered one of his favorite Irish toasts.

Holding his glass high, Timothy articulating his Irish brogue, delivered this message:

"May you have warm words on a cold evening, a full moon on a dark night, and a smooth road all the way to your door. And may God bless this food."

With that, supper was underway.

The evening went well and time passed rapidly with several conversations occurring simultaneously. Everyone, including Jacques, had questions.

"Do you have a hockey team at the school where you live?" he asked Alec. "I like hockey but I don't see games anymore."

"Yes, we have a pretty good team who play other college teams in New England," Alec replied. "Last year, they won every game. We know your father liked hockey but did you play on any team?"

"Papa was a good player with hockey. He played with amateurs but I was not very good. It took me a long time to make a stick but I made a mistake by using apple wood and it snapped in my first game. I never played after that."

"Jacques," Dave asked, "where are the best fishing holes on the lake? Do you have a special one?"

"I like to fish off Patte de Chat, that big rock you can see from the dock. That's where I got those togue today, but if you want small trout they're biting north of the lake way out there," as he waved his arm pointing toward the porch door.

"You called that rock, Patte de Chat. If I remember my high school French," Linda, said, "chat means cat but what does the other word mean in English?"

"Patte is a paw," Jacques replied.

"Cat's Paw," she said. "That's a cute name."

"Are there any other camps around here?" Dave inquired. "This seems to be an isolated area."

"There is a good camp on the logging road about four miles from here that belongs to the Maine Fish and Game wardens who watch for poachers. The other day I met Warden Tom Hillson of Greenville and a doctor who are living in the camp for a few days while they fish.

"If you people don't know, all this land belongs to the big paper companies. No one else owns land in these woods excepting maybe a power company. Some people can use it if the owners say so."

"Oh, Timothy," Jacques said, "I forgot to tell you when you asked me if there were other people here now. Yesterday, I saw two men setting up a tent at a clearing on the other side of the lake. They have a car like Alec's, a long one with number plates that are different than yours. They brought a canoe on top of it. I didn't see them close as they turned around when I looked from my boat. Guess they don't want to talk with me. We don't have people around here often unless someone knows them. Monsieur Barker told me that."

Brett listened attentively as Jacques described them as big men that he and the warden hadn't seen before.

"You said you have a cabin not too far from here." Dave said. "Is it one that you built or was it a camp that belonged to the paper company?"

"No, I build it myself. I'll show it to you tomorrow before we go fishing if you like."

"Randy and Ruth can see it too, if we're going to fish with you," Dave added.

"Okay. After breakfast I'll take you there. We'll go fishing after."

"Jacques, you said we had to be careful whenever we cross the lake," Jan remarked. "What do you mean. The lake doesn't look rough to me."

"Don't let that fool you, Jan. It can be a lot of danger. Sometimes, like today, it's smooth like they say, as a papoose's bottom, but when the wind blows strong it can be rough as an old squaw's face. I have seen waves three and sometime four feet high. Watch the sky! You got to be careful when you cross and don't none of you use a canoe unless you paddle along the shore which would make it a longer way. The motor boat is more safe and faster."

"If the three of you plan to go with Jacques fishing in the morning, then I would like to go with someone in the other larger boat," Timothy said.

"Alec, let's go with Brett and Jan and troll the waters beyond Patte de Chat and see if we can land a togue. Is that all right with you?"

"It's fine with me," Brett replied while Jan said, "I'd love to go."

"Now, that's settled," Timothy remarked. "We have a minor problem I'm sure Ted and Linda can handle while everyone's away from the lodge."

"What's on your mind, Timothy?"

"Earlier, Jacques and I were discussing tomorrow night's supper and although we haven't finished this one yet, it's well to make plans now.

"Anyhow, we decided on baked beans and red frankfurts. As you probably have surmised, Jacques is a good a cook as well as a top-notch baked bean chef. I'll leave a pan of beans to soak tonight and when Jacques comes to breakfast in the morning, he'll get them ready. He told me he has a special beanpot. It will take all day to bake the beans. The only necessity during the day is keeping a fire alive in the stove by just adding sticks occasionally. Can you arrange that, Ted?"

"That won't be a problem," Linda answered. "Later in the afternoon, we'll make the salad for supper if Jacques will be back in time to bake another batch of biscuits."

"All right," Timothy remarked. "The daylight is still long as the sun doesn't set until after eight o'clock so that will give us a chance to do a lot of fishing. One more thing, don't forget to bring sandwiches and something to drink. Brett bought several cans of luncheon meat, jars of peanut butter and jelly, and we have plenty of bread. Hungry is what you'll be, if you spend the day on the lake.

"Oh, yes, another reminder for you women. Keep your body protected from the sun. If we haven't mentioned it before, there are life preservers and rain capes in every boat."

"That ends the schedule for tomorrow and today's is over for me. I'm taking a little walk after that hearty supper while there's still daylight. If any of you go out later, remember to take a flashlight. These woods get dark quickly when the sun goes down. And be careful not to run into a bear," Timothy laughed.

Timothy left the lodge alone, watching his steps carefully as he walked down the stairs.

He moved along the side of the building to a path leading past the icehouse a short distance from the lake. Evening shadows faded as darkness began to settle in the woods and light from the sun gradually disappeared beyond the lake's western horizon. As the sun fell, so did the night's temperature. Timothy continued his stroll trying to avoid protruding rocks and sticks that covered parts of the trail. He soon became aware this wasn't the right time to wander too far from camp. He realized daylight was fading too abruptly for a person of his age to explore the wilderness.

Timothy decided it was easier to retrace his steps and take his evening walk on the better cleared camp road. He could hear voices and laughter of others as they cleared the dining room when he approached the lodge for the remainder of his evening constitutional.

Timothy decided to wear something to foil the mosquitoes so he entered the lodge from the porch where he saw a jacket hanging on a coat rack near the fireplace. It was lightweight so he wondered how anyone could leave behind an apparently new tan color coat. There wasn't a spot on it. One of the lodge's last visitors must have forgotten it. Timothy pulled on the jacket to resume his stroll. It was easier walking in this area but he kept his flashlight on the ground to sidestep any obstacles along the way.

The retired priest thought of Jan's remark about a possible argument between Dave and Brett earlier when he, of course, dismissed the idea to avoid any further discussion at that time. He knew she was correct in her assumption that they were quarreling. He pondered what created the situation. If he remembered correctly from Alec's remarks, Brett wanted Dave along on this trip. He would ask Ted what he thought since he was at the *Guardian* when Dave visited Alec.

Too many incidents were taking place involving Brett. This bothered him. It was supposed to be a vacation and a fun trip. He hoped tempers would mellow now that the most difficult day of the trip had passed. His pipe was unlit but he decided to light up tonight. While he was filling his pipe, he heard the hoot of an owl somewhere in the timber. As the call of loons echoed across the waters of Bear Lake, the nocturnal sounds of frogs and crickets were heard nearer the shore.

As Timothy stopped to light his pipe the loons were more audible and becoming more fascinating, so the old priest decided to change his course again as he turned and headed to the lake. He wondered how he could have forgotten the sounds of these uniquely colored birds that inhabited most of Maine's lakes.

There was a flickering of light ahead when he reversed his travel as Jacques had started a fire near the shore. Whatever festivities were in store for the few remaining hours on this Saturday, they were certain to take place here. When he approached the area, he was aware most of the crowd was gathered on the dock listening to Jacques' tales which he assumed would be the highlight of whatever happened tonight. It had been a long day and knowing how the summer air in the Maine woods produces drowsiness, he was sure these vacationers wouldn't be burning midnight wood.

After the dishes and utensils were washed and the kitchen and dining room cleaned, everyone left for the waterfront. Randy started with the others but he returned to his room and took his pistol from his pack and put it inside his shirt. He started down the stairs but turned again and brought the weapon back. Ruth observed him from the porch when he returned both times. She was relieved when he finally came outside without the weapon bulging from his shirt. She thought that his attitude throughout the day had been strange and whatever was annoying him had not vanished.

While everyone was listening to Jacques' stories, she didn't notice Randy move near Brett and soon both walked to the area where the vehicles were parked.

As they stood near the cars, Randy came face to face with Brett and without hesitation he firmly called him a liar.

"Brett, I'm sure you weren't telling the truth when we met at Cedar Lake a couple of weeks ago. You were with Ruth on the night of the storm but I don't know what happened. Your story doesn't coincide with the information I heard from the utility foreman who saw your car parked in front of our cottage that night. However, I can't prove it and I will not accuse my wife unjustly. What do you have to say?" Randy asked as he looked directly into Brett eyes.

"Nothing more than I already told you. I started down the road that night but turned into a camp driveway after I remembered that you were going to be away for a few days. Believe it or not, that's the truth."

"I don't think you know the truth, Brett, " Randy charged. "You're a fibber and I haven't decided what to do. This is a good place to make a decision and the week is only beginning. Anything can happen here."

Randy turned abruptly and walked swiftly to the lake leaving Brett standing alone. Hidden in the woods, Timothy had moved from the shore and was only a short distance away where he heard part of the discussion. Randy and Brett were unaware of his presence.

Jacques was still relating tales about his hunting feats during his growing up days in the Canadian woods when Ted interrupted him.

"Jacques, I only want to change the subject for a minute because I'm curious about the beanpot you plan to use tomorrow. What's so special about it?"

"Ted, it is one of the best beanpots ever made. It is a redstone and was made by Exeter Pottery Company in New Hampshire about fifty years ago. It was my luck to buy it in a secondhand store in Presque Isle and I have cooked many beans in it. All were very good.

To make them more better," he added, "I go to the best store in Bangor to buy yellow eye beans whenever I have a chance. I will need more soon but I have plenty for supper tomorrow night." Jacques hadn't noticed Timothy had joined the group until now so he walked over to him as he remembered the rifle.

"Timothy," he said, "I got an oil can and a cloth from the work shop and left them in the kitchen. Can I help you clean the gun?"

"No, thanks, Jacques. Just keep on telling your stories. Everyone seems to like them."

As the woodsman stepped back on the dock, Timothy had one parting remark.

"My friends, time has come for me to return to the lodge to do a couple of things before retiring. I leave you now, and seeing you in the morning, I'll be doing."

Timothy returned to the lodge and went directly to the work table where Jacques had left the items. He walked to the fireplace and removed the rifle from its mount over the mantel making sure it was unloaded. He soaked the cloth with oil and tried to clean the rust from the shoulder plate. He scrubbed the surface hard but only a little of the stain disappeared so he quit and placed the rifle back in its original place. It

160

was useless, he thought, to continue trying to clean the stain with this oil. In the morning he would look for a better cleaning fluid.

It didn't take long to get into bed after this long day but before he fell asleep he thought about the day's activities involving Brett, especially the argument with Dave. Timothy couldn't understand what created the situation and what brought on the heated discussion between them. A couple of other things went through his mind before he dozed off. He recalled Jacques's account of two strangers setting up camp nearby, something uncommon in this secluded area. His mind also drifted back to the Middleton Police Station when Chief Davidson commented about the long arms of the syndicate reaching anywhere.

Timothy's earlier prediction that the comfortable night air would hinder the vacationers from staying up late began to materialize as Linda remarked she was getting drowsy. Shortly, she left the group who was sitting around the fire and started toward the lodge.

"Don't make a trip to the half moon without me, Linda," Jan remarked. "We'll be breaking up soon and I'll keep you company."

"I wouldn't think of going alone," Linda replied. "I'll wait in the lodge for you."

Until now, she hadn't been aware that all members of the group were not taking part in the discussions. Looking back at the fire, she noted that most of them were there but she didn't give it any thought.

The lodge was only a short distance but she wished she had brought a flashlight as Timothy had suggested. It was pitch dark and only the flickering of the campfire gave her enough light to find her way over the rough path. She was half way there when suddenly she felt a cold chill.

Glancing back, she could make out a shadowy figure lurking among the trees near the shore. It stood motionless and as a burst of sparks from the burning embers cast a spreading glow, she caught an outline of a face staring at the gathering.

Frantically, Linda turned and stumbled on a rock as she ran back to the campfire and into the arms of Ted.

"What's wrong, Linda," he questioned. "You're shaking like a leaf!"

"I just saw someone standing over there in the dark," she declared as she pointed toward a group of trees. He didn't move and he was looking in this direction."

Jacques rose quickly from his seat on a rock and ran to the area where Linda had pointed. He was followed quickly by Alec while Ted couldn't get loose from Linda's hug as she continued to shiver. Jan moved in and put her arms around her.

"It's all right, Linda. There's nothing to worry about," she said as Linda slowly released her grasp from Ted so he could join in the search for an intruder.

"What happened?" Ruth asked while going to Linda's side.

"Nothing, except it was scary," Linda sobbingly replied. "A man just stood near the trees quietly but it appeared as if he was staring at someone in the group. It was dark and I was afraid. I don't think he saw me."

"I don't know who it could have been," Brett remarked. "Most everyone was near the fire listening to Jacques's stories with the exception of Timothy who left earlier."

"Not everyone was here," Jan said. "The only men with us were the three who just left looking for him and you. I don't know where Randy and Dave were."

"I can solve that problem," Randy said as he walked out of the dark. "I was returning from a stroll on the camp road when I heard the excitement down here. I walked about half way to the logging road. Anyhow, what's going on to cause this commotion?" he asked.

"Randy," Ruth answered, "Linda said she saw a person standing in the woods looking at us while we were sitting around the fire. She was frightened and I don't blame her. Who do you suppose it could have been?"

"I can only account for myself and it wasn't I."

"And," another voice from out of the darkness responded. It wasn't I. I've been sitting on the porch since Timothy came back to the lodge," Dave explained. "Similar to Randy, I came down after hearing all the noise."

The men who were looking for signs of an unknown visitor returned as Dave explained his whereabouts, acknowledging they hadn't found any sign of another person.

"Whoever it was, he's not around here now," Alec reported. "It's too dark out there to look for anything, let alone a person who could disappear quickly into the woods."

"Who do you think it was," Ruth asked.

"I have no idea," Alec said. "The only other people to our knowledge who are in the region are the two fishermen Jacques told us about. I doubt they would cross the lake tonight just to listen to his stories. I'm baffled."

"Well," Ted remarked, "There's nothing we can do about it so why don't we call it a night? It's getting late anyhow. We'll tell Timothy about it in the morning." Taking Linda's hand, he led the group as they returned to the lodge.

"Don't worry about it, honey," he said. "Everything's all right."

Jacques was last to leave the beach as he doused the fire to make sure no sparks remained before he went to his cabin. He didn't need a flashlight as he had roamed woods on countless occasions in pitch darkness and many times in blizzards and heavy rain.

Ted extinguished lamps in the living area and climbed stairs to the loft where the others had already fallen asleep.

It was quiet as the day neared its end and the only sound in the building came from Randy and Ruth's room adjacent to Timothy's .

Talking a little louder than she should, Ruth asked Randy why he even considered taking his pistol when he went outside that evening.

"In fact," she asked, "why did you bring the gun along on a fishing trip. You don't usually do this, do you?"

"You never know what you'll meet in the woods," Randy replied.

Ruth looked up in the darkness when Randy blew out the flame in the lamp. She could feel her heart beat as she lay quietly beside him wondering if he was thinking about Brett and what effect it would have on their future.

Shortly everyone was sleeping as stillness descended on the nocturnal woods. The croaking of what sounded like hundreds of frogs intermingled with occasional hoots of an owl were the only interruptions of the night's serenity.

Chapter 14

Bear Lake resembled the opened half of a watermelon as a rising bright red sun cast a pink reflection over its calm surface. Adding to its beauty were the more fascinating calls and antics of loons. Their heads bobbed in and out of the water as they fished uninterruptedly in the quiet lake.

Who, but Jacques would be the first person to witness this colorful view as he stood on the dock in front of the lodge. His sharp eyes scanned the horizon for any weather signs beyond what he already suspected would take place this day. He wanted to awaken the vacationers so they could see this beautiful scene but he thought quarter past five was too early to disturb city folks.

On the other hand, his experience in the outdoors had taught him this morning's loveliness was only a temporary spectacle. A red sky meant something more ominous would change the complexion of this serenity before the sun disappeared that day.

He didn't think Timothy would mind if he woke him and said how pretty it was outside. He entered the lodge and walked softly across the wood floor and knocked on his bedroom door.

A light sleeper, Timothy awoke instantly and asked who was there.

"Timothy, it's me. I thought everyone would like to see a beautiful lake this morning. It's going to change a lot before another day comes."

"Just a minute, Jacques," Timothy whispered. "I'll get dressed and meet you outdoors."

When Timothy stood on the beach looking at the beauty of the lake, he was astounded and lost no time in returning to the lodge to alert the rest by shouting, "Time to rise."

If anyone objected, nothing was said.

"Get up, everyone. Come outside and look at the lake. You'll never see anything more radiant."

Within minutes, all of the gang were standing on the shore looking at an almost once-in-a-lifetime sight.

After the excitement was over, it was time to get breakfast and prepare for the day's activities but not before Ted alerted Timothy about

Linda's experience last night.

"You said that the men could account for their whereabouts. Who were missing from the gathering near the fire?" Timothy asked.

"Randy and Dave but they denied being near the shore at that time."

"Strange, it is," Timothy remarked. "You don't suppose Linda had an illusion. It would be easy to see strange things at night in these woods. The darkness becomes mysterious and anyone not familiar with the phenomenon could be confused and frightened.

"And," he amusingly added, "I'm surprised it wasn't a bear she saw after all our talk about wild animals."

"I don't know what to say, Timothy. She was positive that someone was there. Unquestionably, she was disturbed."

"Ted, I'll have a talk with her a little later."

However, later arrived sooner than Timothy anticipated as Linda approached them.

"We were just talking about you, Linda," Timothy said. "I'm curious about what you saw last night."

"I'm sure Ted told you all about it. Regardless, I did see a silhouette of someone standing near those trees," she said pointing to the location near the shore. "And it wasn't a fantasy," she insisted.

"You said that the person was looking at the people around the campfire. Obviously, it was too dark to see his face. Could you tell how tall he was," Timothy asked.

"That's difficult to say, also. However, he wasn't a really tall man. I'd guess he was under six feet."

"Well, that's something but it doesn't reveal the identity of whoever it was. Tonight, we'll be prepared in the event he should return. Let's hope it doesn't occur again Linda. Now, you and Ted enjoy yourself while the rest of us do the fishing this morning. You'll have your chance this afternoon. You came here for a vacation so make the best of it," Timothy suggested." And, please keep the fire alive."

Before leaving for his cabin with Randy, Ruth, and Dave, Jacques had prepared the beans and placed the pot in the oven and again reminded the group about the weather.

"Remember, mes amis. The sky was very red this morning and that means big storm is coming. Be careful on the water."

Everyone began leaving except Ted and Linda who had promised to stay near the lodge.

It was only a few minutes walk to the cabin that Jacques said would be his home for more than half of the year and no one was surprised when they saw the makeshift camp. It was a simple structure he made from small trees when he was hired to take care of the lodge. It must have been cold when he began construction as it appeared hurriedly built with many logs extending beyond the twenty-foot building. However, there was one advantage to its site. Jacques had built it under the shelter of a group of fir trees for protection against storms.

Heavy roofing paper covering the roof was secured by rough pieces of boards that he must have found at the logging camp. Instead of a stone chimney that should have extended through the roof, he had a stovepipe protruding through an upper side of the structure.

So far, there were no signs of burnt logs near the outlet of this crude chimney. A wood-burning cast iron stove with an oven served for both cooking and heat. The floor was made from split logs. A small soapstone sink connected to a short length of pipe that extended under it through the wall allowed drainage to the outside. There was no inside or outside plumbing so whatever water was necessary had to be brought from a stream flowing to the lake more than one hundred yards away.

Furnishings included a bed and a couple of chairs that probably came from the lodge. A table made of rough lumber that was most likely used to skin animals during the trapping season took up the rest of the space. A small icebox completed the furnishings.

Three small windows furnished sufficient light in the camp during the day while any light at night had to come from a lantern dangling by a rope from the ceiling. A battered screen door let some light in as well as flies while a primitive outhouse was located in back of the cabin closer than it should have been. Jacques had pounded long nails above the inside door where two pairs of snowshoes and a double-barrel shotgun were kept. A weather-worn holster holding a .38 Caliber revolver was hanging on a post at the foot of his unkept bed.

Jacques spent only enough time in the cabin to get his fishing rod and box. He didn't have a padlock so he had to slide a railroad spike in a bolt after closing the door.

Leaving the area, the group followed a path to the lake where one of the lodge's two outboard motorboats was kept. Here they completed preparations for the day's fishing.

Linda and Ted left the lodge together holding hands as they headed on a trail leading to the north shore of Bear Lake. It was a beautiful day without a cloud in the sky and the sun occasionally broke through branches of tall trees along the seldom-traveled path.

The only sounds as they walked slowly into the woods were their footsteps and the chirping of squirrels as they looked down from perches on tree limbs. Moving farther into the dense forest, the sounds of whippoorwills and an occasional cawing of crows could be heard in the distance while calls of loons continued to echo across the waters of Bear Lake behind them.

They had walked about ten minutes when they came upon a brook crossing the trail. Linda stopped and looked into the brush along its babbling waters. Then, she pressed Ted's hand, pulling him closer to her body and stared into his eyes while her lips were partly open, hungry for a kiss. He lowered his face to hers and they embraced tightly for several minutes. When she loosened her grip, she didn't utter the same phrase she had when they met on the banks of the Kennebec a few weeks earlier.

Instead of insisting, "Let's break it up," Linda tugged at both of his hands and pulled him off the trail murmuring." Remember what I whispered to you at Harry's. How about it?" she teased.

She moved carefully ahead of him to the side of the brook until they reached a clearing on its bank.

This time, she put both arms around him and pushed her hips against his body moving them slowly and snugly. As they began another embrace, their kisses became more intense and she opened her mouth while her tongue searched for his. Slowly, they lowered their bodies to the soft grass along the brook. Linda moved from his side and gradually on top of him while pressing her trim frame against his.

Gingerly, Ted unbuttoned her blouse and reached around to unfasten her bra. His fingers touched her firm breast and she began to breathe heavily, panting and murmuring. He moved from under her while taking off her shorts and panties. Now, he placed a hand on her warm thigh and with the fingers of his other hand, he gently touched her nipples. In a few minutes he moved from the closeness of her body to lower his slacks.

She lay quietly with her eyes closed waiting for the love they hadn't experienced together. Everything was so beautiful, comforting and wonderful as she longed for the final moments. The sensation was ecstatic as they gradually became one, giving to each other. Her head began to spin. Her lips burned as they pressed hard against his and she moved her body back and forth to share his rhythm. She opened her eyes briefly and she could faintly see the trees swaying while under her the earth moved round and round for what seemed an eternity of happiness.

She continued to lie on the soft earth only dreaming and hoping this rapture could continue forever. Ted was lying beside her and smiled as he moved his lips to hers for a soft kiss and whispered, "Linda, I love you."

She responded with a hug and whispered, "Darling, you're wonderful. I love you, too. Very much."

Neither uttered a word as they slowly got to their feet and Linda took his hand as they continued their walk to the lake resembling a large mirror. When she reached its edge, she could see her reflection in its stillness.

Nothing was stirring in this vast wilderness and the only sounds were still the occasional cries of loons and ripples in the water when a fish jumped to snatch flies. To an urban girl, It didn't seem possible that this panorama of a cloudless blue sky would transform into a turbulent nightmare as the day continued.

"I'm curious about the fishermen camping on the other side of the lake," Ted said when he caught up with Linda at the beach in front of the lodge. After I check the kitchen stove, let's take a canoe ride along the shore to the place where Jacques told us he saw them."

Ted was only a few minutes in the lodge where he added a couple of sticks of wood to the glowing embers. He soon joined her at the beach where she was waiting near the canoe with two life jackets. Linda had taken Jacques's warning seriously about rough water. An excellent swimmer, she still wasn't going to chance crossing this lake without a jacket.

With Linda sitting in the bow, Ted put one foot in the canoe while moving it with the other. Shortly, the couple was paddling a short distance from the shore toward Patte de Chat where their companions in an outboard craft were trolling off the rock. He figured it had to be at least five miles along the shore to the spot where the strangers had made camp. It was still a long ride on the calm water but it didn't appear the weather would worsen with hardly a breeze or clouds. Trying to find the strangers in this immense lake would be almost impossible. The men could be fishing in any of the countless inlets or they could be hikers who preferred to explore paths or trails in the wilderness.

Jan waved as the couple passed a short distance from their fishing spot near Patte de Chat while Linda and Ted increased speed to meet unknown and maybe not welcome visitors in the region. Paddling in unison, they left a lot of space behind as the canoe glided rapidly along the shore.

Ted scanned the woods in the distance hoping to catch a glimpse of someone. However, the shoreline was too distant so he decided to try a direct route to an area where Jacques said he had seen the men. The sky was still cloudless without any sign of changing weather as he spoke to Linda.

"Let's cross the lake instead of following the shoreline. Of course, it's shorter and won't take as long to get to our destination. We are wearing life jackets and if a storm should arise, we will see it approaching and head for the nearest shore. We would be paddling most of the day if we continue on this course."

"You heard what Jacques said about crossing this lake," Linda responded. "However, if you think it's safe enough, it's all right with me. Let's go."

They were about a half mile from a clearing on the opposite shore when Ted thought he saw something moving near the rocks. Suddenly, the calm waters began to change as a brisk wind created tiny waves. He strained his eyes trying to recognize objects and it appeared that someone was pulling a boat from the lake. Although his curiosity wasn't satisfied, he was positive of his next move now that the calm water began to change. They quickly reversed their direction and headed straight to land where they would follow the shoreline back.

It was a long way but with a steady and fast pace Linda and Ted were paddling the canoe, they were close to Timothy's boat within the hour.

"What's the hurry?" Timothy asked as the canoe came alongside the larger boat. "It's not noon. There's still plenty of time to fish."

"It must be a case of paranoia after listening to Jacques' numerous warnings of unpredictable storms," Ted replied. "We were close to the other side of the lake to find the men Jacques said were camped when a stronger wind developed. It probably was nothing serious as the water is calm on this side. However, we didn't risk being caught in the middle of the lake when a storm developed. It appears quiet now."

"You're telling us you were almost across the lake to meet someone you apparently have never seen before," Jan remarked. "You must have a reason but I can't imagine what it would be."

Timothy knew the purpose but he remained silent wondering what explanation Ted would offer.

"There are a couple of answers, "he replied. "It was a good reason to learn how fast Linda and I could cross the lake, and I thought if other people visited the region there might be places unknown to me. I have spent most of my life in Maine and I always look for new sights to explore."

The response seemed to satisfy Jan while Timothy smiled as he turned his head.

As the canoe was close to the other craft, Linda looked carefully on the bottom of the boat for fish.

"Unless I'm losing my eyesight," she said, "you've had a fruitless, or should I say fishless, morning."

" We had only a couple bites," Alec said. "We aren't going to fish any more today as Timothy wants to go back to the lodge and Brett would like to take some pictures of wildlife. He'll probably catch more with his camera than we did with fishing rods. Jan and I thought we might join you and Ted on a canoe sight-seeing cruise. How about it?"

"Great," they answered. Let's go back to the lodge for a snack and then we'll cruise along the upper side of the lake. This time we'll keep closer to shore."

Both boats headed for the dock as larger waves began to form.

"I have a suspicion Jacques and his companions will be coming this way soon," Timothy said. "It doesn't seem like a storm now but the wind is becoming brisk and I'm sure Jacques won't stray too far from the lodge if the water gets rougher."

No sooner had the boats reached the shore near the lodge when the sound of an outboard motor was heard and soon a craft could be seen plowing the lake toward them. Everyone waited for the outboard to reach shore and Ruth and Randy stepped out.

"It doesn't appear you had any better luck than Timothy and his crew," Ted said as Jacques and Dave walked onto the beach.

"We had a beautiful ride," Ruth said. "The scenery was gorgeous but the fish must have been enjoying it too because they weren't biting."

"We might have better luck this afternoon," Jacques remarked. "But," again he warned," we must keep on this side of the lake. There are only a few clouds now but I think it's going to get bad."

All of them walked to the lodge except Timothy who asked Jacques to come to the workshop with him. They searched the building but were unable to find any solvents so Timothy decided to forget it. Jacques stopped as they were about to leave the workshop when a thought occurred about the mantle.

"There's got to be a hole near the chimney for water to get in the fireplace," he said. "I'm going to get a ladder and go to the top of the roof to see where it is. If another storm comes, more water will get in if I don't fix it."

"Do you need someone to help you?" Timothy asked. "I'm sure any of the men will be willing."

"No, no, Timothy, I have enough stuff to fix anything myself."

Timothy entered the lodge where the rest were sitting at the table but he went directly to the living room and reclined on a sofa. He fell asleep and when he opened his eyes no one was in the lodge but he could hear sounds on the roof where Jacques was making repairs.

Feeling better after his nap but hungry, he saw the jars of peanut butter and jelly but decided to have something more substantial. He went to the cupboard and took a can of luncheon meat and a jar of mustard from a shelf and made a sandwich with two thick slices of meat. Then he poured a cup of coffee from a simmering pot on the stove and sat at the table.

After eating he looked at the fireplace and glanced at the rifle above the mantel. He wanted to clean the rust from it but there was nothing he could do without a stronger cleaning fluid. He walked over to examine the gun again. Yesterday he was careful to make certain the rifle was not loaded and he pulled the lever to open the chamber to be sure it was still empty. Replacing the weapon above the fireplace, he noticed a partially open box of ammunition on the shelf with four 38.55 caliber cartridges.

Jacques had spread tar on a sheet of roofing on the roof and planned to return later to fasten strips of boards over the repairs to make sure the wind wouldn't blow the roofing off. He took the tools to the workshop but left the ladder near the lodge. When he reached Timothy he asked what plans were in store for the afternoon.

"Well," Timothy answered, "I'm going to fly fish off the rocks beyond the dock. Afterwards I intend to return to the lodge and read. Are you taking someone fishing?"

Before Jacques had a chance to answer Brett came along and interrupted the conversation. "I plan to do some photography today, Jacques, and if you don't have anything special to do, I'd like to have you along. I'm sure you know the best spots to locate animals. Is that possible?"

"Now, I have two things to do," Jacques replied. "First, Timothy, I am here to help anyone. If someone wants to go fishing, I go. And, if he wants me to show places in the woods, I go, too."

"Whatever, "Timothy said. "Why don't you accompany Brett? You have already done a lot of fishing."

"O.K.," he said. "I'll go with him," knowing all the time he would rather be with someone with a camera. He liked to have his picture taken and he felt sure Brett would.

"How about the rest of you?" Timothy asked as he moved closer to the group.

"Ted and I changed our mind about canoeing with the women this afternoon," Alec responded. "We thought we would fish with the outboard on the south shore near Patte de Chat. If the weather changes, it would be safer."

"Well, if this is the case," Dave said, "I'll go with Timothy and cast off the rocks and probably try the stream near Jacques' place that we passed this morning. It seems to me there must be trout there and I'd rather fly fish than troll. When you leave, Timothy, I'll go with you."

"It appears that most everyone is changing plans as Ruth and I have already decided to try our luck fishing from a canoe," Randy remarked. " We're going to fish the waters beyond where Dave and Timothy plan to be."

As the afternoon hours passed, a noticeable difference was taking place in the weather as the wind whistled through the woods bending branches on the trees. Ruth and Randy were first to head for shore when the canoe started bobbing as the wind shifted directions and waves nearly tipped the light craft on its side. They tried to paddle to the dock in rough waters but high waves pushed it against the rocks.

Aware of their plight, Randy shouted, "This is as good a time as any to get our feet back on land," so they got out and started carrying the canoe along the water's edge toward the dock. They hadn't traveled more than fifty feet when it was obvious the canoe was too heavy to carry while trying to avoid rocks. Their only choice was to beach it and return another time. Ruth took a cape from the canoe and walked alone along the shore to the lodge while Randy remained to secure the boat.

Mindful of the wind velocity, he used the rope to tie down the craft but instead of following Ruth along the beach, he made his way to the stream where he took the trail leading to Jacques' cabin and the lodge. About the same distance in a northern area, other boaters were experiencing a similar problem.

"This isn't the time to be out here," Ted remarked. "Let's quit fishing and head for the lodge."

Although their craft was more stable, its outboard motor began to sputter and soon stalled. Like the occupants in the canoe, they got out when it drifted to shore and carried it on land to avoid heavy damage by pounding waves.

In an area between the two fishing parties, Timothy and Dave were fly fishing, casting from the rocks.

When the wind gained strength Dave walked inland from the shore and fished the stream. He continued casting without even a nibble so he quit fishing and began walking to the trail leading to the lodge when the rain started.

Timothy, who was determined to catch a trout if he had to spend the remaining two hours before supper fishing and in spite of his earlier promise to stay in the lodge, gave up when the rain came. He followed the shore back to the lodge.

Heavy rain was falling when Timothy reached the dock and saw Dave coming from the lodge.

"You made better time than I did," Timothy remarked when they met on the beach. "Let's go inside where it's dry."

Timothy joined Ted and Linda at the table in the kitchen while Dave went into the living room to read. It wasn't long before the sound of thunder caught everyone's attention and Dave got up and looked out the porch door.

"A heavy rain squall is coming across the lake, he said. "Maybe I should find out what is happening to the others. They have been gone a long time and the storm is fast approaching. Perhaps I can be helpful," he added as he took a jacket from the rack and rushed outside.

Several minutes after Dave left to help the others, Ruth entered the kitchen soaking wet. She put the cape she had brought from the canoe on the clothes hanger and immediately went to her bedroom to change into dry clothes before returning to the kitchen.

She poured a cup of coffee and joined the others at the table.

"It's going to be an ugly night, " she remarked. "The rain is getting heavy."

"Where's Randy?" Timothy asked. "Dave left a few minutes ago looking for you. Did you see him?"

"No, but Randy is on his way," Ruth replied. "We were fishing until the lake got rough then we were forced to beach the canoe. I made my way back through the woods while he wanted to be certain that the boat was secure."

As the wind picked up, waves across the lake reached a height that Jacques had mentioned last night of nearly three feet. Thunderheads appeared overhead as clouds raced from the southwest. Gradually, the sky began to turn gray as the storm intensified. Flashes of lightning streaked across the distant sky followed by the rumbling of thunder.

Just as she was comfortable again, Ruth realized that she should make a trip outside before the rain became heavier. She went to her room and it took her awhile to find a something suitable to cover her head. She put a wide-brimmed hat on and threw the same wet cape from the rack over her shoulders. Before going out the kitchen door, she paused and shouted.

"Nature's calling. I've got to go. Be right back"

Four other vacationers who had abandoned their boat hurried through the dense woods to avoid lightning strikes and for the safety of the lodge. The storm was rapidly gaining momentum as it neared shore.

On the south side of the lodge less than a mile down the camp road and a short walk in the forest, Jacques was guiding Brett in a cedar thicket where wildlife often inhabited. Usually it was an excellent location to see deer and yet not too far from the lodge. Until now, the only signs of an approaching storm had been the rustling of tree branches and a cloudy sky.

When Jacques heard sounds of thunder, he discarded any thought of looking for animals or anything else except to get Brett back to the lodge.

"Something bad is coming," he told Brett. "We had better give up taking pictures and get back to camp before we get wet. This is going to be a big storm and it will take awhile to reach the lodge. I've got to finish fixing the roof on the lodge before the wind gets too strong."

"Do you think you'll have time to do it when we get back?" Brett asked.

"Probably, if I hurry," Jacques replied. "It isn't a big job. I only put tar to hold the roofing paper down and I was going to go back and nail some boards over it to make sure it stays. If not, the wind will probably blow everything away. I should do it now.

"Do you mind walking back alone?"

"Will I have any trouble finding my way, Jacques?"

"Oh, no, mon ami. It's not far to the camp road leading to the lodge where all of you came in. I'll be with you on this road and then I'll run to the lodge. I can go faster but you should get there before the heavy rain comes."

"All right, Jacques, let's get going."

They hurried to the road where Jacques left him and began running to the lodge. He thought he had time to do the job before the storm came, but he wanted to go to his cabin first to get his heavy rain coat and hat before he started working on the roof. It would take about fifteen minutes to go from the lodge to his camp and back.

Immediately after walking out of the woods to the camp road, Jacques started racing toward the lodge area. He was nearly fifty years old, but it didn't show as he moved like an athlete on the rough road.

He glanced at the lodge as he ran by and he was about fifty feet from his cabin when all hell broke loose. Daylight suddenly turned into darkness and gale force winds scattered black clouds across the sky unleashing torrential rains. Water covered his face before he entered his cabin. He quickly put on his rain gear and headed back. A flash of lightning lit the inside of the camp and Jacques noticed his .38 Special was not in its holster. He didn't have time to look for it now. He thought he must have put it somewhere out of sight because the door was always unlocked and there were strangers nearby.

His first step out of the cabin was in a deep puddle and water was everywhere as heavy rain fell all the way back to the lodge where he hoped Brett had reached by now. He didn't take time to look into the lodge but went directly to the workshop to get tools and wood strips. When he returned he realized it would be useless to try fixing anything now.

A thunderous roar shook the earth with flashes of light on the camp road and streaks of lightning in the sky. The collapsing of fallen trees sounded like gun shots as they cracked before hitting the earth. Another brilliant ray of light followed by a sharp clap of thunder and crashing trees indicating a bolt had struck again near the building. The storm frightened Jacques as he took the ladder back to the workshop and waited inside.

A few minutes later as he left the shop in a driving rain, he could barely make out someone with a rifle or shotgun moving slowly in the gloom on the far side of the lodge and another motionless figure nearer the building. A sudden blast of wind rained down small branches and leaves that flew in horizontally. The wind strengthened blowing rain in his face which stung like sleet as a flash of lightning lit the sky. Another gust of wind blew off his hat and he struggled to retrieve it as it got caught in an alder bush. He grabbed his hat and when he looked ahead again, the images had vanished. There was another blast of thunder and lightning. It hit somewhere very close as he heard the electrical snap and felt the influx of ozone. Frightened, he didn't think anything more about the person with the gun, if indeed, that is what he had seen. He was shaking from the close call with the lightning strike. He was scared of lightning so he hurried back to shelter from the workshop.

Jacques waited inside for awhile but the rain didn't letup so he ran to the lodge and rushed in the kitchen door soaking wet. He scanned the room looking for Brett but was surprised when he couldn't see him.

"Where's Brett?" he asked excitedly. "Did he go upstairs to change clothes? He must got very wet in storm."

"No, he's not here," Timothy answered. "Wasn't he supposed to be with you?"

"I left him on the camp road about two miles from here about a half hour ago. I returned to fix the roof, but when I got here the storm was so bad that I couldn't do anything. He couldn't get lost finding his way here as it is a straight road.

"I'm going up the road now and look for him," Jacques said. "Do you have a flashlight I can use, Timothy? It's as dark as night out there with those black clouds and much rain."

"He wouldn't get off the road and wait under tall trees in this storm, would he?" Ted asked. "Wouldn't that be dangerous?"

"I don't know. He might have tried to get under some smaller trees to keep away from the rain and lightning."

Ted said, I'll go with you," as Timothy handed Jacques a flashlight.

As he started for the door, Randy entered the lodge from the porch.

"Where are you going?" Randy asked the handyman. "It's rough out there."

"I'm going to look for Brett who should be here now. He must have got lost somehow."

"Wait a minute. I'll get a flashlight and go with you."

"There's no need for you to get wet too, "Timothy told Ted. "Why don't you stay here for now. If they can't find him, then we'll all go."

Ruth had returned from the outhouse and was in her room a few minutes before the remaining boaters came in the lodge from the front door. A little later, Dave entered by the kitchen door. He walked in front of Timothy and went to the fireplace and hung his wet jacket on the rack while Ted was kneeling on the hearth lighting a fire.

"Where are Jacques and Randy?" Alec asked. "This isn't a time to be outdoors. I hope everyone else is here," he said looking around the room.

"Brett hasn't returned and they are looking for him," Timothy explained. "The others are here."

After starting the fire, Ted began lighting lamps downstairs. The beans were ready after baking all day in the oven while supper only awaited Jacques's homemade biscuits. Everything seemed serene but a social evening was not forthcoming with one missing.

Timothy was concerned and worried about Brett's disappearance. It was possible he might have left the road and tried to find shelter in a cluster of cedar trees. However, it wasn't realistic that he could be missing almost an hour on a two-mile stretch of road that led directly to this lodge. There was the possibility of an accident, especially since several bolts of lightning struck nearby.

"Let's hold supper until Jacques and Randy return with Brett," Timothy said as they sat in the living room.

"We'll do better than that," Ted suggested. "If Brett doesn't return with them, I think the rest of us should pair off and join the search."

"All right," Timothy remarked. "We'll wait and see."

Outside, Randy and Jacques weren't enjoying the comforts prevailing in the lodge. The storm center had stalled while heavy wind and rain continued. The roar of thunder resounded throughout the wilderness and streaks of lightning raced across the sky.

Neither of them could see a foot ahead after leaving the kitchen toward the camp road that they knew was only a short distance ahead. As they were slowly trudging in mud already created by pouring rain, Randy tripped over a log and Jacques stumbled over him.

"What the hell," Jacques shouted. "These logs were not in the middle of this road when I came down an hour ago."

Then, they both realized bolts of lightning had hit the trees which had fallen across their path. This road was now impassable. They had to locate Brett who must be farther up the road so they flashed their lights trying to find a way around the huge limbs and branches. It was difficult to walk in darkness even with flashlights as rain blinded their vision. It took a few minutes to circumvent the downed trees and make their way back on the camp road. Getting back on the trail, Jacques flashed his light on the ground where he detected tire tracks.

"Randy," he shouted above the noise of the storm. "There are tire tracks in the mud that were made since the storm began. Someone drove down this road but went back when they saw trees blocking the way."

"Maybe Brett got a ride back to town with someone. To be certain, we'd better walk down the road to where I left him and. It's not far."

They walked down the road to the area where Jacques had last seen left Brett, flashing their lights on both sides of the road.

"Let's go back to the lodge," Randy said. " We haven't seen anything on the road. Maybe Brett could have been hurt by a falling tree. When we get back, we can get more help and search the area."

It was difficult finding their way through the downed trees to the lodge where they realized everyone was anxiously waiting word of Brett's whereabouts He was somewhere in this wilderness amidst a raging storm.

Trying to avoid tracking mud into the kitchen, they climbed the stairs to the porch where gale winds were driving rain through the screens. The couple removed their soggy shoes and placed them on the fireplace hearth to dry. No questions were asked as Alec brought a coat rack from the kitchen and placed it next to the fireplace so the men could also dry their coats.

Randy was first to break the silence.

"We don't have any good news. Jacques and I walked down the camp road where Jacques left Brett about two hours ago now. We flashed our lights on both sides of the road but there was nothing to see except water. There was plenty of that."

"There's more unpleasant news to report," he continued. "Two or possibly three tall trees were struck by lightning not far from here and the road is blocked. There's no way out except by foot until someone arrives to help us. When the storm slows down, we'll go out to the logging road for help at the warden's camp. Let's hope that someone is there."

"I'll go," Jacques volunteered immediately." I can leave right now."

"No, Jacques," Timothy responded. "You've done enough today. No one should leave tonight during this storm and besides it's too risky for a man to travel alone. When daylight comes, we'll make a decision. There's nothing that we can do now although we have a serious problem. Chances are that he's injured or he would have found his way back here before the worst of the storm struck."

"We can't stay in here doing nothing," Alec declared. "Ted, Dave and I will leave now and search the area where the trees are down and the rest can come out later."

"Why should we wait?" Ted exclaimed. "I'm going now."

"Me, I go too," Jacques said as he reached for his wet shoes. I'll see you out there," he continued walking out into the storm.

"We've got rain gear, too," Jan said as Linda and Ruth reached for their capes. "We aren't going to sit here and do nothing."

"Be careful when you walk among those trees," Timothy warned. "I'll be with you as soon as I find something suitable to wear."

Timothy went to his room after the last person left the lodge and found an old raincoat and a fishing hat among the items in his suitcase. He had loaned Jacques a flashlight but he still had a three-cell light he had brought with him to Middleton from New York. Under his cot he found a pair of sneakers, the only dry footwear he had. His shoes similar to the others were soaked. He walked to the kitchen with his sneakers and coat under his arm and sat on a chair near the door. While he was getting his sneakers on, Timothy realized no one had taken the beanpot from the oven since Jacques put it there early that morning.

He found a potholder and placed the beanpot on the stove shelf away from the heat. Before he left, he lifted the lid to get a whiff of the cooked beans. It was tempting not to eat some now but he didn't, thinking it would be unfair to the rest. As he walked by the fireplace to the porch, he suddenly stopped when he noticed the rifle above the fireplace was missing. Astonished, he returned and opened the box of ammunition to discover only two cartridges remained.

Dumbfounded, he wondered what happened to the Winchester. No one asked his permission to use it and he was responsible for the lodge. However, now wasn't the time to dwell on this problem when something more important required his attention. He dismissed thoughts of the rifle as he went outside to join in the search.

As Timothy approached the area where the trees had fallen, he counted faint beams from eight flashlights. An enormous task faced these searchers hindered by darkness and rain to grope through this pile of uprooted trees covered with a mass of broken limbs and branches. Instead of abating, the storm intensified as everyone struggled through the debris for anything that would offer a glimmer of hope.

Alec, who had taken charge of the search admitted to Timothy that it was useless to continue until daylight.

"Timothy," he said, "we're getting nowhere trying to find Brett in this nightmarish weather. Without the storm, we might stand a chance of finding him. That is, if he is under this rubble, but I must confess it's a waste of effort now. As much as I dislike to give up, let's return to the lodge."

"Disagree with you, I can't," Timothy responded. "Pass the word along to those nearest you and I'll tell the others on the other side of the road."

A somber group sat at the dining room table Sunday night. The beans were tasty but no comments were made about them or the lack of homemade biscuits. Jacques had worked hard enough today and he wasn't asked to do anymore. The joviality of last night's festivities was missing. In lieu of a toast that heralded the first evening's welcome ceremony, Timothy offered a prayer. Afterwards, they ate in silence.

When it was over and the table cleared, everyone except Jacques sat around the living room watching flickering embers in the fireplace. He went out on the porch to be alone while rain blanketed everything in darkness.

He was soon joined by Timothy who moved beside him and put a hand on his shoulder.

"Jacques, don't think bad of yourself. You are not responsible for Brett's fate. For all we know, he could have gone to the next town in the car that drove up to the roadblock. If we want to think the worst, he could have been struck by one of the falling trees and is trapped under the timbers. Whatever, Jacques, your fault, it's not."

"I feel bad, mon Pere. It's better I stayed with him."

There was nothing more Timothy could say to console him except to suggest he say a prayer.

Timothy left the woodsman alone on the porch and returned to the living room where it was quiet. He sat in a chair aware this wasn't the situation he had in mind when the trip was planned.

He closed his eyes wondering what could have happened to create a situation. Was Brett's disappearance due to an accident from a falling tree, or did he ride with someone in a vehicle that came close but was unable to get to the lodge? The first thought of an accident seemed more probable as Brett could have walked around the downed timbers to reach the lodge. There was enough light at that time to find his way. It wouldn't make sense to ride miles back when he was only a hundred yards from shelter. It was also possible that he might have taken injured and took refuge under trees somewhere along the two-mile stretch.

He speculated momentarily about the strangers in the area recalling Chief Davidson's remarks that a syndicate has long arms. This possibility appeared remote to Timothy as creditors would rather devise a way of collecting money than to eliminate its possible source. It was doubtful they would send a couple of men this far but he couldn't discard the theory as it depended on what Brett had promised them.

There was another problem to be cleared, Timothy thought.

Where's the rifle? Could it have been possible that whoever drove up during the storm might have stolen it? He hadn't given much thought about asking anyone about its disappearance until Ted raised the question. "Where's the rifle that was above the fireplace?" he asked as every eye in the room focused on the vacant spot. "I'm sure it was there this morning when Linda and I were here."

"Do any of you have an idea where it could be?" Timothy inquired.

No one in the room had an answer to his question so Timothy dropped the subject. Only time and events would resolve this mystery, he thought.

Timothy looked up as Jacques returned from outside and went to the stove where a pot of coffee was brewing. He poured a cup and walked into the living room where he sat on the floor.

After awhile, he looked at Timothy and said.

"I wish I could do something. Not just sit here."

"Jacques, there's nothing any of us can do until the storm passes by and the sky lightens," Timothy said. "Wait, we must."

And so they did. Occasionally, someone would rise from their seat and look through a window or walk out on the porch anxiously awaiting a change in weather. Nothing was mentioned about going to bed.

It was a different sound that awoke Ted, actually the absence of it. He moved his arm to look at his watch, unintentionally awakening Linda who had been sleeping with her head on his shoulder while they sat on a sofa.

Drowsy, she asked. "What's the matter? Is there something wrong?"

"No, honey," he answered. "All of a sudden it seems quiet. I think it stopped raining. I'm going to see what it looks like outside."

He reached for his flashlight and looked at his watch. It was 1:30.

They walked quietly to the porch door without disturbing the others who were asleep on sofas and chairs. Jacques was snoring on the rug-covered floor where he had been for the past four hours.

They closed the door quietly and stepped on the porch where a whole different world greeted them. Rain had ceased and the sky was clearing with some stars appearing between moving clouds as the wind subsided changing direction to the northwest. The only sounds now were waves pounding the shore.

"The worst of the storm is over." Linda exclaimed excitedly. "Now we can resume our search for Brett."

"Let's go," Ted responded as both hurried into the lodge shouting.

"Wake up, everyone! The sky has cleared and we can go out and look for Brett."

Within a few minutes, they had flashlights and were heading for the door only to be interrupted by Alec with a few words of advice.

"We have a good chance of locating Brett if he is under the pile of debris. However, let's work in pairs and look carefully under the tree limbs and leaves. I'll mark off sections and we'll complete a search in one area before moving on to another. There are about three hours remaining before daylight."

"Remember if you lift a limb or branch don't let it fall until you're sure nothing is under it. We'll be working close together so if you see anything, just holler.

"Now, let's get to work," he concluded and the lodge became vacant again.

It wasn't easy moving limbs and branches trying to see what lay beneath the heap. The center of the large mass of rubble was at least twenty feet high and some of the edges were also high. At least three large trees were destroyed when lightning hit and gale force winds toppled the timbers to the earth.

They worked feverishly for more than an hour trying to get close enough to see what rested under the maze of wood. However, their view was limited by the entangled debris and it was only possible to see a few feet ahead.

Jan's partner was Alec during this search and they were covering an area along the perimeter nearer the lodge. Several yards behind, she stepped carefully over the limb of a pine and was pushing a branch out of the way when the beam of her flashlight revealed a shoe.

Anxious, but apprehensive, she moved several feet closer when her flashlight shone directly on a distorted face with eyes staring upward at her.

Chapter 15

"Oh, my God," Jan screamed hysterically, shattering the predawn calmness when she saw a grotesque face. Alec moved quickly through the brush to console her while she continued crying.

Within minutes, all nine members of the rescue team converged on the site where a lifeless body was lying. As Alec tried to calm an emotional and shaking Jan, Ted dug under the brush and reached over as he focused his flashlight on the victim.

He looked carefully at the scarred face with a mustache covered with blood and knew instantly it was Brett in spite of the deformity. Although convinced he was dead, Ted placed his finger on the carotid artery in his neck to be positive.

They all walked away from the scene to the lodge when Timothy asked Jacques if he could find something to cover the victim.

"Oui, Oui, Timothy. I'll get a blanket and come right back."

Then Timothy turned to Ted.

"Ted, would you go with Jacques to the warden's camp on the logging road and tell them what has happened?" he asked. "We can't move the body even if we were capable until a medical examiner arrives. A rescue crew will have to clear the area before anything can be done."

"Sure, Timothy," he replied. "We'll leave when Jacques returns."

In a few minutes Jacques was back and covered Brett with a blanket.

"Jacques," Timothy said. "Ted will go with you to the warden's camp when you are ready."

"I'm going to my cabin first, Timothy," Jacques answered. "I've got to put on dry shoes. It could be a long hike. If there's no one at the warden's camp, we'll have to walk back to the camp road and all the way to Ripogenus."

"That would take awhile," Ted responded. "If other trees are downed along the way, they will have to be removed. This means we would have to walk miles to a telephone."

"In that case," Timothy said, "when officials are told, they'll be flown here by plane from Greenville."

Jacques was tired after twelve busy hours and he knew it was going to be a long day so he didn't hurry as he made his way to the cabin. Storm clouds had vanished leaving the sky filled with glittering stars as Jacques neared his camp. He pulled the improvised lock from the door bolt and moved slowly in the darkness to light the lantern. He found boots suitable for the anticipated tough hike. The holster was empty so he began looking around and trying to remember where he had left the revolver.

The more he thought, he was convinced that he didn't hide the weapon. Someone must have taken it from his cabin. On the other hand, there were no other people nearby except the two men camped on the other side of the lake. But he didn't believe that they would cross the lake to fish this stream. Jacques wondered who stole it. Yesterday, three vacationers were here but he felt that Timothy wouldn't bring anyone to the lodge who wasn't honest. Hoping the priest would have an answer, he hurried back to the lodge.

The aroma of freshly brewed coffee greeted him when came in the kitchen. Timothy, Randy, and Ted were sitting at the table while the others were catnapping in the living room.

"Sit and take a load off your feet, Jacques. I'll pour you a cup of coffee," Randy said, getting up from his seat and walking to the stove. "You must be exhausted after all you have done. And there are still many miles to go."

"Why don't both of you take a short nap before leaving," Timothy said, addressing Jacques and Ted. "It will be daylight soon and much easier traveling. I hope you'll find someone at the warden's camp. If not, you've got a long walk by the time you retrace your steps on the logging road and continue to Ripogenus. It would take most of the day."

"We'll wait until daylight but no longer," Ted answered. "I don't want Brett's body lying under that debris another day."

"I know how all of you feel but I hope you will try to continue with your activities. Ted continued. "Try not to let this misfortune ruin your entire vacation. There's nothing more we can do for Brett. Remember, you came here for a vacation so make the most of it. The weather is good now and maybe the fish will begin to bite."

"We'll do our best," Randy remarked.

Jacques finished his coffee and he asked Timothy to come outside.

Timothy followed him out of the kitchen and he had hardly closed the door when Jacques began talking excitedly.

"Someone took my revolver from the cabin," he alleged. "I know it was there yesterday morning but it's not in my holster now. I can't think of anyone who would do it."

"Jacques, are you sure you didn't leave it somewhere else?" Timothy asked.

"No, no, Timothy. I haven't taken the gun from my cabin since I've been here. I'm sure it was there yesterday when your friends visited my place. Maybe it is better you ask them if they saw it."

"Right you are, Jacques. Let's go inside."

"Sorry to bother you," Timothy announced when he walked into the living room. "However, we have another problem. Apparently, we have a gun collector in this area or a thief. I hope it's no one among us. You know the rifle belonging to my friend is missing and Jacques told me a .38 Caliber revolver is missing from his cabin," Timothy said. "He knows someone took it. Yesterday, three of you went with Jacques to his cabin. Did any of you see the gun?"

Ruth was the first to respond. "There was a weapon in a holster hanging from the post at the foot of the bed with a gun in it. I don't know the make, but it was a revolver."

Looking at Dave and Randy, Timothy inquired.

"Did either of you see it ?"

"I saw a holster but didn't notice any weapon in it," Randy replied while Dave said he was more interested in Jacques's stove pipe and chimney.

"Guess I was more concerned how he kept his cabin from burning up than any other fixtures," Dave remarked.

"Apparently, the weapon was in the camp yesterday," Timothy concluded.

"Now, it's to find who took it. It's weird. We have a mystery of two missing guns to resolve."

Continuing, Timothy added. "It doesn't seem probable that someone in the car that turned last night during the storm had earlier in the day entered the lodge, taken the rifle, and then walked a quarter of a mile to Jacques's cabin to take his revolver. I can't believe that would happen. There has to be another explanation. There's nothing we can do until we learn more about the mysterious vehicle and that won't happen until state and county officials get here," Timothy said. "We can only wait."

Ted and Jacques left the kitchen and walked to the dock where they watched the sun rise over the lake before heading for the warden's camp They had to avoid downed trees that were blocking the camp road

185

and make their way around the debris while trying to hasten to the logging road three miles away.

Trees were down on many sections of the muddy road. The only vehicles able to pass now must have a four-wheel drive. If anyone attempted to reach the lodge from the outside they would have to be preceded by crews with chain saws and no vehicle would be able to leave the lodge until the road was dry.

That might require a couple of days and the vacationers would have to remain here.

While they hurried, a thought occurred to Ted.

"I don't understand why you don't have a chain saw," Ted said. "You certainly can't cut all the wood for the stove and fireplace with a hand saw. Also, there must be many trees felled by wind during the year. How do you manage this?"

"Yes, there is a chain saw but Monsieur Barker took it to Millinocket last week to have it fixed. I couldn't get it started."

"That's too bad," Ted replied. "We could have cut the tree limbs, but, of course, we still couldn't have moved the victim."

It was a tiring trek but finally they reached the logging road and turned east to the warden's camp. Only a couple of big trees had been downed thus far.

Their spirits lifted when a World War II surplus weapons carrier vehicle was sighted parked next to a camp built by Maine Inland Fish and Game Wardens. Help was near.

Ted knocked on the door and a couple of minutes later, Warden Tom Hillman greeted him. "It's early in the day to welcome guests but come in. I see that you have Jacques with you, Ted.

"It must be something important to bring you out here after that storm. It must have been a rough walk over the logging road. I'm sure there were many overturned trees. I haven't seen a storm as bad in all my years of warden service. Now, what can I do for you?"

"A man has been killed by a falling tree at the lodge. His body is still under the debris."

"Come in," the warden said. "I'll go with you. It will only take me a few minutes to get ready. In the meanwhile, I'll wake up my friend and advise him what's happening. He's a doctor from Bangor and we've been fishing for a few days.

"Bernard," he said as he walked into a bedroom. "There's been an accident at the lodge and I've got to leave."

In a few minutes, a silver-haired man came to the kitchen and introduced himself.

"I'm Dr. Bernard Williams. Tom has been teaching me how not to catch fish the past few days," he laughed. "You said there's been an accident. Is there anything I can do?"

"I'm afraid not, Doctor," Ted replied. "A falling tree killed a man at the lodge."

"Ted Graves is my name, and I'm a reporter with the Middleton Guardian. Along with eight friends, we've been staying at the lodge since Saturday. Oh I'm sorry, I forgot to introduce my companion, Jacques."

"That's all right. I met him the other day at Bear Lake," as the physician nodded to Jacques.

"Can we drive down the logging road?" Tom asked.

"Only, if you have a chain saw," Ted responded. "There are a couple of big trees across this section of the road, and I'm sure more pines are down on the way to Ripogenus Dam."

"It's a mess with many limbs and branches covering the camp road where the victim is trapped. We're going to need help before a medical examiner can get to him."

"No problem," the warden said. "I have a chain saw and we'll take a can of gasoline with us. There's plenty of room in the weapons carrier for another person if you wish to come along, Bernard. Your medical services may be useful before we get back. We have to go to the village first to make a phone call to get a crew to clear the camp road."

"I'll go with you," Dr. Williams said.

"Before we do anything," Tom remarked, "I'm going to make a pot of coffee and fry some bacon and eggs. It's going to be a hard day and we had better get started on a full stomach. However," he added, "we'll make this a quick breakfast."

"I'll do the cooking," Jacques offered, "if you make the coffee, Tom."

"And, I'll set the table," Ted said.

Soon, the tempting aroma of bacon sizzling in a large iron skillet and freshly brewed coffee filled the air while Jacques began frying eggs in another pan.

"Now, I have to do something to earn my keep," Dr. Williams remarked. "When the food is ready, all of you sit at the table and I'll do the serving."

When they were eating, the physician inquired about the accident.

"I assume the victim was a member of your party. Was he a Middleton resident?"

"Yes to both questions," Ted answered. "He was a photographer who operated a studio downtown. He came to the city about ten years ago."

"You said he was killed by a falling tree," Dr. Williams added. "It had to be during the height of the storm and he must have been alone when it happened. Where were the rest of you at that time?"

"Some of us were in the lodge while others were on their way to it when a series of lightning bolts hit near the building," Ted replied. "Brett, the victim, was coming down the camp road while the rest of us were returning from the lake in front of the lodge.

"With exception of he and Jacques, everyone had been fishing," Ted continued. "Jacques was accompanying him on a photo taking venture and left him on the road to the lodge while he rushed ahead to finish repairs on its roof. You'll hear more about the incident when we get to the lodge," Ted said. "Now, without being rude, we had better hurry our breakfast and get on our way. We don't know how long it will take to get to Ripogenus."

"When everyone is finished eating, put your dishes in the sink. I'll wash them when I return," Tom remarked.

It took more than an hour to reach the camp road after clearing debris along the way. There was still a long stretch of road which would be blocked at intervals until they reached Ripogenus.

There was an advantage traveling now as the closer they came to their destination, the road became wider so the carrier was able to bypass some of the fallen limbs.

However, they had to utilize the chain saw eight more times before reaching a clear road taking them to Ripogenus where they found a telephone.

Tom Hillman didn't lose time in getting out of the vehicle but it took fifteen minutes running from house to house in this little neighborhood before he found a place with a telephone wire leading to it and someone who was at home.

Finally, after he had knocked several times on the front door of a house, an elderly man opened it who quickly recognized the warden's uniform.

"Morning, warden. What can I do for you?" he asked.

"I have an emergency, I believe that you have a phone. May I use it to call Greenville and I'll pay for the charges."

"No need to do that. You're more than welcome. Come in. The phone is in the kitchen, right through the living room."

Tom made his way to the kitchen and he turned the crank several times on an antique wall telephone before hearing the voice of an operator in Greenville.

"Operator, this is an emergency. I'm Warden Tom Hillman and I've got to reach Warden George Fox in Greenville. Will you please try his home and see if he is there or where we can find him?"

"Hold onto the line," the operator said. "I'll see what I can do."

A few minutes later, she responded.

"I have Warden Fox on the line. Go ahead."

"George, this is Tom at Ripogenus. A man has been killed by a fallen tree at the lodge near Bear Lake. Will you get in touch with Deputy Frank Gray and Medical Examiner Dr. Fred Pingree and fly out to Bear Lake with them? In the meantime, I'll try to get a crew from Kokadjo to drive to the lodge where the victim is still trapped under trees."

"I'll get right on it," the warden replied. "We'll be there later this afternoon."

After Tom finished this message, he called Dan Metcalf, owner of a sporting lodge at Kokadjo, and explained the problem.

"I'll round up a crew," Dan replied. "We'll be on our way to the lake as soon as we can."

After he hung up the phone, Tom offered to pay for the toll charges and he quickly explained that someone had been killed by a fallen tree. The man refused any money and didn't ask any questions.

Tom returned to the carrier and they headed back to the camp road.

Back at the lodge, although it was early on this Monday morning, Timothy was trying to decide what tonight's menu would include. No one expressed a desire for fish today so it wouldn't be included in the evening meal. However, he wanted another opinion.

He walked outside where everyone were sitting on the porch.

"For supper, what will it be?" he asked Jan. "A flair for tasty food, you have."

"I've lost my appetite for anything special, Timothy. However, life must go on and we have to eat. We brought some beef so why not cook a New England pot roast with brown potatoes. How does that sound?"

"Sounds super to me," Linda replied. We can top it off with the rest of Harry's delicious pies."

"Pot roast, it will be," Timothy remarked. "We must also get food ready for Jacques and Ted and whoever comes with them. They probably won't arrive until one or two o'clock but no doubt they will be hungry.

"How about warming up the baked beans and serve them with red hot dogs," Linda suggested.

"You hit the nail right on the head," Timothy answered. "We'll start cooking the moment they arrive. At the same time, we must remember to put the pot roast in the oven so that it will be ready for supper. There are five or six hours remaining before anyone comes so why don't you go boating or swimming? It will be better than just hanging around."

"I won't forget the pot roast and potatoes later. Before we do anything, Jan, let's clear the kitchen table and clean the lodge," Linda said.

"We can all help," Alec added as they all went into the lodge except Timothy who stayed on the porch.

While they were working in the lodge, Linda suggested to Jan, "Let's go canoeing. The lake is calm this morning but we'll stay close to the shore, regardless."

"A good idea, Linda. I'll meet you at the dock after we finish here."

Talking to the group, Alec said, "There's only one outboard motor operating but the rest of us could take a ride around the lake in the other one. The other motor conked out yesterday when the storm broke out. We'll have to help Jacques get it back to the dock when he returns."

Linda and Jan were first to the lake and it didn't take long to get the canoe in the water. Jan sat in the bow while Linda gave it a shove and stepped aboard as it moved from shore.

It was a beautiful day with occasional ripples on the water and a few puffy cumulus clouds aloft. The morning stillness was only disturbed by loons as their lonely calls continued to echo over the lake.

It was peaceful as the couple quietly dipped their paddles in the water and they remained silent as the canoe glided away from the shore. Undoubtedly, both were harboring the same thoughts of a companion lying under a mass of trees.

Jan was first to speak.

"Linda, the sight of Brett's grotesque face is still in my mind. It was so awful."

"I know you must be going through a lot, Jan. It must have really been a shock. All of us were eager to join the search but none was psychologically prepared for what we found."

Until now, little had been said about the tragedy although Jan believed it was strange that one of ten would die as result of a bolt of lightning.

"I was led to believe the odds were one in millions," she remarked. And it's unbelievable that a person in the midst of hundreds of trees would be killed by one of them."

"I agree with you, Jan," Linda said. "It's incredible that lightning was the cause of his death."

However, no other explanation was offered by anyone. They appeared satisfied that he was a victim of the storm. Regardless of some differences of opinion about Brett, he was a popular figure at their parties. It was difficult to erase these memories but they knew that the final leg of this journey would end in a Middleton cemetery.

"I don't know what's on your mind," she continued. "But I've lost interest in continuing this vacation. I suspect Timothy will have something to say to us tonight. He may suggest we return to Middleton early," Linda concluded.

A similar conversation was taking place in the other boat where four vacationers were trying to stop thinking about last night's event. However, unlike the canoeists and others on shore, analysis of the victim who had invaded the lives of these people differed although no specific mention was made of it. Alec was handling the outboard motor from the stern with Dave seated in front of him. Randy had his arm around Ruth's shoulders as they sat near the center of the craft.

"Chances are we will be leaving the area tomorrow or the following day," Alec remarked. "I have a feeling Timothy will want to return to Middleton and I agree with him. With Brett's death, this outing has ended."

Ruth and Randy hardly said a word as they sat looking over the lake. They couldn't hear the conversation of Alec and Dave over the sound of the outboard motor but their thoughts dwelled on returning to Middleton.

"Do you think we will be going home soon?" Ruth asked.

"I don't know, Ruth, but I'm sure everyone would like to get away from here now. This tragedy has overshadowed what we thought was going to be a pleasant outing," Randy responded. "Timothy's probably pondering over a decision and he'll have something to say when we get together again."

Dave listened to the conversations but he made no comment.

However, sitting alone back at the lodge, Timothy was wondering what could have created this situation. The cause of Brett's accident seemed unanswerable as his thoughts coincided with Jan's, that the odds of lightning causing the fatality were slim.

Another puzzle he considered was the disappearance of two weapons. Could there possibly be a relationship between these incidents? But guns weren't responsible for the falling trees. He would like to solve the mystery of the missing rifle and revolver before leaving. When they gathered for supper tonight, he planned to suggest that everyone get ready to go home. There was nothing he could do except wait for Ted and Jacques to return with help as he sat listening to the boat's motor as they cruised along the shore of the lake.

Ted was eager to get back to Bear Lake but not anxious to view the pile of fallen trees as the weapons carrier made its way back to the lodge over the rough road. The four occupants got out of the vehicle walking carefully around the downed pines while Ted avoided looking where Brett was pinned.

They entered the kitchen where Timothy had heard the sound of their approaching vehicle and was standing in front of the stove frying frankfurters while Jan and Linda were setting the table. Alec reached for Timothy's fork and took over the cooking allowing Timothy an opportunity to meet the newcomers.

"Tom," he greeted the uniformed warden, "nice to see you again. I wish it could have been under more pleasant circumstances."

"I'm sorry to hear of the tragic death of your friend," the warden responded. "I have a crew coming from Kokadjo to remove the trees and extricate the victim. Unfortunately, you will be unable to leave for at least a couple of days because the rain has made the road impassable.

"I'd like you to meet my friend, Dr. Bernard Williams, who has been trying to catch togue the past few days."

"It's a pleasure, Dr. Williams," Timothy replied. I believe Dr. Pingree has told me about you and your angling habits."

"I enjoy meeting you, Timothy. Apparently you have been in this area before if you know Fred Pingree," the doctor said.

"We met in Dover-Foxcroft when I attended a police association meeting with J.T., a friend from New York City. I've been a fishing and hunting guest at this lodge for a couple of years and I've met numerous county officials."

"You'll have another opportunity of meeting Dr. Pingree within a few hours," the warden remarked. "He'll be flying in with Deputy Frank Gray and a fellow warden, George Fox. Dr. Pingree will examine the victim before having the body transported to Greenville where he will perform an autopsy at Dean Memorial Hospital."

Alec interrupted the conversation by announcing that food was on the table.

"Tom, you met some of the folks here last year. Ruth was here but the other two ladies are strangers to this place. Say hello to Linda and Jan, and to Dave, who is also a newcomer."

"A pleasure to meet all of you," Tom replied.

There was little conversation as the men devoured a hearty meal keeping Linda busy filling cups of coffee while Jan remembered the pot roast and placed it in the oven for tonight's supper.

When they finished, they all knew what had to be done as they left the table and went outside. "We must be careful not to disturb the body," Dr. Williams said as Tom took the chain saw out of the carrier. "However, you can remove tree limbs and branches near the victim so I can get a better look."

The warden, with Jacques' assistance began cutting small sections of the tree around Brett until they had cleared a path large enough to let the physician get close to view the wounds. Dr. Williams removed the blanket and looked carefully at the victim's skull. Then, his eyes focused on the chest area on the bloodstained shirt. He unbuttoned the shirt and saw a hole leading to the heart. He closed the soiled garment and stood up, slowly moving away from the scene.

"There's nothing any of us can do here," he asserted. "Let's return inside until officials arrive."

As the men headed for the lodge, Dr. Williams walked behind the others with Warden Hillsman.

"I have something to tell you unofficially, Tom. A tree limb hit the victim on the head but there is also a gunshot wound in the chest. However, I don't know what caused his death. That decision remains with the medical examiner. Please remember this information is confidential."

"I'll keep it that way," Tom acknowledged.

Timothy kept away from workers when they were cutting branches but moved nearer when Dr. Williams was taking a painstaking look at the body.

He observed the doctor as he concentrated on a wound under Brett's shirt. Now, he suspected that something unexpected was the cause of death. However, this wasn't the time to ask questions. He would wait until his friend, Dr. Pingree, arrived and issued his report.

When this group entered the kitchen, the women were clearing the table so they continued to the porch while waiting for the plane.

An hour later, the drone of an aircraft engine was heard as it approached the lake and circled for a landing on the water. Tom walked ahead to the shore where they watched as it taxied to the dock. The pilot got out and stepped down on a float. He tossed a rope to the warden who tied it to a post on the dock.

Dr. Williams greeted the medical examiner as exited the plane, followed by Deputy Sheriff Frank Gray and Warden George Fox.

"What do we have?" Dr. Pingree asked Tom after the aircraft was secured.

It was Dr. Williams who responded to the question.

"Fred, I think you had better look at the victim. It's going to require a much closer examination before the exact cause of death is determined."

As they moved from the dock, Dr. Pingree saw Timothy and extended his hand.

"It's always a pleasure to see you, Timothy. Unfortunately, your fishing trip has been interrupted by tragedy. I hope we can resolve this situation quickly so you can return to your homes."

"I'm happy to see you again, Dr. Pingree," Timothy replied. "We don't meet often enough. As for returning home soon, there's another problem confronting us. The road out is impassable and it may remain in that condition for at least a couple of days."

Deputy Gray came forward and shook Timothy's hand.

"Great to see you, Timothy. The sheriff said to remember him to you and hopes he'll see you when hunting season opens next fall."

"The future, no one knows," Timothy replied, "But my plans include serving tender venison liver next fall if someone gets a deer."

"Is the victim someone who accompanied you here on fishing and hunting jaunts in the past?" Dr. Pingree asked as the group walked to the accident scene.

"Yes," Timothy responded. "He's been along on every trip. I knew him when I was in New York City and he came to Middleton before I did and opened a photography studio. I don't believe any of you knew him."

When they reached the area near the lodge where the three cars were parked, a pickup truck with a set of chains on its rear wheels had pulled up at the opposite side of the road blockade. A four-man crew from Kokadjo with chain saws, axes, and cant-dogs left the truck and began cutting the fallen trees.

Dr. Pingree walked carefully as he advanced to the victim. Kneeling, he examined the body beginning at the head. When he reached the chest area, he opened the shirt where the upper left section of the body was covered with blood. He looked at the area carefully then got to his feet and signaled to Deputy Gray.

"Frank, instruct the men to clear this area first so we can remove the body. We must take the victim back to Greenville to perform an autopsy. Also, deputy, I believe it will be your responsibility to advise everyone in the fishing party they cannot leave the area until our investigation is finished," he asserted. "This must include Jacques if he has been around during the period," he added.

"I don't understand, Dr. Pingree. How can I keep everyone here if the man was killed by a fallen tree," the deputy questioned.

"Frank, this wasn't an accident. The victim has gunshot wounds. I don't know if the shots or the tree caused death but it doesn't matter. There must be an investigation to determine who fired them. Obviously, no one shoots at a dead body so there has to be a motive."

Walking back to where Timothy was standing, Deputy Gray asked, "Timothy, will you please get your party and Jacques together in the lodge. I have something important to tell them."

"Certainly, Frank," Timothy answered.

Addressing his group, Timothy asked, "Will all of you come into the lodge? Deputy Gray has a statement to make. You're also included, Jacques."

They went into the lodge living room as the deputy and Dr. Pingree followed and closed the door.

"I have more unpleasant news," Gray declared. "Dr. Pingree has made a preliminary examination of your fishing companion and he believes the man also sustained gunshot wounds."

The silence was deafening when the deputy ceased talking momentarily to catch his breath. Only two persons weren't surprised. Timothy and the murderer.

"None of you could leave here anyway except by foot," the deputy continued. "Regardless, until the investigation is completed, you must remain in the area. Don't let me frighten you. We don't plan on keeping you here the rest of the summer. Some evidence will soon come to light as the investigation continues which, should eliminate most of you from suspicion. There's someone among you who has been involved in many police investigations and he could be of assistance to me. I'm referring to Timothy and I hope he will help us in solving this crime. How about it, Timothy?"

If I can be of assistance, an honor it will be, Frank."

"I would like to add something to this announcement, Frank," Dr. Pingree interjected. "This death is unusual as it is possible the victim died by a fallen tree and not by gunshots. However, we won't know the answer until late tonight. Warden Fox and I will be returning to Greenville with the body. I assume you'll be remaining here."

"Yes, I'll stay. Please relay word of the cause of death as soon as possible, Dr. Pingree."

"Warden Fox will return with the results tomorrow," Dr. Pingree replied.

"Regardless of what was the cause of death, he will be accompanied by other deputies and wardens who will assist with the investigation, particularly trying to locate the weapon," the medical examiner said as he left for the plane. In a few minutes, the pilot set his compass toward Greenville and the plane disappeared in the sky with its passengers and cargo.

"I hope you don't mind putting up with me during the days, Timothy," Frank said.

"At night I'll stay at the warden's camp with the other officers and Dr. Williams now that the roads are clear or should be before the afternoon is over. Other officials will drive in from Greenville and Dover-Foxcroft."

"Frank, you're welcome to stay and eat with us," Timothy replied. "We would enjoy your company. Under other circumstances, we could do some fishing together but it seems we have our work cut out for us."

"Thanks, Timothy. We aren't going to take advantage of you. The wardens will bring supplies and do the cooking. Why don't we examine the area outside where it is being cleared," Frank said. "I doubt if there is any evidence remaining after the storm but we can't risk overlooking anything." "I'll join you in a few minutes," Timothy replied. Jan and Linda came outside to talk with Timothy when the men were walking to the rear of the building. "Timothy", Jan said, "Linda and I haven't forgotten about supper. We'll take care of everything tonight. You have enough on your hands to do and besides we have plenty of help. The rest are sitting around and we can put them to work peeling spuds and doing other kitchen chores. I would like to try my luck cooking on an iron stove."

Timothy was interrupted before he reached the site. This time it was by Jacques. It was obvious the lodge handyman was nervous and wanted to get something off his mind.

"You seem to have a problem, my friend," Timothy remarked.

"Timothy, I'm much worried about my missing gun since the police say someone shot the man who was with me before the storm. They may think I did it, but I did not. Someone took my gun."

"Don't worry, Jacques, until there's something to be concerned about," Timothy responded. "No one has accused you and there's no proof yet that the gunshot wound was made by your revolver."

"What's that all about, Timothy?" Deputy Gray asked.

"Jacques told me yesterday someone had taken a revolver from his cabin Monday so naturally he's worried," Timothy said. "I questioned three persons who were with him Sunday morning at his cabin and Ruth admitted she saw the weapon in a holster. The men said they didn't see it. That's all I know at this time."

"Before we become too concerned, it's better to wait until we have the autopsy report," the deputy said. "Then, we'll learn if the victim was shot with the revolver."

"Relax, Jacques," Timothy added. "We'll learn the truth soon."

When Timothy and Frank reached the disaster area, men were still working cutting trees in four foot lengths and piling them on the side of the road. They began the search at the cleared site where the body was found. If there were any small objects on the ground, they wouldn't be seen as the area was covered with chips and sawdust. Timothy was aware of the two missing weapons and either could be hidden in the rubble. A wider search with more help was necessary and it would be better to wait until morning when more officials arrived, he believed.

"It's been a long day for everyone," Timothy said. I'm going to the lodge until supper, Frank. You can do whatever you wish and join us at the table tonight."

"I'm going to look around more," the deputy answered.

"Oh, before I leave, I want to say something to the men from Kokadjo," Timothy remarked as he walked to the area where they were working.

"Hold on a minute, gentlemen," Timothy said. "After you're finished, you may have supper with us."

"Thanks for the offer," one of the men replied. "But we must get home before nightfall."

"Sorry to hear that," Timothy answered. "But if you can spare a few minutes, we have plenty of cold ale. Do you think you can find time to enjoy some? "

"Thanks. We'll be there in less than an hour," was the reply.

Timothy returned to the lodge while Frank Gray walked from the scene and casually strolled about the grounds looking for anything unusual.

Entering the shop, Frank opened the doors to a cabinet where some small tools were kept, and after he inspected them carefully, he moved to the other end of the room pulling out drawers containing tools. Before leaving the building, he looked at the walls and even at the ceiling to be certain he hadn't overlooked anything. Leaving this structure, he walked another fifty feet to a larger building where the lodge firewood was kept.

As in the toolshed, everything was orderly with logs and stove wood stacked in neat rows. He stepped to the rear of a higher pile of logs and saw nothing. But, while moving away, he caught sight of a metal object partially covered by a burlap bag. He returned and removed the cloth bag that concealed a shiny revolver.

Chapter 16

Someone had left Jacques' missing .38 Caliber Special handgun practically in plain sight on the floor.

During his twenty years as a law enforcement officer, Frank never ceased to be surprised by the almost effortless discovery of stolen property. However, he had also learned that even with the discovery of evidence, persons responsible for the theft were not that easy to find. Nevertheless, this unfolding was astonishing. He hardly anticipated such a swift breakthrough in the search for evidence vital to a solution.

He had participated in too many crime investigations during those past two decades not to realize this discovery was admittedly too easy. In his opinion, whoever left the weapon wanted it to be found quickly for reasons he couldn't understand. Something didn't seem right and he thought a chat with Timothy might be helpful.

Although he doubted any fingerprints would be found on the weapon, it still had to be handled carefully to prevent any smudges. He had to take it to a secure place until other deputies arrived in the morning. Frank wrapped his hand with a handkerchief and picked up the weapon near the end of its barrel. Cautiously, he lifted the gun and smelled the barrel. He didn't detect any powder odor so he assumed it hadn't been fired recently. To prevent anyone from becoming aware of his finding, he covered the revolver with a cloth he found in the tool cabinet and slid the gun inside his shirt. Then, he walked outside where Warden Hillsman was helping with the cleanup.

"Tom," he shouted, "would you come here a minute, please?"

The warden dropped a limb he was carrying and walked over to him.

"What's on your mind, Frank? Or what's in your shirt, I should ask?" as he saw the position of one of the deputy's hands.

"There are some things about this accident which you don't know. I can't explain now but I'll tell you more when we return to your camp tonight where I hope I can spend the night."

"You're more than welcome," Tom responded. "What's your

problem now?"

"I discovered a revolver in the woodshed that someone reported stolen this morning. Do you have a place in your vehicle where we can lock it up until we get to your camp? We can't afford to lose this evidence."

"I have a metal storage box with a lock attached to the floor of my vehicle where I keep records. Come, we'll store it there and tonight we'll take it inside."

The warden unlocked the container and Frank placed the wrapped gun inside.

"Thanks, Tom. I'll see you later at supper. Dr. Williams has also been invited. I want to report this finding to Timothy and I have other details to talk about. I think there's more to this accident than just a fallen tree. You'll be told as time goes on."

Timothy was resting on a sofa with his eyes partially closed. When he heard footsteps on the porch, he looked up as Frank opened the door.

"I thought you were going to inspect the area," Timothy remarked. "It didn't take you long or did you decide to do it later? "

Timothy, I found a .38 Special revolver in the woodshed which I guess is the same weapon Jacques reported missing this morning. I can't understand it. Whoever left it," he continued, "wasn't particularly concerned about anyone finding it because the weapon was partially covered with a burlap bag and left behind a wood pile. Tom has locked it in his vehicle."

"Well," Timothy replied, "that solves half of the weapon mystery. Now we have to locate the rifle."

"I don't understand what you are saying when you admitted half of the problem is solved. What rifle? Was there another gun missing?"

"Sorry, Frank, I owe you an apology," Timothy replied.

"During the confusion, I forgot to mention the rifle, a 38-55 Winchester belonging to the lodge owner. It was taken from the wall above the fireplace sometime yesterday. Everyone in our group was aware of its disappearance. It was a good weapon but its use here was mostly decorative.

"Regardless, we must wait until the autopsy report to determine what caused Brett's death," Timothy continued. "Of course, we must find the other weapon. They will have to be taken to the Maine State Police Laboratory at Augusta. I'm sorry you weren't told sooner."

"It really doesn't matter," Frank said. "When the officers arrive in the morning we'll hold a briefing and lay out a search pattern for the rifle and any other clues. Timothy, do you have other knowledge that might cast light on this shooting?"

"If this is a homicide investigation and it appears we're heading in that direction, it's my opinion there are several incidents that occurred before we arrived here which will come into play," Timothy responded. "We have facts and some unsubstantiated information to be examined involving several in our group.

"Also, a couple of persons who left here last night before the storm shut off the camp road must be questioned. It is also my belief, Frank, Ted should be sitting with us when these matters are discussed. Obviously, you're not acquainted with him, but he's a good newsman I've learned to trust since I've lived in Middleton. He knows more about the victim than any of us. I think he could be of help."

"If that's you're opinion, Timothy, it's all right with me," the deputy responded.

"However," Timothy added, "before we call him away from that attractive young woman he's courting, there's an aspect of the inquiry you can undertake prior to the crew leaving for Kokadjo. That is, unless you want to send Tom to Ripogenus."

"Whatever, you feel is right, Timothy. What can I do now to get this investigation on track?"

"During the initial period of last night's storm when lightning hit the trees barricading the camp road, a vehicle was approaching the lodge. It turned around and headed back to the logging road.

"The occupants could have abandoned the vehicle and walked around the obstacles to seek shelter in the lodge. But it appears they intentionally avoided it. That puzzles me. Apparently, they made it to the logging road before any trees were downed or else Ted and Jacques would have seen the car this morning when they went to the warden's camp.

"On Friday or Saturday," Timothy continued, "Jacques saw two men he thought were fishermen who were camped on the other side of the lake. He never got close enough to recognize them. But he did see the station wagon with out-of-state number plates as he walked by their tent. No one has seen it today so it appears the men must have been in the car that turned around in the road last night.

"Frank, I suggest that you ask one of the volunteers from Kokadjo to call the sheriff's office in Dover-Foxcroft when they return home and inform them of the situation. They could contact state police to be on alert for that vehicle with a canoe on its roof.

"Difficult to locate, it shouldn't be."

"What's so important about those fishermen? " Frank asked.

"If you arrange to have police stop and question them, I'll get Ted and we'll enlighten you on the victim's background which may help in solving this mystery. It's probably not necessary, but it might be prudent as a precautionary measure to have the police search the vehicle when it's located."

As Frank was heading to the working crew, he met Tom who was going to the lodge for a break. When the deputy explained what he was doing, the warden said that he had also seen the fishermen but like Jacques, not close enough to recognize them.

"But," he added, "Dr. Williams and I saw the wagon and it had Connecticut number plates. That should make it easier to find. I don't mind driving to Ripogenus and making the call, Frank."

"Perhaps you should. You've had a long day but it appears we have lost enough time already," Timothy said.

Frank returned to the lodge as Timothy entered the porch door with Ted who had left Linda at the dock.

"I'm sorry to break up your conversation with Linda, Ted, but it's only temporary," Timothy explained.

"We'd like to have you participate in this discussion. I believe you have knowledge Frank would find helpful in this investigation which we think will develop into a homicide."

"Ted, Tom is leaving for Ripogenus to call the sheriff in Dover-Foxcroft," Frank said. "Timothy and I thought it best not to wait for the crew to finish removing all of the debris. I understand you are aware of the victim's past activities."

"I hope that I can be of assistance," Ted replied. "As Timothy may already have told you, the victim is a photographer who has operated a studio in Middleton for the past ten years since arriving from New York City. A bachelor, he had two vices, either of which could prove to have been fatal. He had an urge to bet on losing horses, an expensive habit. Until recently, no one had any idea of how serious his losses had become. Word recently began spreading among financial people of his indebtedness as his property became heavily mortgaged.

"Apparently, the largest creditor was a syndicate in Rhode Island where his bets were laid on the state's horse racing tracks. He placed these bets with a local bookie but we believe they were held by that out-of-state group with plenty of clout.

Middleton police have reason to believe they were preparing to lower the boom.

"The big question is where and how Brett could raise sufficient cash to satisfy the vultures. This is one motive and the reason why Timothy and I placed emphasis on the strangers. "Middleton Police Chief John Davidson last week described the organization to Timothy with these words: 'Their long arms can reach anywhere.'

"The victim's other vice had also become serious but Timothy and I would rather not reveal names yet, Frank. However, it does involves a couple in our group."

"We would like to wait a little longer before questioning them concerning a particular relationship," Timothy instilled in the conversation. "They are truly good friends whose marriage would terminate if we revealed our knowledge of this incident."

"As both of you are aware," the deputy said, "if this becomes a murder investigation after the autopsy reports are made public, no one is excluded. Everyone is a suspect."

"We understand, Frank," Timothy replied.

"Before we end this discussion," the deputy asked, "am I to believe that the field of suspects is wide open?"

"I'm afraid so, Frank," Timothy answered. "A Kentucky Derby, it is."

"Let's go outside and get acquainted with everyone," Frank remarked. "We may learn more."

Jan and Linda were sitting on a large rock on the shore splashing water with their feet as they tried to get something more out of this outing than a headache.

"I realize that we didn't come to Bear Lake to witness a tragedy," Linda remarked. "But, there's no reason why we can't do things to forget it. None of us has caught a fish. It's kind of late this afternoon to go fishing but we have time to take a swim. How about it, Jan?"

"I'll race you to the lodge to change," Jan replied eagerly.

"Do you suppose we can convince Alec and Ted to get wet?"

"Wait until we return. Then we'll get them wet."

For the first time since last night, there were smiles on the faces of the two vacationers as they ran to the lodge.

"What do you suppose happened to those two?" Timothy asked.

"I'd bet they decided to quit having a dull time," Ted responded. "It appears they are starting to liven things up around here with either a happy hour or a swim. My guess is it will end with a water fight and some of us are going to get wet if we remain near the lake. If you don't mind, gentlemen," Ted remarked, "I'm joining the fun."

"Go ahead," Frank said. "You might as well make the most of it today. I have a feeling the rest of the week will reveal unpleasant information."

"You're right, Frank. A little relaxation would probably help. I feel a little libation is in order. Would you like to join me?"

"No thanks, Timothy," Frank responded. "I'll be on duty until this case is solved or until I leave here. But I'll get one for you."

"Let me get it," Ruth answered when she overheard Timothy's wish as she approached the couple. "I know his favorite drink. Besides, I'm going inside to change for a swim. This place is getting a bit gloomy."

"Frank, you haven't met Ruth Perry," Timothy said. "Tonight at supper, you'll have a chance to know her better and meet the rest of our group."

The women's enthusiasm was contagious as the rest of the men except Randy and Jacques hurried to the lodge for swimming trunks.

"Jacques, why don't you have a bottle of ale?" Randy suggested.

"I would like that much better and I'll get it," Jacques volunteered as he headed for the lodge.

Within a few minutes, the sound of splashing water and laughter replaced the quietness of early afternoon.

"Now, this is more like it," Timothy remarked to Frank. "As you mentioned, happy days aren't forecast for the rest of this week so they might as well make the best of it."

Frank was curious about the identities of the swimmers, especially the man with the suntan.

"It's been a warm summer," he said. "But that fellow in the white trunks didn't get that tan in Maine this year."

"No," Timothy answered. "He spends the winter in Florida."

"Where's his mate? Most everyone appears to be paired excepting you and Jacques."

"He doesn't have one here," Timothy replied. "You're going to become familiar with everyone's background so here's the low down on Dave Paxton."

"He went to Florida after the war where he met and married a wealthy widow. They winter at Palm Beach and she owns a large home on Cedar Lake in Middleton where they spend summers. Also, for your information, she is nearly thirty years older than he and his duties are confined mostly as her companion.

"I understand that she's a jealous woman but so far I have never heard any rumors of Dave getting out of line, although it's known he has a roving eye. Is that sufficient data?"

"One more question," Frank asked. "Does he and his wife attend functions with you in Middleton?"

"No," Timothy answered. "This is the first time he has been on any of our trips and in Middleton she remains close to her social friends. She has never joined with us."

"Well, then I have another question. Who invited him this time?"

"I really don't know who wanted him but Alec asked me if there were any objections if he came along. Alec, the largest man in the party, was his commanding officer in the Marine Corps during the war and he knows him well. It seems Dave's wife was going on a business trip for two weeks and he wanted something to do."

"A third question, Timothy, and I'll quit asking. Are any others in your party friendly with him except Alec?"

"Sorry, I don't know. I suggest you ask Ted."

"Thanks, Timothy. Now, what's the status of the young woman who brought you the drink and her husband who also appears to have years on her. Are they a happy couple?"

"Dr. Perry is a professor of mathematics at Chamberlain College and he's probably about twenty years older. They came to the city a few years ago from Illinois and she teaches mathematics at the local high school.

"I never heard of any domestic problems, but a couple of weeks ago, Ted told me something about her having an affair with the victim. However, as Ted said earlier, we would like to reserve judgment until the questioning is over."

"That sounds reasonable. Now, what's the story with the big man.? Looks like he could have been a football player."

"Alec Johnson was a football and war hero," Timothy continued. "He's managing editor of the *Daily Guardian.*

"I have never heard a negative word about him and his only interest in women seems to be Jan but I don't think that's serious yet. "

"Ted could fill you in on more details about these people if you're interested but I believe I've covered a lot of the ground."

Deputy Gray had listened attentively to every word Timothy said.

"Timothy," he said looking directly at him. "We're in the middle of a hell of a horse race."

As the afternoon waned, the workers had completed clearing the trees from the road to allow movement of vehicles when the ground became dry again.

"It will take at least another day of dry weather before the vehicles near the lodge can go to Ripogenus," Bob Taylor, leader of the crew, remarked. "And the drivers will have to be careful driving over the soft spots. We're through," he told Timothy and the deputy when they met at the dock. "Before we return home, we're going to accept Timothy's offer for a couple of brews. It's been a dry day."

"You're welcome to our refreshments and supper, if you like," Timothy offered." We certainly appreciate what you've done. How can we pay you?"

"No way," Bob said. "In this neck of the woods, we like to help each other when trouble arises. That's pay enough. But the cold drinks will be appreciated."

"I'll get the ale," Randy offered, getting up from the dock where he had been sitting with Jacques.

While Randy was going to the lodge, Bob asked the deputy what was going to take place now.

"Tomorrow, more wardens and deputies will come by the Ripogenus Road while I expect another warden by plane from Greenville with the results of the autopsy. We will search for the missing rifle."

"You have your work cut out for you," Bob replied as he joined his friends. " I wish you luck."

With towels wrapped around them, Jan and Linda left the water and passed the men on their way to the lodge.

"We've got to get dressed," Jan remarked, "and get supper ready. It's about that time."

Two additions and a subtraction comprised tonight's supper list with eleven guests seated and ready for a pot roast cooked by Jan and Linda complemented by Jacques, popular biscuits

It was a friendly but even more subdued supper than last night for obvious reasons. On the first night they were anticipating joys that the wilderness had to offer while on Sunday night, although Brett was missing, there was still hope that he would be found unharmed.

Tonight the worst was known. Brett was dead and completion of an investigation and finding the person or persons responsible for his death was top in everyone's thoughts.

Timothy always had a toast to offer on any occasion. Tonight, he again raised his glass and in his Irish brogue said, "It's almost as good as bringing good news not to bring bad." This toast was rather ambiguous implying that although no one had been apprehended, if someone were, he hoped it wouldn't be a member of this group. Aware this wasn't the occasion for small talk, he only had a few comments.

"Tomorrow will be a crucial day as more officials take part in the investigation. My only advice is cooperation. On the lighter side, try to catch a few trout. We promised Harry some and I would like to try another Cajun recipe."

It remained quiet with little conversation as they consumed another tasty meal. They were leaving the table when Tom entered the lodge after his trip to Ripogenus.

"I see you made it all right," Frank remarked. "Did you talk with the sheriff? "

"Yup. Let's talk outside?"

They went to the porch as Tom related, "I spoke to the sheriff. He was about to leave the office when I called. After I explained the situation he asked me to stand by while he made contact with state police. In a few minutes, he called back and said troopers in the New England states would be notified and instructed to stop any vehicle matching the description I gave him. They will hold its occupants.

"He also told me something else, Frank. We're looking for a murderer. The victim died as a result of a gunshot wound.

"That doesn't surprise me, Tom. I suspected that all along. Do they know what kind of weapon was used?"

"They removed two slugs from the body and dispatched them to the state police laboratory at Augusta for analysis," the warden continued. "They'll know more later. As you well know, they must have the weapon for ballistic tests."

"We have a firearm which I'll send out by plane in the morning," Frank said. "And we'll put our efforts tomorrow on finding the Winchester rifle. Did the sheriff say how many men he was sending?"

"He said two deputies and a warden will be aboard the plane while another warden and a searching party will be arriving by vehicles. I almost forgot, Frank, Deputy Calvin Mayo will be bringing a photo taken from the body that might be of value in solving this crime. He said Timothy could probably identify persons in the print as he believes they are from Middleton."

"That's good news in view of all the work ahead of us in the morning," Frank replied. "Tom, why don't you go inside and get something to eat before we return to your camp with Dr. Williams. I want to talk with Timothy for a few minutes."

They walked back into the lodge where Ruth and Randy were standing near the kitchen stove waiting for a hungry warden.

"You must be starved," Ruth said smiling as Tom neared the table. "We saved pot roast and potatoes for you. Please sit and Randy and I will serve you."

As Tom went into the kitchen, Frank motioned to Timothy, who was sitting on a sofa in the living room, to come outside.

"Tom received some interesting information from the sheriff which sheds some light on this case. First, Timothy, a gunshot wound or wounds claimed the man's life so it's a homicide. Police are forwarding a photograph the victim was carrying in hopes you can identify the subjects. Also, state police are on alert for the vehicle that left here Sunday night. All that remains is to find the rifle and send both firearms to Augusta. And, of course, capture the culprit," Frank concluded.

"That's a tall order," Timothy responded. "But a lot of evidence has been gathered in one day. There's much more to be accomplished so I propose getting a good night's sleep so we can start fresh in the morning."

"A good idea. We'll leave when Tom is ready."

Ted and Linda left the lodge holding hands and strolled along the shore listening to loons calling across the lake as darkness enveloped the wilderness. They stopped near the dock when Linda asked him who he thought took the guns and shot Brett.

"I don't know, "he answered. "The most likely suspects are not here although it could have been someone much closer. Let's hope I'm wrong about that."

"Honey, "she said. "I think you're referring to Randy but he wouldn't do anything so awful. He's too intelligent. But, I'm not aware of anyone else."

"There are others, but there's no reason why you would know of Brett's financial problems. That may play a role in this shooting. He had a heavy debt with the an out-of-state group who took his bets on horse racing. Timothy, Chief Davidson, and I knew he had been contacted recently by men who wanted their money. The fishermen we tried to locate the other day could have been sent here to collect, one way or another."

"How can they be found if they left before the storm? I heard you tell Jan they were from out-of-state so they could be home now."

"That's possible, but I believe the sheriff has already notified state police," Ted said. "If they were riding in a car with out of state plates and a canoe on its roof, it makes an easy target to locate.

"Anyhow, Linda, we're just speculating. More evidence will surface before another day has passed and police should be closer to its solution."

"I know you have a lot on your mind, Ted, but do you think we will be leaving here soon?"

"Certainly," he replied.

"Let's take a walk along the camp road," Linda suggested. " Perhaps we can spend the remainder of the evening discussing more interesting subjects or something positive like maybe, our future. If we should meet Jacques on the way, he'll entertain us with his stories of life in the wilderness. But I hope we'll be alone?"

"Good idea ," Ted said. "Wait here while I go to the lodge for my flashlight."

Chapter 17

A beautiful sunrise heralded Tuesday as Jacques opened his cabin door and breathed early morning fresh air into his lungs. Jacques slept restlessly during the night wondering who had stolen his revolver and worrying if the deputy thought he had shot the photographer. He now realized it had not been right to leave the man alone on that road. He thought that a two-day-old fawn could have found its way home.

He stepped back into the cabin and went to the sink. He poured water in a basin to wash and shave. Today he thought it would be better to wear a clean shirt as there would be many people around. Jacques made sure to take a cigar Alec had given him last night and put it in his shirt pocket. Looking into a cracked mirror above the sink, he combed his thick hair before leaving for the lodge.

Moving slowly up the trail toward the lodge, he noticed a large maple felled by the storm that could be used for lumber and firewood. He took a half dozen steps off the path to look it over. When he stooped for a closer look at some low blueberry bushes, the cigar fell from his shirt hitting a branch and bounced onto a mound behind the tree. He crawled over the limb to retrieve the cigar, and as he picked it up, he saw a piece of steel.

It was the familiar length of metal with a hexagon-shape barrel that was usually mounted above the lodge fireplace. This was the missing Winchester 38.55 rifle.

Astounded and troubled, he remained on the ground staring at the weapon that might have killed the photographer. Jacques was confused as he tried to understand why the rifle was so close to his cabin. Was someone trying to place the blame on him? And, why was his revolver stolen if the person who shot Brett already had the other weapon? He was sure of one thing. He wasn't going to touch the rifle. He jumped to his feet and ran to the lodge in search of Timothy who would know what to do.

It was still early but surprisingly everyone was up and milling around in the kitchen as Jacques entered breathlessly. Alec and Dave were standing at the stove cooking breakfast. Jacques had planned to bake another batch of biscuits but finding the gun upset him.

"What's wrong, Jacques?" Ted asked when he noticed the excited woodsman.

"Where's Timothy. I got something important to tell him," he replied.

"He's outside, I think, probably near the dock."

Jacques didn't waste anytime as he raced out of the lodge to the beach where Timothy was talking with Randy and Ruth.

"Mon Pere," he exclaimed, "I got to tell you something." "All right, Jacques," Timothy answered as he excused himself from the couple and walked along the shore.

"What is it, my friend? You look nervous. Is something wrong?"

"Timothy, I found the rifle. It's near the trail about half way to my cabin. I didn't touch it. Will you come and I'll show you?"

"Of course. Jacques, tell Ted that I would like to see him?"

In a few minutes, the men were on their way as Jacques was trying to explain how he found the gun.

Jacques and Ted were walking ahead of Timothy when they reached the downed maple about two hundred yards from the handyman's cabin.

"Look!" Jacques exclaimed. "Over there," as he pointed to a large limb.

Ted moved looked carefully until he spotted the rifle.

"Timothy," he shouted, "It's the Winchester. No doubt about it. What shall we do?"

"Don't do anything, Ted. Do you mind remaining with Jacques" Timothy asked," while I return to the lodge and bring back a deputy? I don't want anyone to touch the rifle as there may be fingerprints on it."

"Sure, I'll stay," Ted replied.

It wasn't going to be long. Timothy had walked less than a hundred yards when the drone of a plane engine and sounds of vehicles on the camp road were audible. An anticipated busy and eventful day was beginning early as officials arrived by air and ground.

Timothy was near the lodge when Frank and Tom alighted from the weapons carrier with another warden while five men got out of another vehicle.

"Looks like you brought plenty of help today," Timothy said when the three officials approached him.

"I don't think you're going to need them, Frank. Jacques found the rifle a short time ago."

A surprised but pleased deputy replied, "Let's get it and we'll send both weapons back on the plane. Tom, would you tell the pilot to stand by?"

"Yup. I'll go to the dock right away," the warden answered.

"Now, Timothy. Show me the way."

"Wait a moment," Frank added, speaking to the other warden, George Fox. "Would you get a tape measure from the vehicle? I want to gauge the distance from the site where the victim was discovered to where the rifle was found. Timothy, let's walk back to the area and start from there. In which direction are we heading, Timothy?"

"We're going down the trail toward Jacques's cabin," Timothy responded. "I'm only guessing, but I'd say it's about six hundred feet. It would seem a long way to dispose of a weapon. Or, plant it?"

"What do you mean by planting the gun?" Frank asked.

"Early in the investigation, it is, to speculate," Timothy replied. "But it seems odd someone would commit a murder and travel a quarter of a mile to dispose of evidence unless he or she wanted to attract attention to a particular suspect. In this case, Jacques. In my opinion, it was impossible for him to have taken part in this crime. Besides other factors, including his inability to remove the rifle from the lodge on Sunday, I can't think of a motive."

Frank was pondering Timothy's analysis of the woodsman's alibi as he began measuring while they walked. He suddenly remembered another necessity.

"Tom, would you look for a towel or something in the lodge to protect the rifle."

When they walked by the lodge, Timothy decided it wasn't essential for him to go along, and he was more interested in the photo the deputy brought from Greenville.

"Frank, you don't need me to look at that site. I'm anxious to see the picture."

"Okay, Timothy, we'll get together later when I'll have both weapons ready for transport to Augusta."

Timothy joined Jacques as the plane taxied down the lake to the dock where three passengers got out. He recognized Calvin Mayo but didn't know the other deputy and warden who followed behind him.

"Welcome to Bear Lake, Calvin. I only wish this could have been a fishing trip."

"Maybe next time," Calvin replied.

"Timothy, meet Deputy Don Jewett and Warden Ben Waters. They gave up their days off to be with us."

"Well, I hope it won't be an extended visit," Timothy responded. "In fact, Don's stay may be brief. We've found both weapons."

"Good," the deputy said. "Now, I have something to show you that might conceivably help solve the mystery sooner if you can identify the subjects. Timothy, they call it an action shot and there's plenty of it.

"Oh, another thing. State police haven't located the vehicle with the two fishermen. However, it's possible they are still in Maine."

"How did you come to that assumption?" Timothy asked.

"According to Tom, the men arrived late Friday or Saturday so they didn't have much time to fish and they probably had sufficient equipment to remain longer. It seemed logical to Calvin if they left because of a storm here, they might try another location. It appears likely that they tried to seek shelter at the lodge but the downed trees blocked their way."

"A theory, it is," Timothy contended. "However, it's probable they may have turned on a wrong road and they didn't intend to be seen. After seeing lights in the lodge, they turned and hastened to find another way out of this wilderness. Obviously, they were unfamiliar with the area or they would have walked around the blockade and sought shelter here."

"Why in heaven's name would they do something that stupid," Calvin asked.

"It's just possible they were not on a fishing trip," Timothy said. "That is, not for fish. I have reason to suspect the victim had a serious problem. Let's get together with Frank and discuss this likelihood further."

"That sounds good," Calvin said.

"Now, Timothy, here's the photo we found in the victim's billfold."

Timothy didn't have a problem identifying the man in the print, especially the suntan. It was an explicit picture of Dave and a young woman making love. But he didn't recognize the female.

However, it's a possibility Ted knew her. He wasn't shocked when he looked at this sex scene, but he was somewhat surprised Dave would jeopardize his comfortable life-style by openly having this affair where he could be photographed. He was too clever for that. Something was amiss here.

It suddenly dawned on him this person might be the fifteen-year-old girl who was reported missing a few weeks ago and who was later found by police near Brett's Studio. She appeared to be more than fifteen but the police chief and Ted had described her as looking older than her age. Timothy was reluctant to disclose other theories to Deputy Mayo or others until the matter of the two anglers was resolved.

But, he did want to know the woman's identity in the photo in the event the strangers were fishermen. Also, he had to know when and where this photo was taken. It would be helpful to know why Brett was carrying it. A lot of questions had to be answered.

"Calvin, you're going to meet the man in this photo soon," Timothy said. "For now, let's keep this information between the investigating officials and Ted, a friend of mine. He's a Middleton reporter who has been working with Frank and me on this case and probably knows the woman."

"All right, Timothy. Let's go to the lodge."

Frank and the wardens were waiting on the porch with Ted when Timothy and Calvin approached. "Frank, we have some important news to share with you, and I think we should find a place   where we can talk about it," Calvin said.

"A good idea," Frank replied. "Don and Ben can take the weapons aboard the plane and make sure that the state police get them to Augusta. We can continue our investigation but it's necessary to have results of ballistics tests as soon as possible.

"George, you can also return to Greenville with your searching party. The hunt is over. Tom and Calvin will remain until this case is solved. Thanks for your help."

"Okay, we're ready to go," the warden replied.

"First, there's something else to do en route to Augusta," Timothy said he as passed the photo to Ted. "Do you know the woman in the print?"

"Wow," Ted exclaimed. "I always thought Dave was a womanizer. Seriously, she is the fifteen-year-old who was reported missing in Middleton. I saw her recently in a store with some friends."

"Do you know her name?" Timothy asked.

"She's Dawn Gronorski. Sarah, a *Guardian* proofreader, would know her address."

"May I see the photo?" Frank asked. "This picture adds intrigue to the case," he remarked. "Is it possible the victim took this photo? Wasn't he a photographer?"

"A photographer, he was. I have a suggestion," Timothy responded. "Instruct the trooper who will be taking the weapon to the state laboratory to drop this print off at the Middleton Police Station.

"In the meantime, if you don't object, Frank, Ted can fly to Greenville and call our police chief friend informing him of developments here and learn where the girl lives. After they interrogate her, they will know where and when the picture was taken and possibly who took it. The girl won't refuse to answer questions when confronted with this photograph.

"What do you think, Frank?"

"I think it's a great idea. Unfortunately for Ted, he'll have to eat his breakfast in Greenville. I'm anxious to get this material down country. Ted, you can return any time after you make your call. The county will pay for the flight."

"Any objections, deputy, if I bring a friend along with me?" Ted asked. "There's room for another passenger."

"None whatsoever. There's not too much to see in town but you'll like the flight."

"Don, I'll get Linda and meet you at the plane in a few minutes."

After the plane became airborne, Timothy suggested, "Frank, why don't we have breakfast. Afterwards, we'll meet privately to exchange information before we hear alibis from the suspects."

An hour later, Timothy met with two deputies and Tom in the lodge's living room to continue their discussion.

"We don't intend to keep Timothy's guests here any longer than necessary so let's try to determine the most likely suspects," Frank said. "We must listen to everyone's story but I kind of agree with Timothy about Jacques. We'll question him with the rest. Also, the two missing fishermen are high on the list of suspects. What's the latest report on them, Calvin?"

"No word yet but I understand it's the opinion of two officials that they haven't t left the state but no explanation has been offered except they don't believe the couple would cut their visit short. I don't know why they are suspects, only that Timothy said the victim had a problem."

"A serious problem, it was," Timothy responded.

"Middleton police believed he owed a bundle to the mob for horse racing bets and their patience for the payoff was exhausted. Collectors had already made a couple trips to his studio. What makes these men suspects is their anonymity. No one including Tom ever got close enough to recognize them. It seems they didn't want to be known."

"Until they are questioned," Frank interrupted, "they can't be overlooked. We should not eliminate suspects until everyone has been questioned as to their whereabouts at the approximate time of the shooting," the deputy continued. "That's just routine police work."

"We've got to establish the murder time, and I believe it must have taken place simultaneously with the deafening roar of thunder that drowned out the sound of gun fire," Timothy asserted. "Obviously, it was only seconds later when lightning bolts struck the pines. You know," Timothy went on, "if we ruled out Jacques as a suspect, he should be a good witness. He was outside and about to climb a ladder to the lodge roof minutes before this happened. If none of you mind, let's call him in and hear his version. I'm certain it will be helpful."

"By all means," Calvin replied. "We're going to need all the help we can get. Bring him in, Tom."

"Hold a moment," Frank remarked. "I would like to know more about Jacques' revolver. Until the ballistics report is released, we aren't sure what gun was used in the shooting. It could have been either or none of the weapons. In any event, Timothy, who do you think took it?"

"No one knows except the thief. I had an interesting talk with three of my guests who were Jacques's fishing companions Sunday. They were in his cabin for a few minutes but only one admitted seeing the revolver. Unfortunately," he added, "I only believe Ruth, the person who said she saw the gun."

"Why were two weapons taken if only one was used in the murder?" Tom inquired.

"That's a good question," Frank answered. "Timothy, do you have an opinion?"

"As we mentioned, we are in an early stage of this case and I would be guessing to express my thoughts now. For some unknown reason it does seem whoever pulled the trigger was trying to cast suspicion on Jacques," Timothy added. "If I'm correct it had to be someone in our group and not the strangers. Let's gather facts before making accusations. Shall we ask Jacques to join us?" "I would like his story now," Frank said. "Tom, ask Jacques to come in."

Apprehensive that he would be blamed for the murder, Jacques entered the room with a worried look.

Smiling, Timothy greeted the woodsman. "Don't be afraid. We

don't think that you did anything wrong. We only want to hear where you were and what you saw when the first heavy bolt of lightning struck the pines Sunday afternoon."

"When the big lightning came," Jacques related, "I was standing on a ladder against the side of this building to get on the roof, but I was scared. There was a big boom and then a lot of light in the sky and on the camp road.

"I can't remember too well but it seemed that another boom and flashes of lightning came again soon and it sounded like gun shots with the trees beginning to fall. I don't know but it looked like lights from the road, too. It was raining hard so I took the ladder back to the shop and stayed inside for a few minutes.

"When I went outside, I thought I saw someone with a gun or stick moving and something else closer to the lodge but it was raining so bad I couldn't tell what it was. The wind blew my hat off and after I found it, no one was around."

"Did you come into the lodge after that?" Frank asked.

"Not right then. I went back to the shop to get out of the rain but I didn't stay long because I was worried about the photographer. I wanted to make sure that he was all right so I ran to the lodge to see if he was there.

"Do you remember who was in the lodge?" Frank questioned.

"Timothy was alone but soon Madame Perry came out of her bedroom " Jacques replied.

"Jacques is right, "Timothy said. "Ruth, who is the wife of Dr. Perry, a Chamberlain College professor, returned from the outhouse a few minutes before Jacques arrived. I'm trying to remember who was next but it would be advisable to invite Ruth to join us now and let her tell us. I think it was her husband, Randy."

"Yes, it was," Jacques said excitedly. "I'm sure because he went with me to find the man."

"Jacques," Frank said. "If you don't know the victim's name, it's Brett."

"He told me his name once but I forgot," Jacques said. "I can't tell you any more about who was in here as we went out trying to find him."

Tom left the lodge and went out on the porch where he called Ruth who was standing near the shore talking with the rest of the group.

"Mrs. Perry, the deputies have several questions they want to ask you. Would you please come in?"

With a pleasant smile, Ruth made her appearance.

"Ruth," Timothy said " You met Frank Gray at supper last night and this other deputy is Calvin Mayo. You're aware of what's taking place so they have a few questions to ask regarding where you were at the time we assume Brett was shot. We think it happened about the time two successive bolts of lightning hit the pines. Can you help them?"

"Well, I don't know when he was shot but I was in the lodge with you, Timothy, during the beginning of the storm. I only left for a few minutes when I had to go outside but I returned and stayed in the lodge until all of us began searching for Brett."

"That is what Timothy told us, Mrs. Perry," Frank said. "We just wanted to hear it from you. Now, can you tell us who were the next people to come into the lodge?"

"I think that Jacques was next. He was looking for Brett. We were surprised because he was supposed to be guiding him on a photo venture. After he learned that Brett was still outdoors, he was worried and asked Timothy for a flashlight to look for him. As I recall, my husband, Dr. Perry, came in and joined Jacques in the search."

"Do you remember how long it was before the next person came in and who that was?"

"I'd say it was about five minutes after Jacques and Randy left when Dave entered by the same door."

"Mrs. Perry, where did you spend your afternoon?"

"My husband and I went fishing in a canoe. I don't know how long we were out but we headed quickly for shore when the water became rough. I'm not sure, but I believe we were the first boaters to head for land as I recall seeing other craft in the water when we got near shore. We tried to paddle along the water's edge to the dock but the waves became higher so we tried to carry the canoe. However, it was too heavy and we left it on land and I hurried back here."

"Why didn't you return to the lodge together?" the deputy asked.

"Randy wanted to secure the canoe and told me to go ahead. Heavy rain was beginning to fall and I didn't want to get drenched. Frankly, I didn't think it necessary to attach the canoe to trees but Randy thought that strong winds might damage it."

"How long do you think it took him to take care of the boat. Apparently, you had been back at the lodge quite awhile before he got here."

"I haven't the faintest. You'll have to ask him."

"Only one more question. You told Timothy you saw the revolver in Jacques' cabin but your husband and the other man didn't see it. Are you certain it was in the holster?

"I have no doubt about it," Ruth replied.

"Thanks for your help. We would like to talk with Dr. Perry. Would you tell him?"

After she left the lodge, Frank remarked, "It appears she was truthful. What do the rest of you think?"

Tom and Calvin had no comments and Timothy replied, "At this time, I can't find any errors in her responses. That's what I remember while in the lodge. I don't know what she and Randy did prior to the storm and how long it was before she came back from the outhouse later."

Randy appeared relaxed when he entered the room and sat on a chair next to Timothy. Accustomed to participating in executive conferences, the educator didn't seem uncomfortable while waiting to be interrogated.

"Randy," Timothy said, "you know Tom and Deputy Frank Gray. The other deputy is Calvin Mayo. You are aware of the investigation. I'm sure you know everyone must provide alibis for their whereabouts prior to and during this tragic event. Deputy Gray has a few questions."

"Dr. Perry, we know you were on the lake with your wife when the storm erupted forcing you off the water. Mrs. Perry told us that after both of you brought the canoe to shore, you remained with the craft while she hurried to the lodge. Is that correct?"

"That's right."

"Why did you stay with the boat instead of coming to shelter with her?" Gray asked.

"It was obvious that a violent storm was developing. In view of impending gusty winds, I decided to take the extra precaution of securing the canoe by fastening both ends to trees. Does that appear unreasonable?"

"No. You possess more regard for the property of others than most visitors. That's commendable. However, I realize it was raining but it seems it took you a long time. How long do you think?"

"Deputy, I have no idea. Obviously, I wouldn't have remained any longer than necessary in that weather. That would be absurd," Randy replied.

"Is it possible you didn't stay with the canoe all that time? Did you return to the lodge on the same route Mrs. Perry took?"

"After I tied the craft, I took the path by the stream and made my way to the lodge. Ruth, I believe, walked along the shoreline. It may have taken me longer but the trail is smoother."

"If my geography is correct, you would have to pass Jacques' cabin," Frank said. "By any chance, did you enter his home?"

Randy hesitated momentarily before answering the question, just long enough for Timothy to suspect he wasn't telling the truth.

"No. I thought about getting out of the rain but realized this storm would probably last for hours and I didn't care about staying there," Randy remarked. "Why do you ask?"

"Jacques's revolver was taken from his cabin Sunday afternoon," Frank replied. "To the best of our knowledge, only three persons besides him knew it was there. One of you had to take it. And only one of you admitted seeing it," Frank related. "It's difficult for me to believe that anyone invited to look at his home could have missed it. It was in the middle of the only room," the deputy continued.

"What would you say the size of the cabin is? Twenty by twenty feet, at the most. Why someone is lying I don't know, especially since the weapon was left where it could be easily found. We'll find out before this is over," Frank added. Until now, Timothy had only asked a few questions aware this was a police investigation. Although he knew they would like his help, he didn't want to interfere during the interrogation.

However, he felt a couple of questions needed answers.

"Randy, you and Dave were the last to enter the lodge before a series of lightning bolts destroyed the pines. Did you see Dave or anyone just before you reached the lodge? Or, did you hear any sounds besides the roar of the storm? Did the noises sound like gunshots?"

"Dave or anyone could have been ten feet from me and I wouldn't have seen him. The weather was so bad," Randy said. "As for hearing any unusual noise, amid the rain, wind and thunder, it was impossible to distinguish any particular sound."

"You told the deputy that when you visited Jacques' cabin you saw his holster but not the gun although Ruth said she saw it," Timothy added. "Dave told me earlier that he didn't see it either. I feel the same way Deputy Gray does about this situation. How could you and Dave miss the gun when Ruth so plainly saw it?" Timothy said.

"Also, similar to the deputy, I believe one of you borrowed or took the weapon for an unexplainable purpose. Dave went by the cabin after leaving me near the stream earlier and you were next and, as far as I can ascertain, the only other person to go near the cabin."

Randy was obviously annoyed by Timothy's remarks but his facial expression didn't change. "I don't know what else to tell you," he asserted. "I didn't enter the cabin nor did I take the revolver."

"My next question is personal," Timothy said. "Did you like Brett?"

"I wasn't particularly fond of him, no different than some in our group," he replied.

"That probably can help explain the argument you had Sunday night. Do you mind telling about the dispute?" Timothy asked.

Surprised that someone had overheard the conversation, he quickly answered.

"It was about the poor quality of portraits he had taken of Ruth and me. I wanted him to take the photos again but he refused unless we paid for another sitting."

"Was that all there was to it?" Timothy questioned, knowing it involved more. Randy wasn't the kind of person to become part of a shouting match over a few dollars.

"As far as I'm concerned, it is," Randy replied.

There wasn't more Timothy or the deputy could ask at this time. They both thought he wasn't telling the truth, but three other persons needed to be interviewed.

"You were compassionate, Timothy," Frank said. "Your Roman collar shows. It's evident you're not a cop or that suspect wouldn't have made out so easily. If my memory hasn't failed, the victim had an affair with his wife. You knew he was lying, didn't you?"

"He's been dodging the truth throughout the questioning," Timothy admitted. "However, he's not going anywhere and we have more evidence to consider before any conclusion is reached.

"As Ted and I discussed with you yesterday, Dr. Perry's wife was involved with Brett but we don't believe Randy is totally certain of this. If he were, he is capable of murder. He loves his wife," Timothy added.

"We want to be reasonably certain of guilt and we should have a good idea after we hear from the Middleton police. If we reveal the couple had a tryst and someone else committed the crime, we would malign two lives unnecessarily. Let's wait awhile," Timothy advised.

"You're showing that collar again, Timothy," Frank remarked.

"How many more suspects do we have," Calvin asked. "I'd like a cup of coffee."

"Why don't we take a break, Frank," Timothy suggested. "There are three others to be questioned."

"Who remains?" Frank asked.

"Alec, Jan, and, of course, Dave. You remember him. He's the fellow with the suntan who's in the photo," Timothy said.

"That should be an interesting interview," Frank said.

"Trying to learn where everyone was at the time of the murder, which we haven't established, and who pulled the trigger on what weapon isn't going to be easy to find out," the deputy concluded.

Following an hour break of roast beef sandwiches and coffee, the interrogators left the building and walked along the shore. Before returning to the lodge, Calvin asked if the photo with the girl was going to be mentioned during the interview with Dave.

"No," Timothy answered. "There's additional information we need. I'm sure Ted will know more when he returns from Greenville. We'll refrain from the subject until then."

"I don't think I'm adding much to the investigation," Tom remarked. "It seems my efforts would be better served by helping Jacques get the watercraft back to the dock so that the others can do more fishing. What do you think, Frank?"

"We appreciate your assistance, Tom. But if you want to help Jacques, I'm sure Timothy and his group would like it. If something arises that needs your help, we'll call. Before you leave, Tom, would you ask Alec and Jan to join us?"

As Tom departed to look for Jacques, both deputies and Timothy walked back to the lodge.

Alec was indeed a large man, towering above Jan as the couple entered the building.

"Thanks for coming in," Timothy said. "You met Deputy Gray at supper last night and this is Deputy Mayo. Anyhow you probably have surmised by now, neither of you including Ted and Linda are high on the list of suspects."

"I understand all of you were fishing together when the storm arose and you came ashore in a crippled boat," Frank commented. "Did you see or hear anything that could be helpful to this investigation?"

"We only heard a lot of frightening sounds and we didn't see anything but rain after we left the lake," Jan responded. "I had trouble keeping up with the rest."

"That just about tells the story," Alec said. "Our only interest at the time of the approaching storm was getting to shore and back to the lodge. We had a few anxious moments when the motor conked out but we handled the situation without problems.

"After we beached the boat," Alec continued, "It was only a matter of how quickly we could get to shelter. I can't recall seeing anyone except our boat crew and there were moments when I couldn't see them. I did hear trees crashing but I considered it part of the storm. I'm sorry I can't be more helpful."

"Apparently the shooting occurred while the four of you were between the lake and lodge," Frank said.

"Mr. Johnson, how well did you know the victim?"

"Not very well, I guess. He was operating his studio when I came to Middleton and our newspaper hired him on a few occasions to do photography but not often as we had our own staff. Outside of these fishing and hunting trips Timothy arranged, I seldom saw him."

"How about you, Miss Robinson," the deputy inquired. "Were you acquainted with Mr. Hartman?"

"Probably not as well as the others. I've only been in Middleton a short time so this is my first outing with the group."

"You knew he was a bachelor. Did he ever ask you to go out with him?"

"No," Jan replied. "However, a few weeks ago he invited me to his studio to look at some of his special photographic scenes but I didn't go in."

"Do you mean you went to his studio but didn't enter?"

"That's right. I changed my mind," she answered abruptly.

"It appears you're omitting a good reason, Miss Robinson. Would you mind telling us about it?"

"I'd rather not," she replied, directing her response to Timothy rather than Deputy Gray. "It's personal and I don't think it has any bearing on this case."

"Frank," Timothy interrupted. "I agree. A reply to the question wouldn't add relevant information at this time. We can pursue it later if you wish."

"Well," Frank said, "as far as I'm concerned, this concludes this interview unless you or Calvin have any questions."

"I have no questions" Calvin remarked.

"Alec, I only have one but perhaps you don't have an answer," Timothy asked Alec.

"When you called about Dave coming on the trip, you said his wife was going to be away for a couple of weeks and that he would enjoy a fishing trip. It didn't mean anything to me at the time, but later I wondered why he would want to go with a group he barely knew. Did that occur to you?"

"No, Timothy, I never gave it a thought. Now, it does seem strange. I never knew any of his friends. I had the impression he kept to himself," Alec answered.

"Did he associate with Brett?" Timothy asked.

"I can't answer that question either, Timothy. I don't know."

"I believe that ends this session," Frank said.

"Again, thanks for your cooperation."

"That didn't take long," Alec remarked. "Let's see how Jacques and Tom are making out with the boats, Jan. I'll give them a hand and we can take a canoe ride."

"That sounds great," Jan said as they walked toward the door.

"Alec," Timothy asked. "Would you tell Dave we would like to see him."

"Certainly," he answered.

While they waited, Timothy reminded the deputies that the next person to be interrogated was the man in the photo.

"Frank, I'm not acquainted with this suspect. You know as much about the reason he is here as I do," Timothy said.

A tanned and erect Dave entered the lodge with a brisk walk.

"It looks like I'm next on the chopping block," he uttered. "How can I be of assistance?"

"Dave, we had supper with Deputy Gray last night and this other officer is Calvin Mayo. They have questions to ask," Timothy answered.

"Two men who were in the area prior to the storm have disappeared and they remain prime suspects," Frank remarked. "However, until they are located, a preliminary investigation is being conducted, and everyone who was here at the time of the murder is under suspicion."

"Why are they prime suspects," Dave challenged.

"Mr. Paxton, we'll ask the questions," Frank retorted. "Now," the deputy began, "Will you tell us where you were when bolts of lightning hit the trees near the lodge? We believe that was the approximate time of the shooting."

"I can't separate one flash from another, "he answered. "They became so frequent. However, I was near the lake looking for Alec when the storm erupted."

Timothy listened carefully to Dave's response trying to remember when he left the lodge, more importantly he was waiting to hear when he said he returned.

"I'm getting ahead in my questioning, Mr. Paxton. Let's go back earlier in the afternoon. Were you fishing from one of the boats?"

"No, I went with Timothy casting from rocks along a stream near Jacques' cabin. I don't know how long we were in the area but at least two hours, probably more. Timothy can confirm that. However, we stayed until the storm neared and it began raining. When that happened, I went upstream to fish while Timothy remained where we had been most of the afternoon. I didn't see him again until we met at the lodge."

"When you went upstream to fish, did you pass Jacques' cabin on the way back to the lodge?" Frank asked.

"Sure, I had to go by it."

"Did you enter the cabin?"

"No, I came directly here," Dave said.

"What bothers me in this investigation, Mr. Paxton, is that you and Dr. Perry passed Jacques's place and neither of you admitted going inside. Also, earlier, you and Dr. and Mrs. Perry went inside with Jacques and only Mrs. Perry saw a revolver that was later reported missing. As I told Dr. Perry during questioning, it's difficult for me to believe neither of you saw the weapon. In our opinion, someone is not telling the truth."

"That's your prerogative, deputy. I didn't go into the camp that afternoon and I didn't take the revolver," Dave declared.

"Dave, when I was returning to the lodge, you were coming from it," Timothy said. "It's a longer distance by way of Jacques' cabin than the direct route I took. How did you manage to arrive before I did?

"At the time I mentioned you made better time but nothing else was said."

"Without boasting about age, Timothy, I'm younger and I ran most of the way."

"You left the lodge before the brunt of the storm," Timothy said. "And you were gone for a long time. Two questions, Dave. Exactly where did you go and did you talk with anyone?"

"I went outside in the pouring rain so I can't tell exactly where I was. Somewhere between the lodge and the lake. I was looking for the boaters to help them if I could. But it was impossible to see anyone."

"Mr. Paxton," Frank interrupted. "I wasn't there but that is a vague response to Timothy's questions. I interpreted from your answer only that you were outdoors in the rain. Can't you do better than that?"

"You said you weren't there, Deputy," Dave snorted. "So what else could you conceive from my answer?"

Abruptly changing the subject, Frank asked, "Were you a friend of the victim?"

"We were friends. We went to lunch occasionally and he did our photography."

"Did you visit him at his studio often besides business?"

"Once in a while I'd stop by for a chat," Dave replied.

"A minute ago, you said Mr. Hartman was your friend. Did that shouting argument you had with him Saturday have anything to do with your friendly chats?"

Dave's tanned face flushed as he paused for words. "Well, it's not unusual for friends to disagree. We didn't always see eye to eye," he replied.

"Do you mind telling us what the disagreement involved, Mr. Paxton?"

"Not at all. He was planning on expanding his business and he wanted a loan from Mrs. Paxton and me. We weren't interested in the venture."

"Why didn't Mr. Hartman apply to a bank instead of asking you," Frank inquired.

"I have no idea."

"It seems odd to me," the deputy added. "Two friends would go on a vacation and on the first night have such an intense argument that everyone could hear."

"Unless Timothy or Calvin have any questions, the interrogations are over for today," Frank concluded.

"Tomorrow, we probably will have all the reports pertaining to this investigation and more word on the strangers."

"It's been a long day," Timothy remarked. "If no one needs me, I'm going to the dock."

"Calvin and I are going for a stroll," Frank said. "The plane should be here with the deputies and warden by the time we return."

The lodge emptied after they left.

"Well, what do you think after listening to the suspects?" Frank asked.

"There's suspicion enough for the three of them plus the strangers but little evidence as far as I'm concerned," Calvin quickly answered. "However, more convincing motives are missing."

"I thought only two were lying among the six we questioned today, but you come up with a third. How did you arrive at that decision, Calvin?"

"Similar to a few deputies who got this job through politics, I haven't had much training. The only shootings I ever investigated were dairy cattle that were mistaken for deer by hungover hunters. Sheriff Leon Badger told me to come here to lend you a hand and return with a prisoner, if and when, someone was arrested.

"But, I've read Agatha Christie's mystery novels about her famous character Belgian Detective Hercule Poirot's philosophy 'Cherche la femme' in a crime of passion. I think romance is involved. In this case, the professor's attractive wife is the woman. She had been in bed with the victim and probably had second thoughts about him."

"You could be on the right track, Calvin, but she is the only person who went into Jacques's cabin that morning who admitted seeing the revolver in a holster."

"I'm aware of that. But, I also overheard her friends telling about her hunting experiences. She's a good hunter and bagged a deer on both trips they made here. She is considered an excellent marksman by her companions."

"We won't overlook anyone," Frank replied. "We have an advantage that most police departments in this region don't have," he added. "An unofficial but nevertheless competent investigator, Timothy, is offering his knowledge of crime . I'm confident that we won't walk away from this case empty handed and I'm going to let him hold the reins tomorrow."

As they reversed directions and headed back to the lake, it was Cal's turn to ask a question.

"Frank, do you think Timothy has an idea of who's guilty?"

"That wouldn't be surprising. Although there seems to be many pieces of the puzzle missing at this stage of the investigation, he's a crafty one. You might be right. It could possibly be any of the three or the strangers."

When they heard the drone of a plane engine, Frank remarked, "another piece of that puzzle may be coming closer. Let's go to the lake."

They reached the lodge before the plane taxied to the shore where Timothy waited. Ted stepped out first and was helping Linda when the others arrived. The deputy and warden reported to Frank. Ted was telling Timothy what he had learned from his phone call to Middleton.

"Sorry, we'll have to wait another day for a report from Chief Davidson," Ted reported.

"However, the men from Connecticut were located and are en route to Greenville where Don will accompany them here by plane in the morning.

"He will also be carrying a ballistic report and a Middleton police account of the activities of the allegedly missing teenager. I think the day's delay will be worth the wait, Timothy."

"You said allegedly missing, Ted. What does that mean?"

"Sgt. Davis was vague when he told me about the girl incident but I got the impression police know more than he admitted. However, in fairness to the department, I'm certain their report will be thorough. I had a feeling he didn't want to say more until he talked with the chief."

"In that case," Timothy concluded, "I'm going to have a chat with Frank about your phone conversations. Why don't you and Linda take advantage of what the lake offers. I have a feeling this will be your last opportunity. Tomorrow has the potential to be a busy and possibly our last day here."

Timothy walked toward the lodge where Frank was waiting with his deputies to hear what information he had acquired.

"We're anxious to hear of Ted's day. I've already talked with Calvin and Don about tomorrow's procedure and we have agreed to let you conduct the interrogation. We'll intervene if vital questions aren't asked but I know you won't leave anything out. Of course, we have to make the final decision."

"An honor, it is, gentlemen," Timothy replied. "It's more faith you have in me, than my parishioners had in New York. An interesting investigation it will be, with an unquestionably surprising ending. It's a pleasure to accept your offer."

"I don't know you well, Timothy," Frank said. "But, I have a feeling you already know who committed the murder."

"I think so," Timothy answered. "But let's make the most of the remaining hours today. I'm sure the answer to this mystery will come to light tomorrow."

Chapter 18

The vacationers were greeted Wednesday morning by a colorful sunrise as they prepared their gear for a couple of hours of fishing before the plane arrived with additional evidence. Until now, no fish had been caught and even Timothy's promise of trout for the Haneys and Harry was in doubt.

Time passed rapidly without any catches and the unlucky anglers returned to the lodge where they began packing belongings, aware this could be their last day at Bear Lake.

Within an hour, the plane landed and Don accompanied by two men was met in front of the building by Timothy and Frank. Their conversation continued while reports brought by Don were studied.

When Timothy appeared satisfied with the information, they entered the lodge and found seats in the living room. The curtain was being readied to fall on the final act of this drama.

Frank opened the proceedings, announcing Timothy would be leading the interrogation.

"However," he warned, "We expect all questions to be answered honestly and accurately. A man has been murdered and one of you is guilty."

"Nine of us departed Middleton Saturday set for a vacation," Timothy related. "Unfortunately, not all will be returning together. Those of us who are going home will have memories of a tragedy.

"Naturally, when a crime occurs, we are inclined to suspect someone among us who is unknown," Timothy continued.

"In the beginning, Jacques was the only stranger and it wasn't long before we heard about two fishermen with-out-of-state number plates on their vehicle who were camped across the lake.

"They became suspects to Ted and me before we had a victim because we were aware Brett had financial problems created by gambling.

"Brett Hartman owed money to Rhode Island bookies on horse racing bets. He was practically broke and he believed they were out to collect one way or another. He conceived an idea to stall them until after this outing by promising a payoff.

"In a few minutes you'll know how he planned to come up with the cash.

"Obviously, we weren't aware of Brett's strategy so when we heard Jacques mention strangers, we immediately thought they were hit men.

"However, there was nothing we nor anyone could have done to prevent this type of crime.

"I want to thank these two men for volunteering to join us this morning. Obviously, they aren't killers. I'll introduce them later but I have reason to withhold their identity temporarily. Please bear with me.

"The other stranger, Jacques, who has become our good friend was never considered a suspect. When he reported his revolver was missing I felt he was being set up.

"Except for an argument Saturday evening between Brett and Dave, everything appeared serene. Our first supper and I might inject this comment, 'Last Supper' with Brett, was a success from Jacques's togue to Harry's apple pies.

"I thought we were off to a terrific vacation until calamity struck on Sunday."

Timothy rarely lit his pipe, but this morning he reached in his pocket for a pouch and a match.

He carefully filled the pipe with an Irish blend of tobacco and inhaled gradually while holding a lighted match until puffs of smoke curled and lifted to the ceiling.

Composed, he continued with the summation of his investigation.

"This crime was not on the mind on any of the suspects when we left Middleton last Saturday. It was a last minute idea so it was not carefully planned. An unforeseen incident created a perfect target for the murderer.

"From the beginning of this tragic event, I disregarded Alec and Jan as possible suspects. Of course, Ted and Linda were never even considered.

"Although an investigator feels some individuals are not implicated in an incident, it's essential to be certain that they could not have been involved because of positive evidence. In this case, I saw all of them returning from fishing prior to the devastating lightning strikes. They entered the lodge together where they remained until a search began.

"Now, we are left with six persons who could have committed the crime. Jacques, Randy, Ruth, Dave, or the two strangers. We need a motive."

"Few murders are committed without a reason so our new friend,

Jacques, was deleted from the list of suspects. There are rare instances when a guide shoots a person for whom he is responsible and such incidents would be accidental and usually occur during a hunting season," Timothy said. "Like the rest of us, Brett had known Jacques a day.

"The motive for the strangers was more perceptible. We thought the two men were representatives of a syndicate and that they were here for revenge. Although their leaders may not be tolerant, they are not stupid. How would they profit from killing a deadbeat, especially a skilled photographer whose talents could be used in other ways?

"Why would leaders of a group send a couple of men hundreds of miles to kill someone when it could be accomplished in a populated area with less fanfare? A murder in Maine would create much more publicity as you will observe when you see newspapers back in Middleton. My thoughts began to falter relative to their involvement in this crime..

"When the storm approached, they broke camp and headed for Ripogenus. However, they took a wrong turn off the logging road as heavy rain obscured their visibility. They were lost when they saw lights in the lodge and would have sought shelter here if someone waving a gun hadn't been threatening. They had been running from the storm not a murder.

"Regardless, we had to interview these suspects before arriving at a conclusion. As I said a few minutes ago, the deputies and I had to be certain of their innocence, and we arrived at that decision after our meeting with them this morning. I'll explain their position in a few minutes.

"It's disheartening to even consider a friend to be involved in such a situation. When Deputy Gray asked if I would assist with the investigation, I was hesitant because of my relationship with most everyone involved.

"The deputy and I had earlier compared this investigation to a horse race with a field of contestants, in this instance, suspects, and we agreed it was a wide open field.

"Well, the entries have narrowed to three. Within the hour, it won't be a winner but a loser who will be exposed.

"Most of you think of this case as involving only two guns. You were aware of two weapons missing but there was another firearm that was not mentioned except in a bedroom during a conversation I overheard.

"The wall separating my bedroom from the Perrys is not soundproof and it was not intentional eavesdropping when I overheard a discussion of a weapon. Ruth asked Randy why he brought his pistol on the trip as she believed he only took it on hunting trips. I had seen this weapon before and it was only a .22 caliber. He responded haphazardly and their conversation ended when Ruth asked him not to do anything foolish. I didn't hear his reply but I heard her sobbing.

If Brett had been shot by this handgun, it should have been sent to Augusta for a ballistic analysis. I am responsible for this error. I wasn't close enough to Dr. Williams when he was examining Brett to observe that there were two separate wounds in the shoulder area of his body. I assumed that his death had been caused by only one bullet fired from a larger caliber weapon. Later, my knowledge of Randy's pistol almost threw me off the trail as my suspicions began to focus on him.

"Unfortunately, I must divulge some of Ruth and Randy's personal life in order to relate events leading to this assumption.

"Again, it was another conversation I overheard that brought me on this course.

"While I was taking a late evening walk on our first day, Randy and Brett were having a discussion near the vehicles as I was approaching. It was a spirited talk and I couldn't help overhearing Ruth's name and their cottage mentioned.

"At first, I thought they were talking about our meeting on that Sunday afternoon but then Randy added other words of night, storm, and finally emphasized liar, nothing applying to our afternoon session.

"I continued without being noticed and walked to the dock where the others were gathered. It was getting late so I returned to the lodge where Jacques had left a can of cleaning fluid to remove stains from the rifle. I had noticed rust on the weapon that afternoon that apparently was caused by a leak in the roof.

"Incidentally, Jacques was attempting to make certain his repairs were sufficient when the storm erupted.

"After hearing remarks concerning Ruth, it suddenly occurred to me Brett had been or was making passes at her that were annoying Randy. So much so, Ruth believed, he brought his pistol along to kill him. How determined was he to achieve this deed? No one but he knew the answer. Randy had to be considered a serious suspect and I'm sure Ruth was worried.

"When Jacques' revolver was stolen, my distrust of Randy

intensified. Ruth was the only one of three who was aware the gun was in the cabin and who admitted seeing it.

"Why would she acknowledge that the weapon was in the cabin that morning while the others denied it. The answer was clear. She had no use for it.

"My interpretation of her answer and the fact that there was no opportunity for her to take the rifle eliminated Ruth as the thief. The time element indicated she came directly to the lodge after leaving Randy with the canoe and I was here when she arrived although she left the lodge later for an outside visit.

"I had to ascertain why Randy wanted this weapon when I knew he already had his own pistol. I felt certain that he and Dave were the only persons besides Jacques who were near the cabin again. Randy passed it after he left the canoe and he took the trail by Jacques' place instead of following a shorter path to the lodge Ruth had just traveled .

"Incidentally, although I never considered it important to the investigation, Linda's account of seeing a man standing alone in the darkness watching the group sitting around the campfire could only have been one of three persons. Randy, Dave, or one of the fishermen. "I dismissed the occurrence but I still gave credence to Linda's story. It wasn't an illusion.

"Dave passed by Jacques' cabin when he left me fishing at a brook closer to the lake while he was going upstream fishing. This puzzled me and still does. I still have to conjecture why either of them took the revolver, because I'm holding a ballistic report from the state police laboratory verifying that one of the bullets taken from the victim's body was fired from a 38.55 caliber rifle.

"That was the weapon taken from the lodge on Sunday."

Timothy was calm as he continued with his evaluation of events leading to the murder. No one moved as they listened attentively to him.

"It's my opinion, Randy, that this police report eliminates you in the race for Brett's murder purely on circumstantial evidence. It's a fact that he was shot by a bullet fired from the rifle that was kept above the fireplace in this lodge and from another handgun but not Jacques". Whatever purpose you may have had for taking Jacques' revolver, if you did, is now irrelevant. If you were the individual Linda tried to describe that evening, that too, is immaterial.

"As I said, it's only a guess why either of you took the revolver from the cabin. If it were you, Randy, I think your intentions were to use it, but you either had second thoughts or someone beat you to the draw.

"If Dave took it, which is also inconsequential, I think it was originally intended to cast suspicions on Jacques. The fact that the revolver was abandoned in a conspicuous place indicates there was no longer a need for it. The intended murderer already had a weapon, a rifle, a firearm he had been trained to use while serving in the Marine Corps.

"Approaching the homestretch down to the wire, Dave, you have an uncomfortable lead. When Alec called to ask me if you could go on the trip I wasn't concerned although I did wonder why you wanted to associate with a group who were practically strangers.

"Only a few persons making the trip had ever talked with you, none had ever been invited to your home, and I don't believe any of them had met your wife. There had to be someone besides Alec with whom you had a recent relationship. Your loud argument with Brett that was overheard by everyone Sunday was not eavesdropping. Your voices almost carried across the lake. A discussion of this nature required prior familiarity and it certainly involved a significant problem. Yesterday, you admitted having a difference of opinion with Brett involving money. That made me suspicious.

"Now, I realized it was essential to concentrate on the disappearance of the rifle to solve the crime. Who had the best opportunity to take the weapon? It came to me when I recalled you were walking from the lodge as I came from the lake. I had a shorter distance to travel and you had to go upstream and possibly in Jacques' cabin but yet you were here long before me.

"You didn't do any fishing after we parted but you ran all the way to the cabin and lodge. You are in excellent physical condition. You proved it again later.

"You took the rifle from the lodge and went to the workshop to hide it. You didn't dare to leave it in the other buildings since Jacques frequented them often for wood and ice. So you decided that the workshop would be a more secure place.

"If you had attempted to hide a rifle on the previous day, Jacques and I would have found it while looking for a cleaning fluid.

"You had to hurry but you still had to conceal it well. At that time, you didn't know exactly when it would be used. This was going to be a crime when an opportunity presented itself. The severity of the storm provided the perfect setting.

"Oh, yes, another stroke of luck, you had.

"How you managed to acquire these breaks is amazing. It seems incredible your victim could become a lone target camouflaged by elements of a violent storm.

"Also, the probable odds were one in thousands Jacques would ever leave anyone he was guiding.

Timothy turned to Jacques and said, "To relieve your conscience, Brett wasn't in any danger until he encountered a bullet.

"However, it requires more than opportunity in the investigation of a crime. There has to be a motive. Dave's argument with Brett about refusing to enter into a financial arrangement hardly qualifies for a murder unless a lot of pressure was involved. The motive didn't surface until the victim's clothing was searched.

"Dave, this was your biggest mistake. With all of the breaks you had in the limited planning of this crime, you had one major stroke of bad luck You didn't have time to remove a picture I'm sure you knew Brett was carrying. The storm had provided you with an excellent opportunity to commit a murder, but it also denied you a chance to retrieve this incriminating evidence. Here's a photo that should interest you," Timothy continued as he handed the print to him. "I'm certain you've seen a similar copy and I'm betting there's another print in your pocket."

Dave took the photo from Timothy's hand. His face was grim as he stared at a scene revealing him and Dawn Gronorski making love. Smirking, he returned the print to Timothy.

"This doesn't mean a thing," Dave responded. "I must have shown that to Brett when we first became acquainted at his studio. I believe I asked him to make another print of it."

"Dave, you don't look like a person who would keep copies of that print," Timothy asserted. "What if Mrs. Paxton ever saw it?"

"What I did before our marriage doesn't affect our relationship," he answered.

"Would it make a difference if the photo was taken in Middleton recently?" Timothy questioned.

"Well, it wasn't, so we can forget it," he retorted.

"Not so fast, Dave," Timothy responded.

"Brett Hartman took a photo of you and a fifteen-year-old girl in his studio less than a month ago. To refresh your memory, her name is Dawn Gronorski. The report I'm holding from Middleton Police Chief John Davidson substantiates this contention. There's no doubt in my mind you were a victim of blackmail," Timothy disclosed.

"That doesn't prove I had anything to do with his death," Dave replied.

"Perhaps, not in itself. Allow me to present additional evidence that will bring us across the finish line," Timothy added.

"The two men who are with us today are Connecticut vacationers who cut their stay short at Bear Lake because the storm leveled their tent. As I explained earlier, they lost their way during the storm and wound up near the lodge before realizing their error.

"Fortunately, they were turning their car around to return to the logging road when lightning hit the pines illuminating the area and revealing a man holding a gun."

"Not knowing the intentions of the person bearing the weapon, but now that their car was heading in a direction taking them away from any danger, they didn't linger when they heard a tree snap that sounded like gunfire. They continued to Millinocket where they spent the night and drove to Bar Harbor at daylight on the following morning. It wasn't until yesterday that they read in the *Bangor Daily News* about a man shot at Bear Lake and that police were on the lookout for two Connecticut men who left after the shooting. Immediately, they contacted police, identified themselves and offered to return to the scene.

"Both men are detectives with the Hartford Police Department who were trying to get away from crime in the city. They offered to testify in court after seeing Dave today that he was the man they saw waving a rifle."

The silence in the room was quickly broken as chairs moved when the spectators turned to look more closely at the strangers who turned out to be police officers instead of suspects. Most probably they were men who would play a part in solving the crime.

But Dave didn't share their optimism about the role these detectives would play in a courtroom as he vehemently expressed his dissension. "Because they are police doesn't make them perfect witnesses," he added.

"How in hell could they make a positive identification during a rainstorm through windshield wipers in a darkened sky? My attorneys will make them look like idiots," Dave declared

"We shall see about that," Timothy rebutted.

"However, Dave, the race is not over. There are more obstacles on the track."

"Don't try to tell me Brett took my picture," he laughed mockingly.

"Dave, if the testimony of these witnesses is not sufficient, here's another surprise. I believe a jury will consider it the 'coup de grace'!

Let's return to what took place in this room after we returned from fishing Sunday afternoon. I think you were sitting in the same chair you're in now. Within minutes, there were rumbles of thunder so you decided to check on boaters.

"It was raining hard so you went to the coat rack near the fireplace and put on a jacket, the same one hanging there now. Then you walked out the front door.

"A short time later, Ruth arrived and she went to her room to change into dry clothes. Afterward, she came into the living room where we had a cup of coffee. Some time later, she said that she had to make a visit to the half-moon outside commenting that this was the time when inside facilities should be available.

"I was alone until Ruth returned a few minutes before Jacques came running in the kitchen door. He looked like he had seen a ghost but it had been only the storm that had frightened him.

Dripping wet, he walked toward the stove and kept looking around the room. Finally he asked about Brett.

"Jacques was really upset now, repeating over and over that the photographer should be here by this time. He said he left him on the camp road half an hour ago and that he couldn't lose his way back. He added that the storm was making it dark and asked for a flashlight to look for Brett."

"About that time, Randy entered the lodge from the porch and joined in the search.

"Dave, think carefully before you answer this question. Where were you when those exceptionally brilliant flashes of lightning hit the trees?"

"You're repeating yourself. I told you yesterday I was somewhere between the lake and the lodge. How in hell do I know where I was during that storm!"

"Let's see if I can make it easier for you. Were you in the front or rear of the lodge after you left to find the others?" Timothy inquired. "You couldn't have been that bewildered."

"A Perry Mason, you're not, Timothy. How could I be in the rear of the building if I was at the shore with the rest?"

"No, Dave, I'm not Perry. However, I want to be certain of my facts before continuing. Were you in the back of the lodge anytime during this early period of the storm?"

"You're difficult to convince," Dave smirked. "No, I was with the others in the front." "Then, Mr. Paxton, how could you enter the lodge by the kitchen door?" Speechless, Dave was baffled.

"That would be a problem," Timothy remarked. "But, since you just ran from Jacques' cabin, it was the shortest way into the lodge. Dave, we are getting closer to the finish line."

Everyone was motionless and silent as Timothy's words left his lips.

The next words came from the mouth of the accused.

"You may be an amateur detective but you aren't dealing with an incompetent now," he shouted. "You had better have more proof than you've given so far or else you will spend the remainder of your life in a monastery."

"The scenario goes like this, Dave," Timothy described.

"You left the lodge when the weather began getting wild, not to help Alec or anyone else at the lake. You knew Brett would be returning from taking photos so you went to the shore first to make an appearance but doubled back to the workshop where you had concealed the rifle.

"Luck was with you again when you stepped outside in the rain and saw Jacques running down the road and onto his cabin trail without stopping. Of course, you weren't aware of his purpose but this was the opportunity to complete yours.

"Brett would be along soon and you were ready with a rifle.

"You waited on the lodge side near the pines for Brett to make an appearance. You must have been surprised when you saw Jacques returning and run directly to a building where you had just left. It was a driving rain but you could still see moving figures but the one you wanted was approaching from the camp road. You knew it had to be Brett. What a perfect setup! You couldn't have had it better. What happened in the next few minutes, I can only guess.

"From my conversation with Jacques, it appears you waited until Brett was a good target and fired about the same time the bolts of lightning struck the pines. Jacques said he saw flashes of light on both the camp road and sky followed by snapping of trees that sounded like gun shots. Then the Connecticut car's headlights became visible as it turned around on the road. That's when the detectives said they sighted you so you ran down Jacques's trail where you partially hid the rifle. Unfortunately, you didn't have time to get the picture from Brett's pocket.

"Your next move was a bad one. You entered the kitchen door which

238

you denied a few minutes ago but more incriminating, you walked in front of me to the coat rack where you removed your wet jacket. That was the same coat you took from the rack when you went outside earlier. The jacket is still hanging there."

Timothy got up from his chair and slowly walked to the rack where he removed the jacket. He turned to Dave and asked if he would put it on. Dave started to object until a deputy moved toward him.

"I suggest you put that jacket on," Frank said adamantly.

"This isn't my jacket but I'll wear it if you insist," Dave replied. He stood and put the coat on.

"What's so incriminating about wearing this jacket?" he asked.

"Look at that spot on the left shoulder," Timothy remarked.

"That stain came from rust on the shoulder plate of a 38-55 caliber rifle that was mounted above the fireplace until you removed the weapon Sunday," Timothy explained.

"The rust on the rifle was caused by water dripping from the roof that Jacques tried to repair on the night of the crime. I explained earlier that I tried to remove the rust Saturday night. I wasn't successful as you can observe. In fact, I created a larger stain by applying oil during the attempt," Timothy continued.

"Tests taken at the state police laboratory will confirm this evidence.

"Dave, I wore that coat Saturday night while taking a walk. No one else has worn it except you," Timothy said. "The stain on that jacket was acquired from the shoulder plate of the Winchester rifle you were holding Sunday night when you shot Brett Hartman."

"David Paxton, I'm sure Deputy Gray will charge you for the attempted murder of Brett Hartman but not for his demise. Someone else is responsible," Timothy added.

Chapter 19

Astonishment covered the faces of everyone, particularly Frank who appeared that he couldn't believe what Timothy had said.

"If Dave didn't kill Brett, who in hell could have done it? You have eliminated everyone in the room except the professor's wife. How could she have shot the victim when she was in the lodge with you and why would she do it."

"I'm sorry to have led you to a wrong conclusion," Timothy answered. "Ruth was in the room most of the time but she went outside as she admitted to go to the privy which is also in the rear of the lodge. When she returned, she also entered by the kitchen door."

"Unfortunately for a dear friend, I believe that I have the answers to both questions," Timothy replied solemnly. "It's disheartening to perceive. At this stage of the investigation, my evidence is primarily circumstantial but I'm convinced that she performed the act in defense of someone she loved very much but whom she had deceived. She believed that her husband was going to kill Brett."

"However, I must have Ruth's permission to have the deputies search her belongings for a .22 caliber pistol that she left Sunday afternoon when she returned from a walk to the outhouse or wherever she went. And, we must have the firearm sent to Augusta for ballistic tests before any final proof is confirmed. Ruth, you have rights under law but I have a feeling that you won't object to accompanying the officers to your room and show them the weapon? I doubt that you have concealed it elsewhere."

"Before you say anything, Ruth, " Dr. Perry interrupted, "We'll get a lawyer. Timothy has already admitted that he has only circumstantial evidence. I don't believe that you are responsible for Brett's death. Physically, do you think that any jury would convict you of killing a man almost twice your size with a small handgun? That's absurd. I think that Timothy's contention that Dave can only be charged with attempted murder is incorrect. Dave not only had the capability of killing Brett but he also had a convincing motive. I'll admit that on Saturday evening a thought did enter my mind of ridding the earth of this gigolo but I changed my mind. It wouldn't be worth the consequences. I left the lodge that night carrying that pistol but returned to our room and put it back in my suitcase. I'm positive that you didn't do it, Ruth."

"Randy is right, Ruth." Timothy added. "Listen carefully to him."

With tears in her eyes, she ignored Randy's advice and nodded agreeably to Timothy's request. She gently moved from her chair and led deputies to her room. They returned in a few minutes with Deputy Gray carrying a weapon partly concealed by a handkerchief.

"Timothy, I must have more proof than this weapon to charge Mrs. Perry with any criminal act," Frank declared. "Please continue with your allegations."

"The motive is easier to explain than the act," Timothy replied. "What all of us involved in this investigation wanted to avoid is now wide open. We wanted to make certain that an affair between Ruth and Brett had taken place before arriving at a conclusion so that her secret could be kept confidential if it had no bearing on the case. It doesn't matter now. The cat is out of the bag.

"Ted and I were certain that Brett had visited Ruth at her cottage in Middleton one evening when Randy was on a Boston business trip. Ted saw Brett's car when he drove down at my request to inform Ruth of a meeting planned for the next weekend. He couldn't reach her by phone because of a power outage. Although we discussed it, there seemed no reason to call off this fishing trip. As far as we were concerned, it was a private affair. Soon more activities involving Brett, his gambling debts and photography at his studio, especially with a young girl began to surface. We still didn't think that these were sufficient reasons to curtail the outing.

"However, three incidents took place that caused me some concern but not to the extent of a murder. Before the meeting at the Perry's cottage, I observed Randy talking with a worker from the Central Maine Power Company and when Randy returned he seemed upset. Following the meeting I also noticed Ruth and Brett having a serious talk while away from the crowd. I was sure that something was wrong.

"However," Timothy continued, "the third incident, a motive for murder, didn't occur to me until our first night here when I heard Randy and Brett having a serious argument. I then suspected that trouble could result from this confrontation because I was also aware of Randy's temper. This is when I first considered Randy as a prime suspect.

"As I have already related, the appearance of a third weapon changed my entire opinion. When Frank found Jacques's revolver and determined that it was not the murder weapon, there was only one remaining firearm. It had to be the .22 caliber pistol. But, who fired it, and when, and how?

"Only three persons knew of its existence. Randy, Ruth and myself. Now we have two suspects. Randy couldn't have done it because he entered the front door about a minute after Jacques got here. The murder had already been committed.

"Ruth, who had been in the lodge with me when the storm erupted, was the only person who could have fired that pistol. She left the lodge for about ten minutes with a pretence of going to the privy, but before leaving, she went to her bedroom for her rain gear. Also, to acquire the handgun.

"What happened next is only conjecture on my part. Ruth is the only person who could explain what really took place. She disliked Brett but her main purpose in killing him was that she thought her husband had already made a similar decision. Ruth didn't want Randy to face a punishment for an act which she had brought on.

"She knew that Brett would be returning soon after the storm erupted and she took a chance that she might see him before he reached the lodge. An excellent marksman, Ruth would be in a perfect position to intercept him by waiting near one of the half-moons

"Until Ruth tells her story, if she chooses to do so, my theory is unquestionably speculative. I think that she, like Dave, was surprised when Jacques ran ahead of Brett and down the trail away from the lodge. She must have also been aghast when she saw Dave holding a rifle. But her biggest surprise happened when a shot rang out and Brett fell to the ground. Unsure of just what to do next, Dave made it easier for her as he ran from the headlights of a vehicle as it turned on the camp road. Undaunted and unseen, she raced to Brett's body, pointed the muzzle of the pistol directly to his heart, and fired. It seems she wanted to make certain that he would never again interfere with their lives.

"The rest of the story is simple. Ruth came back to the lodge and went directly to her bedroom. She changed her clothes, concealed the pistol, and returned to her seat.

"Deputy Gray, this is the theory that I have to offer. I've done my best. I sincerely regret that it has such a pitiful ending, "Timothy concluded.

"Mrs. Perry, unless you can disprove Timothy's testimony or offer more defense for your whereabouts when we believe the shooting took place, I have no choice but to hold you on a charge of murder for the death of Brett Hartman," Frank declared. "You will have to come with us to Dover-Foxcroft for arraignment."

"I have nothing to say ," Ruth uttered.

With blurred eyes, Randy went to his wife's side and took her in his arms..

"Darling," he whispered. "I love you and always will. I'll be with you all the way. A jury hasn't found you guilty and I'll be in Dover-Foxcroft as soon as I can get there with the best attorney in the state."

"I'm sorry, Randy," she sobbed. "You don't deserve this. You're so kind and good to me. "

"Don't worry, dear. We'll be together again soon," Randy assured her.

There were also tears on Jan and Linda's cheeks and the room was quiet as deputies lead Dave and Ruth to the plane where the pilot was waiting.

Frank stopped before reaching the dock and returned to the lodge for a talk with Timothy.

"I know this has been difficult, Timothy. Please accept our thanks. We hope to see you next fall at the police conference under better conditions."

"It's more pleasant days ahead, I'm sure," Timothy replied. "I'll be looking forward to seeing you in September."

This parting between friends was the beginning of an end to a shortened vacation for Timothy and his group. They quietly went to their rooms and began packing for the return trip, three days earlier than originally planned.

Standing away from the proceedings, Jacques looked on the downcast faces of his newly acquainted companions as they prepared for departure.

Suddenly, Jacques felt alone and helpless. A rare emotion for a robust woodsman who endured years in wilderness solitude. He knew of no words he could say but a thought occurred. He could do something they might like so he rushed to a canoe and paddled to his favorite fishing hole.

A somber atmosphere prevailed while the vacationers carried knapsacks and packages from the lodge to the vehicles which were returning to Middleton with three less passengers.

"Does anyone know where Jacques went?" Timothy asked.

There was no response.

"Cleaning the lodge, I'm certain, he'll be doing when he returns. Let's make it easier for him by doing some ourselves, "Timothy suggested.

"It's peculiar he's not here when we're about to leave," Ted remarked. "Certainly, he hasn't gone far."

The words had hardly left Ted's mouth when Jacques appeared at the kitchen door with a big grin brightening his face and carrying two large togue.

Now Jacques found words for the occasion.

"It's unlucky fishermen who leave without a catch. "These big ones were hiding near Patte de Chat."

As if someone had waved a wand over them, smiles appeared on faces of everyone.

"For what would you be doing that,? Timothy chuckled as he put his hand on Jacques broad shoulder. "It's a good man, you are, Jacques."

"You're a darling," Linda and Jan exclaimed as they each planted a kiss on the woodsman's face.

Probably for the first time in his life, Jacques blushed while continuing to smile from ear to ear. He knew he had done the right thing.

"Well, mon ami, it's time for us to leave," Timothy said as he shook Jacques's hand.

"It's possible, we will meet again during the hunting season."

"Good-bye Timothy. Et bonne chance," Jacques responded as he grabbed everyone's hand as they entered the cars.

His eyes were moist watching them departing on the camp road leaving unpleasant memories and picturesque Bear Lake behind.

Randy left first and headed for the county jail in Dover-Foxcroft where Ruth would be held.

Alec and Jan were alone in the wagon on the return trip and they had plenty to discuss.

"Don't you ever get lonely on that farm all by yourself?" Jan asked as the vehicle began moving. "Do you have someone to help with cleaning and the hundred or more chores in a household?"

Alec had survived four decades without a woman sharing his house with the exception of a mother. He was too wise a bachelor to fall for this line of questioning that could result with incriminating answers.

"I manage," he replied. "I'm accustomed to being alone, beginning with college and through the war. On the farm there's a lot to do plus running a newspaper. I don't have time to sit and think. I hire a woman once a week to clean and tidy the house," he said.

" Laughing, he added, "It's more economical than a wife."

"But not as cozy on a cold winter's night," Jan retorted. "I'm not getting anywhere with this approach," she said smiling.

"I wonder how Timothy is reacting to this. Being a priest, he's probably more compassionate, but he played an important role in convicting them," Jan remarked. "Timothy did the same in this case as he would in any other," Alec responded." He believes in justice and has expertise in criminology. Chips must fall some place."

For a while, no one spoke as they drove south toward Greenville.

Thoughts of romance entered Jan's mind while they rode in silence. Maybe she had come on too fast about Alec living alone. Now she realized caution had to be exercised if she was to rope this big man. She liked him and he must have feelings for her or he wouldn't have invited her along on this outing. It was only a matter of time, she speculated.

Alec's thoughts dwelled momentarily on Dave. He must have feared the consequence of Brett's blackmail attempt that meant incarceration in Thomaston instead of Palm Beach. Still a wild stallion, he would have difficulty behind bars.

He gave his companion the benefit of doubt in his affair with a teenager. Dave liked women but he was too intelligent to deliberately get involved with jail bait. The girl must have appeared older. There was nothing he could do about this situation but what about the female sitting beside him.

It was about time he shared his life with someone and Jan seemed like the right person.. She was right. It was getting lonely on the farm and more work was involved than anticipated. He was beginning to think of her more as a companion than a colleague. He was aware his feelings toward her were developing more toward affection than friendship. Each day it was gradually getting difficult to avoid revealing his sentiments.

Alec knew this secret couldn't be concealed indefinitely. He never considered himself as a lover and there wasn't any hurry to let Jan know his true feelings. He would play the bachelor role a little longer.

Trailing the small convoy, Linda sat close to Ted as they moved from the lodge area. Timothy, sitting in the rear seat turned and waved to Jacques, a newly found acquaintance he hoped would be there next fall when he returned for the hunting season.

Many thoughts raced through the minds of these individuals ranging from romance to tragedy.

"It's a sad day, it is," Timothy voiced, "leaving without three of our companions."

"It certainly is," Linda said. "Who would ever imagine our vacation would come to this end? One probably gone forever and the others facing a bleak future."

"Timothy, when did you consider Ruth the most likely suspect?"

"Although a touch and go with Randy and Dave, the ballistic report was the clinching factor which indicated that neither the rifle bullet or Jacques's revolver caused the fatal wound. Although Dave was the only person who had the opportunity to remove the rifle from the lodge, Ruth was the only person who had an easy access to the pistol. She was also outside in the same area where and when the murder occurred. Randy's quarrel with Brett gave me the motive but I was surprised when she instead of Randy fired the fatal shot," Timothy continued.

"Now, behind us, is all this. Let's pray we can resume our activities and hopefully return in the fall for a more enjoyable gathering," Timothy concluded.

With the incident over but perhaps never forgotten, Linda focused her thoughts on Ted.

Although they met less than two years ago, she was positive he was the man she wanted as her lifetime partner. Not a schemer, however, she did intend to pursue a course eventually leading to an altar.

Ted had several thoughts wandering through his mind but foremost was getting an in-depth story of the murder written and on the wire service.

Now he shifted his attention to Linda and their future. Obviously, Ted would have no problem to get to the altar but he wasn't in a hurry. He hadn't forgotten Sheila, but it seemed unrealistic that they would meet again.

At this point, it appeared that the two couples were headed to a similar destination.

How about Timothy?

Where was he going? Whenever Timothy lit up, it was an omen something exciting was entering his mind. As he relaxed in the Chevy while blowing whiffs of smoke from his pipe, he thought of the trip to his native land with the Haneys. Fortunately they had the same ideas.

His next adventure could probably take him to Ireland. Until then, he looked forward to Bear Lake again when the hunting season opened in the fall.

The End